GIRL & THE MACHINE

VICTORIA RIVERA

First published in the United States by Prosey Books, an imprint of Pocketful of Prosey LLC.

GIRL AND THE MACHINE.
Copyright © 2024 by Victoria Rivera.
All rights reserved.

Layout, formatting, and cover design by Victoria Rivera

www.toririv.com

Hardcover ISBN 979-8-9900218-0-8
Paperback ISBN 979-8-9900218-1-5

First Edition: March 2024

For Nano

Some parts of this novel may deal briefly
with sensitive subject matter.

For a detailed list of content warnings, please visit:
www.toririv.com/cw

THE SIX CALIFORNIAS

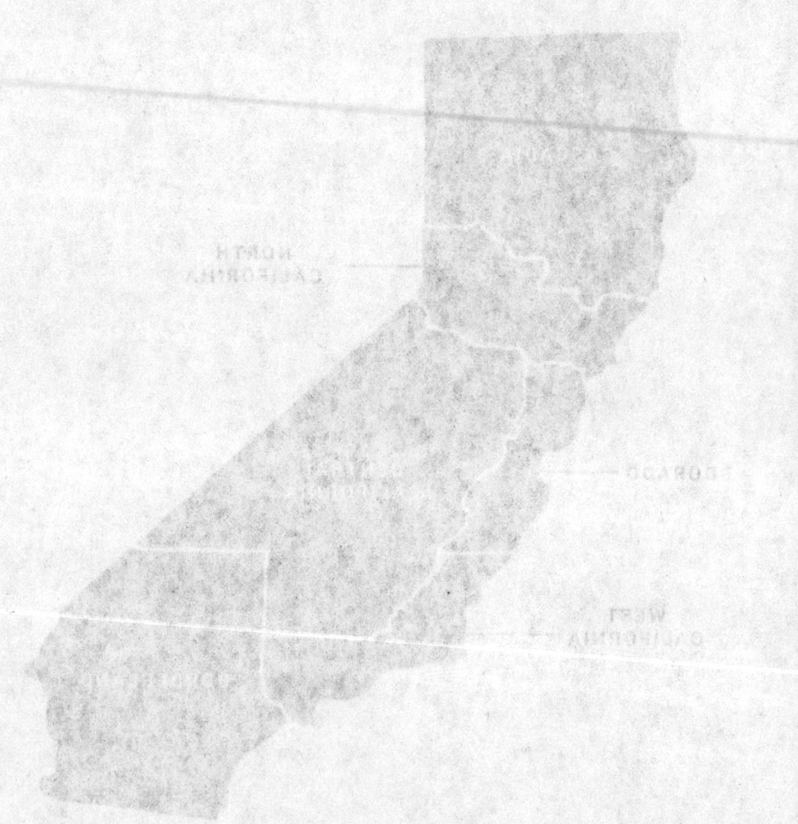

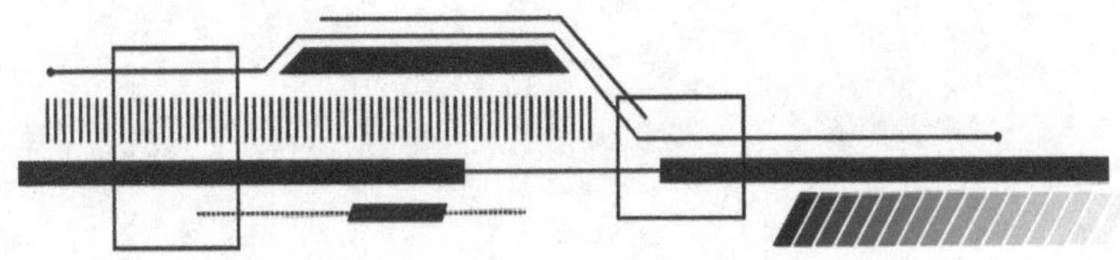

To insult someone we call him "bestial."
For deliberate cruelty and nature,
"human" might be the greater insult.

Isaac Asimov

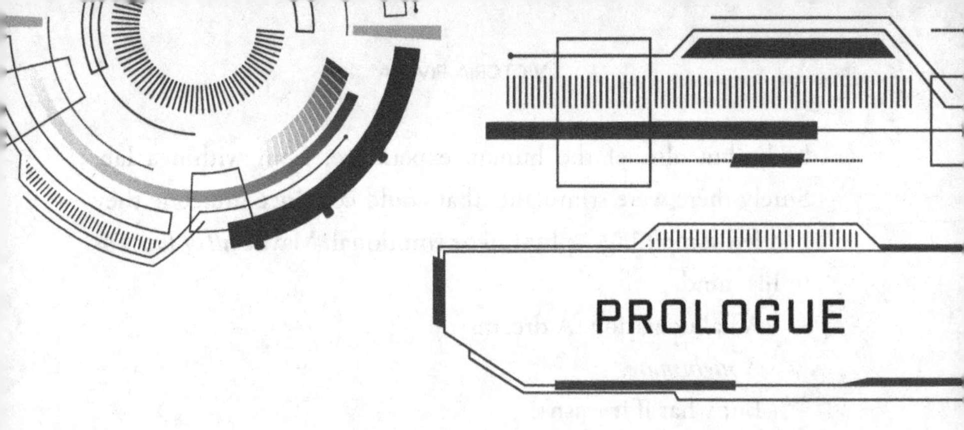

HIS BODY WAS ALL WRONG.

His heart—or whatever was inside him instead of it—was racing as he moved through the night, palpitations that mimicked the rapid pumping motion of human panic.

The footboard of the stolen hovercraft hummed beneath his bare feet, which looked as much like his own as they always had—but were they? Was *any* of him authentic now?

His right hand was a glaring reminder that he couldn't be sure. He gripped the steering handle with those strange, metallic finger bones, the meager moon reflected on their surface. The metal ran up his wrist and his right arm and shoulder, spreading across a portion of his chest—everywhere the fire had caught before he'd been able to extinguish himself—exposed to open air. Without having seen the full extent of the damage, he knew the side of his face had taken significant fire too. He knew it because, while the sensations on his "skin" were deceptively natural, the sensations surrounding his metal bones were dampened and, in some cases, non-existent.

But he certainly felt a churning in his stomach. A throbbing in his head. A crushing weight against his lungs. Were these feelings real? Or some trick of the mind? He knew that it was possible to recreate not only certain elements of the human body, but also of the human experience, from within a lab. Surely there were stimulants that could convince someone they had felt something—physical or emotional. Maybe *all of this* was in his mind.

A hallucination. A dream.

A *nightmare*.

But what if it wasn't?

He clenched his teeth and forced himself to focus. This was no time to let the horrors sink in. He couldn't yet pause to think about what had happened to him—or who was responsible for it. He had to get to safety.

He didn't *know* the way, technically speaking, but he knew the coordinates—the ones he'd memorized since childhood—the ones he never thought he'd ever have to use.

Thirty-four degrees, 41 minutes, 57.0309 seconds north …

For a long time, he thought the forest would never end, with its lurking silhouettes and the unsettling resonance of whatever lived among them. With the pervasive darkness, and the thin, waxing crescent above struggling to spread enough light.

But eventually, the hovercraft readouts told him he'd arrived. The single headlight shone on a hillside that looked as ordinary as any other. A veneer like his own skin.

He had to scour the moss and lichen along the craggy surface for several minutes before he found the panel. With trembling, unfamiliar fingers, he pried it open, worried that the system wouldn't recognize him—because he wasn't sure he'd be able to recognize *himself*, were he to catch sight of his own reflection.

Since he was certain that the external appearance of his right eye had been damaged, he placed his left in front of the retinal scanner.

The scanner beeped.

The surface of the rock parted to reveal an entrance.

Inside, safety lights flicked on. He followed them through another set of doors and down a long corridor and, finally, into an electrical room.

Metal doors lined the walls. Tubes and wires ran across the ceiling. He opened a few of the doors to look at the switches inside—little rows of black breakers neatly labeled. A larger compartment was labeled CENTRAL CIRCUIT and he went to it, hesitating before he switched it on.

What would he see when the light flooded the room?

After the snap of the switch, everything came alive. A buzz filled the entire structure, the kind of subtle, underlying noise most people wouldn't have noticed unless it had come immediately after dead silence.

He crept back into the corridor, which led him to an open space with marble floors and white pillars and a petite grand piano.

Slowly, he approached the instrument, surveying its black surface—shiny, reflective. Not quite a mirror. A mirror would be too clear, too much of a shock, but *this* …

With caution, he lowered himself onto the bench, not yet turning his eyes toward the gleaming surface of the music rack in front of him.

He waited.

He swallowed to assuage the lump in his throat.

Then, he looked forward.

For a moment, he couldn't breathe.

When he finally did, he screamed.

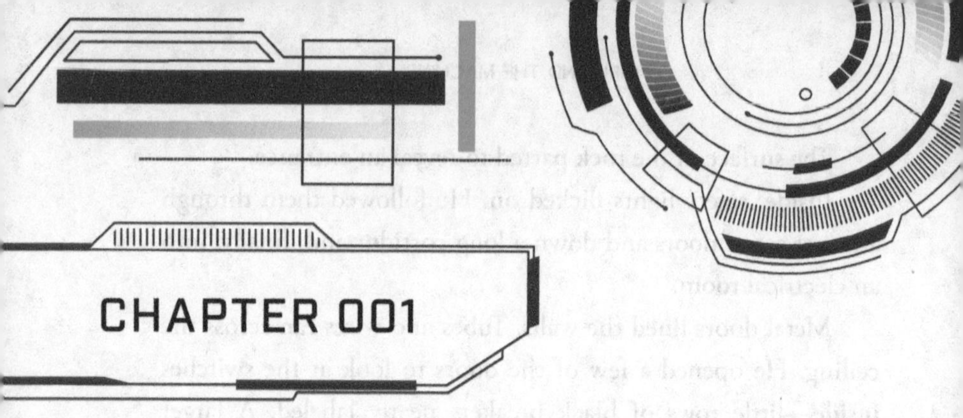

CHAPTER 001

THE HOLOGRAPHIC SCREEN GLOWED blue against the night, displaying a terminal full of commands that would be incoherent nonsense to most people. A flat, six-by-three-inch rectangle sat face up projecting the information. Warm, West California air blew a few loose strands of Bel's dark hair against her face as she positioned her hands over the keys.

"You look like you're about to perform a concerto," Aly said over her shoulder.

Bel looked down at the way her fingers were curved, wrists held high, like her piano instructor had taught her. She never would have imagined that anything from those lessons would stick, let alone leak into other tasks; she'd hated those lessons, fought with her mom every time she'd had to go. Thinking of it now, that version of her life seemed like it belonged to someone else entirely—and it might as well have, for how little she was allowed to acknowledge it to anyone in this version.

The two girls sat on the catwalk of a panopt—one of millions of electronic billboards installed throughout the nation, fitted with advanced security cameras and identification software—looking out over the old, abandoned highway that ran below. This panopt had fallen out of use, a blank screen and a (hopefully) non-functioning lens.

Regardless, Bel instinctively felt along the edge of her hairline until her fingers ran over a one-millimeter bump—a freckle or a mole as far as anyone else knew. It was a comforting ritual, to remind herself she was still safe, and that the microdot device would continue to emit signals that would mask her true identity in front of panoptical scanners.

She sat with her legs crossed while she worked at the holopad computer, whose base rested on the metal grate in front of her. The branches of a nearby tree came up high enough and were angled just right, allowing her good visibility while also keeping her activities somewhat private. Meanwhile, Aly's green electric car was parked down the road and hidden in the bushes.

Aly squinted into the distance. "They're here."

Bel's mouth twisted into a smirk as the boys came into view down the road. All five of them pulled up on skimmers. The single-rider hovercrafts made a v formation like a flock of silver birds in the darkness, illuminated by the glow of their own headlights. Branxton was dead center.

His skimmer came to a halt, levitating a foot or so off the ground. Branxton's legs hugged the sleek vehicle, which Bel had already researched in advance.

SUMMARY	
Brand	Voltellus LV4
Fuel Type	Electric
HIN	1Y70031QK582
Year	2081
Dimensions	81.5 in x 27.8 in x 45.7 in

Branxton's biceps flexed as he gripped the handlebars, revving the vehicle as though it had an engine, even though it should have been silent. These boys liked to add aftermarket sound effects for show.

"I don't like this," Aly said.

"Yeah, well," said Bel, "I don't like what Branxton did to your arm."

Aly put her hand to her bicep, which showed the remnants of four small bruises in a curved row. She watched Bel pull up a terminal window as the skimmer came into range.

"I've never driven a Voltellus before," said Bel. Within a few seconds, a clone of the skimmer's dashboard appeared on the holographic screen. "This should be fun."

Aly bit her thumbnail.

The boys spread out behind a line of neon yellow spray paint. Branxton's friend Thane sat to his left.

When she looked at Thane, Bel's nostrils flared, tightening her thin, silver nose ring against her skin. She hated the way his sand-blond hair fell into his eyes. She hated that stupid plaid button-down he always wore on top of his "vintage" t-shirts. She *really* hated the fact that she'd made out with him last summer—repeatedly—and even more that she'd actually liked it. He'd also noticed the "little freckle" on her head once (even said it was "cute"), and that was when she knew she had let him get too close. He hadn't seemed to suspect anything amiss, but she wasn't going to risk it.

Bel waited, twisting the frayed threads around the hole at the knee of her jeans.

"Bel ..." Aly said warily.

Pulling her jagged, shoulder-length hair into a ponytail at the nape of her neck, Bel readied her fingers over the holokeys again. "Someone has to teach him a lesson."

The boys hovered at the line for a few more minutes while some people from school showed up in cars or other small hovercraft and gathered into a sparse crowd spread out at different points along the road. Some of them brought drinks and food. A couple of them had sacks of Sparkfyre, a grainy substance that they poured into the hole of an old tire. Someone pulled out a small, silver tube on a keychain and pressed a button on top, sending out a thin, red laser beam. The second the beam hit the Sparkfyre, it went up in flames, and everyone gathered around.

Three of the racers, including Branxton, had open beer cans, which they drained, crushed, and tossed aside.

Aly grimaced.

Branxton's dashboard waited in front of Bel, which included fingertap buttons to control brakes, acceleration, ignition, and alerts.

So many choices, Bel thought.

Meanwhile, a notification popped up in the corner of her screen.

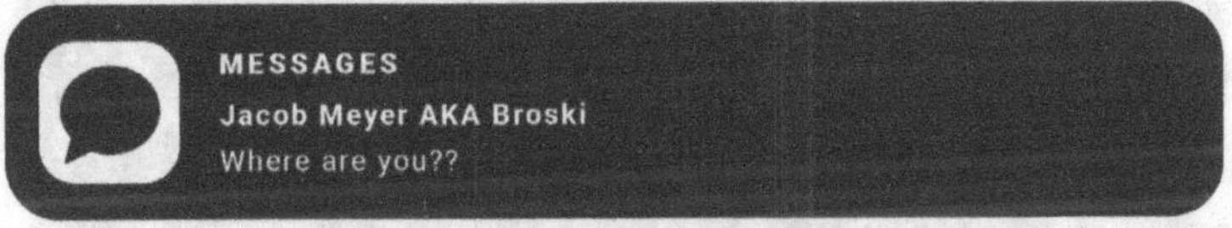

Bel tapped to dismiss the message. Her brother had made it a point to know exactly where she was at all times by tracking her device, but last week she'd programmed a hack that would allow her to *look* like she was in one place even when she'd gone somewhere else. He must have figured it out, and now he was about to blow a gasket. She sighed. The routine was getting old—her trying to live like a normal teenager, him trying to keep her "out of trouble." If she was going to be trapped in this nothing little town, and forced to pretend she was someone else, the least he could do was let her have some fun. He may have been her legal guardian—up until she'd turned 18 last month, that is—but he was only three years older than her, and he was paranoid beyond reason.

She also had to dismiss a slew of Atmosfera notifications. The all-encompassing social media app always seemed to be busier at night, blowing up with requests. Her secret, paid hacking account had become popular lately.

It had been hard to keep up with, but a great way to make money on the side. Not all of the requests were things she was willing to do, but most were pretty reasonable—and easy. She'd saved up enough for two semesters of college tuition and was on track to make enough for three by the end of the school year. But she'd have to deal with them later.

The boys were close enough now that Bel and Aly could make out the numbers and letters on their license plates. Little rectangles that said West California across the top, with a watermark off to the side showing the outline of the state highlighted among the other five Californias within the shape of the original one.

They revved while the onlookers hollered. A girl from the dance team unhooked her bra from inside her shirt and pulled it out through her sleeve, then ran into the middle of the road in front of the boys and waved it around over her head like a flag.

"Ready?" she shouted.

The boys nodded. The two in the back pumped their fists. Students on the sidelines cheered.

With her free hand, the girl drew her wrist close to her mouth, speaking into a small device.

"Count down from ten," she told it.

An AI voice obeyed with surprising volume despite the tiny speaker it came from. "Ten, nine, eight …"

Alternating artificial revving sounds bounced off the pavement.

"Seven, six, five …"

Bel whispered, "Ready or not …"

"Four, three, two, one …" A long beep followed and the boys took off.

After giving the boys a few seconds to get going, Bel set off Branxton's horn. Branxton, who had just taken the lead, frowned, and glanced over the front of his handlebars. The other boys turned to him with looks of confusion.

"What the—"

Bel turned up the volume.

The other boys laughed as one of them pulled ahead. Branxton leaned forward, pressing into his handlebars and accelerating, his horn still blaring.

When Branxton once again passed everyone else, Bel disabled his accelerator. He pushed his foot down over and over on the pedal but without any reaction from the skimmer. He shouted curses at the guys and demanded to know which one of them was responsible for this. He put more force on the pedal, and just when he stomped into it with the most effort, Bel reactivated the accelerator, launching the vehicle forward so hard Branxton almost flew off the seat.

Back in the race with a vengeance, Branxton caught up, shoving into Thane with his shoulder and whipping the back end of his skimmer against one of the other boys to throw them both off.

"What the hell, dude?" the boy shouted.

Bel let Branxton reclaim his place at the front again and coast for a few seconds before her next move.

"Enjoy it while you can," she whispered.

Aly continued chewing her nails, eyes pinned to the race.

On the dash clone, Bel tapped into the steering mechanisms. Buttons for left and right faded in. She alternated tapping the buttons, moving Branxton's vehicle in a serpentine pattern, slowing him down and speeding him up, weaving him in between the other boys and jerking him dangerously close to hitting them several times. Everyone was going insane, his friends shouting at him and the students on the sidelines telling him to knock it off.

For the final stretch, Bel let up again. Branxton made it back to the front one last time as all the racers approached the finish line. He had the accelerator pedal pressed flat. His chin edged past the handlebars. He put almost a yard of distance between himself and the others. Another five yards and he'd have his victory.

And that's when Bel cut the power.

The headlight flicked off. The vehicle's hum went silent. The invisible energy that had been buoying up the vehicle dissipated, and the vehicle slammed against the cracked asphalt, metal grinding and shooting sparks as its lateral motion slowed in ragged scrapes. Branxton struggled to hold on, but from the look on his face it wasn't clear whether he wanted to. His friends whooshed past him one by one, and his vehicle came to a full stop just after the finish line, the final jerk skewing its tail end sideways, thrusting Branxton off.

Bel gasped and covered her mouth. She hadn't meant for it to *throw* him—just for it to thunk, and skid to a lackluster halt.

Branxton landed in a clumsy roll on the other side of the paint, coughing, as a dotted pattern of blood formed over his forearms from the abrasion.

The other boys rushed to check on him. They hoisted him up, one of them on either side taking an arm.

"What the hell was that?" one of them demanded, still on his vehicle, hovering over to join them.

"I don't know," Branxton said. "It wasn't me."

Thane narrowed his eyes. "What do you mean it wasn't you? Who else would it be?"

"The skimmer was out of control," Branxton insisted.

The boys looked around at everyone, at each other, at the crowd of students who were gathering to see what had happened. Branxton glanced around for an explanation.

Then his eyes turned up toward the old panopt.

Bel minimized her holoscreen, darkness spilling over her and Aly as the glow disappeared into the holopad like a genie slipping back into its bottle.

"There!" Branxton pointed to where the girls were.

It was too dark for anyone to see them clearly. They scrambled across the catwalk and down the ladder. Aly's car waited for them down the road, but it would be a mad dash to get there before Branxton and his friends caught up. They'd all hopped back on their skimmers.

Aly's feet hit the grass and she ran, tapping on her wrist device to start the car's ignition remotely.

Bel landed after her and followed.

They raced for the bushes—the hum of skimmers resonating behind them—barely outrunning the headlight beams that would reveal them.

The car's gull-wing doors were already opening automatically up ahead, lifting to permit passengers. The headlights glowed blindingly as Bel and Aly climbed in.

Just as the skimmers approached, Aly peeled out from obscurity. The car doors didn't start lowering to close until the vehicle was already in motion.

Bel looked out the window as it settled into place. She caught a glimpse of Thane at the head of the group, staring after her, growing smaller in her view—with a flicker of recognition on his face.

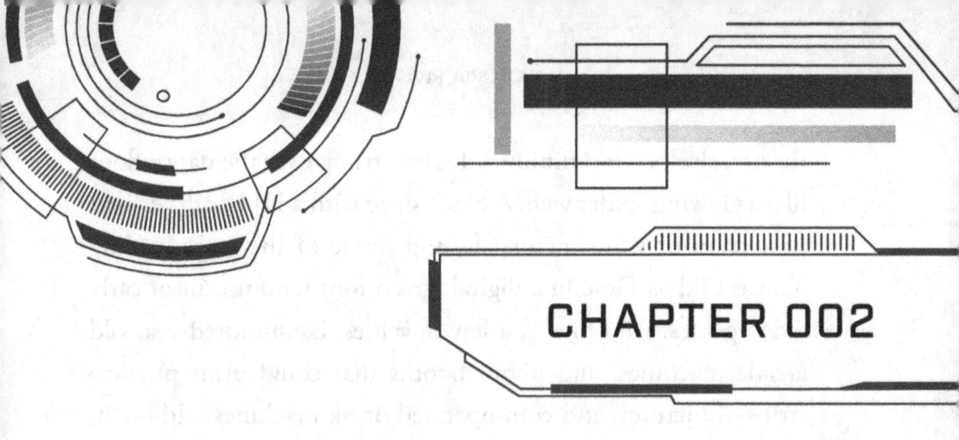

CHAPTER 002

"IT'S FINE," BEL SAID as she checked her eyeliner in the reflection of the gold elevator door.

It had now been approximately twenty-four hours since the incident on the highway, and while there was a chance that Thane might have recognized her, the boys couldn't prove she'd done anything wrong—or, for that matter, anything at all.

Aly fluffed her brown curls and sighed. "I really hope so."

"Let's try to have fun tonight. I mean, we only get to do this once, right?"

"Go to prom? Or employ your own brand of guerrilla war tactics against the social hierarchy?"

Bel patted the small holopad in her dress pocket. "Why not both?"

When the elevator doors parted, hip-hop music hit like a throb in her own chest. Bel stepped out and let her gaze trail over the scene—the rooftop of the Hotel De La Rosa cluttered with her classmates in a range of formal attire (some modern, others following the theme by incorporating the retro dresses or tuxedos from times past) bodies pulsing with the beat. The view of Ventura, West California sprawled out all around them, a glimmer of the ocean in the distance, palm trees swaying gently. Mission-style historical buildings, fashion boutiques, a VRplex theater, sleek condominiums. Lights strung over the dance floor like a glowing spider web. A black stage with a DJ booth. A light projection of words across the top frame of the stage reading Tale as Old as Time in a digital, green font reminiscent of early video games. And finally, a few novelties like hundred-year-old arcade machines, and photo booths that could print physical strips of pictures, and coin-operated drink machines (although, thankfully, they seemed to be dispensing beverages for free).

From the east side, a large panopt flashed above the roof's ledge, cycling through 3D ads and news clips. Its scanners' green lights remained steady at the bottom edge of the screen. As always, Bel absentmindedly felt for her InVisor. The scanners were intended for United Watch to keep an eye on criminal activity, with the ability to pick out the face of a wanted person almost instantly. They should have made her feel safe; instead, they made her wary. Still, she was determined not to let them intimidate her. The InVisor was her defiance, and she would do as she pleased.

Bel looked over at Aly, who was busy adjusting the tulle at the bottom of her knee-length, pink retro prom dress. Bel's own dress was purple and contoured, with a voluminous, draping bow at one hip, a sweetheart neckline, and a silky sheen. She'd struggled at first to squeeze her curves into it, but now she thought it hugged her body rather nicely.

Bel sniffed the air dramatically. "Do you smell that?"

Aly wrinkled her nose. "No. Why? What do you smell?"

Bel smiled. "I smell a RAT." She reached into her clutch purse and withdrew a strip of black dot stickers—dot drives, to most people—which she had programmed to act as remote access trojans. "*Several* RATs, in fact."

Aly, having spent enough time with Bel by now to at least

vaguely understand her jokes, rolled her eyes.

Perpendicular to the stage, a row of holographic screens stood out against the theme of vastly outdated technology, four screens in all, projecting out of flat devices set up on a table.

Cast your vote! they all demanded in scrolling letters. *Prom Monarchy 2087.*

With Aly in tow, Bel casually made her way past the arcade machines (where several of her classmates amused themselves trying to work the mechanisms and make progress on the games) and over to the voting screens. She waited for a couple of girls to finish voting, then nodded to Aly.

Aly nodded back and moved around to the other side, keeping lookout.

Carefully, Bel peeled one of the black dots from its backing and stuck it onto the first device. She repeated this for the next three, glancing up between each one to ensure no one saw her, then tucked away the other dots and motioned for Aly to follow.

Together, they slipped behind the curtains of the old Photo Booth and sat down.

"So, those will really just *give* you remote access?" Aly asked. "I thought you had to get a user to install malware first or something."

Bel set her own device on her lap and flicked it on, fingers ready before the screen and keys had even projected out. "These are special." She opened up a program called RAT King, which quickly displayed a list of all "entangled" devices. She tapped on the first one and began typing commands into a box that had popped up.

"TapResponse 1 ..." Bel muttered to herself as she typed. "Selection equals ... 'false.' Interface simulation ... equals ... 'true.' Input equals 'selfsame.'"

She paused for a moment and peered through a sliver of an opening between the curtain and the edge of the Photo Booth, through which the voting screens were visible. Another few students had accumulated there, one standing in front of the first screen. It beeped to confirm the girl's identity—a necessary facial scan to prevent duplicate votes—then presented her with a series of rectangles, each bearing the name of one of the prom monarchy nominees.

The girl tapped a rectangle. It highlighted in response to her touch, then gave her a *ping* and a confirmation screen. *Thanks for your vote!* chimed a voice.

Bel looked at her own screen for the incoming data. Text appeared character by character, in quick succession, in front of her.

StudentID 01343
Input = WriteIn
WriteIn = 01343

"Did it work?" Aly asked.

Bel nodded. She typed another few commands. "And *this* will update all the votes that have already been cast."

"Who do you think it would have been?" said Aly.

"Based on this data set? Vanessa Hester and … Branxton Lowes."

Aly huffed. "Of course."

With a few more taps, Bel finished up her work, minimized her screen, and turned off her device. "Now," she said, "Let's go enjoy this party."

They pushed between bodies and made their way up close to the front—because of course that's where they would want to be when the winners were announced—and found a small niche with a prime view of the center of the stage.

Not far off, Bel spotted Branxton and Thane standing with a group of friends and dates. Both were wearing oversized pastel blazers with t-shirts underneath, as a nod to some caricature of the decade this theme was trying to emulate. Bel wondered if any of the fashion attempts here tonight (including her own and Aly's) were even remotely accurate, or if they had just been assumptions passed down over the last century, with inspiration taken more from parody films and Halloween costumes than from any logical source.

Bel turned so her back was to them, straightened the large bow on her hip, and then let the beat of the music move her. Meanwhile, she watched the panopt within her line of sight, as it flashed an ad for Neon Sniper II, the sequel to the VR game she'd been obsessed with for the past year.

Coming July 3, 2087

Then it switched over to a tribute screen.

In Memoriam

ELODIE ACERO

PRESIDENT, CEO, AND FOUNDER OF VIVOREX LABS

2037-2085

For her outstanding accomplishments in biotechnology, advancements in restorative medicines, and contributions to medical charities.

Bel recognized the photo of the Afro-Latina scientist and businesswoman alongside the text, the same portrait that had been on the cover of *Time*. Elodie stood proud, arms crossed, her dark skin glowing, black spirals grazing her shoulders. She'd been in and out of the news since Bel could remember, a beloved revolutionary when it came to biotechnical developments. Cancer treatment machines that had made the disease and all its variants virtually non-existent, organ replacements that mimicked human tissues, advanced prosthetic eyes that were better than the real thing. The last miracle she'd produced before her death had been much more simplistic in comparison—Sanaflamm, a topical medicine that could rapid-heal skin through some nanotechnological component suspended in a liquid solution, particularly in the case of burn wounds. The drug still hadn't hit the market yet, but it was supposed to be groundbreaking. Unfortunately, she'd died before fully developing a treatment for agnemia, the rare but emerging blood disease that had killed her two years ago.

Due to the subject matter, Bel had also always remembered vividly the news that had followed a little over a year later, the report that Elodie's teenage son, Andro, had died by suicide—cocaine overdose, in the wake of depression related to his mother's death. Bel remembered because she had immediately thought that she didn't blame him; when she'd lost her parents, she'd all but wanted to die too, just so she didn't have to keep thinking about what the rest of her life was going to be like without them.

The DJ's voice startled her back to the present, reminding everyone one last time to vote, as the music shifted to a new song. Bel and Aly danced alongside other girls from school, the casual friends with whom they shared classes (and the occasional lunch table) but whom they didn't otherwise spend much time with.

Three songs later, the music stopped and the DJ's voice came over the speaker again.

"Alright, alright. The moment you've all been waiting for. Give it up for Orwell High's student body president, Hazel Haines!"

Hazel Haines took center stage, along with the mic, and gave a little curtsy in her silky teal party dress. Her dirty-blonde hair had been combed and teased into oblivion, and her lips were dark pink. "Thanks, everyone, for coming tonight!" Her voice echoed cheerfully, and the ninety-four students in attendance applauded her words. "Okay, let's do this!"

She raised a mini holopad so everyone could see the hologram floating above it—a 3D envelope, spinning mid-air. "Ready?"

The students cheered their assent.

Hazel smiled and tucked the wireless mic under one arm while she tapped the envelope.

Dramatic techno music played in the background.

The envelope spun the opposite direction and flipped open. A digital card slipped out and upward.

"Your 2087 prom monarchs are …."

She brought the holopad closer to herself, frowning at the words on the card. "Um …"

She glanced back at the DJ like he might have an explanation, then back at the audience, which has begun to murmur their confusion amongst themselves.

"I'm not really sure what's going on," said Hazel. "This must be some kind of prank."

"What does it say?" someone shouted.

Vanessa Hester had a pronounced crease between her perfectly manicured eyebrows as she whispered to the other monarch nominees.

"It's, um …" Hazel hesitated. "It's … all of us …?"

She tap-flipped the card, revealing a list of names so long it had to scroll continuously."

A few of the students laughed, or slow-clapped their approval of the joke, but the majority leaned in to one another and exchanged befuddled whispers.

Except for Vanessa, who boldly stated, "This is *ridiculous!*"

Watching from within the mass of her peers, Bel tried to suppress a smile, but she could feel the amusement breaking out on her face.

That's when she spotted Branxton staring right at her. He nudged Thane beside him and pointed.

Thane zeroed in on her too, nudging the guys around him to move out of the way as he marched toward her.

Reflexively, Bel took a step backward.

"*You* did this somehow," he said. "And it was you last night, too, wasn't it?"

Branxton came and flanked him. "You almost *killed* me!"

"How'd you do it?" Thane demanded

Bel looked from him to Branxton and back. "Do what?"

"You're going to pay for that skimmer," Branxton said. "And I don't just mean what I'm going to do to make your life miserable from now on. I'm talking about actual money."

Bel feigned confidence as every student turned to watch the confrontation, a musical pulse beating in the background. "I don't see how you being a drunken jackass with your friends has anything to do with me."

"That's not what happened," Branxton argued.

"Really? Because that kind of seems 'on brand' for you."

"Don't play stupid, *Belinda*," said Thane.

Bel recoiled at the sound of her whole name—the one that wasn't really hers. "I don't have to listen to this."

With clacking heels, she walked away, off the dance floor and toward the east side of the roof.

"Bel ..." Aly said.

The panopt cast its light on the open concrete, flashing a mascara ad.

Lashes for days. Voluminate.

Thane followed her, cornering her near the ledge as she headed for the stairwell.

"Since the second you came to Orwell, something about you has been off. You don't have any Atmo posts from more than two years ago. You always seem to know everything about *everyone*. And I'm pretty sure—" he snatched her holopad out of her dress pocket.

"Hey!" She reached for the device as he held it just out of her grasp.

It woke at his touch, revealing all her notifications.

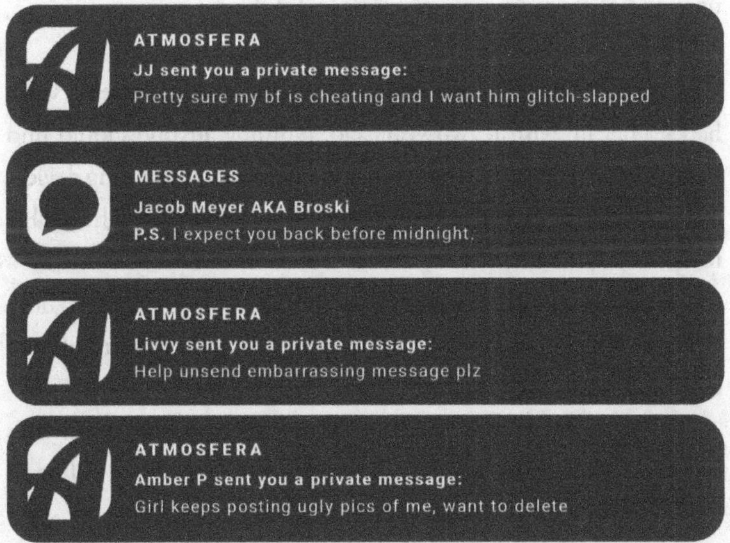

"You're the glitch-slap girl," he said. "The hacker. I *knew* it."

Thane moved up close to Bel, who stood her ground.

"Taking hacking jobs for money?" he said. "Of *course* you're capable of hacking a skimmer system. But that's still not everything you're hiding, is it?"

She took back her holopad, shoved his chest, and went to move past him, but he grabbed her by the wrist, spinning her around so that the panopt light was directly in her eyes.

He seemed to be searching her face—and only an instant too late did she realize why.

His fingernail scraped the skin of her hairline, and pried off her InVisor.

She immediately turned her face away, but not before one of the green lights at the base of the panopt turned red.

Her pulse quickened.

Thane held his finger up to the light, showing the microdot. "Trying to pass this off as a birthmark?" He scoffed. "My cousin uses one of these to get into clubs in LA."

Bel pursed her lips, trying not to panic.

The InVisor technology had been fairly obscure when VOLT had set her up with it two years ago. Nothing anyone should find suspicious, the operatives had told her. But it seemed masking devices weren't so secret anymore. People with enough money might be able to get one (a low-end one, at least) and have it programmed—a sophisticated fake ID for entry into restricted areas or events. Still, Bel hadn't imagined someone her own age would have heard of such a thing, at least not as anything more than fiction.

Thane seemed to be waiting for her to respond, mere inches away, with her entire alternate life coded into a spec on his finger. "Who are you really, Belinda Meyer?"

In response, she delivered a palm-heel strike to his face—and ran.

Bel was halfway down one flight in the stairwell when Aly came clacking down after her.

"Bel! Are you okay? Where are you going?"

"I have to get home."

The elevator would have stopped at every floor on the way back to the lobby, and she couldn't stand the thought of waiting as people got on and off, over and over, while her whole life might be falling apart behind the scenes.

The red light of the panopt still flashed in her mind.

"Fine," Aly said. "I'll drive you. But can you please tell me what just happened back there?"

Bel didn't reply and she didn't slow down. After another flight, she abandoned her shoes on the steps, letting them fall off her feet as she ran.

It was only as they reached the car that Bel finally noticed the sensation of the cool concrete on her bare feet. Everything around her was muted, blurry. What had she done?

She touched the bare spot on her hairline, and a sense of dread consumed her.

It might take a few hours to process in the system, but the panopt had seen her. The *real* her. And she was in trouble.

She looked at Aly, who waited patiently for an explanation, and finally said, "I'm not who you think I am."

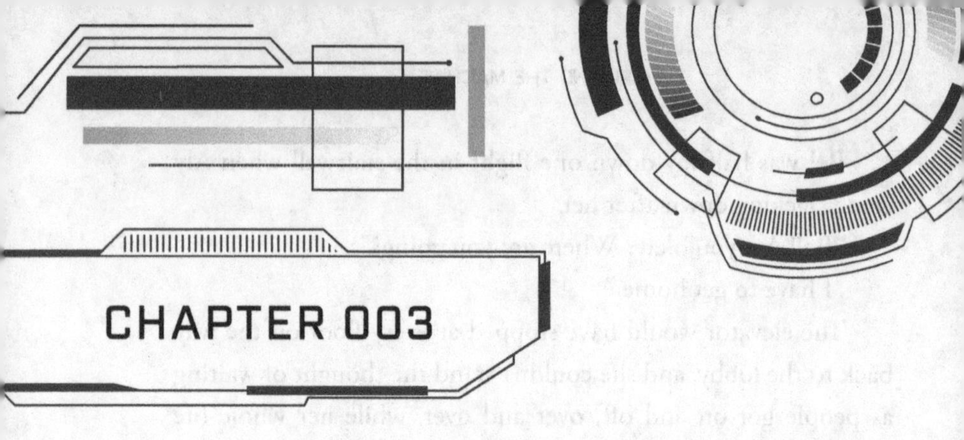

CHAPTER 003

MATEO STEPPED OUT onto the tiny porch of the blue and white house nestled snugly between all the others on the street. It was a cluster of little ramblers with bay windows and tropical-plant gardens, all crammed together with barely any room to breathe the salty ocean air, but it was a perfect place to disappear. A quiet neighborhood with no panopts for at least a mile, and no affluence to draw any attention—although the neighbors could be nosy at times.

The sound of the news anchor's voice on the holoscreen TV followed him out from the living room. Ignoring it for the moment, he inhaled slowly, trying to calm his nerves. The entire street was quiet and empty, with nothing but the shadows of palm trees in the glow of the streetlamps, but he couldn't help feeling anxious.

It's just a high school dance, he reminded himself.

Except that it was several miles away in Ventura, and Bel sometimes had a way of making normal events more … interesting.

She wouldn't tell him what she'd been doing out by the old highway last night, but he knew she hadn't been there to watch those dumbasses race; she'd been up to something. And if he had had any control over her at this point, he wouldn't have let her go off with Aly tonight. But alas, he was "not Dad," as Bel so vehemently reminded him whenever she got the chance.

"*Today marks the two-year anniversary of the death of Elodie Acero,*" said the anchor, drawing Mateo's attention and pulling him back inside, "*beloved biotechnical mastermind responsible for curing multiple diseases and the development of groundbreaking medical and surgical technologies.*"

Mateo took a seat on a black futon and picked up a bag of open Flamin' Hot Limón Cheetos.

"*Vivorex Labs reports a delay in progress for several of the company's projects since the founder's passing. However, current Vivorex president Soto Acero, brother to the late Elodie Acero, stated in an interview last July that the stall may have more to do with internal politics, particularly after the company's Vice President, Veronika Mandersloot, was ousted from her position for misuse of company resources and leading unethical experiments.*

The woman in question appeared on the screen, dressed in a tailored blazer, her blunt-cut blonde hair grazing the shoulder pads. It was a clip from the day she'd been dismissed, where members of the press swarmed her as she exited Vivorex Labs headquarters, while she hid most of her face behind oversized sunglasses and refused to comment.

Vivorex had often been a topic of interest to Mateo, ever since his internship with Kleid Co. Security. Vivorex had been a loyal client, but seemed prone to scandal. Mateo supposed biotechnology was inherently dicey, though, manipulating nature for industrial purposes. It was bound to get out of hand, and people were bound to take things too far at some point.

Mateo set down the Cheetos, wiped the red finger-dust on his jeans, and picked up his holopad, whose open window of code had been hovering in the air. He stared at the symbols, the back end of a site for a company selling biodegradable shoes. It was the type of work he could have done in junior high—in his sleep. He took a deep breath and held his fingers over the projected keys, scanning the code and preparing to make edits.

The code had begun to blend together into an incoherent jumble, along with the endless string of similar, menial tasks he received each week. Product landing pages, login authentication, plugins, modal popups.

He stopped, rubbed his eyes, sighed, and closed the screen, setting the device back on the futon. He looked around the room, at the wrappers and socks scattered all over, then moved to the kitchen, where empty dishes sat on the counter with the remnants of his breakfast, lunch, and snacks that barely passed for dinner. Remote work was one of the better developments of the early twenty-first century, but he had to admit it was tough on housekeeping. Or maybe *he* was just tough on housekeeping.

"In other news, two members of the dismantled Knight Crew syndicate were apprehended yesterday afternoon."

Mateo looked through to the other room as the Knight Crew's symbol flashed onto the screen—the outline of an upside-down triangle with three vertical lines intersecting it, along with its Latin motto: Metallum Foris, Metallum Intus.

Mateo clenched his jaw.

"The crime syndicate has struggled to regain territory over the past three years, ever since an attempted sting operation by the anticrime agency VOLT—the Vigilant Order of Lateral Tactics— went awry in the midst of an unexpected turf war that left many wounded and several operatives dead. The following members, however, are still on the loose ..."

The anchor rattled off several names, mostly ones Mateo didn't recognize. Then, one stuck in his mind like a harpoon.

"*... including Damian Knight, a high-ranking family member and self-proclaimed digital sicario of the Knight Crew, currently believed to be hiding somewhere south of the border.*"

"Digital sicario," Mateo repeated bitterly. A hitman who didn't *kill* his targets but who could destroy lives by altering personal records and fabricating criminal histories.

Mateo clenched his fists and went to the kitchen to pick up some of the clutter. There were four near-empty bottles of Tapatío in various places, and two empty boxes of Brown Sugar Cinnamon Pop-Tarts. A few more dirty dishes sat around, which Mateo took to the sink, along with those from the living room.

Then he spotted a handful of mail envelopes on the counter. He picked them up, leafing through the stack. It was obnoxious how these small towns still used paper mail, he thought, although the marketing technique made sense—when digital messages could be deleted instantaneously, a physical document could persist, and stand out—and likely wasn't going anywhere no matter how advanced technology became.

A booklet of coupons for DiMaggio's pizza, addressed to Current Resident. A utility bill addressed to Jacob Meyer. A credit card offer from the local credit union for Belinda L. Meyer.

Mateo tacked the coupons and the utility bill to the fridge with magnets, then scoffed as he tore up the credit card offer and tossed it in with the recycling.

These aliases were ridiculous. Mirabel couldn't pass for a "Belinda Meyer." "Belinda Meyer" was a white woman in her forties, not a teenage girl with a dark complexion and a nose ring. Ironically, his sister had been happy to receive the name.

"People can call me 'Bel' again," she'd said. In the years they'd been in hiding, only *he* ever called her Bel anymore—in private, of course—and, whenever she'd pissed him off, he'd had to remind himself not to call her by her *full* name—Mirabel Alondra Dayana Solís, complete with its intended pronunciation and inflection.

Mateo had immediately discouraged her enthusiasm. He didn't like the idea of anything that might tie them to their real identities. But Bel was tenacious. After three relocations and three different aliases, she'd been determined to take something of herself back.

As Mateo passed Bel's room on the way back to the living area and glanced through her wide-open door—a perfect example of how lax she was about keeping secrets—he realized she'd slowly been taking back more and more over time. Aside from conventional teenage things, like a bottle of black nail polish, the VR headset with which she spent hours playing Neon Sniper, and a few items of clothing draped over the bed, her desk was strewn with wires and circuit boards, CPUs, and old holopads ripped open and reconstructed. A wireless soldering iron sat upright in its dock.

Then there was the Ecker, a handheld Van Eck phreaking device Bel had built from scratch and tried to enter into the science fair during their Iowa relocation—which Mateo had explicitly forbidden. Showing everyone that she knew how to cobble together something with a built-in SDR that could pick up electromagnetic waves, and software that could intercept and manipulate basic data transfers and crack passwords, was officially crossing the line into conspicuous. Then again, Bel's digging through the physical parts of electronic devices was nothing compared to the digging she'd been doing through their *digital* parts; more than once, he'd caught her taking money to get background information on someone or to recover messages that had been sent during a drunken rage.

Mateo shook his head woefully. It was partially his fault. He'd taught her too much. His profession had stoked her curiosity at a young age and now she was ablaze with a never-ending drive for information. If anyone knew what she was capable of, they'd never believe she was just boring old Belinda Meyer from Orwell. Mirabel Solís would be visible through that already-thin veneer of false identity. People would start to ask questions—and questions were dangerous.

The sound of the news crept back to him.

"Authorities continue the search for the missing members of the Knight Crew, along with several conspirators from the same operation that have yet to be apprehended. Any information on these individuals should be reported immediately."

Mateo stepped back into the living room and stood in front of the holoscreen. A grid of headshots filled it from top to bottom. The last one was a mirror image of him, except for the hair on his head and face—a trim cut with a nice part and fade, jaw shaved clean. Now he hid beneath a dark, scraggly mess, accentuated by persistent scruff. Below the photo was a name: Mateo Solís.

His throat tightened. Thanks to his InVisor, the panopts couldn't identify him—and thanks to his current appearance, even people who adamantly watched the news wouldn't be able to either—but knowing this didn't ever fully ease his anxiety at seeing himself lined up with criminals. He croaked at the AI system. "TV off."

The holoscreen faded into silence and darkness. He sat back on the futon and rested his head on its top edge, taking a deep breath. If he tried hard enough, he could almost make himself believe that Mateo Solís really was someone else, that the young man sitting in this house right now was just Jacob Meyer, web designer, skateboard enthusiast, lover of Hawaiian pizza. He ran his hands through his hair, then clapped his hands onto his knees, preparing to get up again when his watch beeped. He held it up and tapped once.

A small holographic notification flew up.

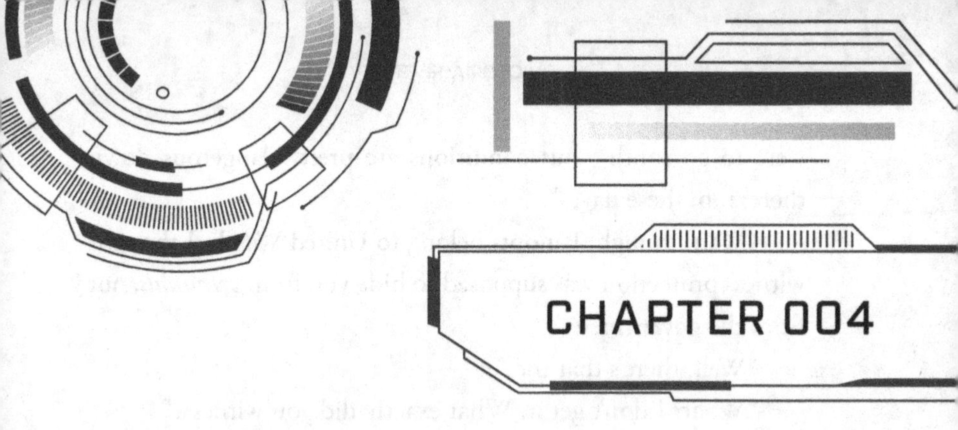

CHAPTER 004

"WHAT DO YOU MEAN YOU'RE NOT who I think you are?" Aly hit several buttons on the car's touchscreen in sequence, which immediately kicked up the speed.

The vehicle's screen view then turned to a map, showing the car's current location as a blinking blue dot.

"It's a long story. My name is Bel, but not Belinda. It's Mirabel. I didn't grow up in Santa Fe; I grew up in Palo Alto. And there are some very bad people who want my brother dead."

"Why are you telling me this now? What happened back there?"

"The panopt," Bel said. "Usually I have a device that blocks me from the scanners."

"*Blocks* you? Why?"

"It's called an InVisor. It's really small, hidden at my hairline. It ties my face to a whole other profile so they don't know who I really am."

"And Thane ripped it off ..." Aly realized aloud. She seemed to be mentally working out the other details. "So, you're in, like, witness protection or something?"

"Sort of."

"Why didn't you just, like ... leave the country?"

"Customs will check now for masking devices. Unless we

were to go south—but conditions are pretty dangerous down there, too, these days."

"Wait, though. Panopts belong to United Watch. I thought witness protection was supposed to hide you from *criminals*, not from the government."

"Well, there's that too."

"What? I don't get it. What exactly did you witness?"

"Not me. My brother. There's this criminal organization—traffickers, mostly. He was working with our dad and an anticrime initiative to take them down by hacking into their network records, intercepting product shipments and all that, but one of their operations went wrong."

"Anticrime? Like, the police?"

"No. It's called VOLT. It's a whole other thing. Law enforcement can be paid off. There's too much corruption. Anyway, there was tons of shooting back and forth. My brother got away; my dad wasn't so lucky. But the operation destroyed a huge shipment of product and killed a bunch of the organization's leaders—and the ones left standing were furious. They have powerful people, people who can take your whole identity and turn you into a fugitive of the law. So anyone they couldn't kill, they found other ways to ruin their lives. Now my brother's identity is tied to a whole string of crimes—vidrinium trafficking, cyberterrorism, financial fraud, armed robbery, *murder*. He's got a huge bounty on his head. They've been looking for him for years, along with any relatives that could lead them to him."

"You're saying one scan to *your* face could lead them to your brother?"

"Yes. Everything's connected in the database. Those cameras see and hear everything—and Thane said my alias out loud right before the alarm went off. My whole identity's been compromised, my record as Belinda Meyer, my address, anyone I live with—all of it."

"So, what now? I drop you off and then … you disappear? I never see you again?"

"I don't know. Now that the system's flagged, it's only a matter of time before they connect me to Mateo. Jacob. Sorry—it's hard to keep it all straight. I have to get home and make sure he's okay."

"How will you know for sure?

"The organization that's protecting us has a tap into the UW database. They get alerts if any of their stewards show up in the system, and they're supposed to let Mateo know. With so many reports, it can take time for United Watch to assess threats and decide whether to dispatch authorities, so I've got a bit of time, but there's no telling how much."

"If you're questioned," Bel added, "you say whatever you need to say to protect yourself, okay? Tell them anything they need to know. Don't try to keep me safe."

"What are they going to ask me?"

The car pulled up to the front of Bel's house.

"Maybe nothing. But Mateo and I will figure this out. And for now, you need to get as far away from me as possible." Bel touched the screen to open the door. She took one last look at Aly, then reached over and hugged her. "I'll contact you as soon as it's safe."

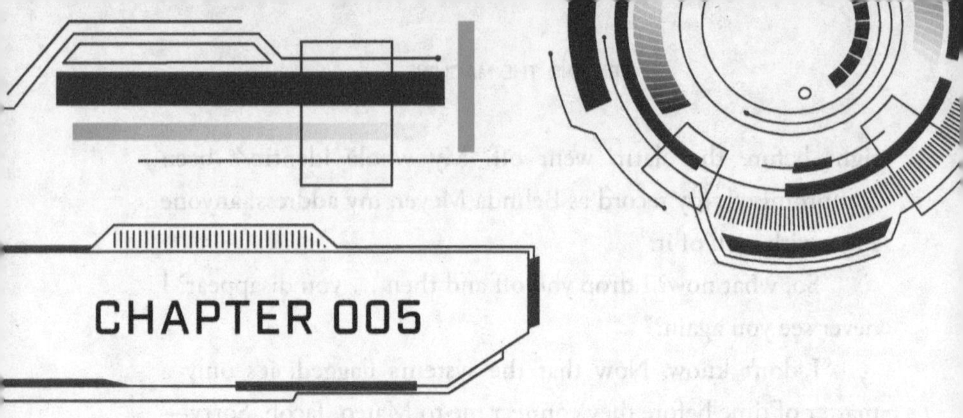

CHAPTER 005

WHEN BEL RUSHED INTO THE HOUSE, she nearly tripped on the pile of supplies in the entryway.

Two large backpacks, like something belonging to a couple of long-distance hikers, were propped up on the floor with sleeping bags attached, ready to go, along with a duffel bag.

Bel was all too familiar with the contents, having prepared for this moment from years ago. The packs contained tarps and thermal blankets, water bottles, dehydrated food, packages of Sparkfyre, multi-tools, flares, paracord bracelets, water purification tablets, and flashlights—for starters. The duffel contained an old GPS device, a first-aid kit, a compact camping tent, and a pair of extra clothes for each of them.

Mateo's face appeared at the end of the hall. "We have to go."

"What—"

He picked up a laserlighter from the side table and shoved it into his pocket. "VOLT sent me a message five minutes ago. Grab anything you don't want to leave behind—within reason. I'm going to get the bikes down."

"The bikes ..." she repeated.

That could only mean one thing.

Bel hurried to her room as her brother disappeared toward the garage. There were a thousand things she didn't want to leave behind, works in progress and random trinkets, but there was no time or space to take them all. She grabbed a bullet-sized digibank from her desk—which contained every penny she had—then grabbed a set of two-way radios she'd barely finished repairing, a keychain full of tiny drives that held photos and documents, and the Ecker. She quickly changed out of her dress and into a pair of jeans, slip-on vans, a gray tank top, and her green cargo vest. She stuffed the bank and the drives into the different pockets of her vest. She deliberated over her soldering iron, but finally grabbed it along with its battery-powered dock and a small roll of solder. She'd just returned to the backpacks and slipped the larger items inside when Mateo reappeared.

He picked up one of the backpacks and Bel slung the other one over her shoulders.

They reached the garage, where two bicycles were propped up waiting for them. No electronics, no enhancements, just regular, old-fashioned bikes. Vehicles that couldn't be tracked or hacked.

Bel was about to mount hers when Mateo pulled the inciniforge off the wire shelf and set it on the floor. He opened it from the top of its glossy black barrel, and dropped in a handful of electronic devices, then unlatched his watch and dropped it in too. He nodded at Bel.

Hesitating, Bel slipped her holopad out of her pocket, held it over the opening, and let go.

Mateo shut the lid, with its heat-resistant ceramic-glass window, and pressed IGNITE.

In a matter of seconds, the unit glowed with heat. Within its depths, the screen of each device began to crack, the metal melted, the CPUs became exposed and then curled and shrank and turned to ash, releasing streaks of colored flames along the way.

Bel felt herself die a little as she watched. Without looking up yet, she asked, "Where are we going?"

"Northeast." Mateo mounted his bike. "VOLT sent me coordinates. I already programmed them into the GPS. Somewhere in the Los Padres National Forest."

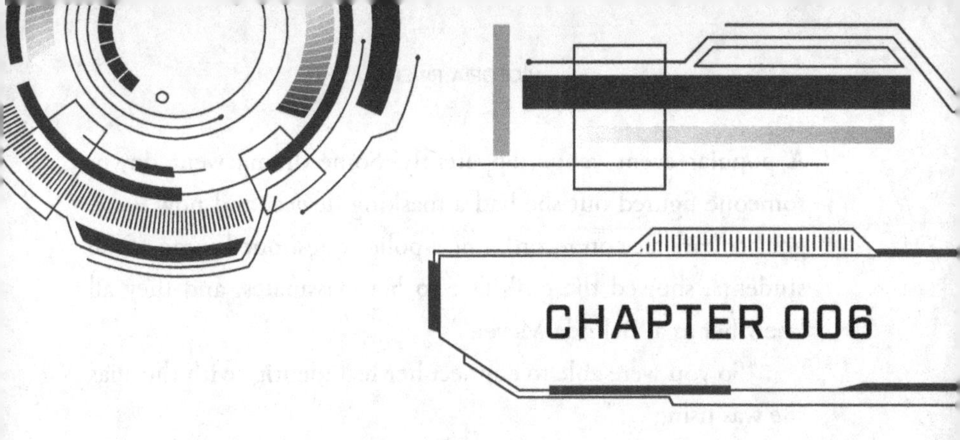

CHAPTER 006

DETECTIVE REYNOLDS SCANNED THE HOLOSCREEN at his desk, looking over the panoptical report on one frame, and compared it to the profiles on a second frame. "This guy's managed to keep hidden for almost three years now."

His co-worker, Detective Jimenez was busy scanning other documents for another case at her own work station adjacent to his, and only nodded halfheartedly. "Criminals are good at that."

"Not this good. Not the younger ones. Unless they're working with someone who knows what they're doing—and I'm betting Mateo Solís definitely is."

"Like who?"

Detective Reynolds shrugged. "Probably one of those vigilante organizations. His record shows he was still a kid when he started making serious trouble. Barely eighteen. And it looks like he's been dragging his younger sister along with him. It'd be hard to keep them both under wraps without help."

"I'm surprised it was a panopt that caught them. It's getting easier to fool scanners these days, what with InVisors and EchoMasks and Ghostrs and all that."

"I don't think it would have been that easy, if it weren't for the girl. She was the one who was spotted—caught by a panopt in Ventura overlooking the rooftop of the Hotel de la Rosa.

A popular event venue, apparently. Some drama went down, someone figured out she had a masking device, and now we've got her bare face on record. Local police questioned some of the students, showed the girl's face to her classmates, and they all knew her as a 'Belinda Meyer.'"

"So you were able to connect her real identity with the alias she was using …"

"Yep. And this 'Belinda Meyer' has a brother, 'Jacob,' not unlike Mirabel Solís, whose brother we've been hoping to catch sight of for quite some time now. With that information, we got an address."

"Except you still didn't get *him*."

Detective Reynolds shook his head. "Skipped town. The place was already abandoned when the police arrived. Someone must have tipped him off. He might have helpers with the skills to keep tabs on reports that come in about anyone they're protecting."

"So how are you going to find him?" asked Detective Jimenez. "He's apparently good at disappearing. Probably already a ways off."

"Already requested the communications record from his data provider. If he *is* working with someone—and I'm sure he is—they'll have communicated recently. Maybe given him the location of a safe house or a rendezvous point. That'll be a good start."

"And if he's already off the grid? Somewhere remote, with no tech? How will you catch him before he moves on?"

Detective Reynolds smiled. "That's what panoptical drones are for."

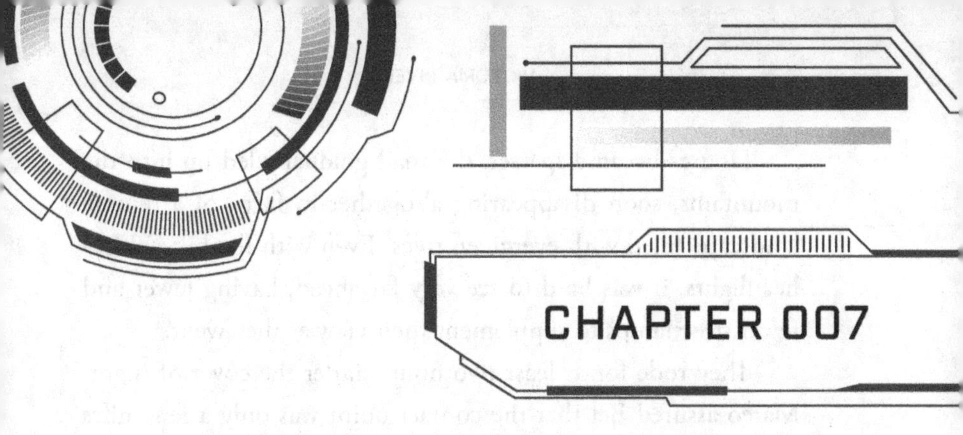

CHAPTER 007

BEL RODE BEHIND MATEO, who steered the bike with one hand while he checked the GPS with the other. The device was so old they'd had to order a special battery to power it, but Mateo had insisted on having it for emergencies. It was so outdated that United Watch wouldn't be able to track it—wouldn't waste time trying. United Watch knew people couldn't live off the grid very well for long, anyway.

"Someone from VOLT will meet us and take us to a safe house," Mateo said.

Bel remembered this plan vaguely. They'd gone over contingencies before. She hadn't expected to have to go through with any of them, though. She could only hope that they were at least a few steps ahead, based on their history of misleading aliases and the fact that they had gotten out of town so quickly.

After this, Bel figured they'd start the re-identification process all over again and move somewhere new, like Ohio, and she would get a new name she hated and work at an outlet mall or a VRcade.

The bike ride was long and a lot of it was hilly. Bel's calves ached and her underarms were soaked with sweat. The coordinates were for twenty-six miles out, based on the GPS unit, to a place called Ojai.

Houses became sparser, the road gradually led up into the mountains, soon disappearing altogether in favor of a remote landscape filled with evergreen trees. Even with the bikes' LED headlights, it was hard to see very far ahead, having fewer and fewer streetlamps to supplement their view as they went.

They rode for at least two hours under the cover of night. Mateo assured Bel that the contact point was only a few miles more.

Pulling off the Maricopa Highway led them onto a smaller, country road, where they rode a little farther until they reached an open space overlooking what used to be Matilija Dam, now deconstructed.

They turned off the bike lights in favor of dimmer, alkaline battery-powered flashlights and looked around. Bel sucked down most of a bottle of water in a matter of seconds.

"This is it," Mateo said. "Someone should be here soon."

There were still remnants of the dam, portions of concrete rising much higher than the river itself, cut away in the center to allow the water and its sediment to pass through, part of an abandoned removal and restoration initiative from long ago. Bel gazed up at the partially demolished walls, shining her light on them for a moment, then took off her pack and sat down on a boulder.

Mateo raked his fingers through his dark hair and scrubbed his hands over his scruff. "Since it's going to be a while, do you wanna tell me what's going on?"

"You assume I have something to do with all this?"

"Don't you?"

"I don't know. Maybe. Probably."

"I've told you a *million* times—"

"I know." She pulled her knees to her chest and draped one

arm over them. "'Be careful,' 'Don't draw attention to yourself,' 'Keep your distance from other people.' Don't eat or breathe or walk out in the open where anyone can see. Act like I don't even exist. Be a ghost."

"I never said *that*."

She threw up her hands. "I'm not *you*, Mateo. You don't even try to have a life. You never leave the house, you don't have any friends. People try to get to know you and you act all skittish and weird. That's way more conspicuous than just socializing like a human being."

"I've *sacrificed* a life to help keep you safe. But here you are doing everything possible to cancel out my efforts."

"It doesn't take any effort to be afraid."

"It actually takes a *lot* of effort."

"Well, it's *wasted* effort."

"Clearly." He threw her a pointed look.

"Look, I'm sure everything will be fine. We'll have to start over, and that sucks, but we'll make it work; we always do."

"No, *I* always do." Mateo slapped a palm to his chest. "If you keep acting this way, this is going to keep happening. I know about that second Atmo account you use to make money—leaving a trail of security breaches that eventually someone is going to figure out."

"I'm not sorry for what I can do. I'm not sorry for finding a way to get the money I need to have a life and a future. For making sure people pay when they hurt people I care about."

"That's not how you're supposed to handle these things, Bel. Otherwise we wouldn't be here right now, would we?"

"You didn't see what Branxton did to Aly. Or what he's been doing for months now."

"Then you talk to an adult—or the police," he chided. "You

don't hack people's devices and take matters into your own hands! And that's not even the half of it. The way you act at school, getting into trouble every other week, not even trying to hide what you're capable of. You're supposed to *lie low*."

"You want me to just pretend I'm an idiot?" She kicked over her backpack. "Let the Knight Crew drive us under a rock? You didn't die that night with Dad, but you might as well have, because you're definitely not living. Do you think that's what Mom or Dad would want?"

"It doesn't matter what they'd want. It's what we have to do. Damian Knight is still out there somewhere. The Crew's in the process of regrouping, and eventually they're going to be back in full force."

"And meanwhile, we're supposed to let them erase us like we never existed?"

Mateo clenched his jaw. "He's not some guy at school who pissed you off. You can't just puff out your chest and tell him where to go. He's dangerous. Someone who has the hacking skills to infiltrate United Watch is not someone you screw around with. It's not about *letting* him and the Knight Crew erase us— or, more accurately, letting them make *me* into a criminal—it's about not letting him take more from us than he already has."

"You want to cut our losses."

He sighed. "You can rebel and try to take back little pieces of your former life and who you are, but it won't change anything. For every criminal that died that night, at least two more got away. They could be anywhere, trying to blend in just like us. I follow the news every night; UW is still looking for dozens of them. Some are barely older than you. Just last night, the anchor mentioned they were looking for a guy named Silas Fine, son of one of the leaders of the Knight Crew—nineteen years old, killed six people over a shipment of raw vidrinium less than an hour from Orwell."

Bel couldn't say she was surprised. Vidrinium was the center of an ongoing battle, and had been for years. Despite evidence of the detrimental side effects of its decay, its potential to provide large amounts of power for long periods of time with a very small amount had become highly coveted among criminals. Entire factories and facilities could work off of vidrinium for months at a time, completely independent of the electric power grid and difficult to trace—perfect for anyone running shady operations or trafficking networks.

"It's not like I've been hanging out in back alleys and abandoned warehouses, Mateo. What happened earlier was a freak accident. How was I supposed to know Thane had any idea what an InVisor is?"

"All the reason to be even more careful, to not let anyone—anyone at all—get close."

"There are only a *few* people who actually want to kill us. You realize that, right?"

He shook his head. "There's no risk worth taking if there's even the slightest chance I could lose you too. But I guess you don't feel the same way about me ..."

"Mateo, come on." She reached for him but he pulled away, muttering a few curses in Spanish before standing and putting some distance between them.

He reminded her of their dad, the same peppered language, the choice to slip into the tongue of their heritage when English didn't quite capture the moment.

She and Mateo hadn't been taught to speak Spanish initially; they'd just been a couple of "no sabo" kids with whatever limited vocabulary they might have picked up in passing. More often, the language was a way for their parents to have private conversations when they couldn't be completely alone. Bel used to commit certain overheard phrases to memory and repeat them to her holopad translator—some of her earliest efforts to crack codes or gain information she wasn't supposed to know. But eventually she and Mateo were enrolled in a dual immersion school so they could become fluent. After that, the words came naturally, a curse or an exclamation, a phrase here and there to convey emotion. Most of the time, though, Bel felt like it was some distant part of her, one she kept trying to connect to, but which kept slipping away.

Hours passed. Bel had tried to sleep on the ground, using one of the thin blankets from the backpacks that did nothing to protect her from the prickly, dry grass underneath. When she couldn't sleep, she paced, or sat on the boulder again, feeling lost without her holopad, forced to stare into silence with no distractions.

Mateo had found a boulder shaped like a reclining chair and was lying with his arm over his eyes.

Desperate for something to do, Bel pulled out the flashlight again and reorganized the backpacks, rearranging items to be more easily accessible.

Each item she touched reminded her of all the times Mateo had forced her to learn to use it. Reading a compass. Deploying a paracord bracelet and weaving it back together. Utilizing all the features of the multitool. Implementing first aid procedures. As if that hadn't been enough, he'd also enrolled her in multiple self-defense classes over the past couple of years. Of course he hadn't been wrong to do so; under these circumstances, they had to be ready for anything.

When she came across the Ecker, she turned it on. The LCD

screen lit up. It wasn't fancy; she'd built it with rudimentary parts and pieces—cheap stuff—and tried to keep it small. In the old days it would've taken a whole van full of equipment and an antenna array to pack all these features together. But this one fit in Bel's hands and ran on a lithium-ion battery with wireless charging. After a while, she set it down and lay on the grass to rest.

Soon, the sun's reflective light peeked up over the horizon before the sun itself, throwing pale pink hues across the sky, mirrored on the surging waters of Matilija Creek that ran to the Ventura River.

The Ecker beeped, startling Bel from sleep. On the screen, several blips appeared.

The blips were moving toward her and Mateo, coming from a quarter mile away.

A second later, Mateo sat upright abruptly. He scrambled to his feet, eyes aimed at the sky. He grabbed his pack and took Bel by the elbow, dragging her to her feet, guiding her to the trees. Bel stuffed the Ecker back into her own pack as she went.

A low hum filled the air, growing louder. It couldn't be VOLT; the agents would never be that inconspicuous. And the sound was coming from the sky.

When Bel realized what it was, her stomach dropped.

Pandrones.

CHAPTER 008

BEL AND MATEO RACED INTO THE TREES, deeper and deeper. Searchlight beams swung back and forth as the pandrones scanned for movement, propellers tearing through the air, buzzing like giant wasps. They were closing in quickly. There must have been four or five, Bel thought, but she and Mateo didn't stay in one spot long enough to be sure.

"Citizens: Halt!" The robotic drone voices called in unison. "You are in violation of West California law. Please remain where you are until higher authorities arrive. Estimated time to arrival: Approximately nine minutes. / If you do not comply, these devices are authorized to administer projectile tranquilizers."

The humming of the drones faded and swelled, over and over as they combed the area and repeated their chant. They were designed to keep fugitives in place until human officers could come to apprehend them, with sophisticated darts that could knock someone out in an instant. But if Bel and Mateo could increase the distance between themselves and the drones, hopefully human officers would come up empty-handed.

Bel whimpered, exhausted from lack of sleep, from the persistent rush of adrenaline that filled her limbs and kept her running for her life.

Finally, they reached a point where the drones were only

audible in the distance. Then, barely audible at all, and no longer visible.

"I think we lost them," Mateo said.

Cautiously, they searched for water. Insignificant streams trickled nearby, with the dam site only a few miles off. Bel quenched her thirst, cupping her hands in the small rapids and drinking, not caring what the water carried with it.

When she was finished, she wiped her face with her knuckles. "How did they find us?"

Mateo splashed water on his face. "The agent coming for us must have got caught. UW could have intercepted the message that had the coordinates before I destroyed my watch. Or maybe they recovered the data somehow."

"We should go back for the bikes," Bel said. "If we need to move quickly—"

"No," said Mateo. "Too risky. The pandrones will probably keep combing that area, especially because there's a lot of water back there; they know we won't get far without it. Plus, those bikes won't work on a lot of this terrain, and the drones'll most likely be watching the trails."

"Well, we have to go *somewhere*. If VOLT isn't coming, we can't just stay here forever. We'll run out of food."

Mateo pulled out the GPS and switched to a full map view. "The only thing we can do is try to get to someplace where someone might be able to help us." He dragged his finger over the screen, moving the map around. "A place where we can find other campers, say we're lost—which isn't a lie—and hope one of them has a device they can let us use to contact VOLT so we can try to get a new rendezvous point set up."

Bel peered over his shoulder. "Won't there be drones around the campgrounds? Won't they figure that's a place we might go?"

"Probably," said Mateo. "But we don't really have a choice. If we leave the forest, we've got targets on us the second we step back into civilization—or anywhere close to the highway. We're safer on the inside, at least on that front. We just have to tread carefully, use the Ecker to make sure the drones aren't close enough to spot us before we head in anywhere."

Watching until Mateo's finger settled on a point called Spineflower Creek Campground, Bel said, "That's the closest one?"

"Looks like it," said Mateo. "A lot of the older ones aren't showing up. Probably shut down after all those appropriations lapses."

"What?"

"Never mind."

"But ..." Bel looked at the distance. "That's another twenty-five miles ..."

"Got any better ideas?"

Bel frowned. "No."

"We stock up on water, ration the food, keep all devices powered down unless we need them for something specific since we don't have any way to charge them. It should take the rest of today and most of tomorrow to get there, but that's our best shot."

Even though it was still early morning, the sun was already blazing. Bel and Mateo refilled their water bottles and tried to keep moving without taking breaks. Waves of land stretched out before them, rounded hills and gulches between, dotted with pines that grew thick and bristly in some places and sparsely in others. The hills at the farthest extent of their view were faded purple.

Later, when the trees grew closer together and more

abundantly, Bel and Mateo traveled under the shade, which also kept them hidden from the view of any drones they might come across.

At night they used the Sparkfyre to heat water and reconstitute a portion of dehydrated food, but they had to extinguish the flames quickly. "Open flames are illegal out here," said Mateo. "Not to mention we don't exactly need to be making ourselves easier to spot. There are probably ranger drones that would be drawn right to us."

"Can ranger drones really do anything, though?"

Mateo nodded. "They can dispatch pandrones, I know that much. Probably can't shoot a trank, or scan a face, but if they were to call others to the site, we'd be in trouble."

By nightfall, Bel was so weary it pulled her into a heavy sleep. Dawn and birdsong woke her the next morning, along with the sun's heat that was already spreading and creeping into every crevice of the land. Mateo suggested they try to get some extra miles in before the sun reached its highest, hottest point, and by midday, Bel couldn't fathom taking one more step.

Somehow she mustered the strength, her heels blistering in her Vans, and her skin hot and reddish from the stretches between shade. She drank the least amount of water she could manage, but she wanted to inhale it.

They were sunburnt. Bel's heels had blisters within blisters, and her shoes were now stained not only with dirt but with dried blood and the fresh gushing that broke through every hour or so. She felt like raw meat, torn open, oozing.

They tried to make the food last, but midday came with a hunger neither of them could ignore.

"If we don't eat enough," Bel argued, "we might not have the strength to make it the last seven miles."

Reluctantly, Mateo agreed, and they ate the remainder of their supply.

They pushed themselves the last seven miles, dehydrated, empty, and ready to collapse at a moment's notice.

"We're almost there," said Mateo. "Another half mile."

But they walked that half mile, broken, weak, desperate, and arrived to ...

Exactly nothing.

Spineflower Creek Campground was a mountainous, tree-clustered wasteland just like the whole of everything they'd seen so far. And there was no creek to speak of, no water to console them after they'd used every last bit of strength and resolve. Only more dry grass, more ominous forest, more rock-strewn terrain that dipped down and rose up and dipped back down, over and over and over again.

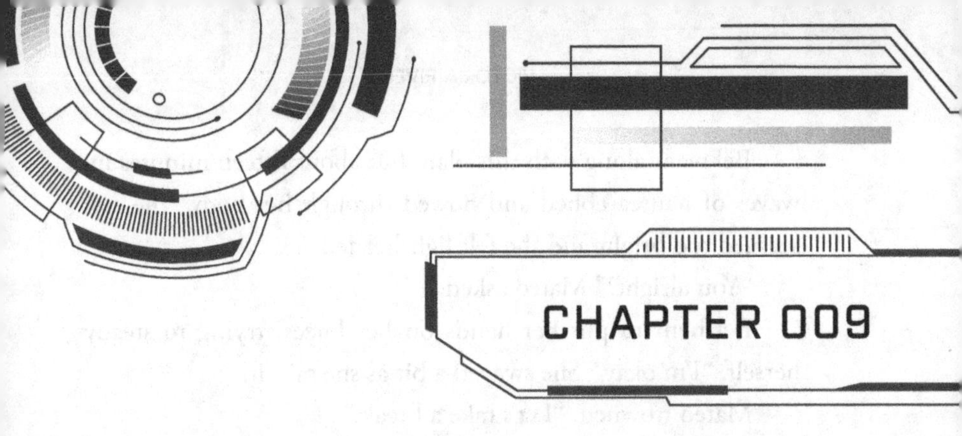

CHAPTER 009

THE NEXT MORNING, BEL AND MATEO found their way to a small stream, mostly dry, with muddy trickles running over rocks and damp sediment. They gathered what they could, but it was nothing substantial. Bel stared at her arms, scratched and tender, and wished she could rub cool, clean water over them.

Mateo searched the GPS, looking for something that might be useful. Another trail, another potential campground.

Bel turned on the Ecker in case there was anyone close—other hikers, or rangers maybe. Even small devices would give off a signal, but so far, literal radio silence.

Sometimes Bel imagined she heard drones, but whenever she checked the Ecker, the screen was blank. She looked above the trees, through the holes in the canopy, and saw only sky, the occasional bird, small woodland rodents scurrying among high branches.

Mateo had talked about maybe using the handgun to hunt some of them but decided against it for now; the gunshot would be too loud, and even far-away drones might hear it. With no panopts out here to put camera-lens eyes on suspicious noises, the drones would be programmed to come and investigate.

"There's another campground about two miles off," Mateo said once they'd rested a bit. "We should at least try it."

Bel went along with this plan, but about fifteen minutes in, waves of nausea ebbed and flowed through her body. The sun seemed too bright and she felt lightheaded.

"You alright?" Mateo asked.

Bel bent to put her hands on her knees, trying to steady herself. "I'm okay." She swayed a bit as she said it.

Mateo frowned. "Let's take a break."

"No," said Bel. "It's fine. There's only a mile left. I can—" She scrunched her face and took a slow breath through pursed lips.

"There's some shade over there." Mateo pointed. "We're going to sit down for a while. The last thing I need is you getting heatstroke."

Bel didn't try to argue anymore. She let Mateo direct her to the shade of a scrub oak, and sat on the grass with her head between her legs until the nausea faded to a queasy thrum. Mateo rustled around nearby, for how long Bel couldn't be sure, but when he came to sit beside her, he brought a handful of brown nubs.

"It's not much," he said, "but it's protein."

Bel sniffed one. "What are these?"

"Pinyon pine nuts. They fall out of the pine cones and you can collect them off the ground. I saw a thing about it on 'The Natural Man.'"

Bel gave him a suspicious look but put one in her mouth. Even though it tasted like actual dirt, she hadn't expected how her hunger would grip her. She ate the rest in a single mouthful.

"Pace yourself." Mateo looked at the GPS, dragging the image of the map laterally with two fingers. "Looks like there's some water a few hundred yards out of the way. I'm gonna go for it."

"I can come with you," Bel said as she chewed gracelessly.

"You can wait here"—he removed both of the two-way radios and switched them on, tossing one onto her lap—"and we'll use these to keep in touch until I get back."

Bel grimaced. She didn't like the idea of splitting up, but one attempt to go from sitting to kneeling made her compliant.

Mateo also left her the handgun in case she ran into any trouble. She tested the weight of it in her hand, curled her fingers around it. She wasn't sure she could bring herself to shoot it if an opportunity arose, but it was good to know she had options.

There was a gentle wind moving over everything. After a while, the shade, the warmth, the breeze, and Bel's exhaustion all lulled her into a doze.

Then, half-asleep, she heard a low hum. She jolted awake, heart pounding, and scrambled to her feet too quickly, having to steady herself on a tree so she didn't topple over. The skies were empty and quiet, as they had been since leaving the dam. Bel calmed herself, reacquainted herself with her surroundings, and settled back down. The nausea was better now that she'd eaten the nuts, but her throat was sticky, raspy, and her energy waned.

Still, she couldn't shake the feeling that something was near. She told herself she was being paranoid; she'd been living a lie for two years, and then had recently had it all exposed in the face of sophisticated, predatory machines. And the memory of those drones would haunt anyone.

Remembering that she could always look at the Ecker for reassurance, she turned it on. The battery was getting low, so she'd need to be quick with it. When the screen lit up, though, she saw a strong signal nearby. She held her breath and watched the blip, waiting. But the blip didn't move; it remained in place and radiated from the same spot.

She went toward it a few steps and it came in stronger. A few more steps, a stronger signal, and the blip continued to remain in place. Estimating it visually, Bel guessed that the distance was still within range of the two-way radio, so she could hail Mateo if anything went wrong.

She slipped the handgun into the front pocket of her jeans, then picked up her backpack and pulled the straps over her shoulders, holding the Ecker out in front of her as she moved toward the signal's location. She had to move slowly, to not push her body too much.

According to the GPS map before Mateo had gone out for water, there was nothing out this way, only more trees, more mountain land. There hadn't been any recreational hikers out this far; there were certainly no special sights that might draw anyone into such remote forest depths. But a small device wouldn't create a signal this strong anyway; not even a drone would. She continued onward, glancing back and forth between the Ecker and the unbeaten path ahead, moving uphill at a gentle incline, gradually closing in on the mystery blip.

About ten minutes later, she reached the spot in question, a large rock formation with a niche in the middle, sloping up into the next mountain. She eased toward it, as though someone or something might jump out, and then spotted a light inside.

A small LED flashed amid lichen and moss.

Bel scraped at the light's surroundings until she revealed a metal square, using a stick to dig into the square's edges. A metal panel, twelve inches wide. She gathered a variety of other sticks and sharp rocks to pry it.

Finally, the panel popped open.

Inside were all the elements of a security system—a flat display with a touchscreen keypad and a retinal scanner.

What could be this far out in the wilderness that would require digital security? Her brain tingled at the thought. A prepper's stockpile? A survivalist bunker designed to outlast some kind of nuclear armageddon?

If that was the case, then breaking past security could potentially open something that would lead to a storage of tools, supplies, maybe even canned food. It *had* to be. There would be no point in locking something up out here in the middle of nowhere if it hadn't been the work of someone who expected the world to end and wanted to be ready when the time came. Or it could be nothing—something abandoned and empty, no harm, no foul.

There didn't seem to be an entrance anywhere nearby, but the code input looked to be about eight characters wide.

Bel pondered a moment. "That's thirty-bit strength, approximately one billion permutations, and depending on the hashing function ..." she muttered aloud as she navigated the Ecker's software to get to its password cracker. Then she paused. "But it might not be vulnerable to brute force. Probably has an anti-jammer, too."

However, the passcode was just one of two entry methods. The box also had a retinal scanner that, based on the data Bel was able to intercept, unlocked the system with a rolling code—a code that would change with each entry attempt, based on an algorithm—and would be highly complex.

If she could impersonate the device, though, she could do a platform reset to try and retrieve the encryption key from the data remanence.

She picked up her end of the two-way radio. "Mateo? I think I found something."

A second later, a burst of static came out of the speaker, followed by Mateo's voice. "What? What do you mean you 'found something'? A campground? Water?"

"Something better. I mean, I *think* it is. Go east from where you left me, for about a half mile."

"Half a mile?! You weren't even supposed to—"

"That's all for now. See you in a bit!" She set the radio by her feet and set to work. Mateo tried to keep their connection, but after she continued to ignore him, he seemed to have given up and come after her.

From the Ecker, Bel wormed her way into the security system settings, pulled up a terminal, and entered a few commands to bring up a working directory, where she obtained the address for media access control. She disabled the Ecker's interface and changed its own address to match that of the security system's device, allowing her to impersonate and control it. With this, she performed a platform reset, found the most recent rolling codes within the memory contents, and copied them.

A couple of final steps and she'd be in.

Mateo showed up a few minutes later. He was covered in dirt with a couple of twigs clinging to his jeans, carrying both their water bottles.

"Any luck?" Bel eyed the bottles in his hands.

Mateo proceeded carefully toward her. He seemed to be observing the setup: Bel with the Ecker, an electronic panel open in the middle of a craggy section of the hillside.

"What is this?" He moved to the box to get a closer look.

She took a bottle from him, opened it, and chugged. Her throat flexed over and over as she swallowed, draining the whole bottle and pulling it away with a cough.

"The Ecker was picking up a signal." She coughed again. "I followed it here. All I could see was an LED light, but then I cleared away some junk and found this box. It's a security system, and I almost have the passcode to get in. I just have to decode this."

"You 'almost have the passcode'? How?" He didn't wait for her to answer. "This could be dangerous. We don't know what this is."

"Relax. I've heard about things like this before—hidden bunkers out in the middle of nowhere. It could be full of food, weapons, whatever we need. We barely know where we are and we have no idea where we're going. We need anything we can get our hands on."

He shook his head. "This is a bad idea."

"Either we die doing this, or there's a good chance we die out here in the next few days." She gestured at the vast and seemingly endless woodland mountains around them. "I personally think we have a better chance with this."

The Ecker's software analyzed the recent rolling codes Bel had copied in order to determine the next code in the sequence. "If it *is* a bunker," she said, setting down the empty water bottle, "it's weird that there's something private here, right? Can you own land inside a national forest?"

"If you have an inholding, you can." Mateo went over to look at the screen. "Families that have owned properties for several generations—far enough back that they predate the national forest establishment—are allowed to keep that private land. And they can sell it to other people too. Whoever owns this would likely have a lot of money."

The software provided the next code.

"Well," said Bel, typing into the terminal to copy and transmit the rolling code to the security system, "That could only be a good thing. More supplies, better resources."

"And if there's someone in there? Someone who doesn't like the fact that we've just broken in? What then?"

"Oh please," said Bel. "There's no way anyone actually *lives* here. It's probably just a storage hole."

Just as she was about to send the transmission, the Ecker beeped. Bel and Mateo both looked at the screen. Bel switched over to the radar, which showed a series of moving dots.

"We have to go," said Mateo. "Those are definitely drones."

"I'm almost in. The drones are *barely* in range, and they don't know we're here. They're probably just patrolling the campground we were headed to before."

"Bel …" He reached for her hand.

She swatted him away but he tried again, then he went for the Ecker to force it from her. They wrestled over the device until the handgun slipped out of Bel's pocket and fell to the ground.

It didn't misfire, but Bel jumped back abruptly at the clatter, her foot landing on her end of the two-way radio and cracking the plastic surface. A high-pitched squeal came out of it, along with loud static.

Mateo swore as he fumbled with the radio to try and stop the noise.

Still holding the Ecker, Bel watched the drone blips gathering and moving toward them quickly. The volume had drawn them, and it would only be less than a minute before they arrived.

Mateo broke open the back of the radio with some difficulty, as the cracked plastic had jammed the battery cover into its own tabs. He ripped out the batteries to silence it.

Bel kept working on the breakthrough. She wasn't about to

have a repeat of the other night, hiding and running and taking cover and hoping for the best with the drones. She was going to get into this bunker if she died trying. Mateo would probably say there was a good chance she might.

Mateo gathered up the gun and the broken radio and a few other items that had fallen loose back into the backpacks, then looked to Bel, who was concentrating on the code.

"Is this seriously the hill you're going to die on?" he said. "*Literally?*"

"Just give me a few more seconds."

"We can come back later!" he grabbed her by the elbow.

"Or we can get in now and take cover in *here* ..."

Mateo glanced up.

The familiar chopping of propellers, whirring and buzzing.

"Get down!" he said.

Bel got down, but she didn't stop typing. She was sure she could finish before the pandrones came within shooting range, but it was taking longer than she expected. When the buzz overwhelmed her ears, she knew it had been *too* long.

Mateo pulled out the handgun.

"Are you crazy?" said Bel. "The second you shoot, there probably won't be any warning calls—they'll start firing tranks immediately."

It was too late, though. The drones were almost close enough to scan them now, and all the miles Bel and Mateo had traveled to make sure the authorities had lost their trail would have been for nothing. Bel knew her brother wouldn't let them get a reading if he could help it.

Mateo grimaced and aimed the gun. He followed the first approaching drone's path waiting for a good shot.

Bang.

The drone wavered but remained in the air while Mateo dragged Bel toward the bushes and additional drones approached.

Warbling, the drone attempted to recite its usual speech.

Ciiiitizens, Haaalt! You are in violaaaaaation of West California laaaaaw. Pleeeeease remain where you aaaaaare until hiiiiiiigher authoooooooorities arriiiiiiiive.

Crouching, with bristles tickling her face and neck, Bel transmitted the code.

Back by the box itself, a crevice between two adjoining rocks parted like a pair of sliding doors, revealing an entrance just big enough to allow one person through at a time.

Mateo and Bel exchanged glances. They were mostly hidden, but Bel peered through the overhanging tree branches. A second drone appeared and started to shoot along with the first. Tranks hit the ground directly in front of Bel's feet, spewing up dust.

"We have to go in." Bel raised herself enough to determine the clearest, fastest path back.

There were enough trees over the bunker's opening that the drones wouldn't be able to get a visual on it. If Bel and Mateo could get inside, the drones would register having lost sight of them the same way they had at the dam site, then keep combing a while and eventually go back to their usual, wide-range patrol.

She sprinted toward the opening, running through a rain of tranks, ducking and veering left or right to dodge them. Finally, she reached the crevice, panting, and tossed her backpack inside. She looked back at Mateo.

He stared at her in disbelief, then glanced up at the shooting drones.

Bel slipped into the crevice, then peered out, waving her brother forward. It was dark behind her, but she used the dim light from the Ecker's screen to locate how to close the bunker's opening from the inside.

"Mateo!" she shouted.

Mateo looked up, then back at Bel, then up again, and gritted his teeth. For a second, he seemed to sink down deeper, making himself small within the bushes. Then, like a runner crouched on starter blocks, he got even lower and propelled himself forward, handgun in the air, shooting back at the drones. He sprinted, catching himself before he slammed into the rocks, and rolled into the crevice with Bel.

Bel let out a breath and touched her finger to a lit plate on the inner wall. The entrance closed itself on them.

"Never do anything like that to me again!" Mateo shouted. "Never. Do you understand? I swear, Bel—"

Lights on the ceiling illuminated, row by row, revealing a narrow hallway that led to a set of double doors at the end. Except for the jagged rock through which the tunnel was cut, the elements of the entrance were sleek, white marble.

"Welcome to the Submundo," said a male voice, gentle and low, with a British lilt.

Bel shrieked when a man appeared a few feet away. She covered her mouth and backed toward the wall, until she realized that the man was translucent, with a vague blue hue to his features. A holomorph.

"I am Lucius, at your service," he said.

Mateo looked to Bel with wide eyes. "What the hell did we just walk into?"

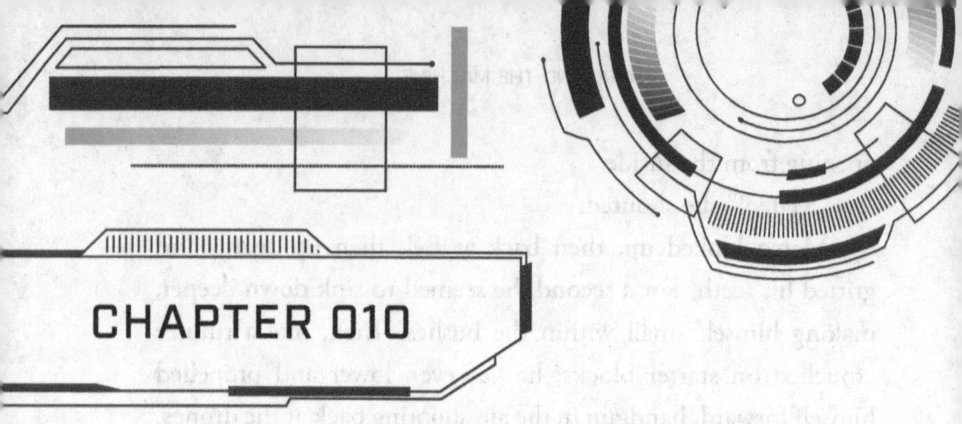

CHAPTER 010

THE HOLOMORPHIC HOST was modeled after an older Caucasian man, with dark silver hair combed back, a pair of brown-rimmed glasses, and impeccable posture. He wore a blue dress shirt and tie under a sweater vest, and he clasped his hands at his front and waited patiently.

"The Submundo?" Bel glanced at the ceiling, from which several tiny dots projected Lucius's form. "What's the Submundo?"

"The Submundo," said Lucius, "is a protective shelter, equipped with enough resources for up to ten adult individuals to live comfortably for approximately fifty years."

Bel looked around for a door. This couldn't be all there was—not if there were enough 'resources' for ten people. This must have been an anteroom. "Is there anyone else here?"

"My system detects two human organisms within the Submundo at this time," Lucius replied. "Located at the West Entrance."

Bel turned to Mateo, who was examining the tunnel walls, running his hand over the surface like he was looking for a seam to indicate a doorway, probably thinking the same she had been.

"I think he means us," Bel said. "If the rest of this place expands from here, this would be the west side. The west entrance. No one else is here."

Mateo stopped what he was doing. "That doesn't mean someone won't be coming."

"Lucius," Bel said again. "Has anyone else been here recently?"

"My records detect no human activity in the past seven hundred and thirty days. Would you like me to access records predating this time period?"

"No, thank you." Bel turned to her brother. "That's two years, Mateo."

"Thanks, I can do math," said Mateo, "Lucius, are you expecting anyone else at the Submundo in the near future?"

"There are currently no scheduled arrivals in my database."

Bel raised her eyebrows.

Mateo threw up his hands. "Fine. Let's have a look around, see if we can find anything useful to take with us, maybe map out a real plan for where we're going to go and what we're going to do from this point. But then we're leaving—as soon as possible."

"How do we get in?" Bel asked Lucius.

"Please proceed forward. Follow the lights. Doors will open automatically as you approach."

Mateo and Bel proceeded toward the end of the tunnel. When they reached the last of the lights, the wall parted in front of them, sliding into invisible pockets and revealing a white marble foyer that expanded into a lavish living room.

The high white ceilings were speckled with more dots— more projectors, Bel thought. Lucius was probably programmed to be able to go anywhere. Bel gawked at the space, which was supported by marble pillars and filled with sleek, black couches and chairs, and a baby grand piano. Twenty-foot floor-to-ceiling windows took up what would have been the entire back wall, looking out to a garden.

"Is that a skylight or something?" Mateo whispered.

Bel couldn't imagine what that would look like from the outside, above ground—a huge panel of glass in the middle of the dirt?

"Does the Submundo system have any kind of tour feature?" said Bel.

"Certainly," said Lucius. "Allow me."

"Are you kidding?" Mateo said to Bel. "What did I just say about finding stuff and getting out of here as soon as possible?"

Bel nodded. "And the fastest way to find things is to look at the inventory. The AI is a walking, talking inventory guide."

Mateo sighed. "Touché."

Lucius gestured to the living room. "This is the Common Room." A round table in the center of the furniture ignited with purple flames. "The fire is artificial and produces no smoke, but does emit heat at adjustable temperatures, for ambience and comfort. The Submundo's heating and cooling system is otherwise entirely geothermal. All furniture is genuine leather. The piano you see is a Fazioli Model F156, quite old but in perfect condition."

Bel stared at the shiny black surface of the piano and approached it slowly. She had a distinct urge to reach out and run her fingers over the keys, to press a few of them and let their notes ring out—but she couldn't bring herself to do it. Her mother would have loved to have had the chance to play something so fine, probably would have scolded her for holding back. A scolding didn't sound so bad now, though. Bel would have given anything to hear her mother's angriest voice again, to have another argument with her over piano lessons or finishing homework on time or picking up clothes off the floor.

"The end tables are functional art pieces," Lucius continued, drawing her back to the moment, "steel sculptures that also provide a useful surface. Through the windows, you'll see what we refer to as the Terrarium, an indoor garden space with a VR sky that reflects the current sun and moon cycles, as well as a visual representation of the weather. The plant watering schedule, however, keeps the plants thriving regardless of dry conditions."

Entering the garden, Bel gazed up at the VR sky, which was a stark blue with a blazing sun that looked all too real. No wonder Mateo had thought it was a skylight.

If she had to guess, she would have said the garden was only two stories high, although the optical illusion above made it seem like miles. A cobblestone walkway curved throughout a series of raised soil beds, some of which were coated in bright lawns, with full-sized trees that reached the second story, and a variety of plants and flowers, many of which were tropical. The space was warm and humid. Holomorphic birds projected through the space, flying or perched on trees.

"All the plant life you see in the Terrarium is monitored closely by the Submundo's sensitive ecosystem, which provides appropriate light and water specific to each plant's individual needs, in addition to trimming and grooming services performed by a team of robotic devices, scheduled at appropriate intervals by Flora," Lucius said. "Would you like me to introduce you to Flora for further information?"

Bel said, "Sure."

A female holomorph appeared beside Lucius. She was tan, with blonde hair pulled into a low bun, and she wore a plaid shirt under a gardening apron. "Hello, I'm Flora," she said. "I oversee all operations inside the Terrarium. I can assist you with plant species information, scheduling plant nutrition, and environmental conditioning during your use of the Terrarium. How may I help you?"

Mateo huffed impatiently but Bel nudged him with her shoulder. He rolled his eyes and said, "Fine. Tell me about this plant right here."

"Certainly. Monstera Deliciosa, also known as the Ceriman. This is a flowering plant native to southern Mexico, and south to Panama. It grows best in tropical regions. The plant produces edible fruit, which is why it is called Deliciosa, or 'delicious,' and can grow to heights taller than sixty feet, which is why it is called Monstera, or 'monstrous.' Would you like to know more?"

"No, thank you," said Mateo as Bel opened her mouth.

"You're welcome. Let me know if you need anything else."

Lucius continued the tour. "This way, through the Terrarium's west exit, you'll find the west corridor, which will lead to the Dining Room and the Virtual Reality Dome."

"There's a VR *dome*?" said Mateo.

Lucius nodded. "A space adequate for the wide variety of physical activities available within the Submundo's VR system. Large-scale games, exercise routines, or far-off virtual experiences, should Submundo guests like to run laps around an Olympic-sized track, play cyber chess on a human-sized board, or simply go for a stroll through the Himalayas or along the beach."

"Kind of seems like whoever built this place was planning on being stuck down here for a long time," said Mateo.

"Or *preparing* to be stuck," Bel reasoned, "Just in case."

The Dining Hall had more floor-to-ceiling paneled windows looking into the Terrarium, and a long table with ten chairs. Synthetic LED Edison bulbs hung from industrial pipes protruding from the ceiling over the table in an upside-down runway.

The kitchen came next, a stainless-steel culinary sanctuary complemented by seamless white cabinetry, with robot arms positioned to do all kinds of culinary work. Electronic sliding doors encased a pantry full of foods preserved with a variety of technological means Bel had never heard of before, ways to keep food even longer while maintaining appropriate textures, flavors, and consistencies.

Bel's stomach clenched at the mention of food, after days of subsisting on rations of dehydrated meals and the handful of pine nuts she'd eaten just before breaking in. She took a mental inventory of what they might be able to stock up on before they left, once the tour had finished. There were still other kinds of resources to be on the lookout for. They needed Lucius to show them to rifles, maybe, or camping supplies.

Throughout the corridors that connected each space, there were displays of artwork. Sculptures and paintings along the walls.

The sculptures seemed to be modeled after ancient Caribbean gods or figures from island folklore, with more abstract features and decorative, geometric patterns engraved onto them.

The paintings were all vividly colorful, mostly showing scenes from warm, distant places. A faceless man and woman pressed together in a dance, shown from the waist up, wearing brimmed straw hats, surrounded by pink flowers with broad leaves. An angled view of four stucco houses in a row—goldenrod, blood orange, royal blue, and magenta—with clay-tile roofs and iron gates holding back tropical gardens. Dark-skinned people leaning over baskets of fruit. A woman, mid-spin, wearing a three-layered skirt in red, white, and blue, with a waving Dominican flag behind her. A cluster of dozens of bananas hanging in front of a teal wall.

Bel tried to get a better look at one, but Mateo kept urging her along. They weren't here for entertainment, he reminded her with his glare; this was a last-ditch effort to survive. But it was hard to remember that when they were in a place like this, full of wonders and mystery.

Finally, after Lucius explained how each corridor had its own utility closet with robotic cleaning devices programmed to take shifts at regular intervals, they came to some sort of arsenal.

"Here we go." Mateo said. He'd never been big on weapons, but being caught helpless enough times could make a person more accepting, Bel figured, especially when he considered himself her grand protector.

Glass cases spanned the walls, lighting up as the group entered, filled with traditional rifles and pistols, followed by laser rifles and blaster pistols, knives, machetes, and steel crossbows.

"The Armory provides a selection of fine weaponry for personal defense," Lucius explained, "in the event of emergency."

"This really *is* a doomsday bunker." Bel let her eyes trail over the collection. She set her sights on one of the blaster pistols, which was silvery blue and compact. "That one's nice ... "

"Ah, yes," said Lucius. "The Pulsar 13. Four inches in length and 3.75 inches in height, single and sustained firing modes, powered by coin cell vidrinium batteries—purchased *prior* to the Vidrinium Ban of 2071, of course."

Mateo didn't say anything, but from the solemn look on his face, Bel knew he was thinking of the crime syndicates; the war over vidrinium usage had hurt a lot of people, and she and Mateo were just a few of the victims. Ever since the Callidus rover had discovered the element on Mars in the mid-2050s, vidrinium had been controversial—incredible properties when it came to electrical power, but highly volatile when handled improperly, with the potential to create irreversible environmental damage. Groups like the Knight Crew were all over it, trafficking it in from countries where the ban was barely enforced, if at all, sometimes selling it raw, but more often selling it in the form of power cells or vidrinium-powered weapons.

Lucius continued, gesturing to a set of laser rifles with thick barrels and squared-off silver grips, guards, and stocks. "The most powerful of these laser firearms is the Relámpago Z-101. Its weight and output have been calibrated to operate well in hazardous conditions and—"

"Let's just move on," Mateo said. "What's next?"

"Congruent with the Armory is the Medical Resources room next door." Lucius led them onward, but Bel caught Mateo looking over his shoulder as they went.

Medical Resources was like a hospital stockroom, Bel thought. In her mother's line of work, she'd seen enough of them to know. There were large medicine cabinets full of every kind of drug imaginable, along with adhesive bandages, gauze, medical tape, cotton swabs, sanitizing chemicals, latex gloves, ointments, and beyond. There was even an operating table with monitoring equipment. Bel figured if there *were* to be an apocalypse, these people would be well-prepared for it.

"Now," said Lucius, "we've come to the Garage." He pronounced it *GEH-rej* and led them to a more industrial-looking room with an unfinished concrete floor. In it, a series of five skimmers stood lined up in a row.

Transportation.

Bel thought about walking mile after mile in the blistering heat outside, for hours, days, and. how one of these hovercrafts could have taken her the same distance in a matter of minutes. It almost made her sick.

And yet …

"Don't even think about it," said Mateo, while Lucius prattled on in the background and pointed to some small, compact vehicles hanging from hooks on the wall.

Bel furrowed her brow. "Are you kidding? One of these skimmers could outrun a pandrone if it had enough of a head start."

"It's too much." He lowered his voice to a whisper. "Don't you think it's bad enough we're planning to take *small* things that don't belong to us? You want to steal a *vehicle*?"

" … and actually much more versatile than you might think," said Lucius. "In fact …"

"Borrow," Bel whispered back, ignoring Lucius. "We could feasibly return it when things calm down. I don't like the idea of stealing any more than you do, but I also don't want to die."

Mateo scoffed. "Could've fooled me."

"… similar to a bicycle without wheels …"

"We clearly have different ideas about what constitutes a death wish," said Bel.

"… while utilizing hovercraft technology. Quite convenient for short, recreational trips or even for use within larger cities, as it can be folded up and carried easily onto public transportation vehicles without taking up more space than a traditional duffel bag."

"Wait—what?" said Bel. She looked over the slim, silver contraptions. Each one measured about two and a half feet long and maybe a little over a foot wide, with a retractable bar and seat folded against a footboard. "Those are portable?"

"Yes," Lucius replied, "a proof of concept that only its earliest investors had the privilege to own. The Lightfoot F1."

She might just have to come back for one of those.

As she examined the lineup of Lightfoot skimmers, a third type of vehicle caught her eye—one that did not belong. A green SkimShare scooter, leaning up against the wall. "What's that doing here?"

"Based on my image search feature," Lucius said, "it appears to belong to a shared mobility service called SkimShare, for the purpose of short-term rental within urban areas."

"And you don't know how it got here?"

"I'm afraid it is not part of the Submundo's inventory. I cannot confirm the reason for its appearance."

As they moved on from the garage toward the main stairwell, a sound snagged Bel's attention. A soft tapping on the marble floor, almost like footfalls. Bel tried to listen over Lucius as he explained the geothermal heat pump, something about evaporator coils and freon. She glanced backward and craned her neck, focusing on environmental noises, but she didn't hear it again.

Lucius said there was no one else here, she reminded herself. And if he received notifications when someone would be coming, there was a chance he'd mention it. She'd almost convinced herself the sound had only been an echo of her own steps, or Mateo's—it would be reasonable with so many slick surfaces and nothing to absorb sound—when something moved in her periphery. She jerked her head toward it, but there was no one there. Nothing.

It could have been a cleaning robot or another AI staff member like Lucius or Flora. Then again, the holomorphic AI wouldn't make sound on the floor …

"While the Submundo is equipped with multiple stairwells," said Lucius as they came to the end of the hallway, "along with a grand staircase in the Common Room, it also features multiple elevators." He paused suddenly, almost like he was experiencing a glitch. After a moment, he said, "My apologies, but my system has told me to have you proceed forward to the left."

There were two elevators, side by side. Bel and Mateo moved toward the one at the left and, when the doors parted, entered without giving it much thought. Once inside, however, Bel noticed something strange.

"Wait," she said, pressing her hand to bare concrete. She glanced down at her feet, where she stood on a concrete floor. "There aren't any buttons. The floor's totally stationary. Where's the—"

Mateo tried to step out, but a set of glass doors—which must have been at least four inches thick—slammed shut so fast Bel was surprised they didn't shatter.

Pounding on the glass, Mateo grunted. He turned to Bel with a venomous glare.

"What just happened?" Bel looked through to Lucius outside. "What is this?" She wasn't sure he could hear her, but she imagined he had ears in places besides the projection of his head—receptors in the walls or the ceiling.

"I'm sorry," said Lucius, "But security has required that I contain you both."

"Contain us?" said Bel. The security shouldn't have caused this. Everything she'd done had successfully tricked the system into believing she had full access without suspicion. She'd retrieved the correct passcode, something the owner themselves would have entered on the keypad. It wouldn't have registered as a breach.

That's when another figure—a solid, non-holomorphic one—appeared through the glass, in the shadows just beyond the lights.

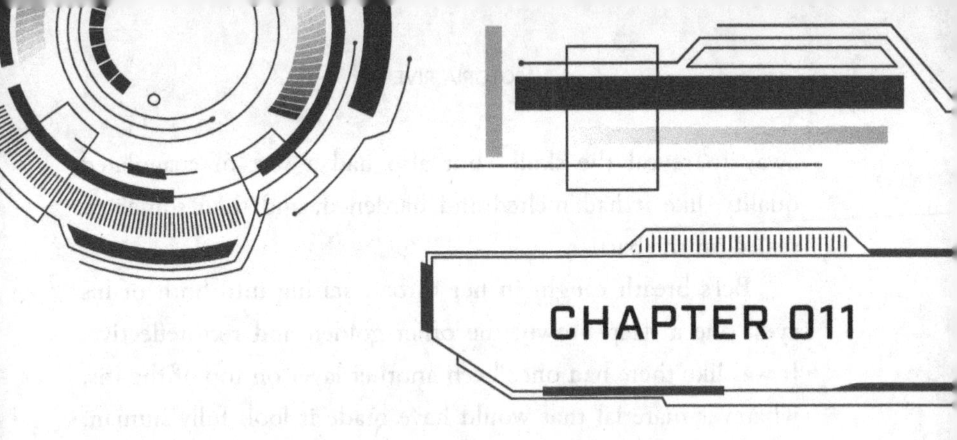

CHAPTER 011

THE FIGURE WAS MOSTLY A SILHOUETTE from where he stood, with only a hint of his features at the edge of the tour's guiding light-path. The hood of a gray sweatshirt obscured parts of his face—dark skin, with what looked like a partial mask along the right side of his jaw. Subtle reflections bounced off his eyes, but one eye had a different quality to it, almost like a cat's eye, iridescent.

He crept toward the glass, then stopped short and pressed something just out of frame.

A click. Then a subtle white noise, like the background of an intercom.

The figure spoke in a gruff voice. "Who are you?"

Bel moved to the glass, squinting as she took him in. Now that he had more light on him, the shadow of his hood wasn't enough to hide the details of his face. A portion of the skin on his right side was missing, baring a dark metallic skeleton, surface plates pieced together with blue lines of light flashing through between them. His nose and lips were still intact, still humanlike, but the exposed metal extended up around his left eye and probably over the top of his head—although the hood hid the full extent of it. The edges where skin turned to metal were rough and charred—as though the skin had been burned away to reveal the skull—but also had a sort of coagulated quality, like it had melted and hardened, and then somehow sealed off the barrier.

Bel's breath caught in her throat, staring into both of his eyes, one a deep brown, the other golden and retroreflective. It was like there had once been another layer on top of the iris, whatever material that would have made it look fully human, burned away like his skin.

It was hard to be sure with the deformities, but he seemed relatively young. Not exactly a teenager. Maybe a young adult. Probably not older than Mateo. But it was stupid to try to guess. Who could say how much of him was man and how much was machine? If part—or all—of his skull was artificial, his skin might be, too, and therefore ageless. Based on the tech in this place, it was impossible for Bel to know what she was really looking at, what kind of advanced science contributed to (or entirely made up) this person. But his appearance did explain why Lucius had claimed to have only detected two human organisms. Maybe this person was a *cybernetic* organism. A cyborg. Although cyborgs were still partially human, weren't they? Only enhanced? Bel wasn't sure, but "cyborg" seemed a good enough classification for the moment, at least.

"Who are you?" the cyborg asked again.

Bel thought of all her assumed identities. Small-town Iowa cheerleader Ari Mendoza. Quiet and well-behaved Elena Vega of Maine. And of course her most recent, the one that had brought her back to within three hundred miles of where she'd been born—the one she hadn't been able to fully hide behind—Belinda Meyer of Orwell, West California. Not the best student, not so good at hiding her technical talents, not wanting to pretend anymore. And then there was the persona she'd assigned herself behind the holokeys, ReBELi0u5. But despite pretending for so many years, she couldn't help feeling like each identity was somehow a genuine part of her, so much that she wasn't quite sure which, specifically, was who she was now.

She looked up at him with sharp eyes. "That's a loaded question."

Mateo came and smacked the glass with his palm. "Who are *you*?"

"I live here," the cyborg said calmly. "I don't owe you an explanation."

"Okay," said Bel. "I get it. This looks bad. But we didn't mean anything. We're not dangerous. You don't have to lock us up."

"We're just hikers," Mateo said. "A couple of idiots who didn't plan well, got lost, ran out of food and water, and we were desperate. We stumbled onto the entrance and took a chance that no one would be here."

The cyborg stared at them, his mutilated face blank. "'Stumbled onto,'" he repeated. "And how did you know there was anything to 'stumble onto' in the first place?"

"Every system gives off electromagnetic waves," Bel reasoned.

Mateo shot her a look.

The cyborg's metal glinted when he tilted his head. "And you expect me to believe that a man on a recreational trek just happens to know how to hack a security system ..."

Man? Bel opened her mouth, but Mateo spoke before she could say anything.

"I used to work in security analysis," Mateo said. "You can't just assume that being in the middle of nowhere is its own protection. Frankly, your system could use an update—and that's an evaluation that normally would cost you a lot of money—"

"Not like he doesn't have it," Bel muttered.

"—so let's just call it even, alright?" Mateo held up both hands in surrender. "We haven't taken anything. We can walk right back out of here like nothing happened."

The cyborg regarded them both, looking from one to the other without saying anything for a minute. Finally, he said, "You're running from something."

"You seem like you might know something about that." Bel glanced pointedly at the mansion beyond the corridor—a decade's worth of hiding-out supplies and amenities.

He ignored her comment. "Tell me who you are."

"We're nobody," Bel said through a sigh. "You want a couple of names that won't mean anything to you? Jacob? Belinda?"

After a few more seconds of silence, the cyborg pressed something else out of frame and the door closed over the glass, trapping Mateo and Bel in darkness.

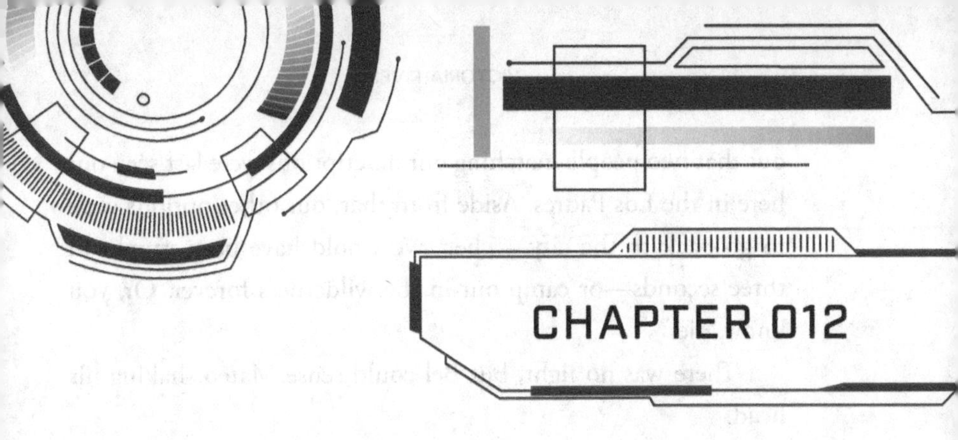

CHAPTER 012

IT MUST HAVE BEEN AN HOUR that they waited, sitting on the cold concrete floor in the dark. Bel fiddled with the Ecker, which brought a faint glow to the darkness as she tried to hack the doors, but she wasn't getting any signal from them—like the cyborg had cut power to the whole room so there was no signal to pick up, or set up a jammer.

Smart.

Mateo hadn't said much at first, but Bel knew what he was thinking. This was her fault. Just like everything else. Being forced out of their home, and now getting locked up by a mechanical tyrant in a strange place filled with technology that was probably more advanced than they had ever seen.

"I'm sorry," Bel offered. "I know that probably doesn't mean much right now, but—"

"You're right. It doesn't."

"It was this or scavenge for pine nuts for the foreseeable future," Bel argued. "That's how I saw it, anyway. I mean, seriously, Mateo. Even if we found other people, with devices and a signal, it wouldn't have guaranteed our safety. Any connection to the outside world would mean they could get a clue to who we really were. If any hiker had the slightest reason to think we were suspicious, they'd be one holopad search away from finding out that two people matching our descriptions were last seen out here in the Los Padres. Aside from that, our other options were to go back to the city—where we would have been caught in three seconds—or camp out in the wilderness forever. Or, you know, die."

There was no light, but Bel could sense Mateo shaking his head.

"Doesn't matter," he said. "The campground was still a better chance than we have right now. We don't even know if that guy's coming back. He could leave us here to starve. Scavenging doesn't sound so bad when you consider that, does it?"

"Mateo ..."

"No. No more excuses. If you had just *listened* to me, for once ... if we'd hurried up and grabbed a few things and run, instead of doing that ridiculous tour ..."

"Fine. Okay? You're right," her eyes began to water. "I'm sorry you got stuck taking care of me. I'm sorry it wasn't me who ended up dead instead of Mom and Dad."

"Can't you ever just accept responsibility without being *so—*"

A burst of light blinded them both suddenly as the doors wrenched apart again. Mateo blocked the brightness with the back of his hand. Bel squeezed her eyes shut, and only cracked them open one at a time after she'd given them a few seconds to adjust.

The glass, of course, was still intact, keeping Mateo and Bel contained. Their captor stood behind it, looking in and waiting. Lucius wasn't with him this time.

Bel looked at Mateo, then stood and moved toward the glass. Mateo followed.

The cyborg held a holopad in one hand, a hand that

appeared normal enough—brown skin, five fingers, no marks or blemishes. The other hand, which he now used to push the intercom button again, was made of metal, with shiny bones, and blue-tinted wires running through them.

The white noise rushed in again, right before he flicked on the holopad, and an intersphere frame bloomed up holomorphically.

The cyborg began to read aloud from the text that accompanied two headshot photos—one of Bel and one of Mateo.

"'Two criminals, a twenty-one-year-old male and eighteen-year-old female, both of Mexican heritage, fled United Watch investigations on the evening of May 10, 2087, escaping pandrones near Matilija Creek in Ojai and disappearing into the forest. United Watch continues to search the area but has yet to apprehend them.'" He looked over Bel and Mateo in turns, like he was comparing them each to the corresponding photos in front of him. "'Mateo Solís,'" he continued, "'also known as Eric Mendoza, Eduardo Vega, and Jacob Meyer, is charged with illegal systems infiltration, cyberterrorism, distribution and sale of illegal substances and products, financial fraud resulting in losses totaling more than twenty million dollars, identity theft, falsification of government records and documents, and resisting United Watch officers.'"

"What?" said Mateo. "I never resisted United Watch off—"

"Pandrones," Bel clarified. "And *that's* the item you take issue with?"

"Those metal *vultures* are supposed to be 'officers'?"

"Are you going to continue with the story that you're 'just a hiker'?" the cyborg said to Mateo. "Because I'm certain it would only take one call to United Watch and you'd never see life outside prison walls again."

"Guess you're just trying to prepare me, then." Mateo rapped on the concrete beside him with his knuckles. "At least in a real prison I'd have a place to piss and sleep."

"None of that stuff is true," Bel told the cyborg. "That whole record is fabricated."

The cyborg flicked to another frame showing a news article. "It also says here that you graduated high school at the age of sixteen, earned a full-ride scholarship to Caltech, and went on to intern for two summers at Kleid Co. Security under the security analysis team. Is all of *that* fabricated as well?"

Mateo glared at the cyborg. "No. That part's true. So what?"

"And right before your disappearance, it looks like you were …" the cyborg scrolled down the text, "working in advanced software development, along with your father—also an expert in software and systems—in association with anticrime efforts." He looked at Mateo flatly. "*Anticrime*. Seems ironic …"

"I don't have to explain anything to you." Mateo went up to the glass. "You know nothing about me—about us."

"That's fine," said the cyborg. He gestured at the holoscreen. "This is all I really need to know anyway. Your skill set, and the fact that it would be very easy to get you locked up if you don't do what I say."

"You'd have to give up your own location, too," Bel pointed out, "if you were to turn us in. Considering how you've clearly gone out of your way to be as hidden as possible—and the fact that you look like someone has it out for you—I doubt you'd want to bring United Watch here just to spite us."

"It may look like I have a lot to lose," said the cyborg, "but I only care about one thing, and that's the only reason that I'm talking to the two of you now."

"And what's that?" said Bel.

He pressed his thumb to the inner side of his wrist, as though he were easing a pain there. "I get limited information on you, you get limited information on me. Enough to finish our business together and then we can all go our separate ways."

"Business?" Mateo shot back.

"What—you want us to help you commit a crime, and then you'll let us go?" Bel mused.

"Essentially," the cyborg replied. "You need to get somewhere safe, undetected, and I need someone to get me information I can't get myself. We can help each other."

"'Help' doesn't quite seem like the right word." Mateo gazed up the length of the glass that separated them. "I think 'blackmail' might be more fitting …"

"So, it's a hacking job," said Bel. "Great. Just give me—*us*—a holopad and we'll be out of your nonexistent hair in ten minutes."

The cyborg made a brief sound in his throat that was almost like a laugh. "If only it were that easy." He came closer to the glass. "Unfortunately, all the data I need will be on a closed network, on secure servers, unhackable from the outside."

"Where?" asked Mateo.

"Vivorex."

Mateo furrowed his brow. "You want us to go all the way to Dorado. Into the city?"

"Not both of you," the cyborg replied. "Just you."

Mateo glanced at Bel, who glared at the cyborg.

"No way," Bel said. "I'm not staying here with you. Especially not if this is how you treat guests."

The cyborg remained firm. "I have no reason to put my complete trust in two criminals *who broke in*."

"I'm not saying it was right," Bel argued, "but people will

do a lot of things they wouldn't normally do when they're afraid they're going to starve."

"*Your* track record also implies a criminal history. Petty cybercrime. Assaulting a peer."

Bel crossed her arms.

"Why wouldn't you just contact the authorities?" Mateo asked, ignoring his sister. "Or call a friend? I mean, with your attitude, I'm sure it's difficult to *make* friends, but surely you have someone who could help you out besides *me* ..."

"The people I need to investigate are powerful beyond what you can imagine; there's nothing they can't cover up or pay off. And any 'friends' or acquaintances who might be *willing* to help ... wouldn't have the ability or the means."

"Under the circumstances," said Mateo, "I get that you don't trust us, but you're not exactly inspiring a lot of camaraderie. I'm not about to leave my sister alone with some guy who's been threatening me for the past two hours."

"It's lucky for you that you have the precise skill set I need, otherwise I would have already alerted United Watch," said the cyborg. "And as far as Mirabel is concerned"—Bel flinched at the sound of her real name spoken aloud, which the cyborg seemed to be reading from the holoscreen as though he'd forgotten already—"you have nothing to worry about. I swear to every god anyone has ever worshiped, I won't touch her."

"Like you even could," said Bel.

The cyborg seemed to regard her comment but didn't acknowledge it out loud. "Try any tricks and I'll turn her and myself in to the UW authorities. Help me, and that won't be necessary."

Bel narrowed her eyes.

"Obviously you don't have to stay in the cell," he told her.

"There are eight bedrooms in the Submundo, and many other spaces to occupy—as you've already seen. You and I will never have to interact." He closed the digital frames and pocketed the holopad. "Trust me, I'm not interested in being around you for any amount of time. I only need to be sure I get the necessary information and that no one sabotages me in the process. I'd be glad to have you two trade places, except for the part where I need someone who actually knows what he's doing."

"Okay, wow," said Bel. "Just so you know—"

"Fine." Mateo stepped in front of her. "You're right. I have experience at Kleid Co., and Vivorex was a client of theirs. And you need someone to go there." He glanced sideways at Bel, a look that warned her not to argue. "But what *doesn't* make sense is the fact that I'll be recognized as soon as I'm within range of a panopt. I can't go anywhere *near* the city."

"You had the means to do it before," said the cyborg. "Or the technology, more accurately. You were probably using an InVisor, right? I have a few here, and the software to program them."

"Of course you do," said Bel.

"I can provide you with whatever you need. I have plenty of money; I'll get you transportation, defense weapons, an apartment overlooking Vivorex, all the information you would need to infiltrate."

Mateo considered this. "That could take weeks of nonstop work. Even then, I might not be able to get into anything."

"You'll make it work," the cyborg said. "Interning for Kleid Co., you helped to create software that could break through Vivorex security so you could test the system's limitations and determine how to improve upon it. Now you just have to outdo yourself."

"Are you going to tell us who you are, though?" asked Bel. "Or why you need this information?"

"I'll tell your brother what he needs to know to do this job. That's it. And in the meantime, there'll be no contact between you two—just in case you get any conspiratorial ideas."

"That's too far," said Bel. "You have to let us communicate somehow."

The cyborg rubbed his wrist again and shook his head. "Sorry. Too risky for me."

"What about the risks for *us*?" said Bel.

The cyborg shrugged. "According to what I read about you both, and the way you were willing to hack into something you didn't know anything about … it seems like you *like* taking risks. Not sure why it bothers you now."

Bel shook her head. "That isn't the same thing."

"I'll give the two of you a few minutes to talk it over."

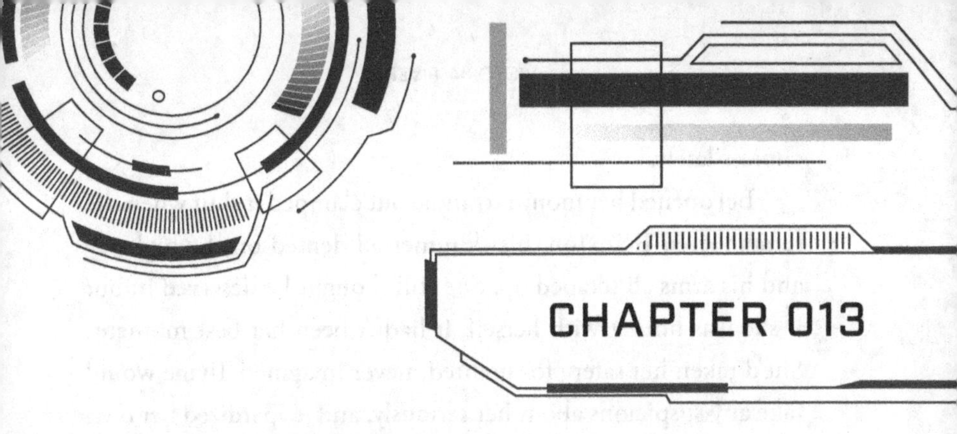

"ARE YOU CRAZY?" BEL SAID once she and Mateo were alone. "Are you actually considering this?"

Mateo combed his hair back from his forehead with his fingers. "I don't know. Maybe."

"*What*?"

"Look, just because he pissed you off by assuming—"

"He wants to keep me as *collateral*."

"Only because he doesn't know you have any skills. I'm the one who can do what he needs, so it makes sense for you to stay."

"I could figure it out," Bel argued.

"This isn't some girl's Atmo profile. It's an advanced biotech company with high-class security—and you didn't help work on the Vivorex system like I did. I'd still have to be the one to go."

"You're seriously going to leave me with that monster?"

"I'd think you'd be more offended if I got all protective and acted like you couldn't take care of yourself."

"It's the principle. He can't just hold me like a prisoner."

"In some cases, prisons are the safer option," said Mateo.

Bel paused, and then her eyes widened. "Wait a second ... You *don't* think I can take care of myself—do you? You want to leave me because you think I'll be safer here than out there ..."

"Well, you haven't exactly proven that you can make good

choices lately."

Bel opened her mouth to argue but clamped it shut when she remembered Branxton, his skimmer all dented on the highway and his arms all scraped up. She still thought he deserved it, but if she was honest with herself, it hadn't been her best moment. She'd taken her safety for granted, never imagined Thane would take any suspicions about her seriously, and jeopardized her own life and her brother's.

"I didn't want to hide anymore," she whispered.

"Well, now you'll be hiding underground, cut off from the whole world. And who knows when you'll ever be able to come out again."

It felt like Mateo had slapped her in the face.

Thankfully, the cyborg didn't give them more time to wallow in their mutual misery. The doors slid open.

Before the cyborg pressed the intercom, Mateo said, "Don't tell him what you can do. His ignorance can play to your advantage. If you really need to contact me, I know you'll figure out how."

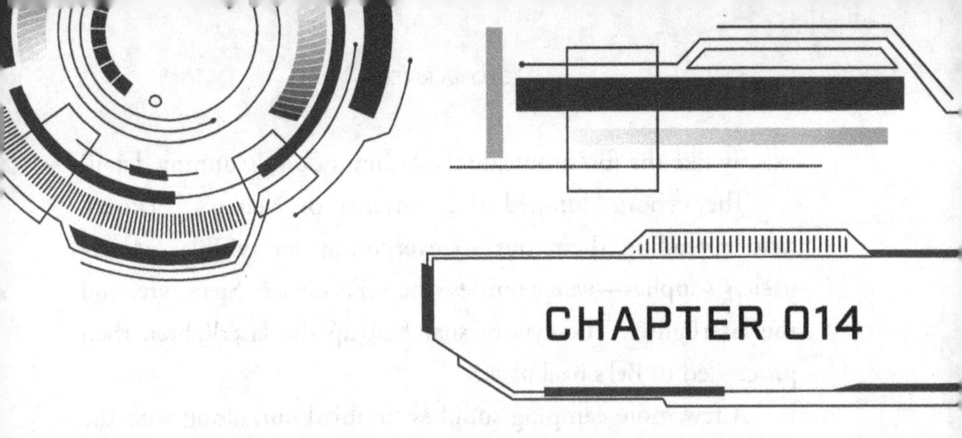

CHAPTER 014

"BEFORE I RELEASE YOU," THE CYBORG SAID, "you should know that, if anything happens to me, Lucius is programmed to put in an alert to United Watch instantaneously. He already has facial data on you both, and I personally input your names so he can identify you. Plus ..." he turned sideways and lifted the back of his sweatshirt, removing a blaster pistol stashed in his waistband.

Like his face, the dark skin of his lower back was disturbed by sections of exposed metal, although Bel only caught a glimpse of this before he let the sweatshirt fall to cover it.

Lucius was nowhere to be seen, but Bel imagined he had eyes everywhere, that he was the personification of all the hidden security cameras under the guise of being constantly available to every guest's beck and call.

The glass opened and the cyborg reached for their backpacks—which they handed over without any fuss—and immediately began to walk away. Bel and Mateo looked at each other, then followed.

They ended up in the elevator—the real one this time—and ascended in silence. When the doors opened to the second floor, they followed the cyborg to a spacious office with black walls and a glass desk and a picture window with a VR scene that looked exactly like the forest outside the Submundo in stunning detail.

The cyborg dumped the contents of Mateo's backpack first, spreading them out so everything was visible. Mostly useless supplies—water bottles, the GPS device, Sparkfyre, and the laserlighter. The cyborg snatched up the laserlighter, then proceeded to Bel's backpack.

A few more camping supplies tumbled out, along with the soldering iron, the handgun, and the Ecker.

Of course the handgun was the first to be confiscated, but then the cyborg picked up the Ecker and examined it, turned it on, tapped through a few of its screens. "Impressive," he said.

"Thank you." Mateo threw a pointed look at Bel.

Bel had to bite her lip to keep from correcting either of them.

Once the cyborg was satisfied that he'd checked everything thoroughly, he handed back some of the smaller items—Bel's digibank and keychain of drives, their water bottles—and their empty backpacks. Then he brought them to a supply closet full of electronic accessories. Earbuds and gaming controllers and batteries. He located an unopened package of InVisors with ten to a box, a collection that would have been valued somewhere in the neighborhood of twenty-five thousand dollars. Thane's cousin must have been using a Ghostr, Bel thought; significantly cheaper, but not always reliable.

After unboxing, the cyborg handed Mateo one of the cleaning wipes that came inside.

Mateo took it and brushed the dark waves of hair off his face. He had to rip off the old InVisor first, then wipe his skin clean before applying the new one.

The cyborg peeled off one of the tiny dots, handing it delicately to Mateo.

It took a few minutes to connect it to the software on the cyborg's desktop holoscreen, but soon Mateo had his fourth alias.

"Liam Hollinger?" Bel read from the screen.

"Trust me," said the cyborg. "Where he's going, he'll need a name like that. He has to fit in with trust fund beneficiaries and CEOs."

"You mean he needs a name that cancels out his skin tone," said Bel.

"An unfortunate requirement, especially in this day and age," said the cyborg. "But yes. If he had some clout—and nothing to hide—it might be different; under the circumstances, though, it's best for him to blend in any way he can."

"Why do you even have these on hand?" Bel picked up the box with the rest of the InVisors and peered inside.

"You never know who might be running the world next," said the cyborg. "It's good to be prepared for anything."

Mateo looked over the rest of his profile, the fabricated backstory about himself he'd need to memorize. "What's keeping *you* from going back there, using one of these to get around, and actually *hiring* someone to do this job for you?"

The cyborg scoffed. "I think my face would turn a lot of heads, don't you? An InVisor might make me look different to the panopts, but it won't do anything to confuse human eyes. Besides, that's not the only issue." He went back to the closet and scanned the shelves until he found a packaged holopad box and unwrapped it. "There's vidrinium inside me. It interferes with the InVisor—something to do with the signals it gives off—and makes the masking spotty."

"More vidrinium ..." Mateo said.

"Hence the reason I'm trying to get information," the cyborg told him. "There shouldn't be vidrinium in any tech newer than 2071. I've got vidrinium wires *and* a vidrinium-ion battery—not exactly your run-of-the-mill prosthetics."

That must have been the reason he'd confiscated the laserlighter, Bel thought. Exposed vidrinium would easily explode under its beam. She'd have to know right where the battery was located, though, in order to aim the laser properly. She looked him up and down, like if she searched hard enough, she'd be able to see through his sweatshirt to the other metal he might be hiding.

A few taps later and the holopad was running, and the cyborg was inputting all of Liam Hollinger's fake information.

"So, what do I call you?" Mateo asked. "If I get a fake name, I'm assuming you get one too. How do I address you when we communicate?"

"You can call me Mr. Steele." He raised his metal arm as if in demonstration—*steel*, although probably ossteel rather than the original alloy—then handed the device to Mateo, along with another small, cylindrical device.

"An expense account?" Mateo mused, turning over the digibank.

"That's got a lot of money on it," said the cyborg. "Let's hope your sister's worth more to you than that amount."

"I'm not going to run off with your money," Mateo replied. "I'm not *actually* a criminal. And I care about my sister."

Bel rolled her eyes. "Your sister cares about getting a shower and something to eat—and maybe not being talked about in third person."

The cyborg handed Mateo the holopad. "I programmed the address in here. Use it to navigate your way, and by the time you get to the apartment, the building attendants will be expecting you. I'll set it up while you're on the move.

"You'll also find notes about your assignment, but the gist of it is that I want everything you can find on Project Iterum. What it is, the objective, the process, who's in charge of it, who's affiliated with it, and where experiments are being carried out."

As they left the office, the cyborg closed the door behind them and locked it with the fingerprint on his non-metal hand. Bel groaned internally, knowing it would be that much more difficult to get her hands on a device if she couldn't get back into that office. She wouldn't be able to hack the lock, either, with her Ecker inside. She just hoped there were other devices stashed somewhere else.

Next, the cyborg led them to another room they hadn't yet seen, dark walls with strips of light illuminating four mirrors with black salon chairs facing them. He gestured for Mateo to sit down at one of the stations, at which point another holomorph appeared.

"Welcome to the Studio," said a French-accented voice. It belonged to a platinum-blond Caucasian man with a black muscle shirt and tattooed arms. "I am Frédéric. How may I assist you today?"

"Please make this man presentable," the cyborg said flatly.

"Certainly." Frédéric displayed a series of images with different styling options—fade haircuts, undercuts, crew cuts—floating in glowing frames beside him. "Would any of these be to your liking?"

The cyborg tapped a basic, clean, businessman's haircut, eliciting a confirmatory chime.

"Very nice," said Frédéric. "Let's get started."

Thin lightbeams coming from the ceiling sensors scanned Mateo's head, measuring and assessing, and then mechanical appendages emerged from the station at several angles and began to trim and shave, not only his head but also his face. In a matter of minutes, Mateo was completely transformed.

Bel stared at him in awe as small cleaning machines came out of nowhere to remove the mess of hair on the floor. He'd gone from a shaggy mountain man to a clean-cut scion.

Once Mateo had showered, and emerged in a black bathrobe, the cyborg led him and Bel to a large, open compartment of the Submundo, sectioned off by sheets of glass that slid apart to let them through. The height of the space, similar to the Terrarium, reached the second story, with a display of clothing racks—behind more glass—that ran along the entire remaining three sides of the compartment's perimeter, blocked only by floor-to-ceiling mirrors midway through. It was almost like looking into clothing shop windows, except that the racks were not only long but several layers high. Glowing strips of light bordered the ceiling and floor. There were two, round, spotlit platforms at the center, and a few lounge chairs and tufted benches arranged throughout.

A new holomorph appeared. This one was a slim, dark-haired woman who wore a collared blouse of white lace and a pencil skirt with stilettos. "Welcome to the Wardrobe," she said with a Spaniard's accent. "I am Isabel. Please proceed to one of the platforms for a fitting scan, or if you already know your sizes, let me know what I can find for you."

Warily, Mateo stepped onto a platform. More thin lightbeams moved over him, this time for almost a full minute, and then a series of numbers hung in the air next to Isabel.

"Thank you," said the AI. "What kind of attire are you looking for?"

"Business casual," the cyborg told her.

Isabel nodded and the hanging clothes began to rotate behind the glass, along with multiple conveyor belts of accessories, and then shoes, underneath. There were what appeared to be feminine and masculine sections, with everything from casualwear to formalwear, from henley tees and cardigans and denim pants to lace blouses and blazers and chinos, to cocktail dresses and suits, and of course jewelry and watches. Most of the styles were simple, nothing too wild or flashy or particularly distinctive, but still there were a surprising number of options and, presumably, sizes, all shifting past like train cars on a track. The center panel of glass at the back of the room seemed to be the focal point, and soon a selection of men's dress shirts, slacks, suit jackets, and ties came into view, slowing as they approached. When the racks settled, the glass panel lifted to allow access to the clothing.

The cyborg went to it and began pulling out pieces, until he'd amassed a collection of approximately four sets of clothing and dress socks, with two pairs of shoes and a luxury holowatch.

"Put this one on," the cyborg told Mateo, handing him one set. "We'll pack up the rest."

Once that had all been settled, Bel—still a ragged, filthy mess—and the brother she now hardly recognized in his pale-blue button-down, fitted dress pants, and Oxford shoes, followed the cyborg to the Garage.

"At 760 miles per hour, the Mag is the fastest way to get to the city," he said, "but we need to get you to the Mag depot first. I will provide you a vehicle, which you will abandon at one of the depot lots—making sure to erase all navigation history—and then you'll purchase a new vehicle upon arrival, using your allotted funds, so that you'll have short-range transportation as needed. The Submundo's vehicles are not registered, so they won't have any traceability."

The cyborg operated a holographic console and remotely started one of the skimmers, which rose to a hover and came to a stop in front of him. "You'll take this one."

Mateo stared at the skimmer with shining eyes.

SUMMARY	
Brand	Celeritas 1350T
Fuel Type	Electric
HIN	1Y70075PL312
Year	2082
Dimensions	80.5 in x 26.8 in x 44.3 in

It had a sleek body with white fairings and black accents, a cushioned seat, a crystal-clear polycarbonate windscreen, and ergonomic grips. Bel pursed her lips, trying not to be resentful of the fact that her brother would get to drive it and she wouldn't.

The skimmer drove itself toward the hatch and waited for them.

"Lucius," said the cyborg, "open the East Entrance."

The wall opened into an anteroom, similar to the one Bel and Mateo had come in through earlier, only more spacious. Then, the outer wall—a hatch—lifted too.

Mateo was fully outfitted with a handful of electronic devices for his use on the mission—which also contained instructions and contact information for relaying his findings to the cyborg—along with a few supplies he'd need on his way to the city, like water and prepackaged food from the pantry. Everything was packed into a cognac leather travel bag stashed in the skimmer's cargo attachment.

The cyborg had already remotely sent navigation instructions to the skimmer's dash. Mateo's InVisor was securely in place, and all that was left to do was get on the skimmer and go.

Mateo looked at Bel, who stood with her arms crossed and didn't meet his eyes. "Well, I guess this is it. I'll get this done as quick as I can," he assured her. To the cyborg, he took a warning tone and said, "Anything happens to my sister ..."

The cyborg stared at him blankly. "Just get me the information I need."

Mateo flashed him a glare, then pulled Bel into an embrace. She resisted at first, but finally lifted her arms to reciprocate. Tense as things were between them, she couldn't let him leave without a little bit of compliance. He was the only family she had left, and what he was about to do would be dangerous.

"I love you," he told her.

"I love you too. Be careful."

He climbed onto the skimmer, which hummed quietly a foot off the ground and dipped a couple of inches until it readjusted to his weight. Bel and the cyborg stood back. Mateo looked over his shoulder once, gave Bel a flat smile, then squeezed the throttle and zoomed off into the woods.

Bel watched him for several seconds, his figure getting smaller and smaller, until finally she couldn't see him anymore. The cyborg waited without saying anything.

As soon as there was no sign of Mateo left, Bel said, "What now?"

The cyborg pressed his metal thumb to opposite his wrist again, and shrugged. "Like I said before, there are eight rooms. Pick one. Explore the Submundo, entertain yourself however you want, use what you need." He pushed the button on the hatch's inner panel manually this time without calling Lucius. The door came down, slowly blocking out the daylight as it sealed shut. A beep implied that it was locked.

The lights on the ceiling flicked on the same way they had at the West Entrance, and the cyborg followed their trail back into the heart of the Submundo.

Bel stood still for a moment, then hurried to catch up to him. "Can I ask you a question?"

"You can ask. Doesn't mean I'll answer." He shoved his hands into his sweatshirt's front pocket and kept walking.

The East Entrance doors parted to let him in.

Bel thought about what Lucius had said when she and Mateo had first arrived.

I detect two human organisms.

Cyborgs were usually *part* human, at least—enhanced with mechanical prosthetics—but for whatever reason, this one didn't seem to have registered that way. Still, he didn't seem to be a robot, despite the metal and the wires.

She followed him all the way back to the elevator and watched as he pushed the button.

"What are you?" she asked. "I know that's probably a rude thing to ask. I just don't really understand—"

The doors parted and he stepped inside, turning to face her from within. He withdrew his mechanical hand from his pocket. Not that the other hand wasn't mechanical, too, Bel thought—it very well could have been, even though it didn't look it. If the skin were burned away …

"I mean, are you, like …" Bel wasn't sure of a better way to say it. "'Real'?"

The cyborg glanced down and flexed his metal fingers. Just before the doors slid together and completely closed him off, he looked back up at Bel and said, "I used to be."

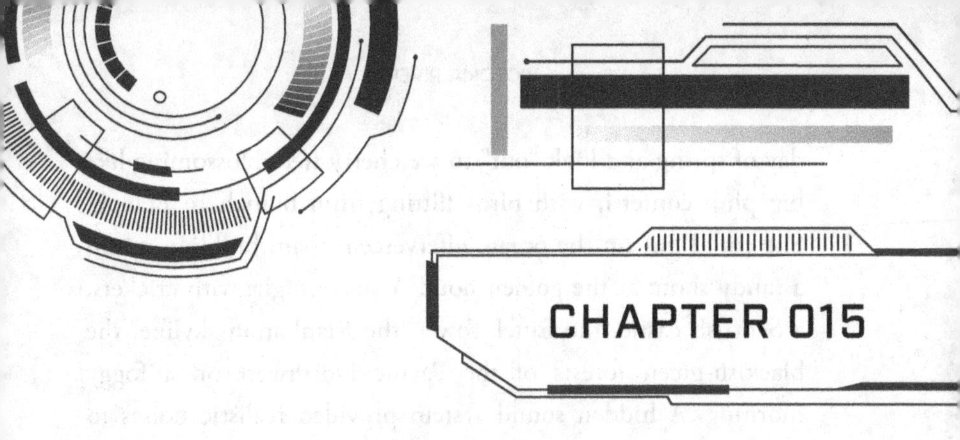

CHAPTER 015

BEL WAS TOO TIRED to hunt for the perfect room, so she took the first one she found. The door to the room was automated like the rest, sliding into its own wall pocket as she approached. She took a second to program an access code for herself on the touch panel, for privacy, although she didn't suspect the cyborg would come anywhere near her if he could help it. Then she dropped her empty backpack on the floor, deposited her smaller items in a pile on the first surface she saw, and looked around.

White walls, plush carpet, a king-sized bed on top of a black platform with a lit-up headboard. After playing with the controls, Bel discovered that a holoscreen would project downward from the ceiling, creating a small theater.

Black chairs flanked a marble table between them. A floating-shelf vanity took up part of the wall, in front of a square mirror surrounded by adjustable lighting. Many of the surfaces held wireless lamps, along with plants in high-tech pots that apparently provided sufficient water, light, and heat for themselves.

The adjacent wall—which acted as a partition between most of the room and what Bel quickly realized was the room's private, hidden bathroom—had three artificial windows with VR scenery behind them. Bel found she could put on the first day of spring and look "out" to see cherry trees blossoming like big pink confetti, with birds flitting from branch to branch. She could put on the ocean, effervescent foam building up on a sandy shore at the golden hour. A starry night with crickets, a Scottish castle, the Eiffel Tower, the Manhattan skyline, the blackish-green forests of the Pacific Northwest on a foggy morning. A hidden sound system provided realistic noises to add to the ambience. She cycled through several dozen scenes before she finally left the VR on a view of outer space, looking at Earth as if from the moon, since that's about as far as she felt from home—whatever that was for her now.

Then she searched the room for devices, something she could use to hack into the security cameras, to reprogram Lucius's auto-alert, or even just to dig around and get more information about the guy who was keeping her here. And, of course, to figure out how the cyborg would be communicating with Mateo so that she could intercept. A mini holopad, maybe, or even a holowatch. She asked Lucius where she might find something like that, but he informed her that he was not authorized to grant her access to such devices or to the knowledge of their whereabouts.

Bel plopped down on a chair for a moment and sighed.

She glanced around the room again. Everything was so clean. In contrast, Bel was filthy, dried sweat and dust layered over her, her hair knotted and greased with the secretions of her scalp. More than ready to bathe, she explored the bathroom. Charcoal granite covered the floor and climbed most of the walls. The shower was nestled in the corner, enclosed in big sheets of glass.

She undressed. A circular hole in the wall revealed itself, previously undetectable—a laundry chute of some kind, and she inserted her dirty clothes and then stepped inside the shower.

Goosebumps formed over her exposed skin while she stood there and examined the unsightly tan lines on her arms and around her neck, and on her legs where her jean holes had been—light brown, with a drastically deeper brown, and a distinct shift from one to the other.

The water came out of the ceiling like rain, from corner to corner. Bel rinsed away the past few days, murky water dripping over her body and swirling down the drain. When she'd finished, a rush of warm air dried her as she stepped out, and the drawers beneath the sink slid open gracefully, presenting her with a pile of folded towels.

Afterward, she wandered into what appeared to be a closet, curious what it might hold since the Wardrobe had already contained so much clothing. A door slid open, revealing a much smaller version of the Wardrobe—only one story, with only one platform, and a glass-enclosed clothing rack less than ten feet long.

The Isabel hologram appeared again. "Hello. Please proceed to the platforms for a fitting scan, or if you already know your size, let me know what I can find for you. This closet contains only essential clothing; for a wider variety, please visit the Wardrobe."

Bel stepped onto the platform and allowed the lightbeams to move over her body, resulting in a set of numbers similar to what had appeared for Mateo. She asked for "something comfortable" and the rack sped through several sets of mostly solid colors, mostly basics like cotton shirts and plain jeans and slip-on sneakers.

When it stopped, she looked through the section and found some black leggings and a gray, long-sleeved shirt. She also slipped on a pair of soft socks, and grabbed a pair of lace-less sneakers similar to her Vans, for later.

Now that she was dressed, she explored the contents of a cabinet across from the bed, and discovered that it was full of bottled water and light snacks. She took two bottles, along with a jar of chocolate-covered cashews, and consumed it all while she lay on the bed, sinking into the soft comforter and sighing.

She asked Lucius to show her what she could watch on the holoscreen. There were thousands of movies and shows available on the local server, but for now she put on *Rise of the Saturnians*. She lay relishing the pillows and her own cleanliness while she watched, although she could hardly concentrate on the movie.

She kept thinking of the cyborg, of all his grisly features, the way he hid himself pointlessly with the hood of his sweatshirt. She wondered how much of the rest of him had been burned away, what parts were metal and what was flesh. What had happened to him? What disaster had forced him to barricade himself underground? Not that this was an uncomfortable place to be.

It reminded Bel of the summer storms in Iowa, of going underground to wait them out. Most towns there had been equipped with storm sirens that would blare a warning when windspeed was high. She'd never actually seen a tornado while they'd lived there, but she and Mateo had gone to the cellar many times to wait for the "all clear" alert while the wind whipped violently above the surface. It had happened enough times that they'd started to keep the cellar stocked with snacks, pillows and blankets, a few rudimentary devices for entertainment. It was fun, in a weird way, living on the basics for a couple hours, eating chips and snoozing on thin mats on the floor with blankets that smelled like the musty cellar, watching movies on the ancient 5K Smart TV the previous owners had left down there. It had been fun because it had been temporary.

If this was the cyborg's version of a storm cellar, Bel couldn't imagine what a regular home of this caliber must be like.

Twenty minutes into *Saturnians*, Bel's stomach groaned again. She'd known the cashews wouldn't be enough, but the thought of trekking all the way down to the kitchen with the long hallways sounded exhausting. She lay in bed for a while longer and then, finally, forced herself to get up in search of something more substantial.

"Lucius," she said, "Can you please guide me to the kitchen?"

Everything was empty as Lucius led Bel through the corridor. No trace of the cyborg. No trace of anyone or anything, really. Just the occasional cleaning robot and the sound of water jets spraying the plants in the Terrarium. The fireplace lit automatically as Bel and Lucius passed through the Common Room and faded as they left.

Lucius brought Bel to a quartz-topped bar that ran the length of the kitchen, looking in over the whole of it. He lit the space and gestured for her to sit on one of several galvanized metal stools.

"The kitchen will prepare anything you like," he explained. "The Submundo kitchen staff consists of 534 unique appliances that gather, measure, and assemble ingredients from the pantry, following a database of recipes."

A holoscreen projected a vibrant menu display, with a list of dishes and their descriptions, three-dimensional animated photos, and sections where 3D videos demonstrated the cooking process. Bel stepped closer and looked over the items—meals she couldn't believe a mechanical kitchen would be able to prepare from food meant to be preserved for decades. Paella, lobster risotto, hanger steak, heirloom vegetables, spanakopita, sushi rolls, cilantro-tomato bruschetta, Waldorf salad.

"How is all this even possible?" Bel asked. "Fresh vegetables? Raw fish? How's that supposed to last fifty years? How's it even supposed to last fifty *days*?"

"The Submundo pantry is stocked with food items that have been preserved through various technological means, including but not limited to freeze drying, flash freezing, cellular dehydration, instastasis, immerglas containment, and sempiterne canning. Would you like to know more?"

Bel shook her head in disbelief. "Not right now. I'm sure I'll have more questions later." After some of the things she'd already seen at the Submundo, she knew it wasn't a far jump to imagine what was possible in food preservation technology. Still, she was skeptical that any of the ingredients in the pantry could hold much flavor. But all she really cared about was getting something in her stomach. "Is there anything less … extravagant? Like, a burger or something?"

"Certainly. Let me connect you to Reuben and he will assist you with your meal preparation."

Another AI holomorph materialized beside him, a man with olive skin and a trim salt-and-pepper beard, wearing a chef's coat.

"Oh," said Bel, "You meant *the* Reuben …"

The holomorph had apparently been modeled after real-life, world-famous chef Reuben Delessio, known for his cutthroat tactics in the kitchen. He was brutal to his employees and tolerated no nonsense. Everybody loved to hate him—because, despite being a terrible human being, he was also a culinary genius.

"You want a burger?" said Reuben. "Done." He turned to the kitchen mechanisms and spoke like he was giving orders to a full staff. "Ground chuck, grilled onions, heirloom tomatoes, loose-leaf lettuce blend, garlic aioli."

Lucius nodded. "I'll leave you to it." His image dissipated.

Bel's eyes went wide. "Wait, I just wanted—"

"Smoked gouda or Somerset brie?" Reuben asked her.

"Um … brie, I guess. But could I have it without onions?"

"No onions?" Reuben said in disbelief. "*No onions?*"

"I just don't like the texture—"

"You would sacrifice the sweet, smoky, caramelized flavor?"

Bel raised an eyebrow. "Yes?"

Reuben stared at her a moment before he said, simply, "No."

"What do you mean, 'no'? I thought I was in charge here."

"Wrong. I'm in charge. This is *my* kitchen."

"Did they program you to be hostile?"

"The Reuben Delessio model is programmed for maximum authenticity. If you don't like it, take it up with your IT officer."

"Right," Bel said bitterly. Something told her having a conversation with the cyborg about his kitchen's bad attitude wouldn't get her very far. She was a guest here—if using the term 'guest' loosely—and really had no right to complain about the way her otherwise very expensive food was given to her.

When Bel didn't say anything further, Reuben clapped his hands together once and said, "Very good. Cook time is approximately seven minutes."

Classical music began to play, loud and clear as a live symphony. A dissonant harmony of stringed instruments provided a suspenseful introduction as the preparation counter divided itself, half its surface rising lengthwise to twice its original height, black metal hinged mechanisms dangling—

robotic arms—some with pincers waiting to grasp ingredients or containers, others with small tools or appliances permanently attached: graters, a hand blender, a whisk, a mixing paddle, knives of every shape and size and sharpness for every purpose, a blow torch …

The wall connected to one end of the counter opened and produced packaged ingredients on a conveyor system: cheese, herbs, brioche dough, something that looked like meat, a few other items in opaque containers, and a bottled liquid—possibly some kind of formula to reconstitute ingredients. From above the counter, mixing bowls, pots and pans, and cutting boards descended on hooked rods, like a military airdrop of supplies. Everything arrived in order, perfectly timed, perfectly coordinated, and the music swelled around it.

Bel sat, eyes wide and unblinking, taking in each movement. The counter itself seemed to be a cooking surface when necessary, but also opened to receive things—to discard trash, in some cases, to lower raw foods into convection ovens below.

Within minutes, the air was warm, and saturated with evocative smells. Bel's stomach churned in response.

Finally, everything finished, and the arms drained, combined, and plated the food, placing it on another conveyor system, which carried a copper tray to the receiving table beside Bel as the music stopped with an intentional, closing cadence.

The lights dimmed to a relaxing, diffused amber, and Reuben concluded with, "Thank you for joining us in the Submundo kitchen. Please enjoy your meal."

Bel took her tray to the dining hall.

Ten seats in all, a long table, edges straight, chairs evenly distributed along both sides and one on each short end, lined up like soldiers waiting for command. She chose a random chair somewhere in the middle.

Her first bite was incredible, the flavors and the textures unaffected by the fact that every ingredient was meant to last several decades. She never would have known it had been made from food that had been cellularly dehydrated or stored in immerglas—whatever that was. Reuben had been right to insist on the onions, which were grilled to perfection and didn't present any of the same problems she'd had with onions on burgers before. She guessed it made a difference, having a world-class chef—or his likeness, at least—make her food.

The Terrarium filled the space behind the big windows as she ate, like a lush garden outside a massive estate. The VR sky wasn't so bright now, the sun clone moving toward the west end, the plants casting oblong shadows onto the lawns and walkways. It must have been past five o'clock.

Bel returned to the kitchen with her plate and asked if it would be possible to get a bottled soda to take with her to her room. She had to argue with Reuben, who insisted that she follow her gourmet burger with a cabernet sauvignon or at least a Manhattan.

"You know I'm under twenty-one, right?" Bel said.

Reuben seemed to be programmed not to care. He only complained that this was the first time anyone had used his kitchen in seven months and it was a huge disappointment.

Bel had to hand it to Delessio's designers; the AI man was true to character, from his rage scowl to the way his accent got thicker when he was complaining. Finally, he consented to direct her to the place where the dishes were kept so that she could get an empty glass to "fill with whatever swine's beverage" she preferred, and then he disappeared with a disgusted huff.

Bel frowned at the now-empty space where the holomorph

had been, and wondered about Reuben's earlier comment, that no one had used the kitchen in seven months.

What had the cyborg been running on all this time?

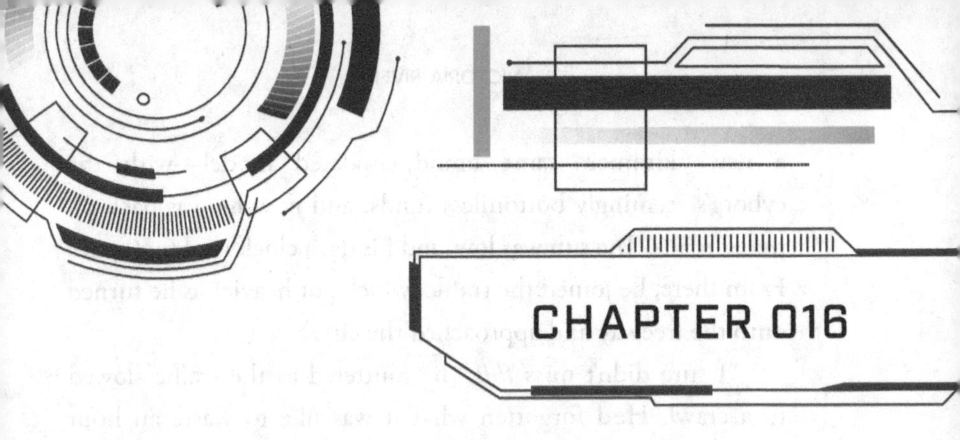

CHAPTER 016

MATEO'S JOURNEY THROUGH THE LOS PADRES on the skimmer was significantly shorter than it had been on foot. The seamless navigation and the vehicle's ability to skim over rough terrain without missing a beat made the whole thing stupidly easy.

A few miles out, he'd spotted a fleet of pandrones in the distance. He hadn't imagined they would have been out so deep into the forest normally, but after what had happened with the ranger drone before he and Bel had gone into the Submundo, he knew it was reasonable that the authorities might have sent more drones to comb the area.

He was fairly confident that the ranger hadn't gotten a full visual on him earlier, but a shot-down ranger would still be likely to draw suspicion—because no one who wasn't guilty of something would bother to shoot one—especially with a criminal on the loose in the same region.

He'd resisted the urge to drive off-course into the trees. Thankfully, it hadn't been necessary to run. The drones had approached, whirred and beeped, scanning him, and the InVisor had done its job. They flew away and left him alone.

He'd made it to the nearest Mag depot, where he'd ditched the skimmer as instructed, ridden the Mag to the city, purchased a new skimmer—same brand, updated model—with the cyborg's seemingly bottomless funds, and now he was back on paved roads. The sun was low, and his dash clock read 6:30 p.m. From there, he joined the traffic, which got heavier as he turned onto the freeway and approached the city.

"I sure didn't miss *this*," he muttered as the traffic slowed to a crawl. He'd forgotten what it was like to waste an hour between exits that were only a few miles apart. Everyone around him didn't seem to notice, though; music blared from within different vehicles, most of which were electric and self-driving now, and at least half were hovercraft. Some passengers or drivers were having conversations with holomorphic heads—people on the other ends of holopad calls—to pass the time. This was their normal. It had been his normal once, too.

Soon there were panopts every hundred yards, and then every dozen or so. The skyline that had previously been minuscule in the distance behind the hanging smog began to turn clear, growing in Mateo's view. His heart pinched at the sight of so many familiar buildings, with the silvery water beyond them. Even the smell was familiar, briny and dusty and a little bit sulfuric.

Finally, he reached the city streets themselves, all aglow with urban lights. Many of the panopts flashed ads.

Sign up for Atmo Premium

The Mystical Bones *in VRplex theaters now*

McDonalds 2 for $10 Big Mac

Other screens played news clips, where giant news anchors' heads protruded out three-dimensionally. Streetlights and traffic lights remained relatively steady in between the changing color casts of the panopts. Buildings with lights in the windows showed human activity—business meetings running late or cleaning staff moving around.

Mateo inhaled deeply, taking in the scent of garlic and butter, grilled meat, and alcohol, trying to separate it from the less-pleasant scents of garbage and urine that punctuated every few streets.

Soon, the buildings became larger, more sleek. The vehicles flanking him became more expensive. The attire of the pedestrians became more posh.

When he reached the apartment building, he had begun to seriously doubt that his appearance was sufficient.

It wasn't so much an apartment building as a boutique luxury community that was practically its own small city: high-rise units with outspread balconies and huge windows, expensive shops on the first level, restaurants with sophisticated outdoor dining, a terrace with steps down to the waterfront, a gym, multiple swimming pools, and a lobby to rival that of a five-star European hotel—or what he *imagined* what might rival one, considering he'd never been to Europe.

The valet took his skimmer and he entered the building. A beep echoed in the lobby as he passed under a silver arch, prompting him to look up; it was hardly visible, but Mateo recognized the facial scanner.

"Welcome back, Mr. Hollinger," said a woman behind the desk.

Mateo nodded his thanks.

He tried not to walk too quickly, even though he wanted to sprint to the elevators before anyone could see him. He was sure his body odor was seeping through his new clothes, that his complete lack of confidence would give him away in a second. His clothes, which had seemed to fit fine at first, now felt all wrong; the pants were too baggy around the ankles and the shirt didn't conform enough around his shoulders, unlike the perfectly tailored attire of everyone that meandered through the lobby—the investment bankers and the socialites and the B-list celebrities.

By the time he reached the elevators, he had to force himself to breathe, to relax his shoulders. Another scanner beeped over his face, although this one was an eye-level panel beside the elevator door. This would act as a key, the cyborg had told him, instructing the elevator to take him to the appropriate floor.

Thankfully he didn't have to share the elevator with anyone else.

When the doors parted, Mateo found himself staring directly into his new apartment. No hallway, no upper-floor lobby. His face must have been the key to the apartment *itself*, Mateo thought. The kind of luxury he'd only ever seen on TV shows.

It wasn't a huge apartment—almost none in the city were—but it was sleek. The entire back wall was a window overlooking the city, with the Vivorex building—a great, silver, double helix—directly in view from behind the balcony's iron rails. The floors were white wood, with fine-textile area rugs dividing the leather furniture. The kitchen had quartz countertops and backsplashes and an island-bar. Abstract art hung on the walls. A snake plant sat in the corner, almost touching the ceiling. All the sinks and lights were automatic. Everything Mateo used or walked close to seemed to sense him, to anticipate him. Not quite as extreme as the Submundo, but there were touches of the same technology in each room. The kitchen had the ability to prepare a small menu of meals automatically, provided the refrigerator and a specific shelf on the pantry were fully stocked—which they were.

After walking around for a few minutes, Mateo figured he

should stop gawking. Even though he wanted to settle in, he could hardly relax knowing that Bel was alone in the Submundo with someone who wasn't fully human. He had to get his thoughts together. The entire trip, he'd been thinking on and off what he could do to turn this thing around, to get Bel out of that place without the cyborg alerting anyone that they'd been there. But he knew if he contacted VOLT and they tried an extraction, there was always a risk something could go wrong. Mateo knew that all too well. Any mission that double-crossed a tyrant could backfire—and hurt the ones he loved the most.

No, he thought. For now, he'd try to do his job. He unbuttoned the collar of his shirt, rolled up his sleeves, and opened the holopad the cyborg had given him. He could do this quickly; he had to believe that.

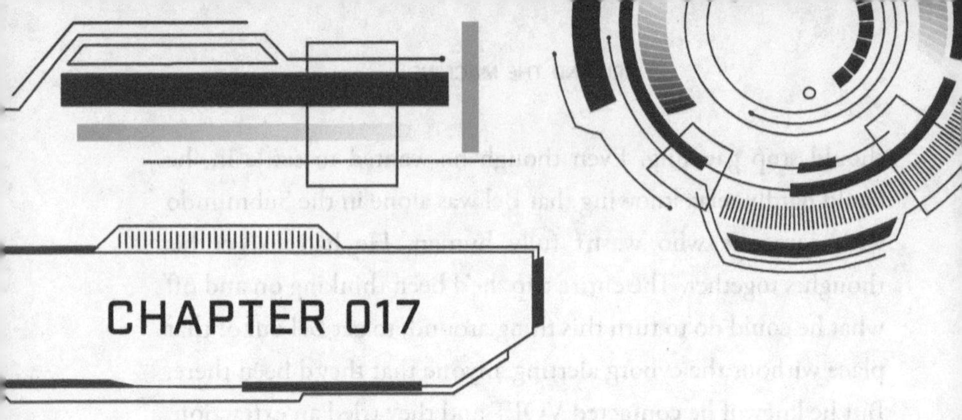

CHAPTER 017

THE CYBORG STARED AT HIS OWN shirtless reflection in the bathroom mirror. Exposed wires and internal mechanisms gleamed in the dim lights, which he always kept low so as not to have to take in the full effects of himself.

Most of the right side of his face and top of his head had been burned, along with part of his right shoulder and his entire right arm. A portion of his chest was also exposed, right where his human heart would have been—if he'd still had one—as well as a portion of his hip and left thigh.

He reached for the clippers. The blade was bare, ready to get close to the skin, and he held it to his head. Automatically the clippers began to buzz.

It was only the left half of his head that required attention, as no hair grew on the metal where his scalp had been burned away.

The hair that did grow wasn't the way he remembered it. His black hair had always been coarse and thick, with a deep wave when grown out. High humidity would have coaxed it to a full-on curl. But this hair was different; it was thinner, softer. Only vaguely so, and it wouldn't have looked unnatural even to anyone who had known him well. It was only his own deep familiarity that allowed him to feel the difference.

His mother had told him once that the human finger could discriminate between surfaces patterned with ridges as small as thirteen nanometers, something he'd forgotten he even knew until the first time he'd shaved this partially burnt head.

The buzzing relaxed him a bit. Each tuft of hair that fell brought him momentary peace, knowing that he wouldn't begin to feel the nanometrical difference in each strand again for at least another week. He wouldn't have to remember the random facts his mother had shared with him, and he wouldn't have to keep asking himself if the sensory cells on his one apparently normal hand were real, or whether they were a disturbingly accurate recreation.

He wanted to believe he wasn't all machine, but there wasn't a single exposed part of him that indicated otherwise. Only his mind was original, he thought. It had to be. Would he feel real if it weren't? Would he question himself and his realness if he had none to question?

Occasionally, the memories would come back to him in fragments, flashing through his mind like a strobe light—some parts blindingly bright and clear, others doused in shadow. The imperfect nature of his true, organic memory. He'd learned, however, upon his arrival at the Submundo, that this new machine in which he lived was capable of storing memories like a computer, as files that could be downloaded to any of his local devices—he only had to confirm access with a pairing code that appeared in front of his eyes—and then he could watch them like video footage. But of course the earliest files only began with what had happened *after*. Everything from *before* was still much more abstract.

He'd been looking into a mirror like he was now, but in a different place, music pulsing outside the walls. Splashing water on his face—a face with clean, dark skin on every inch of it, no metal peeking through. No metal hiding underneath it, either.

The InVisor had gotten him through the door to Paragon, even though he wasn't quite nineteen yet and the law would have otherwise kept him outside the club.

Lights had been fading between purple and pink as he'd sat down at the bar. Then there'd been the blonde girl one seat over. Glass clinking. Ice jostling. That's when things had started to get blurry.

A strobe of light on the memory of his body slumping to the ground. A strobe of light on the memory of an ambulance wailing in his ears. A strobe of light on lasers scanning him from crown to toe, machines beeping, a man typing something on a holopad. "Overdose," a voice had said.

It was like he'd been a ghost, not yet willing to leave his corpse, still listening but unable to speak.

Darkness in between the lights. Darkness for a long stretch before another strobe on the memory of waking in a cold room, staring up at an industrial ceiling with sore eyes that didn't feel like his own, stainless-steel surfaces and glass cabinets and holoscreens of data all around. A row of other bodies extending from either side of him. Trying to stand but stumbling on weak legs. Alarms blaring. The panic that had filled him with an animalistic urge to run. His desperate attempt to evade the swarm of white lab coats. Hands wearing verapiel medical gloves reaching for him. Thrashing and flailing. Framework collapsing. A deafening blast. Shards of glass spewing. Searing pain across his face and limbs. Flames whipping everything in sight, climbing the curtains that divided the space from whatever had lain beyond, consuming enough of his pursuers that he could escape.

Into darkness again, but different kinds of darkness this

time. The night that had awaited him outside of that sinister place. The haunting reflection that had been staring back at him every day since. The rage that burned hotter than the fire on his flesh ever could have.

He'd watched portions of his downloaded memory footage *since* the incident, from his abrupt awakening and onward, studied them and searched them for answers. But unfortunately, the footage he needed preceded the first recordings of his mechanical mind. Even with a perfect re-creation of his waking and escape, he couldn't learn enough to know for certain who had done this to him. Only the vaguest of clues.

It sickened him, the way he'd been reduced from a human soul to little more than a robot. The way other devices could detect him, like he was a mere device himself. Not only had they been able to detect his files, they had sensed an energy meter—a timer on his very life, although he couldn't say what that life meant to him in this state. He only knew he still had the instinct to survive, no matter how miserable he'd become.

Through an app called ROSE (a remote observation status emulator) he'd been able to display all the statistics of the battery that powered his body. And while he knew it was vital information to have, he couldn't bear to look at it from day to day—like a ticking clock, or worse, an hourglass with sand running through in one direction, and no way to refill it or flip it back over—so he'd left the app running on a mini holopad, but kept it tucked away in the storage zone, like some looming demon in a dungeon temporarily contained by the wards of superstition.

Now, he clung to the possibility that his intruders might be the key to better understanding.

Under normal circumstances, he might not believe that

Mateo Solís wasn't the criminal his record had presented him to be, but having had his own identity stripped down and rebuilt with new material, he knew anything was possible. He could only hope that a tech prodigy hadn't landed at his door for nothing.

He worried that the girl might complicate things, though. She was like a wild cat, with a certain inherent elegance and confidence, but also with the tendency to hiss and scratch in response to very little provocation. As long as he stayed clear of her, he might be able to avoid any issues. He didn't need or want the drama.

When the last tuft of hair hit the floor, he silenced the clippers. He set them down and flexed the fingers of his exposed hand, watching the metal and the wires move. This hand had lost most of its sensation, as had every other exposed part of him. He had so little of himself left, and there was a good chance the rest was only a facade.

He looked at himself again in reflection. He curled his fists. Heat rose in his body—whether electrical or organic, he didn't know. He pounded his metal fist into the glass, cracks spidering across its surface. He pounded again and again and again. Bits of glass broke loose and rained over the sink, collecting into a glittery mass near the drain. Heaving, he braced himself on the vanity and glanced down, only to see the image of his mutilated face yet again, now multiplied in every shard.

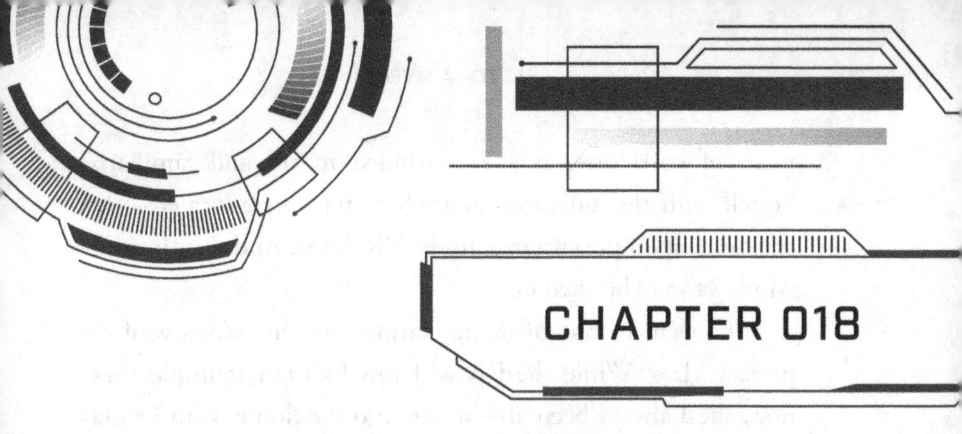

CHAPTER 018

BEL SPENT THE FOLLOWING THREE DAYS exploring what she could of the Submundo, eating gourmet meals with the Delessio holomorph, and watching movies and playing Neon Sniper with the VR headset in her room. Despite her exploratory efforts, however, she hadn't gotten any closer to finding a way to get in touch with Mateo. All devices seemed to be out of sight, behind closed doors—and of course this was on purpose. The cyborg didn't know of all her talents with a keyboard, but any device could be a means of communication, and allowing her to communicate with the outside world was a threat to him.

In all this time, Bel hadn't encountered the cyborg even once, and she was sure he must have set up notifications through his surveillance system in order to avoid her. Which was fine. But being all alone in this strange, enormous place was somewhat unsettling, too. The holomorphic staff members were realistic, sure, but she could only hold a conversation with any one of them for so long. The chef was by far the most entertaining, but she had to stop herself every time she remembered she was arguing with a caricature. She wondered how long the cyborg had been here by himself, and how he hadn't lost his mind yet. Or maybe he had, and that's what all of this was about.

It was on yet another one of her explorations through the

maze of corridors—as she continued to try and familiarize herself with the amenities and where they were located—that she came upon the entrance to the VR dome. And this time, the windows were blacked out.

She went to one of them, staring into the darkness of the privacy glass. While she'd passed this location multiple times now, she'd always been able to see into the dome, with its gray interior and thousands of sensors and projectors embedded in every surface.

He must be in there.

A panel off to the side glowed with blue icons.

She tapped the third icon. Immediately the glass became a screen, showing the interior of the dome—but with VR effects applied.

A familiar nighttime skyline in a futuristic city. An inky sky, and moody skyscrapers illuminated only by pink and purple color casts from neon signs that glowed between them. All the signs were made up of alien symbols, mostly geometric shapes and lines.

Neon Sniper.

Suppressing a grin, Bel tapped the fourth icon, which allowed her to see the view from the perspective of whomever was playing. The visuals on the screen shifted to a lower angle, close to one of the streets, then a gaze that swept over the broken windows of a gritty, industrial zone.

Bel tapped the audio icon and a musical bass filled her ears, along with the empty echo of a mostly abandoned, dystopian city.

She made sure to avoid the mic icon, probably an intercom. The last icon, however, allowed her to toggle-switch to additional views and then swipe the window-screen to change them. She zoomed out a little and came in from slightly above and in front of the player—and there he was, crouching in a dark alley, peering around the corner.

From the neck down, he wore a virtual armor all sleek and black and fitted, with thick seams at every joint. His face, however, looked the same as it did in real life. He must have scanned himself in as-is, not bothering to alter his avatar.

He also held a large weapon, two feet long, black grip and stock with a thick silver barrel that had a glowing orange line running through its center. It buzzed with electrical charge.

Bel watched as a large, red, alien beast emerged from the darkness. An orange laser zinged from the cyborg's weapon and struck the alien. The number 13 flashed above the alien, changed to 12, then faded.

Her whole body itched to get in there, muscle memory ready to take over and blast the NPCs. She'd only ever played on a small scale, knowing that the vast expanse of city was only an illusion and, if she wasn't careful, she'd crash into her bedroom wall. Within the dome, she could actually run the full length of some of the streets, or spin-shoot a group of opponents without fear of knocking things off her desk.

"Lucius," said Bel. "Can I enter the game?"

Lucius manifested beside her and said, "Certainly."

Gesturing toward the wall, he highlighted a panel that slid out to reveal racks of equipment—haptic vests, haptic gloves and boots, haptic headgear, even full haptic suits, along with several simple, lightweight, mono-lens headsets, and a number of other types of more elaborate headsets.

"Place a headset over your eyes," Lucius told her, while she removed one of the simple ones and held the frame up to the light to observe its details, "and when you're ready, tap the stem at your temple."

"Will the game alert him"—she nodded at the image of the cyborg on the window-screen—"that I'm in it?"

"You may enter in Stealth Mode, if you would like."

"I would like." She put on the headset and stood in front of the dome entrance. Lucius parted the doors for her and she stepped inside.

The room was bare and unaffected at first. Now that she had a better look at the inside, the floor seemed to be porous in some way, a sort of metallic mesh—maybe to allow floor sensors to track movement from below the user.

Bel tapped her headset, and then her surroundings turned to an abyss of digital matter.

"Whoa." She glanced around.

Lucius's voice came like he was in her ear, something that must be coming through where the headset pressed lightly at the side of her head. *Bone conduction sound*, Bel thought.

"At any point," he added, "in any scene or game within the system, simply tap anywhere with two fingers to see a menu."

Bel looked down, where she found herself standing on a rooftop. She wore the same armor as the cyborg, the same armor she always wore in Neon Sniper, but it felt different somehow. It *felt*. It was like the material was touching her body. Like the electric charges were moving through it, vibrating against her.

"The system within the VR dome has scanned your face and body," Lucius explained, "and thereby recreated your likeness and adapted thematic accessories to fit you. However, if you'd like, you can alter the appearance of your avatar at any point.

"The dome is fitted with thousands of sensors and sensifiers, which will track your movements and produce realistic alterations to the room's temperature, humidity, sound, and scent. The system also employs nanotechnological sensification that will mimic the feeling of force against your body or textures on the skin. While not as powerful as the effects of hapticwear, it can provide a relatively immersive tactile experience in addition to the other sensifiers.

"Finally, as you approach the dome walls, a blue boundary warning will show up along the edge of the floor. When you see it, you have two feet of clearance before collision."

His voice faded and she was left alone on the rooftop, stunned at how real it all felt. There was a night-air sort of chill that moved against her, even from below. The armored suit felt surprisingly stiff, for not being real. The boots she virtually wore weighed against her feet. The weapon was somehow heavy in her hands. Nanotechnological tricks of the senses, she supposed. Sensory illusions.

She steadied herself and scanned her surroundings. She raised her weapon and looked out. In her periphery, something moved. Quickly she spun and caught sight of someone jumping from a ledge onto the rooftop. A masculine humanoid with blond hair. Instinctively, she fired.

An orange laser zinged from the weapon and struck the opponent, whose suit flashed as it absorbed the energy. As soon as he recovered, he returned fire. Bel ran, but she was hit. Suit flashing, she raced to take cover, ducking behind a huge air system pipe. The number 20 appeared in the air, changing to 19, and faded. She panted as smoke puffed out a few yards away, its realistic scent filling her nose. She grinned.

This was amazing.

She leapt between buildings like she was superhuman, climbed down fire escapes, raced through abandoned city streets dodging laser beams and shooting from dark spaces. She was hit a total of fourteen times, but she'd managed to obliterate two opponents entirely—one human and one alien—depleting all twenty of their lives.

As she stalked one of them, who had disappeared around a corner, she thought she caught a glimpse of his shoulder, and raced toward him. She'd been following the sound of scraping boots. In fact, most of the opponents made subtle noises when they moved.

Then she heard the opponent's weapon power up and she instantly ducked into a roll. Her body hit the pavement, illuminating the blue boundary line.

Two feet of clearance.

Getting back up, she crouched low to avoid another hit in case the opponent fired again. But the sound of different footsteps—coming from behind her—startled her. She swung around and aimed her weapon at another oncoming opponent— one she recognized.

It was the cyborg.

His weapon powered up, aimed directly at her.

He wouldn't know it was her, she told herself. He'd just think she was another NPC.

She backed away as she powered up her own weapon, the blue boundary line steady and growing brighter in her periphery. She dodged a blast from him just before she reached the line's glow with her foot, and immediately fired back. Except that the realistic kickback pushed her one inch too far.

She stumbled—and smacked right into the dome wall.

The cyborg let his weapon hang at his side and took a step

forward, a confused look on his face that quickly turned sharp.

"*You*."

CHAPTER 019

ONCE BEL HAD REGAINED HER COMPOSURE, she picked up her virtual weapon that she'd "dropped" when she'd fallen, and rested one hand on her hip, breathing heavily.

The cyborg stood amid the wreckage of a rusted hovercraft. "What are you doing here?" His voice sounded closer than he was, like a bug in her ear.

"You said I could do whatever I wanted."

"How long have you been in my game?"

Bel sighed. "Oh, I don't know. About forty-five minutes. Maybe an hour. It's easy to lose track of time in here. This is seriously incredible."

She took in her surroundings. Once she'd gotten going, she hadn't had the chance to continue appreciating the complexity of the graphics. She now stood on an empty street corner with concrete walls at every turn, most of which were covered in graffiti.

"Come back another time," said the cyborg, "when I'm not here. Anytime after that, knock yourself out—again."

Bel caught the hint of a smirk on his face, although he otherwise maintained a serious expression. She thought of how ridiculous she must have looked, smashing into the wall—what would have appeared to be her flailing over thin air, thanks to the game's environment. She hoped the VR sensors wouldn't digitally recreate the flush of warmth now creeping onto her cheeks.

"You want me out of the game?" she said. "Fine. Take me out yourself."

"What?"

She raised her weapon. "Take me out. Kill my avatar."

He stood still, but his weapon hummed at his side, charging up. Deadpan, he aimed at her and fired.

Bel ducked behind an air unit as the laser streaked past her. She waited a moment, then peeked out carefully.

She caught sight of his shoulder and took a shot, but he was too quick. The laser zinged against the concrete and a spray of sparks flew out as he slipped into the darkness.

"You must play this a lot," she said.

His footsteps echoed a ways off, heavy as though his avatar's boots were real. "Good way to blow off steam," he replied flatly.

As before, his voice had come directly into her ear. She couldn't use it as a gauge for the distance between them, so she continued to listen for boots on the pavement or the charge of his weapon.

He darted out from hiding and she fired twice, but he dodged both lasers and disappeared around the side of another building.

Bel held her weapon out and crept to where he'd gone. She waited, straining her ears. After almost a minute of relative quiet, she said, "How long have you been down here? At the Submundo, I mean."

He didn't answer. The audio of his breath told her he was listening, but he remained otherwise silent.

"I'd lose my mind if I had to stay underground, alone, for a long period of time," she told him. "Although, I have to say, when it comes to being forced into hiding indefinitely, this is one of the better places for it." She charged her weapon in preparation, continuing to creep down the sidewalk. "You must come from an important family. Not a lot of people have the means to live like this—in *general*, and especially not as a last resort."

His breath came in heavier again, like he was on the move. Then, a pause. She imagined him with his back against the bricks, weapon close to his chest, glancing sideways.

"But we're all mortal in the end, though," he said. "Aren't we."

She assumed he was referring to his own condition. No amount of money had protected him from that, from whatever had happened to him.

"So what is it, then?" she asked. "Venture capitalism? Aerospace manufacturing? Software development? I'm guessing you're not a celebrity, otherwise I'd probably at least vaguely recognize you."

"Not much left to recognize."

Bel peered around the next corner, certain she'd find him there. She raised her charged weapon.

Screeeeeeeeeeech.

A looming, hairy creature emerged. It stood upright like a human, but its body was all animal, jaws wide open and sharp teeth dripping with foam.

The sight of it knocked Bel backwards, but not before she took a shot.

The blast threw the unarmored creature into the nearest wall. Its number appeared, dropping from 9 to 8, and then it scurried off.

By the time Bel had gotten back on her feet, the cyborg

reappeared and blasted her dead-center in the chest. Her suit flashed, and then her own number, already partially depleted from her earlier playing, appeared as 6, then 5.

She shot at his back as he fled, striking him between the shoulder blades.

15 ... 14

Damn, he's good, Bel lamented internally. He'd been in the dome longer than she had and still had more lives remaining. Although, to be fair, he'd also had more practice in this particular version of the game. She was used to a much more contained environment. While the ability to move around freely was great, it had also worn her out more quickly, physically. She was sure she'd be sore from this later.

For several minutes, they stalked one another. Circling. Creeping. A shot in the dark here, a semi-lit shot there, but no hits.

Finally, Bel said, "Why don't we make this a little more interesting?"

"I'm not *interested* in doing this at all," he said.

"Then why don't you just leave?"

"I was here first. And this is my place."

"Sure. But you're the one who insisted I stay at the Submundo with you. I'm bored. And you have *got* to be going crazy after what—I'm guessing—has been a torturous amount of time." She waited for him to say something but, again, he was silent. "How about every time I hit you, you answer a question."

"And why would I do that?"

"Because I'll have done something to earn it," she said.

He laughed bitterly. "That doesn't benefit me in any way."

"If you hit *me*, you can ask me a question and I'll answer it."

"I already know everything I need to know about you."

"You know what's in a database," she countered.

"Doesn't matter. If all goes well with your brother at Vivorex, you won't be here long anyway."

"You get two passes," she told him, as though he had actually agreed to her terms. "Say 'pass' and I'll come up with a different question."

"No thanks."

As she turned another corner, she stepped up to an almost mirror image. The cyborg faced her, his weapon raised to the same level as hers. A standoff.

"I'm not telling you my name," he said, "if that's what you're after. Or where to get your hands on a device."

Bel fired and the laser struck him, lighting him up. She smiled.

"Cheap shot." He aimed back at her, but she'd been ready, twisting her body out of the way and scrambling behind one of the EVSE ports of a vehicle charging station.

She caught a glimpse of him and lowered herself to a crouch. "So … What do you think happened to you?"

"Pass."

She peeked out again, but his avatar was gone now. A shallow puddle of stormwater—or maybe leaked machine oil—remained where he'd been, reflecting the light of a pink, neon sign from one of the buildings.

While craning her neck to look for him, a zap struck her, and her suit flashed once more. The number 5 appeared in the air and changed to 4.

Bel raced down another alley where she encountered a blue alien NPC with four hands and large, pointed ears. She hit him on the first try, grabbed him, and used him as a shield against the cyborg's next attempt to shoot her, then shoved the alien toward him and sprinted to the outlet at the alley's far end. She didn't stop until she reached a freight truck, where she climbed inside and sank to her knees, panting.

"Aren't you going to … ask me something …?" she said.

"Fine. Here's a question: Why can't you stop prying?"

She smiled, pleased to have worn him down even though he was trying to be difficult. "Because knowledge is power. Obviously."

The cyborg passed right in front of her, his face angled away. He stopped.

Bel slowly pointed her weapon in his direction.

Zing.

She climbed out of the truck and slipped behind its cargo bed. "What does your family do to make all this money?"

"Pass."

"Okay. Where did you go to school?"

"Nice try. You're going to have to hit me again." He ducked to dodge her immediate attempt to shoot him, and rushed around the corner. Once he was safely out of sight, he said, "And that's going to be a 'pass' too."

She rolled her eyes and slipped out, sauntering to where she'd seen him go. She was sure he was still a ways down, but then he jumped out. His laser struck her. The number 4 appeared in the air and changed to 3.

A feminine humanoid NPC with green hair ran along the adjacent building, but the cyborg shot her before she could attack either of them.

Bel dodged laserbeams coming from one of the nearby buildings' windows and moved for cover behind a pile of bulldozed rubble. It was too late, though. The cyborg's next laser caught her upper arm, setting her aglow. Number 3 changed to

2. Panting, she said, "Question?"

The cyborg only replied, "Sure: Have you had enough yet?"

"Never." Bel ducked behind an angled concrete slab, then slipped her weapon through a crack, and fired.

The cyborg froze, glancing down at his flashing suit.

"Have you ever killed anyone?" Bel asked.

"Not on purpose."

"What does that mean?"

"Exactly what it sounds like." He crept closer.

Bel searched for a clear path to a new safe spot. She located another abandoned, rusted hovercraft that she could probably reach within a few seconds at a sprint. Just as she sprung for it, the cyborg appeared in her path. Her shoulders sank.

Zing.

Two changed to 1.

The cyborg slipped around the corner.

Bel followed, listening.

The creak of old metal echoed off the concrete. Carefully, Bel watched the movement of the shadows ahead. The cyborg was moving upward, on a fire escape. Or, at least, that's what it would *look* like he was doing. In reality, he would still be standing in the same spot within the dome, miming a climbing action.

She gazed up the length of the building, modeled after something that must have once been industrial and later converted to a stack of rundown apartments that now had smashed-in windows. A second-floor unit would be accessible from the top of a dumpster.

With another glance at the cyborg's ascending shadow, Bel pulled herself up to the dumpster's lid—impressed at how true-to-life it felt as she made the appropriate motions—and "climbed" in through the apartment window, avoiding the shards of glass that remained around the frame, forgetting that they weren't real and couldn't hurt her. From the inside, she located a freight lift, all rickety and musty and closed off from the shaft by a metal cage. The buttons were dirty, but she pushed one and the lift rose, vibrating.

The detail of this VR was seriously so incredible.

In a minute or so, she'd reached the top floor, where she took a short stairwell to the roof, then crept to the edge as the cyborg continued to climb, now just one level down. One corner of her mouth twitched up as she prepared her weapon. The second he appeared over the ledge, she shot him—but this time, she'd aimed for his weapon.

He gasped and dropped it. Bel had hoped it would "fall" to the ground level, shattering in the street below, but instead it landed on the roof, only a few feet out of reach.

She shot him again, flaring up his suit. "Why are you hiding at the Submundo?"

"Pass." He reached for his weapon, but she gritted her teeth and shot him again, jolting him backward and nearly sending him back over.

She wondered what it would feel like, how real the sensation of falling would be for him, even though, in reality, he'd only stumble and then collapse right where he'd been standing. But the mind could play tricks when sensations were this detailed.

"Who are you hiding from?" she said.

He panted as he regained his balance. "Pass."

"You've already used your passes."

"I never actually agreed to this game. *Either* of these games, in fact."

He stepped forward and she shot again. Another step. Another shot. Each time, she deterred him away from retrieving his weapon. His number changed so fast she didn't bother to look at it.

Zing. "Why are you hiding?" *Zing.* "What do you expect my brother to find?" *Zing.* "Who are you?"

He abandoned the weapon and charged at her instead. He got hold of her gun's barrel, instantly accepting another shot to his suit, light radiating from his chest out to his limbs. But he didn't stop.

They wrestled over the weapon. Bel was relentless, but even in a virtual reality the cyborg's true strength came through. He was taller than her, and his muscles—whether real or synthetic— were overpowering. Bel held on but eventually lost her footing. The cyborg was on his knees beside her, his grip threatening to tear the gun away. He twisted the weapon until Bel was staring down her own barrel's orange glow, so close she could hear the electrical charge rev up just before its laser jolted through her body.

One turned to 0.

GAME OVER

The darkness around them faded.

The buildings that had been towering over them, and the smoggy night sky, and the neon color casts, dissolved into pixels that dissolved into the reality of the gray panels of the VR dome, leaving Bel staring into the cyborg's face through nothing but her thin headset, while, together, they gripped an invisible gun.

Both panting, they each seemed to be waiting for the other to say something.

Had the cyborg set the game to end this way? To just shut

down when one of the players died?

Bel's pulse thrummed. Heat flowed to her face when she realized his mechanical hand was still clasped over her wrist, from when he'd forced her to turn the gun on herself. His metal was warm and smooth on her skin, on her bare flesh that had never actually been protected by the armor she'd worn in the game.

The cyborg's eyes were piercing, a tragic and menacing force behind them. His lips trembled.

Who was he? *What* was he? Bel tried to find the answers in his broken face, but all she saw was a monstrous glare.

The cyborg seemed to snap to attention. He looked to where his hand was, metal fingers curled, and drew back.

He released her and got to his feet. Then, hesitating, avoiding eye contact, he reached for her with his other hand—the one that, had Bel not known better, looked as human as her own—and slipped the first shamefully into the front pocket of his hooded sweatshirt.

She frowned, analyzing him, but slowly accepted his gesture of assistance.

The second she was standing, he let go.

How had she allowed herself to lose control like that?

What had begun in hostility had, at certain moments, seemed lighthearted—until, of course, it hadn't anymore. As with the effects of the game, it was difficult to tell the difference between what was real and what wasn't.

The cyborg turned to leave, pressing his wrist. As he passed between the sliding doors, he glanced over his shoulder and muttered, "Better luck next time."

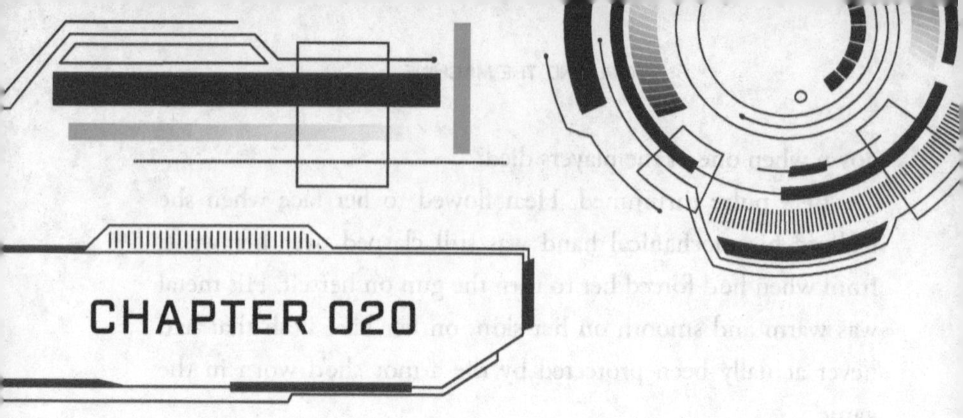

ONCE MATEO HAD GLEANED all he could remotely, he faced the unfortunate truth that he was going to have to leave the apartment.

He had crafted several counterfeit messages from legitimate associates to Vivorex, with embedded spyware links, and sent them to the appropriate inboxes (the help desk, the investors' department, and a general information recipient) based on contact addresses listed on the intersphere for the company. The messages would go to lower-level employees, for sure, but from there he might be able to obtain passwords to different networks within the company, or additional contacts, which would allow him to get spyware through to upper-level employees who might have more data-viewing privileges. However, despite his skills in crafting a visually trustworthy message, he'd gotten very few bites with the bait. He couldn't keep waiting for someone at Vivorex to fall into his remote traps. It had already been four days.

The next thing to do would be to go into the Vivorex building in person and pose as an interviewee. He would need to apply for an important enough position that he could be interviewed in one of the upper offices, where there would be devices connected to network drives with more valuable information. While there, he could plant a physical RAT on one of the current employees' holodevices, and then he'd have a whole new world of information open to him. Except that he'd need to purchase some dot drives first, and program the RATs onto them.

The closest electronics store was The Circuit, located three blocks away, just before the tech district began to merge with expensive clothing stores, high-end beauty salons, and cosmopolitan eateries.

Mateo practically hugged the base of a Silicon Valley Bank skyscraper as he walked along under a section of scaffolding, keeping himself out of the panopts' easy range. It was ridiculous to be so paranoid, now that he wore an updated InVisor with a new identity not in any way linked to his real one, but he still wanted to keep to the shadows at all costs.

He had to admit, though, that he'd missed the Bay Area in a big way. Growing up in Palo Alto, the lightning-fast Mag could take him into the heart of San Francisco in a matter of minutes, where he could peruse the best electronics stores, get the best coffee, and see the best views of the water. He only wished it hadn't been under these particular circumstances that he'd been allowed to return to his home state. Dorado beckoned him to all the old places he'd loved—but he didn't dare venture too far.

The Circuit wasn't terribly busy, which was a relief. The fewer the people, the better. Mateo took a moment to orient himself within the layout, to determine which aisles might have the supplies he needed. The back wall was, of course, covered in a selection of large, thin, television screens. Smart appliances took up the majority of the left half of the store, while a showroom was staged at the center, with a handful of customers testing devices and chatting with sales associates. The right half of the store contained electronic vehicle supplies, then general computing supplies, and finally, a Nerd Force station in the back corner with a couple of additional customers waiting for assistance with device problems.

Mateo scanned the aisles of the general computing section, looking through the products until he found an assortment of dot drives. They came in packages of four to twenty dots, and there were several sizes, none of which were as small or discreet as he wished they were—not like what he might have found if he'd gone all the way downtown—and multiple brands. FlashDot, Dottr, Eyeletech, Speck. As he compared a four-pack of Specks to a four-pack of FlashDots, he happened to glance over at the Nerd Force station, which was visible at the end of the aisle where he stood. The first customer that had been there had picked up her VR headset and left, and now a young Asian woman took her place at the counter and asked for "the Holopad M4" and gave her name: "Kat Seok."

Mateo let his gaze linger on her a moment.

She appeared to be in her early twenties, and wore her black hair in a long bob, with a dramatic and voluminous side part. She wore a black pleather jacket with elbow-length sleeves, and a bluish-green, floral top with yellow flowers on it. Her eyelids had a bold shadow on them, that same greenish-blue. Teal, Bel would have said, had she been there to correct his analysis. "Mustard" for the yellow.

Humming to herself, the girl tapped her dark red fingernails on the countertop while she waited.

The Nerd Force rep returned with the holopad and explained that he hadn't been able to figure out what the issue was, and that he'd need more time.

"You've had it for three days," said Kat. "I need it back *today*.

I thought you guys were supposed to know how to fix this stuff."

Mateo strained his ears to get more details, gathering what he could about the problem from the rep's explanation. The solution was a relatively simple one, for someone who knew what they were doing, which the rep clearly did not.

"I'm sorry," said the rep. "The only one here who might have a better idea would be Roger. He's been on vacation, although he's supposed to be back sometime this week."

"What day?" Kat said.

The rep shook his head. "I'm not sure. Let me go look at the schedule. Give me just a minute."

He left Kat alone at the desk, holopad open to an error screen. She sighed and stood there for a moment, and then her attention seemed to drift to a display of holopad cases on the next aisle. When she went to look at them, Mateo pretended to be focused on the packaging of the FlashDots until she passed.

Mateo wasn't sure what came over him, but he tucked the FlashDots under his arm and peered around the endcap to see that the girl had begun to busy herself looking at the whole array of holopad accessories. Meanwhile, her device waited. He went to it and tapped into the settings. It only took him a few seconds to get into the terminal, type some commands, and resolve all the errors. Easy as breathing. He rebooted the device and slipped away just as Kat came out with a purple holopad case in her hand.

From the other end of the aisle, he watched.

She gaped at the screen, then looked around as if for explanation. The screen's control center glowed with a selection of icons, now fully accessible and properly functioning. She tapped through them, testing them, and looked around again. Soon the Nerd Force rep reappeared and she asked him what had happened. Mateo felt a twinge of satisfaction when the rep scratched his head and said he had no idea who it could have been.

"I stepped away for a minute," said Kat. "Maybe less …"

Then, as if by instinct, Kat glanced down the aisle, and Mateo felt her attention catch on him for an instant.

Mateo turned and walked briskly to the checkout line. He tried to angle himself so that he was mostly obscured by a pair of teenage girls purchasing a gaming console, and withdrew the cyborg's digibank from his pocket to pay for the dot drives.

When Kat came up behind him, he tried not to flinch, and resisted the urge to glimpse her sideways with shifty eyes. He once again pretended to be reading the back of the FlashDot package, but he could feel her gaze on him.

"That was impressive," she said at his back.

Mateo turned slowly. "Are you talking to *me*?" He made a show of looking toward the girls ahead of him like they might be the true recipients of her compliment.

"Yep."

She was even prettier up close, with a rounded nose, and cheeks that had the faintest, glowy sheen. Her eyebrows were flawless—he didn't know much about women's eyebrows, but he did know hers were perfectly groomed, and he liked their shape.

Her lips quirked with amused suspicion. "I know it was you."

"*What* was me?" His heart rate kicked up a notch.

She raised her holopad. "The idiots who work here got nowhere with this in three days. Then you come in and fix it in three *seconds*? Honestly, I could use your skills at the salon where I work; our scheduling software's been all out of whack for weeks."

Mateo rubbed the back of his neck. "Look, it was nothing, okay? I've got some very … specific experience. I overheard your conversation and it just bothered me. You know when there's something you're good at, and you see someone else doing it horribly wrong, and it feels impossible to stand by and watch it go down like that?"

Kat nodded. "Yeah. For me, it's basically any Vidverse makeup tutorial. Although I can't exactly interfere with pre-recorded videos. But sometimes I leave critiques in the comments."

"Right. You get it. So … no big deal. Glad I could help." He turned his attention forward again.

"I'm Kat," she told him.

"Nice to meet you," he said over his shoulder.

The line moved up a few spaces.

"You don't have a name?"

"I've got a lot of names. None that I really want to share, though."

"Oh … You're going for, like, a mysterious vibe …"

He scoffed. "Sure."

A pause.

"How about I make up a name for you, then?" she asked. "Based on my first impressions of you."

He gave her his attention, but didn't say anything.

Kat smiled and put a finger to her chin and looked him up and down. "I'd go with something like … Miguel? No. Gael, Maybe? Gael … Mendivel. IT Manager, or Database Administrator … at … Blaise Investments. Or *maybe*—"

The line moved up again and it was Mateo's turn. "Sorry. I have to go now." He kept his head down while he checked out, refusing to look back at her.

Why couldn't he just tell her his real name? Three syllables.

Five letters. A ridiculously small and useless bit of information to someone like her. But … for what? He'd never see her again. On the other hand, maybe the fact that he wouldn't see her again was the whole point. She'd forget him almost as soon as he'd told her anyway.

He finished up and ducked out of the store.

From the sidewalk, he paused, watching Kat through the window. She smiled at the cashier, like the guy had just said something funny while he rang up her holopad case.

A small part of Mateo ached to go back inside, to give her any bit of information that was true, just so that he could feel like a real person for a minute.

But that wasn't possible. For his own protection, and for Bel's, he had to keep it to himself. Just like he always did.

Right now, he had a job to do. And he was just getting started.

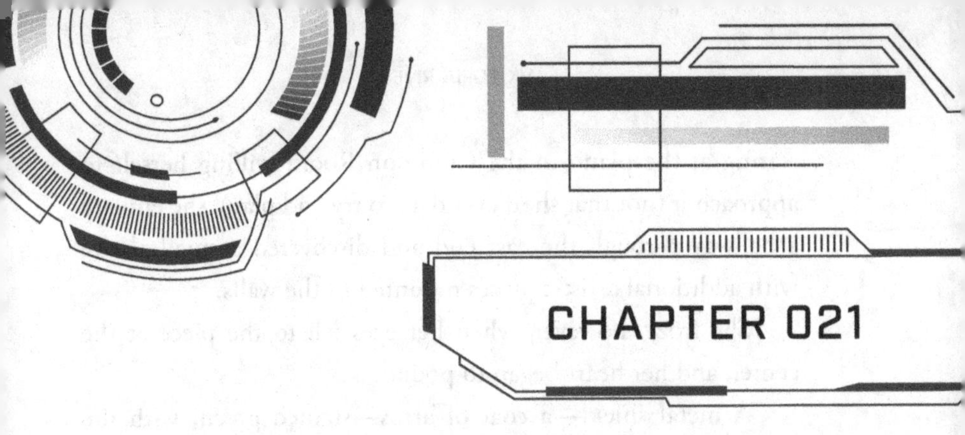

CHAPTER 021

JUST AS SHE HAD SUSPECTED, Bel woke to discover that her arms and legs were sore, her muscles flaring in the aftermath of her physical activity from the day before. She spent nearly an hour in the luxury tub of the adjoining bathroom, physically soaking and emotionally seething.

She couldn't stop thinking about that game, and her body wouldn't let her forget even if she'd been able to take her mind off of it. The cyborg was determined to be an unhackable device—and she hated it. On any given day, there was essentially nothing she couldn't crack into, given a keyboard and a terminal, and no one she couldn't parse digitally for information. It absolutely killed her that she couldn't do the same with him, especially because he was more machine than man at this point.

The irony.

She took her time drying off and dressing, and then after a brunch of duck eggs Benedict (with truffle hollandaise and sliced pancetta and pseudo-fresh dill on sourdough English muffins), Bel wandered the corridors again.

After admiring some of the artwork up close for a while, then asking Flora for a deep-dive on the gardening process (which was honestly fascinating, considering the plants were set up to thrive without a single human touch), and several minutes staring at the piano in the Common Room willing herself to approach it (not that she'd ever dare to try and play), she entered a hallway through the east end and discovered a small alcove with additional artistic pieces mounted to the walls.

She froze, however, when her eyes fell to the piece at the center, and her heart began to pound.

A metal shield—a coat of arms—stained green, with the shape of a knight's helmet at the top and metal feathers and leaves sprouting from it and curling down the sides, and then, on the shield itself, the embossment of a fully armored knight.

Flashes of Knight Crew mugshots sped through her mind.

A lot of crime families were incredibly wealthy, raking in the profits of trafficked goods and illegal operations, extorting money wherever it made sense for them. And all of them had enemies who might force them into hiding. They'd be likely to have extravagant safe houses. They would definitely buy in to elitist ideals and display their heritage on the wall like a trophy.

Don't jump to conclusions, she thought. Most coats of arms had a knight or some kind of knight's helmet on them, didn't they? Knights were a symbol of nobility, a social rank from the Middle Ages or something. This was common. Wasn't it?

Except she was fairly certain that others she'd seen had usually had some sort of animal or symbol on them too. She'd seen one for her own surname once—when her *abuelo* was still alive and had been talking about the family's lineage—with a big red sun on the shield. "*El sol, porque somos Solís*," he had said. Likewise, a shield for a name like Lopez would probably have wolves (from *lobo* meaning "wolf"), or De Leon would have a lion, or Flores might have a smattering of *fleur-de-lis*.

"Lucius," Bel invoked. When the holomorph appeared, she said, "What's this coat of arms for?"

"For decoration, Ms. Solís."

"No, I mean what family does it belong to?"

"Ah. Unfortunately, I am forbidden to discuss any personal details of the Submundo with you."

"Can you discuss coats of arms, in general?"

"Certainly. A coat of arms typically consists of a crest, supporters, and shield. The crest, which heads that heraldic symbol, may consist of a helm or helmet, a wreath, or additional decorative elements. Supporters may include mantling, animal figures, and flourishes. The shield itself bears marks, patterns, symbols, or figures relating to the family name it represents."

"Which family names mean 'knight' … as in 'knights of the round table'?"

"Knight, Knightley, Caballero, Cavaleiro, Chevalier, and Ritter are a few examples."

She took a deep breath.

Maybe she was being paranoid. But she had to consider it. Plenty of the pieces fit.

Then again, a lot of the other displays and artwork within the Submundo implied a Latin American heritage—even the word *submundo*—so it was reasonable to think that the coat of arms might refer to a surname like Caballero. Unless, of course, the art came from the maternal side of the family and had nothing to do with the surname at all.

Bel closed her eyes and shook her head. Who was she really dealing with here?

"Have you ever killed anyone?"

"Not on purpose."

Suddenly she found herself wondering whether she might be the cyborg's next "accident."

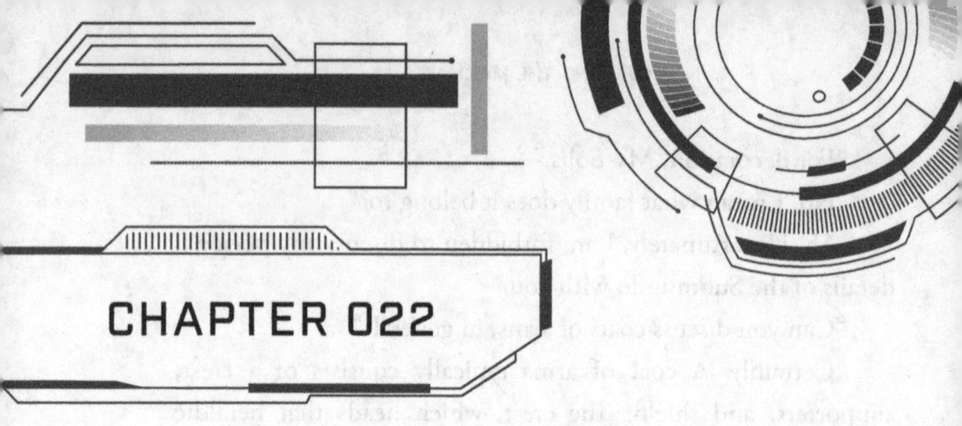

CHAPTER 022

THE NEXT DAY, BEL KEPT AN EYE OUT for the cyborg. He had his ways of avoiding her, sure, but if she could catch sight of him, she could follow him and see what he was up to.

She knew he was probably watching the shared spaces and the connecting corridors through the security feed, or maybe he'd told Lucius to let him know when she was out and about, so she kept the door to her room cracked, peering out periodically and listening for sounds of movement. Not so different from Neon Sniper, only in this case he wasn't targeting her—he was avoiding her entirely. Still, she had to keep hidden, in a way, and plan a stealth operation.

Finally, in the afternoon, she spotted the cyborg descending the stairs. Waiting until he gave away the general direction he was going, she slipped out of her room and followed at a distance, until she realized he was headed for the VR dome.

The memory of the knight shield stuck in her mind like an afterimage, a neon flash behind her eyelids that wouldn't fade.

Bel thought of all the advanced features of the VR dome, of the indoor garden, of the automated kitchen and realistic AI servants, the bedrooms and bathrooms that put top-tier hotels to shame. It was feasible that one of the families might build something like this, large enough to hide and protect a core family and support their indulgent lifestyles for the foreseeable future—a place where one of their own might go when he wanted to avoid capture.

"Son of one of the Knight Crew leaders," Mateo had said. *"Nineteen years old, killed six people over a shipment of raw vidrinium."* Was Bel looking at Silas Fine right now? Or maybe what was *left* of Silas Fine?

Assuming his appearance accurately reflected his age, he fit the bill.

But if that was the case, that meant that Bel was sleeping down the hall from a real criminal. A murderer. Someone who probably deserved whatever had happened to make him look like that. A victim to his enemies, maimed and burned—before or after whatever had been done to his skeleton and organs, Bel had no idea.

All Bel knew now was that she had to find out what the cyborg was up to, and she had to figure out a way to get in touch with Mateo to warn him.

Once the cyborg was inside the dome, Bel gave him a minute or so to get set up so that he'd be distracted when she approached. Not that there would be much to see, considering he was probably only there to play Neon Sniper again, or maybe another game that would give her no clues to his background. But she figured it wouldn't hurt to watch him, to make further analyses of his general behavior.

The windows were blackened again—no surprise there. Bel stepped up to the control panel, and the square screen lit up, revealing the menu of icons.

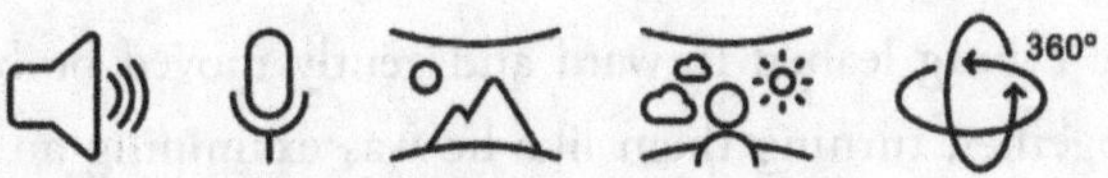

She quickly tapped the speaker so she could hear, and then the 3D viewer so she could control the angle—except that she'd forgotten to tap the scenery button first, so all she saw was a side angle of the cyborg standing at the center of the otherwise empty dome, wearing a headset.

Just as she went to tap the scenery button, Lucius appeared.

"Hello, Ms. Solís. I have been instructed to inform you that you are not to interact with the VR dome while it is occupied."

Inside, the cyborg tapped a few things in mid-air that Bel couldn't see, already immersed in another world, although he only appeared to be standing in the midst of a hemispherical, gray space dotted with sensors.

"But I did it the other day," she said.

"Yes, and my settings have been updated to interfere, should I sense that anyone is attempting to gain access. If you go any further, I'm afraid I must notify the current occupant."

"'Current occupant,'" Bel repeated bitterly. She was grateful she'd gotten as far as she had, with audio and the ability to see the cyborg's gestures, but it killed her that she couldn't see what he was *seeing*.

She expected him to run, or crouch, or aim an imaginary weapon now, but instead, he turned and extended his right hand, curling it slightly, and said, "Mucho gusto. Toma asiento."

Nice to meet you. Have a seat.

His Spanish had a distinctive accent, Bel thought, a softening and slight aspiration in the instances of the *s* sound. Bel narrowed her eyes and moved closer to the window.

"Echemos un vistazo," he said.

Let's take a look.

The cyborg leaned forward and gently moved both hands close together, turning them like he was examining an object.

"Obviamente lo que puedo hacer desde aquí es limitado. Pero al menos siempre podemos resolver algunas cosas, incluso a distancia."

Obviously what I can do from here is limited. But at least we can always work out some things, even from a distance.

The way he spoke was like a river, flowing and burbling rapidly, skimming over certain sounds and bypassing others entirely, almost musical. But his tone soon turned darker, to warning, as he said, "Sin embargo, tendrá que tener más cuidado. Su línea de trabajo es peligrosa."

You'll need to be more careful, though. Your line of work is dangerous.

Dangerous. What line of work?

Drug dealing, maybe. Weapons trafficking. Counterfeit goods?

Bel's shoulders tensed.

Then came a pause, like the cyborg was listening. Further examination of object.

"Pues, esto parece aceptable por ahora. Sigue haciendo lo que ha estado haciendo."

This looks acceptable for now. Keep doing what you've been doing.

While Bel saw an empty room, she tried to imagine a setting around the cyborg. Whoever he was talking to might not be contacting him with a full VR background, but they were showing him something, likely projecting the full 3D rendering of their entire body and whatever they had wanted him to assess. If she could just see who it was, what this person looked like, or—better yet—what was under scrutiny here, she might be able to—

Lucius had continued to stand by, throughout Bel's

observations, and hadn't said a word—because, of course, she had made no further attempts to gain access, even visually, to the dome—but he waited, watching her.

Bel glanced at him, then back at the panel of icons. Maybe she could tap one of them before he had the chance to send an alert. The cyborg would need several seconds to stop what he was doing and come to the door; in that amount of time, Bel could get a solid glimpse of his associate *and* the object of their discussion. Who knew what the cyborg would do when he caught her, but it would be too late; she would already have information that couldn't be taken from her.

She bit her lip. Took a deep breath. Let her fingers twitch at her side for half a second.

Then she reached up and tapped the scenery button.

It grayed out just before her finger made contact. The panel beeped a negative tone.

An alarm went off from somewhere overhead.

The cyborg turned toward the entrance. Bel stepped back, pulse racing.

She made to run as the cyborg went out of frame, but the dome's doors slid apart and the cyborg came through, removing his headset.

"Don't you know when to quit?" he said.

Bel stammered. "I … I just came to …" She kept going over what she'd heard, trying to make sense of it.

"I'm *working*," he growled.

Working. Sure, Bel thought, clenching her fists to keep herself from trembling any more than she already was. That's how someone like him would probably see it. The "family business."

"What are you trying to hide?" she demanded. "Blackened windows, increased security. If you're not doing anything shady, what's with all the secrecy?"

He stepped forward abruptly, causing her to shrink back. "That's none of your concern. You don't belong here. You're a means to an end, and you don't get a say in what goes on in this place. Do you understand?"

Her eyes stung, and she had to clench her teeth to control them. "Let me talk to Mateo."

"I have no reason to trust you."

"And I have no reason to trust *you*. How do I know you're not endangering my brother's life by sending him off to do your dirty work?"

"It *is* dangerous. I never said it wasn't." His jaw hardened with his glare. "Anyway, we're done here."

"*I'm* not done."

"You came here of your own free will. The fact that you and your brother found a place that was supposed to be off the grid completely compromises the entire purpose of its existence—so the least you could do is cooperate while I get the information I need." He put his headset back on. "You're welcome for saving your lives, by the way."

Bel narrowed her eyes. "Don't tell me you've never been so desperate you did something stupid or illegal," she shot back. "You don't end up full of metal and wires with half your face burned off for no reason. Not someone with this kind of money. Who exactly did you piss off to deserve that?"

"If I knew, I wouldn't be here."

"So, that's it, then? No mercy? No exceptions? I'm just supposed to sit around indefinitely, hoping my brother doesn't die by the same hand that put you here? You could at least let me hear his voice, supervise a call …"

"Not worth the risk." He turned away and went back toward

the dome. The doors parted, letting him through.

"Wait!" Bel shouted. But the doors slid shut, cutting her off from him. She slammed her palms against them, once.

She went to the window and stood there for a long minute, watching the cyborg like she could melt him with her glare. Once he was situated again, the windows blackened, and she was left in the corridor with Lucius, who waited calmly with clasped hands. Bel made a disgusted, throaty noise at him, then headed back to her room.

Bel threw herself onto the bed.

There had to be something she could use. This house was full of tech, and anything technological could be hacked. It was just a matter of getting creative about finding an access point.

She stared up at the projector lenses on the ceiling. The holographic videos streamed from a server that existed somewhere in this house, she was sure of it, because there was no media from earlier than a few years ago. Anything connected to the internet would be more up to date, and a place like this probably had limited connections to the outside world anyway.

Bel asked for the menu, which projected downward and provided a group of icons. She tapped on them in the air with her fingers, navigating to the settings. Here she could alter the holoscreen's contrast, tweak the sound equalizer, and change media language and subtitle appearance, among other useless things. It took her a few minutes to figure out how to get to the network settings, where she found that the device was connected to Submundo Network 1. Not exactly helpful. Until she tapped on the network name itself and a schematic diagram flew up.

"*Yes!*" she whispered.

The diagram showed a collection of blocks that represented each room in the house—blank inside except for a dot that indicated network-connected devices and their labels. Her room had several dots: Closet, Bathroom, Media Console, Sliding Door, Plant Pot 1, Plant Pot 2, and Plant Pot 3. All the things that required network access to operate intelligently. The Media Console dot was highlighted, indicating that that's what she was currently using to view this diagram.

Zooming in on the diagram; she scanned the different rooms. Most of them had Sliding Door, all the bedrooms also had Bathroom, Closet, plant pots, and Media Console like hers. The kitchen had one called Delessio, another called Menu, and a few dozen others for the various smart appliances. Only the cyborg's office had devices like Holopad M4 or Holopad Mini K or Holodesk.

Nothing in these settings allowed her remote access to the devices, and none seemed to be located anywhere she was allowed to go. Finally, she closed her eyes and lay back on one of the obnoxiously plush pillows, her thoughts drifting from one impossible hope to the next, until she lost her grasp on every one of them and fell asleep.

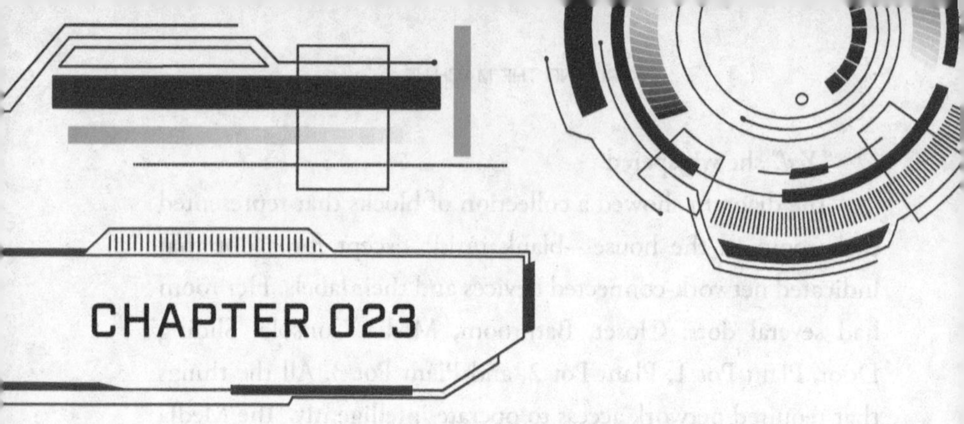

CHAPTER 023

"THANK YOU SO MUCH FOR THE OPPORTUNITY." Mateo shook hands with a man by the name of Tyler Helvig, head of Vivorex bioinformatics, who happened to be looking for an intern.

Mateo hadn't been able to find any openings in IT, which obviously would have been more suited to him, and much easier to pretend to interview for. Instead, he'd had to fabricate a résumé for himself that was relevant to bioinformatics—software and databases that support biological research and analysis—and spend several hours studying the subject on the intersphere and watching Vidverse to even begin to pretend to know what he was talking about. He'd even found a remote service that implemented AI to perform mock interviews for any profession, which had been a lifesaver.

At least he could speak to the technological part mostly on his own. And thankfully the past two years pretending to be someone else had given him a decent set of acting skills, although not as developed as his sister's, considering he tended to avoid social situations whenever possible.

"Pleasure to meet you," said Helvig. "Have a seat."

It was that very seat on which Mateo discreetly installed the dot drive RAT, slipping the adhesive dot onto the underside of the chair's steel frame and fixing it there. As long as it remained within five feet of Helvig's desk, it could work its magic.

Now for the hard part.

Over the course of the next twenty minutes, Mateo fumbled his way through a series of questioning. He was fluid with his answers in relation to programming language proficiency, algorithmic sequencing, and handling corrupt or missing data, and he'd done enough research to talk about FASTA and FASTQ file formats, but had a bit more difficulty when it came to his ability to describe gene expression and the role of alignment in comparative genomics. He completely drew a blank at a question about SNPs, but managed to steer the conversation back toward sequencing, and then everything else was all "why do you want to work for our company" and "how does this internship fit into your career path" type questions. Which were technically easier but required a lot more fiction, as opposed to fact memorization.

When it was over and Helvig saw him back out to the reception area, he thought he might pass out. He held himself together long enough to make a show of thanking the receptionist for her time as well, and slipped a second RAT onto the inner rim of a potted plant that sat on the woman's desk. He speed-walked to the elevator, pushed the button for the main level, put his back against the interior wall, and slid to a seated position on the floor, releasing a breath he felt like he'd been holding the entire time.

The RATs turned out to be a great success. With the ability to see and control key devices within the bioinformatics department, it had only taken Mateo an hour to gain access to the internal messaging system used by all members of the board of directors. Certain security measures might have been tricky for another hacker to attack, except that Mateo himself had helped install some of those security measures during his time at Kleid Co., so bypassing them was barely an issue.

Unfortunately, he hadn't found anything about Project Iterum yet, which was strange. More than a hundred other projects were listed in the database, and while some required additional permissions to view certain details, it didn't make sense that any should be completely hidden.

If Project Iterum *was* hidden, though, someone on the board would have to have access. Of this, Mateo was certain. But hours of combing through the messages between them gave him little insight into any classified projects. It wasn't until he was looking through the message log from more than a year ago that he came across a permissions grant from Soto Acero (Vivorex president and CEO) to Veronika Mandersloot, to allow network access.

"Network access?" Mateo said aloud.

Why wouldn't she have already had network access?

She had been the vice president at the time, after all.

Or—had she?

Mateo couldn't remember for sure when she'd been fired.

The grant was timestamped 2086-01-24 11:32:15 UTC.

January 24, 2086.

Mateo typed "Veronika Manderlsoot" into a search engine, which returned dozens of news articles. He skimmed through the titles and his attention fell on one in particular.

Vivorex VP fired for malfeasance, denies allegations
December 5, 2085

He stared at the screen, frozen. *December.*

Why would Soto Acero give network access to someone he'd specifically *fired*?

To: Mr. Steele

Not sure if it's relevant to your case, but you might want to take a look at these screenshots. Not only was Veronika Mandersloot given Vivorex network access after she was fired, she (or someone using her old company ID) has been accessing Vivorex software and documents—as recently as a few hours ago.

CHAPTER 024

IT WAS WELL AFTER MIDNIGHT, but Bel's mind wouldn't power down, and having fallen asleep for a couple of hours earlier in the afternoon, she wasn't physically tired enough to overcome the mental noise. Sometime in the midst of her restlessness, a sound came through the walls—distantly, and muted.

Music?

The sound was soft enough that she likely wouldn't have woken from it, had she been as fast asleep as she wished she was, but already being wide awake, it caught her attention.

Bel got up and peeked out of her room, instantly raising the volume of the minor-key melody. Piano notes rang out from below, in slow succession, one key at a time, building intensity, and then a chord. Higher notes deepened by the addition of lower ones.

She went out to the top of the stairs and looked down. The UV lights in the Terrarium were off, and the moon was on display, high up and centered.

Appropriate, she thought, because she recognized the piece of music as Beethoven's "Moonlight Sonata."

Drawn forward by the melancholy piece, Bel crept down the stairs. She followed the sound all the way to the Common Room, where the cyborg sat with his back to her, in front of the keys.

If she hadn't known better, she would have thought it was a recorded piece that played over the Common Room's sound system, it was so perfect and clean—with the exception of a soft tap each time his metal fingers struck the ivory. But he didn't even have sheet music out for it; he was playing it from memory.

Bel's breath quickened at the sight: a young man who was mostly—if not entirely—machine, hardened both literally and figuratively, a product of science and technology, creating such exquisitely disturbing sounds.

It's fitting, though, she thought. A disturbed man playing a disturbed melody, all dark and brooding and sinister while possessing an enchanting talent. Like some male siren, drawing in his victims with music.

But no matter what the music made her feel, she had to remember what he might be capable of. He was someone who could be involved in the same sort of "work" that had led to the death of her parents. He may have been young, but she highly doubted he was innocent. The children of syndicate leaders were groomed from the day they were born, prepared to follow in their parents' footsteps and ensure that the empire survived.

As he reached a section of the piece that was a bit more dynamic, Bel instinctively stepped forward, but stopped when she caught her own moving reflection in the dark sheen of the empty music rack.

The music stopped too.

Bel stood still.

The cyborg looked up from the keys but didn't turn around.

Of course if Bel could see herself, then he could see her just as easily. *More* easily, even, as he sat so close to the mirrored surface.

He played a single minor chord. "You're up late."

"You too," she replied.

He pressed one of the pedals to keep the volume low and started a new piece, but he performed most of the volume control with his fingers, with the gentle way he touched the keys, the kind of touch Bel had never been able to master during her childhood lessons.

"You play …" His voice was flat as always, even with his questions. Or *was* it a question?

Bel shook her head. "No. Not really. Not anymore."

The cyborg played another minute or so, and Bel thought maybe she should walk away now, but for some reason she didn't. She just stood there, waiting—for what she didn't know. He ended the piece on a pair of chords that stroked a dark emotion inside of her, then let them dissipate.

He kept his eyes on the music stand, on his own reflection and hers behind it. "It's not something you really forget."

Bel took another few steps forward and gazed through the Terrarium window. "Maybe I *want* to forget."

The cyborg turned toward her now. "Show me."

"Show you what?"

"How you play."

"I told you I don't play anymore."

He pressed his thumb to his wrist, as he'd mysteriously done so many times before, then moved over on the bench.

"It was a year of lessons," Bel said, "and I hated every one of them."

Despite her protests, he only nodded toward the open instrument, which shone like a smooth, dark sea.

He continued to wait.

When the tension of the moment grew tiresome, Bel thought to walk away, but she didn't quite want to do that either. It was true, she'd wanted to touch the keys, to see what she might make of them, out of idle curiosity or some strange form of longing for her mother she wasn't sure. But how did *he* know that?

Finally, Bel conceded and, warily, took up the place beside him. She placed her hands in position, hovering over the keys and readjusting the curvature of her fingers. *Just like a set of holokeys*, she told herself. If she could pretend it was a computer, the muscle memory would kick in. She could think of the notes as data, a code to create sound, and separate her emotions from the music.

"I only remember one piece well," she told him. "It's a beginner version of 'The Blue Danube Waltz.'"

Bel looked to the cyborg for reassurance, although she wasn't sure why. He didn't give it to her. Mentally, she could hear the rhythm, recalling the three-four time signature of the sheet music. At age twelve, she'd practiced the piece over and over; it was the only piece she'd ever really liked. But the idea of playing from her fractured memory, of playing something so trite on an instrument like this … the very thought was like a diamond necklace on a kangaroo.

She began slowly, pausing after the first three beats before she summoned the courage to slip into the first chord—although it was only two keys—and again between the first chord and the second. It took a few more before she was able to build up to the waltzy bounce. Her tempo was all over the place as she paused to remember the fingering for the left hand, speeding up when her fingers seemed to remember certain parts on their own, then slowing down again each time she remembered that the cyborg—who had played so professionally a few minutes ago—was watching. She got further through the music than she expected before hitting a wrong note. But she played through the mistakes, and as she went on, she began to feel the beauty of playing again, a feeling that had always been fleeting and which she'd long ago forgotten. The notes were the cleanest sounds she'd ever heard. Even the most expensive speakers were no match for this fine-tuned instrument, keys like silky butter under her fingertips.

Bel faltered a few more times, mostly on the left hand, expecting the cyborg to react, to show some sign of ridicule, but he didn't, and each time, she fought the warmth rising in her, the blood that rushed to her face, like she was at a recital and toiling along in front of a crowd.

She played only the right-hand notes for a moment, trying to remember how the left hand went for the next part. And then, without missing a beat, the cyborg began to fill in.

His chords were strong and sure, rounding out Bel's sound. Then he added flourishes, embellishing the basic structure of the piece, enhancing it.

Bel caught herself about to smile—in disbelief, but still— and immediately pressed her lips together to regain control.

Meanwhile, the cyborg was serious. Concentrating. Although Bel didn't think he'd *need* to concentrate. This skill seemed to come easily to him, a second nature.

She watched him, entranced, so much that she didn't realize *she* wasn't even playing anymore. He'd taken over without affecting the music at all, a seamless transition from one player to the next.

Bel leaned back a little, allowing him better access to the rest of the keys. His flourishes grew more and more beautiful, and then he slowed the entire piece to a melancholy tempo, playing the high keys in such a way that Bel thought if twinkling stars were to make a sound, this would be it.

She couldn't help staring at his divided face, his mismatched eyes. The edge of his skin—the frontier where it touched his metal skeleton—was more gruesome now that she could see it up close, all burned back and almost nodulous in texture. But although the combination of elements was unsightly, Bel had to admit he was actually quite beautiful from a material perspective.

Dark metal made up the majority of his exposed bones. The joints were copper toned. The vidrinium wires, woven through him in bundles, shimmered silvery blue. Everything picked up the light in a different way. From the intricacy—and accuracy— of his infrastructure, Bel maintained that his metal was probably ossteel—a newer development used in advanced prosthetics that paired the strength of steel with a density comparable to human bones and a surface quality that bonded easily to real or synthetic ligaments. She'd seen part of a documentary on it once.

As far as the cyborg's more humanly features, his smooth, brown skin was flawless, from his high cheekbones to his squarish jaw. One of his eyes was framed by a set of long lashes, while the other had been burned down to the edges of a synthetic lid that must have been the base below the realistic skin that had once covered it. Behind them both, there was a depth Bel hadn't noticed before. This young man was wrecked and alone, trapped—afraid, even.

But he could be a murderer, too, Bel reminded herself. *Or associated with murderers, at least.* It was more likely than not. Associated with the same kind of people she was certain had been the cause of death for her mother for asking too many questions, whose crossfire had stopped her father's heart, who had altered her brother's history and forced him into hiding.

It was possible, though, that she'd been reading everything wrong. He could be as much of a victim to higher powers as she was. But that might be wishful thinking. Not that she was thinking *wishfully*—other than in the sense that she wished she had a better sense of what was happening, of whom she was with, and where she'd end up after all this was over. And there was a lot she still couldn't explain.

The cyborg finished his version of "The Blue Danube," ending on a sad but satisfying chord that echoed a while.

For the first time tonight, he looked at Bel directly. Her pulse quickened and she didn't know whether she was scared or only startled. His cold stare endured, and soon Bel couldn't take it anymore; she looked away, down at the keys, touching them but not pressing them.

"That was … beautiful," Bel said.

He gave her a solemn nod as she slipped her fingers off the keys and rested her hands in her lap.

"You're not bad. Shame you want to forget."

"It reminds me of my mom. That's all."

No response. He just continued to look at her.

"Not that you'd understand." Bel swallowed hard. "She died a little over two years ago."

His gaze faltered now, and he took a heavy breath. "Actually … that, I *would* understand."

Bel tried to read him, searching him for clues. *Even criminals have mothers. It doesn't change who they are, what they've done.* Maybe he'd lost his own mother because of his family business; people like that must be targeting each other's loved ones all the time, as a show of power, or to send a message. Members of crime families were always getting kidnapped for leverage or murdered out of revenge. Or, at the very least, caught up in gunfights.

"I take it you couldn't sleep," the cyborg said. He picked at a few notes that harkened back to "The Blue Danube," keeping the volume low.

"Hard to sleep in a place like this … under these circumstances."

The cyborg didn't acknowledge her point. Of course he wouldn't. She'd agreed to his terms. She'd *chosen* to hack into a strange place that belonged to someone else. He wasn't entirely wrong. But he wasn't entirely right, either.

"You probably don't really stick to a schedule," Bel said. "Right? I mean, you can literally make your own daylight. Whatever's going on in the real world doesn't dictate your waking hours."

"I don't sleep much, if that's what you mean," he said.

"Don't? Or can't?"

"My body doesn't 'power down' all the way. Literally or figuratively." He stopped playing again and looked forward, at nothing.

Bel glimpsed him sideways, trying to be subtle about her growing curiosity. "That … sounds awful."

"It is what it is. Pointless to feel one way or another about it."

"I don't think it's pointless," said Bel. "Feelings one way or another. Good or bad. I think it's fine to acknowledge pain— even if you can't change things."

"And why's that?" he said flatly.

"Because … it makes you human."

He nodded distantly, was silent a few seconds, then stood and removed himself from the bench.

Bel stood too, when she realized the implications of what she'd said. "I didn't mean it like that."

"I know." He pushed the bench forward. "Good night."

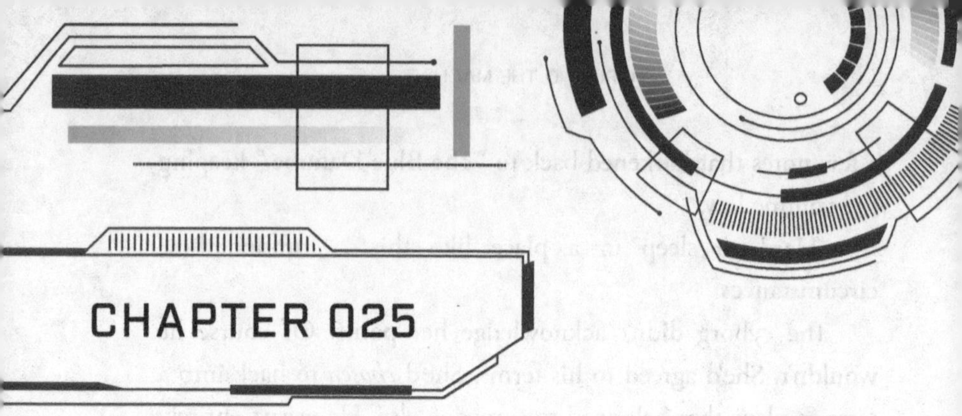

CHAPTER 025

MOONLIGHT POURED ACROSS THE CONCRETE FLOOR as the warehouse rolling door slid up on its rails. Damian Knight stepped inside and looked around, scanning the dimly lit rows of the rack system. Even though everything was packaged up, he could smell the vidrinium, traces of the chemical odor.

A dark-skinned man stepped forward, straightening his lapels. "As I live and breathe. Damian Knight, in the flesh."

"Soto Acero." Damian raised a thick, white-blond eyebrow, and looked the man up and down. "Nice … *suit*."

"Thank you. I spared no expense."

They regarded each other a moment, as Damian fought to keep signs of bewilderment off of his face.

"In any case," Soto finally said, "Welcome back. I trust your time down south gave you the opportunity to regroup a bit. How long has it been now? Just about three years, I'd say?"

"Just about."

"Well, your contributions to my projects have been invaluable. You've kept these warehouses well stocked for me, despite the limitations of your physical absence."

Damian began to walk down one of the aisles, gazing up at the height of the shelf. "This amount of product is highly volatile," he said. "You keep it all together like this?"

"No, no," said Soto. "Of course not. We have it spread out over several locations throughout the city. Only a small percentage of what you see here is vidrinium. Much of it is construction materials—you'll see here that we have spools of vidrinium *wire*"—he led Damian over to the next aisle and gestured around—"along with raw ossteel that we send off to the factory for processing once we have the necessary source-material scans"—he tapped a large box on top of a pallet on the floor—"and of course hundreds of polyvinyl bags of liquid Tactiperone, which has been essential in creating realistic sensations. And, well, the rest is basic medical supplies that we use to conduct our work. Gloves and gauze, scalpels and clamps, sedatives and anticonvulsants. We also store a variety of phakes—in case we need to cover our tracks."

"Phakes?"

"Falsifiers," Soto clarified. "That's the name on the street now; but even the professionals have picked it up as a shorthand. It's certainly easier to say than 'mendacium.'"

"I'm surprised it's known on the 'streets' now. Last I heard, only a select few knew anything about it."

"Well, once word got around, it was hard to keep it quiet."

"I thought the whole point was to make sure those drugs were a well-kept secret. You wouldn't want authorities to start questioning CorpuScan autopsies and start looking for actual killers."

"I agree, but falsifiers have also been the key to helping me make some *very* valuable friends. Not many people can ignore this kind of potential."

"Well, that's your business, I guess. I got what I needed from your 'phakes'—before VOLT interfered, at least." He straightened the cuff of his sleeve.

"That was unfortunate," said Soto.

"Anyway. What am I doing here?"

"I thought this might be a good place to start rebuilding some of your networks. A new hub. Obviously you can't go back to any of your old locations. You've been a valuable business partner; it's the least I could do. There's an office upstairs with plenty of tech for you to start making contacts again. Soon, I'll even be able to provide you with a few units of my own creation—you know, to help you … extend the life of your crew, so to speak."

"And what, exactly, do you expect in return?"

"The technology I've developed is at a critical stage," Soto explained. "It's proven itself to be everything I'd hoped and beyond. But I've been testing it only on a small scale. Now it's time to expand our horizons."

"Meaning … what?"

"*Who*," Soto clarified. "I think we could use this to infiltrate government offices. Legislation. Regulations that have been holding us back for decades. I'll need your help obtaining what we like to call a 'source unit'—securing a particular body so that we can make the appropriate scans."

"Alright, then. *Who*?"

Soto grinned. "I'd like to start with Kella Quintero, senator of Dorado."

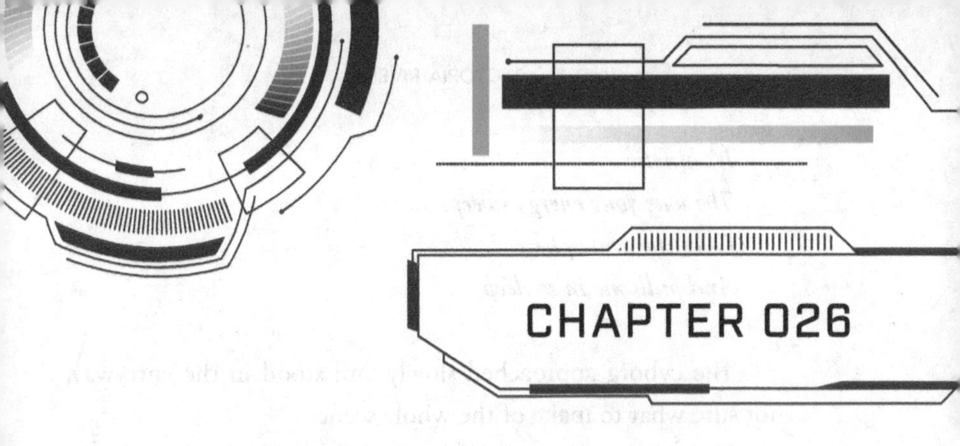

CHAPTER 026

IT WAS UNSETTLING TO HAVE SOMEONE ELSE in the Submundo with him. Even though being completely alone had been a foreign and miserable thing when the cyborg had first arrived, he'd gotten used to it, learned to take comfort in the silence—because silence meant he was safe. Until recently, the only voices he'd heard were the ones he'd asked for—calling on Lucius or turning on the TV. Now, though, he heard footsteps on the stairs or Delessio randomly barking orders at the robotic culinary machines. And he might run into the girl at any turn. Despite the Submundo being so big with so many places to go, Mirabel Solís seemed to be everywhere.

Even as he stepped into the lounge, he found her there, sitting in one of the armchairs with her nose in a book. Her actual nose deep in the folds of the pages. A small stack of books were piled on a side table beside the chair, an element of decoration meant to give the space an antique and cozy feel. Mirabel inhaled.

Meanwhile, a song played over the stereo, some kind of electropunk ballad with an ethereal quality to it. The stereo's holographic letters spelled out "PLASMA" BY WAIVELENGTH. Masculine voices harmonized with vocal enhancements:

It's kinetic
The way your energy sweeps
Over the atmosphere
And pulls me in so deep

The cyborg approached slowly and stood in the entryway, not sure what to make of the whole scene.

He had never imagined that Mirabel would have the audacity to be so comfortable in all the rooms of his house. Although he had given her relatively free range—as a courtesy—he didn't think she would have taken it so seriously. Having gone to the dome, twice now, in the middle of his activities, was an obvious encroachment.

He thought about those last moments on top of that building in Neon Sniper, how she'd struck him in the chest, over and over, lighting him up with her fury. She'd caught him off guard almost as much as the way he found himself staring at her right now.

Why had he followed the sound of her music? Not the same reason she'd followed the sound of his. No—he'd seen her on the security cameras, stopping every time she'd passed the piano. Until two days ago, he hadn't had any idea why, only that she seemed fascinated by it. *It reminds me of my mom.* Of course her mother had died; it hadn't occurred to him before, but it should have. Teenage girls didn't end up this far out in the wilderness if they had parents to take care of them. Something must have happened to her father, too. He wondered what. And then he wondered why he should bother to wonder. It wasn't like he'd *wanted* the girl here—especially not with her sarcastic bite and her tendency to pry—much less to know more about her past.

Today, she was wearing her own clothes. Her ripped jeans and gray tank top with that green cargo vest. She must have finally figured out where to retrieve the finished laundry.

For someone who had apparently been hiding—according to the report that had mentioned multiple locations and aliases—she didn't seem like someone who was trying to blend in. Her clothing style and her black nail polish and the ring on one side of her nose were just the beginning; she struck him as someone who didn't like to fade into the background. Which was terribly inconvenient for him right now.

Hopefully he'd only have to deal with her presence for a little while longer.

He was just about to back out of the entrance when Mirabel seemed to sense him, flinching as she turned up her gaze. She shot him a questioning look.

The cyborg cleared his throat and nodded at the novel she held. "It's called a 'book.'"

She narrowed her eyes and slammed the cover shut. "I know what it is."

"Are you sure? You seem … intrigued by its properties."

She set the book back on top of the others. "My dad used to have a few. Really, really old ones. Classics, mostly. *To Kill a Mockingbird*, *Jane Eyre*, *Things Fall Apart*. Hard covers that were all faded, pages coming loose. I used to look at them when I was a kid, and they all had this certain … smell. And, I liked it."

"You've never seen more than just a handful of books at once." He didn't have to ask. It was obvious.

"No," the girl said. "I haven't."

Suddenly he wondered what she might do if she had twenty more, a hundred more—a thousand more. Would that keep her occupied? Would she hole up in one room and spend the day perusing pages? Would it satiate her curiosity until it was time for her to leave? Sure, she had plenty of films and series to watch, or VR games to play, but those things held little novelty for her. Books like these were rare and fascinating specimens.

"But you don't like to *read* them," he said, testing her. "Only to … relish their scent …"

She crossed her arms. "I do like to read them. I mean, I don't read a *lot*, and definitely not these old paper things. Usually I've got other stuff on my mind. But that doesn't mean I don't *like* it. I always do well in English class. *Honors* English. Not that you care."

He analyzed her a moment, wishing he could look at a page of text and skim her internal monologue. Instead, he simply said, "Come with me."

She trailed him at a distance, with an attitude much less brazen than what he'd seen from her so far. Maybe he'd scared her the other night, gotten too close with his horrific face and body. He hadn't been able to tell whether she'd secretly appreciated the opportunity to play the piano, or whether his insistence had been unwelcome. She seemed defiant by nature, the kind of person who might disagree solely because she could, and so he struggled to dissect the meaning behind her reaction.

Quietly, he led her to an inconspicuous section of the corridor wall, about three-quarters of the way down its length, and stopped in front of an impressionistic painting of palm trees over white sands at sunset. After feeling along the frame's bottom edge, it emitted a beep, and then the wall section shifted and turned perpendicular to the rest of the wall, showing its narrow depth and leaving openings on both sides of it.

Mirabel stepped back and surveyed the transition. She kept

her mouth tight when she looked at him for further instruction.

The cyborg gestured toward the opening on her side.

As she stepped in, the lights automatically flicked on. She gasped as the brightness revealed wall after wall of books, on black shelves that spanned corner to corner and floor to ceiling at least fifteen feet high. Several black rolling ladders were stationed throughout, all surrounding two sofas and five armchairs in various shades of gray. The floor was the same white marble as the rest of the Submundo, but with a plush, charcoal area rug at the center. Everything was monochrome except for the books, whose diverse colors livened the room.

It wasn't an enormous space. In fact, it had been designed to be "cozy," but considering the number of books that filled it, the cyborg imagined it must have seemed overwhelming to an outsider—to someone who wasn't used to collections like this.

Mirabel gaped at the shelves. She moved slowly along for a minute, then reached for one of the titles. "Can I?"

The cyborg nodded once.

In just a few seconds, Mirabel had already gathered a small collection, scanning the rows, gasping, rushing to new shelves, and pulling titles from all over. Her arms overflowed, book spines pressed together as she held them tightly to keep from dropping them.

He took a few under his own arm to relieve her and set them on the round table between the sofas and chairs.

Finally, Mirabel seemed satisfied for the moment and brought the rest. She took a seat and immediately began exploring the pages. She'd leaf through them, thumbing the paper like all she cared about was the texture. And then she'd stop and read random passages along the way, or other times she seemed to be looking for specific parts of the books. First, it was

Their Eyes Were Watching God, then *One Flew Over the Cuckoo's Nest,* then *Brave New World.* Watching her, the cyborg couldn't help but notice a pattern. The titles stacked up beside her also included *The Catcher in the Rye, 1984,* and *The Color Purple.*

"You chose all the banned books," he said.

Mirabel looked up from *Brave New World* and let her gaze drift over her other selections. "Yeah, I guess I did."

"Although that one has some problematic descriptions of people of color. So maybe it *should* be banned."

She nodded. "Well, it's still important—as long as it's read with context. It definitely gives insight into the prevailing attitudes of the time it was written in."

"Right. I was joking."

She raised an eyebrow. "You? *Joking*?"

"In my own way."

He wasn't sure why he was still here with her. He could leave at any moment and she'd be perfectly happy—and occupied—indefinitely with all these books.

"Keeping people ignorant doesn't protect anyone," she said offhandedly. "It just makes them less prepared to deal with things when they eventually come into contact with them. And just because you read something doesn't mean you're going to do it, or support it, or believe it, or think it's okay. Making everything taboo breeds idiocy."

The cyborg nodded. "'Reality ... is something from which people feel the need of taking pretty frequent holidays.'" He pointed at the book she was reading.

Mirabel raised her chin analytically. "So ... you've actually *read* some of these. You're not just hoarding them to show off your money."

"Like I said, I don't really 'sleep.'"

"Right, of course. And I'm guessing you also attended some expensive school where every book report was practically a college thesis."

He felt a sadness seep into his veins—or whatever he had instead of veins. The mundaneness of school and book reports. Essays and math tests. College applications. Things that were behind him now. A world he might never catch up to, if he ever found a way out of his current circumstances. "Essentially."

She scratched at her hairline absentmindedly.

"You can have one if you want," he told her. "Or two. Or however many."

She stopped and stared at him with cinched eyebrows. "You would just … give me books? Aren't these like collector's items?"

"They're just paper and cardboard if there's no one to appreciate them."

She took her time, easing through the titles. Pulling one out, opening it, looking through it, putting it back. She seemed especially attached to a third edition of *Do Androids Dream of Electric Sheep?*

Mirabel paused, and looked at him with suspicion. "Why are you being … nice?"

"I'm capable of being civil."

She nodded slowly, like she wasn't sure she believed him. "Well, in that case … thank you." She gripped the book. "This is … really great."

"No problem."

"While we're on the subject of being *civil* …" she ran her thumb along the book's top edge and then rested it on the corner. "Can I … *please* … talk to my brother?"

The cyborg clenched his jaw. It was instinctive, like if he could hold his teeth in place, he could hold *himself* in place, and not show any outward signs of his internal crumbling.

What the hell was he doing? He should have just kept his distance. This had been a terrible idea.

Maybe it would be harmless to let her have a call, he thought. But would it? He'd have to give her access to a device, or supervise her in his office, where she might be able to gather more information without him realizing. She might not be a hacker like her brother, but she'd spent at least two years lying about her life, pretending to be someone else—acting.

No. He couldn't risk it. Not when he was this close to getting answers. Even if her dark, pleading eyes made him want to give in.

He swallowed a lump in his throat. "The answer ... is still ... no."

Mirabel's gaze hardened. "You're seriously going to keep up this whole prison warden persona?"

"Better not to complicate things."

"Not *complicate* things? Things are already complicated. A few weeks ago, I was living my relatively normal life—a fake life, but one that at least kind of made sense—and now I'm in some underground tech palace, completely cut off from the outside world, holding a physical book and trying to negotiate with ... whatever it is that you are."

"As I've said, coming here was your choice. Keeping you here is a matter of my own survival. Sorry I'm not nicer to look at." He flipped the hood of his sweatshirt up over his head and turned back toward the stairs.

"Why won't you just tell me who you are?" Mirabel shouted at his back. "You've taken a look at my past, who *I* am, a whole record of my mistakes."

"You know as much about me as you need to."

"You're choosing this, you know. Choosing to deal with whatever you're dealing with, alone."

He shoved his hands in his sweatshirt pocket and shot her a glare. "I don't have time to explain to you why that's not true."

"You 'don't have time?'" Mirabel said. "Don't you have all the time in the world down here? What could you possibly have to do that could take up so much time?"

The word 'time' hung in the air, ringing in his ears, taunting him. He stared at her for a long moment, then finally told her, "Close up the library when you're done."

When the cyborg reached the office, his holoscreen remained open, a cluster of frames in the air. A notification hung in the corner. He went to it and stood in front of the screens. It was the same message that had been popping up for weeks.

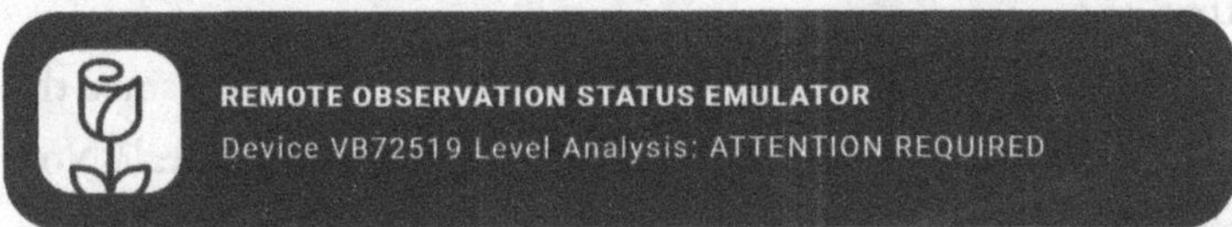

The cyborg's machinery hummed inside of him, a rush of chemicals and electricity that flooded his mind. Steadying himself, he reached for the notification and, as always, tapped **DISMISS**.

CHAPTER 027

BEL COULDN'T SEEM TO GET COMFORTABLE in her room. She adjusted herself in the chair and the book in her lap, but it felt awkward no matter how she sat. Unfortunately, she wasn't sure it had entirely to do with her setup, with the bulky text and the fact that it wouldn't lay open flat, or the fact that the chair was too comfortable for its own good. It was more than that.

Her pulse hadn't fully settled to its natural rhythm since the cyborg had stormed out of the library. What was his deal? Now that they'd had a civilized conversation, he had been starting to show signs of humanity—some kind of deep pain or regret, a sense of loneliness when at first he'd seemed to *prefer* to be alone. And then ...

She'd had to keep reminding herself he was probably a criminal, that all this money and wealth likely came at the expense of someone else's life or livelihood, even if indirectly. At least it had been easier to believe that in the beginning, to antagonize and defy him.

Bel shook her head and reread the same passage of the book again. She'd read it three times already but had failed to concentrate and get its meaning.

"The spider Mercer gave the chickenhead, Isidore; it probably was artificial, too. But it doesn't matter. The electric things have their lives, too. Paltry as those lives are."

Bel's eyes rested on the phrase "the electric things."

The story was talking about mechanical creatures. Animals and insects that were electronic but which resembled organic bodies. In the case of humans, they were called replicants. They were incredibly realistic—so much that very specific psychological tests had been created to determine whether they were human or not.

She thought about Lucius—how, if he weren't translucent from certain angles, he'd be as realistic as any other member of a household staff—provided, of course, that she didn't try to touch him. Even with the visual flaw, her mind had let her feel like he was a person, given her permission to talk to him and ask him questions as though he were. She hadn't thought of him as "an electric thing," but now that she considered it, he was.

She thought about the entertainment console in her room, with its settings, its diagrams and modifiers. She thought about how the console's settings diagram had shown her all the rooms and their devices—how the AI were listed among them. Delessio in the Kitchen. Isabel in the Wardrobe.

She gasped.

All this time she'd been scouring the Submundo for a device, when the device had been with her all along. The very thing she needed was a shout away. And it hadn't even occurred to her, simply because he didn't have a screen. Except that he *was* a screen. A three-dimensional, holomorphic screen!

She slammed the book shut. "Lucius!"

The AI appeared. He adjusted the buttons of his vest—

another programmed feature no doubt designed to humanize him—and clasped his hands. "How can I help you, Mirabel?"

"I want to customize your appearance. I can do that, right?" Bel stood to face him.

"Certainly. I can appear as any gender, age, body type, and/or ethnicity. You may alter my voice, mannerisms, and attire to suit your personal preferences. I even come with a selection of celebrity personas to choose from, similar to your kitchen model. Allow me to provide you with a customization menu."

A frame flew up beside him, a menu board hanging in mid-air. It had all the customization he mentioned, along with a few others, and an "advanced settings" button.

He smiled and gestured to the menu. "Simply touch the items you'd like to alter."

Bel nodded and hit "advanced settings." A secondary panel replaced the current one, while Lucius's form stood waiting. Here, Bel found she could alter Lucius's ability to remember faces and memorize the preferences of anyone in the house, or change the way he conducted conversations (follow-up questions, small talk, greetings, politeness), or even what rooms he could or couldn't appear in. There were also several preferences that were accessible only by voice command—specifically, an "emergency SOS" feature, programmed with the United Watch main line and a pre-scripted message. Bel tried to alter this feature but Lucius simply said "voice pattern not recognized" and continued to wait patiently while she explored her other options. She tapped in and out of several more settings until she finally found something that said "developer mode" and a grin spread across her face.

As soon as she tapped it, she had the option to toggle certain features or switch to a terminal view. She opened the terminal, which then came with a projected keyboard.

Bel felt her blood thumping through her limbs. This was it. She could do anything now.

She typed into the terminal. A simple command gave her the entire directory of other commands she could use for this specific system. From there, she disabled the cyborg's voice-locked permission to Lucius, and then deprogrammed United Watch from the SOS feature.

Now to get in contact with Mateo.

Thankfully, Lucius was the one AI that would be connected to everything in the house. Where Delessio and Isabel and Flora would probably be limited to their isolated regions, Lucius had to have access to every room and every server, to be able to appear for any little thing and answer any question about the entire Submundo.

First, she accessed the main network, which had outside internet connection. Definitely not something the Submundo inhabitants would probably have during a worldwide apocalypse, but she was glad to be able to have it now. She logged in to her personal Atmo account, which was flooded with messages from Aly and other kids from school, wondering if she was okay, along with tags linking her to news stories about her and Mateo's escape and Mateo's criminal history. She felt queasy looking at it all and ended up closing it without reading anything else or responding to anyone. Instead, she logged in to her secret account, which was equally flooded, but in this case with assignments she hadn't been able to take, and tags in threads where other users were questioning whether she'd been caught or shut down.

I don't have time for this.

Then she had the sudden urge to try and send a message to Aly, although she wondered whether it would be okay to do so.

Aly had been the last person to see Bel before she'd disappeared; the authorities could be monitoring Aly's devices. Thane had probably already been questioned, and no doubt would have revealed that Bel was ReBELi0u5, so Bel couldn't even use that account to keep a low profile in Aly's inbox. So she decided on creating a new account with a generic name; that way, anyone who saw it probably wouldn't think twice about it.

The message would be vague, but Aly would know what it meant. She would know Bel was (relatively) safe.

To: Alyson Kae Zaffino

You've just been glitch-slapped ;)

After she sent it, Bel tapped to bring the terminal window back to the front again. With a few more commands, Bel pulled up a list of every connected device in the house. It took several minutes, but soon she was able to locate the cyborg's office holopad and pull up the screen remotely. She quickly pulled up the camera feed to the office first, though, to make sure the cyborg wasn't sitting right in front of the device she needed to attack.

All clear.

She began remotely looking through the cyborg's files and history. Anything she could ever need was visible—everything he'd accessed, viewed, created. All she needed was to get into his messaging program and she'd be sure to find Mateo's contact info.

408-555-6552
89 Wentworth Place
Cupertino, Dorado

Bel copied all the information and saved it in a message to herself on Atmo, just in case she had to access it later and didn't want to go all the way into the cyborg's device. That's what she'd use to message Mateo's number, but first she wanted to have some information to give him. Some solid facts. There had to be something in the cyborg's documents to tell her who he was or what business he was involved in.

She tapped into folders and previewed files. The first few were mostly research—scientific articles on cybernetic implants or information on companies that manufactured them. There was also a collection of information on vidrinium, specifically vidrinium batteries and how to make them last longer. Unfortunately, it seemed that the cyborg had more questions than he did answers.

Within a fifth folder, however, Bel discovered a single video. She assumed it was a piece of security footage that the cyborg might have set aside for some reason. She opened it and tapped the play button.

At first, the screen was mostly dark. Hazy. Then a crack of light—still hazy. A ceiling, white paneled, coming into focus. The view panned over to a sideways wall of white cabinets, some with glass, and medical supplies behind the doors. Curtains, like a hospital. Between the curtains: beds … or, maybe lab tables, each with a still, naked body lying on top and only a sheet for cover. Touch panels, holoscreens, IVs.

Bel glanced at Lucius, guiltily, as though he knew exactly what she was doing. He said nothing, just continued to wait, fully open to any commands she might give. He was an "electric thing," Bel told herself; he didn't have the ability to judge her.

A soft beep sounded in the background of the video.

The back of someone's hand lifted toward the camera. A

tag on the wrist, showing a scannable code, the words PROJECT ITERUM, and the number A309.

It's like someone had a camera attached to their forehead, Bel thought.

Abruptly, the perspective shifted as though this unnamed person, who had appeared to be lying down, had now sat up.

Hands showed again, first the backs and then the fronts. Long fingers, brown skin, nothing out of the ordinary. Then a glance down at the body: a bare, masculine chest, a sheet covering waist to knees.

Chest rising and falling. Audible breaths, slow at first and then increasing in speed.

The view went dark for a second, then bright again. Black faded in simultaneously from the top and bottom of the screen, meeting in the middle, before fading out the opposite direction.

Like ... blinking.

Breaths turned heavier and heavier until the whole view went unsteady and then there were feet swinging over the table, landing on the floor.

Out of view, one of the hands seemed to be grasping something, Bel guessed from the way the arm was positioned. The sound of a soft snap, like a plastic cord—no, a wire, maybe—breaking. Then, a grunt, like that of someone in pain.

A glance at the floor, a disconnected wire dangling in the periphery.

Rapid, persistent beeping.

A sweeping gaze across the entire space—a laboratory.

Bel felt like she was in a memory, living it moment by moment. It was footage, sure, but it had a quality that was something more. It was like she was *inside* the viewer. Her blood rushed at the movement. Her instincts were on high alert as though she could steer the perspective. But of course she couldn't.

Medical technicians, or assistants, maybe—some with white lab coats, others with scrubs—swarmed the area.

The view jerked back and forth, then swept downward. More curtains, set up on metal frames to divide the space. Oxygen tanks. Imaging machines and computer equipment.

Another grunt.

Hands on the concrete floor, pressing, pushing the viewer back up, grabbing hold of a curtain. Pulling, as if for leverage. The framework began to collapse, then came hurtling toward the viewer. Everything turned on its side in a blur, like he was rolling out of the way. A crash.

Metal striking metal. A violent hiss.

The tanks, Bel thought. Oxygen was combustible, especially spewing the compressed gas right next to electrical—

An explosion rocked the scene. Bel flinched.

Flames quickly erupted on the curtains, the equipment.

Screaming and shouting.

Everything shaking up and down like a cameraperson running with handheld equipment.

Another scream, louder this time, rattling the view. The viewer looked at his right arm, fire devouring the top layers of skin and revealing layers of metal below as it spread up his chest and, presumably his face, with flames consuming the entire right side of the screen.

Bel covered her mouth, her own heart pounding.

Another downward sweeping view. Concrete floor again, flames lapping. Then a rolling view—smothering the flames.

A voice shouted, "Source units are top priority! Get them out the north exit!"

Alarms blared.

The cyborg—what Bel was *sure* was the cyborg now—seemed to have gotten his own flames under control and begun to crawl. The view slowly panned upward, like he'd managed to get to his feet, although still unsteadily.

He stumbled away from the explosion site, through a set of swinging doors that led to another room full of equipment, and several bins—some that appeared to be for biohazardous materials, others for dirty laundry. He did a double take, then began to fish around in the laundry, removing a set of dirty scrubs and shakily slipping them onto himself before he stumbled toward an EXIT sign

The sign led to a hallway, where another EXIT glowed above another set of doors.

Finally, he stepped into a dark alley.

Panting, he looked at a heap of old pallets, a dumpster, the brick walls, then down at his bare feet on the pavement.

In the darkness, a light flashed, bathing everything in pale green. He glanced at his chest, where exposed metal and wires surrounded the light source—a small black box with a green LED light and the word Sequitor® stamped onto it.

A tracker.

He touched it, tentatively at first, then with a more exploratory nature, feeling around the edges and pushing his fingers underneath. Without the exposure from the explosion, he might never have known it was there, but now it was right out in the open. Now it was clear that whoever had brought him to this place had wanted to not only experiment on him but also control him somehow. He grasped the tracker, grunted, and pulled until the outer casing cracked loose. He stared at it for a few seconds, then let it fall to the ground, where he crushed it with his bare heel. Its light faded.

The cyborg turned down the alley, his gait steadier now—evident because the video view was steadier—and gradually picked up speed. Sirens went off in the distance, along with shouting as people escaped through the exits on the other side of the building.

Bel watched for several minutes as the cyborg navigated the streets at night. He stopped at the nearest SkimShare, a hovercraft EV rental station where several stand-up skimmers were lined up at charging docks.

She suddenly remembered the one she'd seen in the Garage. It hadn't made sense at the time; it had been harshly out of place. Now she understood.

Not having a device with him to unlock a vehicle through the app, the cyborg had to use the main kiosk, where he entered payment info manually. He typed in numbers that he'd apparently had memorized, along with the name "Adam Steele" in the required registrant fields.

"You can call me Mr. Steele."

Now having a full name, Bel paused the video to search the intersphere, but results came up inconclusive. If the cyborg was anyone important—as Bel remained certain he had to be—then the name would have pulled up news articles, social media accounts, and multiple photos of the same person attending events. But that would have been too easy, wouldn't it? It was the same last name he'd willingly provided to Bel and Mateo that first day; it couldn't have been real. It had to be an alias. High-profile people probably did that kind of thing all the time, to hide financial activity—because financial activity was a dead giveaway to *general* activity. The only question was, what was so secret about this guy's activities that he'd need to cover it up with a fake ID and accounts?

With a beep, one of the skimmers unlocked itself and the cyborg stepped onto the footboard. He programmed a set of coordinates—also apparently memorized—into the GPS on the small dash. The ETA read as 5 HOURS 23 MINUTES. Then he tore off down the street.

Bel tried to place his location by the buildings he passed. It looked like it might be on the outer edges of Silicon Valley, but he kept moving further from the city center. He was headed south.

Another quick search told Bel that the distance between Silicon Valley and the general location of the Submundo was approximately five and a half hours. This must have been the night he arrived.

Then, the video abruptly cut out.

Bel stared at the blank video frame, her body frozen. She struggled to process everything she'd just seen—even having already witnessed the cyborg up close—and also how she'd even been able to view such a thing. Like his eyes were inherent cameras, his ears inherent audio recording devices, producing tangible memories in video format. And somehow he'd downloaded and saved a piece of them ... but for what?

She thought of all the times she'd tried to "replay" her own memories, going over past events repeatedly trying to see what might have gone wrong or to capture a certain lost detail that might make something make sense. How much easier would it have been, had she had an actual video to refer back to? Maybe that's what the cyborg had been doing: replaying this bit of his experience to look for more answers.

How could he not? Who knew what kinds of things had been done to his body while he slept?

No, she thought. She couldn't be too sympathetic. She still didn't know who he was, or what he had done. Maybe he'd deserved it. Maybe this had been his punishment.

She shook her head. As tempting as it was to dwell on all these new questions, she still wasn't finished getting the answers she'd originally set out to get.

She tapped out of the video folder, moving backward through the file network toward the main folder again. In one of the subfolders, she spotted a text document titled "Notes." She opened it.

Project Iterum
A309
source unit
vidrinium batteries
metallum intus

Bel paused on the last item. *Metallum foris, metallum intus.* The Knight Crew's motto.

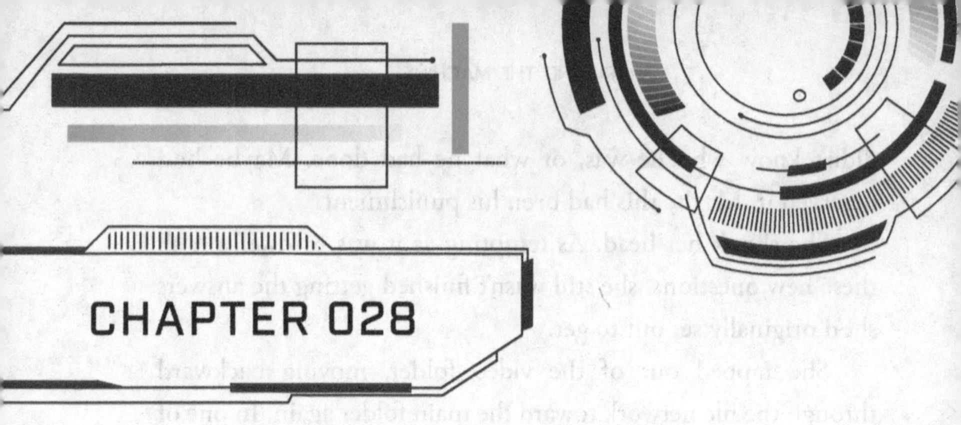

CHAPTER 028

AS USUAL, THE CYBORG STRUGGLED to rest. Aside from the persistent humming in his ears—a sound he didn't really notice during the day but which plagued him whenever he made the effort to do anything even *resembling* sleep—he felt a nagging in his mind, too. For all his internal machinery, he was feeling painfully human at the moment, and for the first time in a very long time, he didn't want to.

The girl shouldn't be here. It had been a mistake to demand it. It should have been a simple thing, for him and her to each mind their own business and never interact, but he hadn't known how she would be—how persistent.

Yes, she might be able to understand what it was like to live in fear, like him, and to keep her name hidden behind a lie, and to not know who to trust. But for him it was more than that. He had his entire family's legacy hanging in the balance, the awareness that there had been people in his life who were capable of things he never would have imagined, the fact that his body was now full of foreign gears and chemicals, and the complete lack of certainty as to how much of him was real anymore. All of that was too much to risk on a girl who was basically a stranger. And if he could get answers—something he could not jeopardize—his time with Mirabel would be over soon enough anyway.

If only he could leave it at that.

But no.

Her dark eyes came to his mind again. Her sharp gaze. That resilient facade that held a mess of secrets he continued to pretend he didn't want to know. He was sure she didn't see him with the same curiosity; hers ended at whatever information might benefit her. To her, he was just a mechanical monster. He'd seen the discomfort in her eyes at the touch of his mechanical hand. Disgust at worst. At best, pity.

Except he *was* a monster. Whatever his reasons, it was cruel to keep her here without contact to the outside world, under threat of revealing her to United Watch. He knew that. It wasn't something he'd *enjoyed*.

Would it be so risky to allow her a brief conversation with her brother? After all, what conspiratorial ideas could she possibly convey during a one-minute call?

There was always a chance it would backfire, that she'd find a way to run, and her brother's assignment would go unfinished.

He felt sick at the thought that he might die here and never know the truth, but he also didn't like what he'd become, desperately digging in his claws to get what he needed. That wasn't who he wanted to be. He had so little control over what he was now; all he *could* control were his choices.

Finally, when he couldn't take the mental back-and-forth any longer, he left his room and looked for Mirabel in the library, but everything was closed up, as he'd asked her to do. She might have gone to bed—he couldn't be sure, since he'd sometimes seen her out in the later hours—and could very well be asleep in her room now, but he preferred not to wake her. If she was still up, and happened to be in one of the Submundo's common spaces, then the solution was simple: He only needed to call on Lucius to locate her.

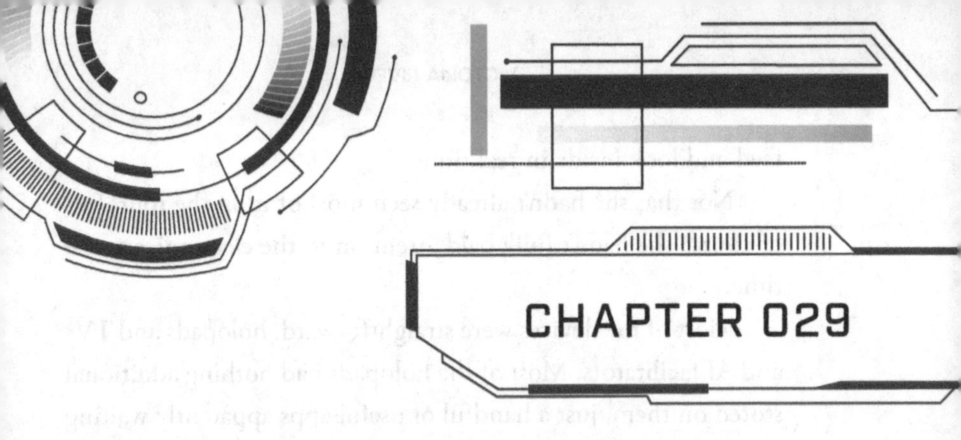

CHAPTER 029

HEART RACING, BEL BEGAN FRANTICALLY looking through the Submundo's main network for additional drives or devices that might help her get more information. She had pulled up a schematic of every connected device, divided by regions of the building.

Metallum foris, metallum intus.

The phrase continued to repeat in her mind.

"Metal without, metal within." Or "metal on the outside, metal on the inside."

Of course it didn't mean the cyborg was Knight Crew. Not for certain. After all, it was in his *notes*—along with other items that had appeared to be clues he'd been piecing together. If that motto belonged to his own family, it wouldn't make sense to list it like that. But that didn't mean he wasn't part of a rival crime family, or that he wasn't involved in some shady business.

While some part of her had begun to want to assume the cyborg was as much a victim to larger powers as she was—and even more so—she had to be sure first.

For each region, or room, of the Submundo on the schematics, there were holographic representations of the devices and their general location within the floorpan. Bel found that if she tapped on a specific room, she could also access the security feed and look inside in real time.

Not that she hadn't already seen most of it on the tour. But of course she hadn't fully paid attention to the electronics at the time.

Most of the devices were straightforward, holopads and TVs and AI facilitators. Most of the holopads had nothing additional stored on them, just a handful of useful apps apparently waiting for someone to utilize them. There were several drives within the server room, most of which seemed to be designated for the vast media storage required by whomever would be stuck living here during an apocalypse.

Then, a mini holopad in the storage zone caught Bel's attention.

Mini Holopad V103 - ROSE

"Why would there be a random holopad, online, in a storage room?" she wondered aloud.

She tapped the security feed to get a peek at the space.

It was an unfinished room with concrete flooring, and rows of metal shelving with clear containers lined up on them.

Bel zoomed in on one row of containers, which was full of cleaning supplies and toiletries. Others were full of dish sets, linens, light bulbs, batteries, and sensors. There was also an entire section of electronics, devices offline and still in their packaging: holoscreen TVs and holopads, watches, a whole supply of holoprojectors—the kind that were embedded all over the ceilings so that Lucius could show up in different places—enough to replace all those currently installed throughout the Submundo as the years passed.

Along one wall, there were stacked chairs and sofas wrapped

in plastic. Everything appeared to be arranged by category—household items based on the rooms they applied to, the place from which the Submundo's seemingly endless resources could be refilled, from which worn-out items might be replaced in how ever many years it took to break them down from use.

Then, at the back of the room, Bel spotted the mini holopad connected to the network.

Why had it been shown up as ROSE on the schematics?

She raised her finger to tap-zoom, but Lucius—along with every window she'd left open—disappeared into thin air.

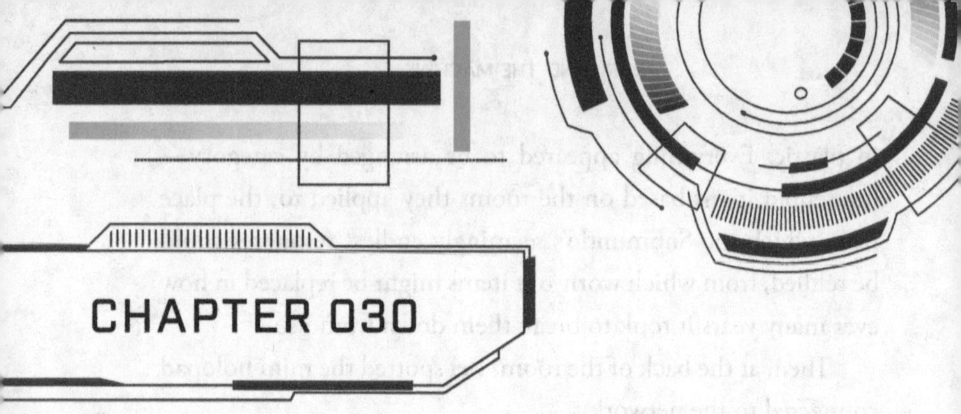

CHAPTER 030

BEL BURST OUT OF HER ROOM and caught herself on the railing overlooking the Common Room.

The cyborg was standing below, in front of Lucius, whose settings were wide open under layers of browser, terminal, and file manager frames. He looked up at her, a bitter expression on the part of his face that was capable of showing any emotion.

Bel froze. "I ..." Slowly, she descended the stairs. "Look, you wouldn't tell me anything, okay? You can't just expect me to be locked up down here with a complete stranger without any other information and not—"

"You're a hacker," he said, with a kind of disgust in his eyes Bel never would have expected at the revelation of this secret. "And you let me think you were just ... just ..."

"Just what? Just some dumb ... *girl?*"

"Just—"

"Yes, *I'm* the one who built the Ecker. *I'm* the one who picked up the Submundo's signal. *I'm* the one who hacked in. Mateo told me to leave it alone and I didn't listen. He had nothing to do with any of it."

"Did I even send the right person to Vivorex?"

"Of course you did." She scoffed. "He's capable of doing *all* that, and a whole lot more."

The cyborg clenched his jaw.

"I know we made a deal"—Bel continued moving down to him—"even if it was completely coerced, but it's wrong for you to not let me talk to Mateo. It made sense when I'd just broken in and you'd never met me before, when I could have been a threat. But you have to know by now I don't want to hurt you. You should be able to tell that you can trust me."

He turned quiet, sullen. A darkness seemed to pass over his face as she came down and stood in front of him.

"You know, it's funny," he said. "I was starting to think so, too. I was starting to think I'd been acting like a psychopath, and that I'd read you completely wrong." He pressed his thumb to his opposite wrist again. "I was about to tell you I changed my mind. But then, when I wanted to locate you, I called Lucius."

Bel's stomach twisted as she imagined Lucius appearing in his current state, settings all splayed out like that.

"I saw how you hacked my security cameras," he told her. "I saw your Atmo account—where people are messaging you, offering to pay you to dig up personal information on someone else, or get rid of intersphere photos they don't have access to, or change their grades. I saw *my* video memory, opened, played to the end."

"I needed to know—"

"You don't *need* to know anything," he said. "I told you that. Just because information is available doesn't mean it's your job to look at it. My past is not your business. You don't have a right to know about my pain if I don't want you to."

"Knowledge is the only power I have," Bel replied quietly. "Finding information, manipulating it, using it to my advantage, making money off of it. I'm not allowed to let anyone else know about me, so I make sure I know about them. For years,

I haven't had the freedom to show my own face without some kind of masking device attached to me. I would think you could understand that feeling."

"You and I are not the same."

"No, we're not. I wasn't anyone important like you probably were—big family business, lots of money, prep schools and good connections. Nobody misses a *nobody* who goes missing. But still … We share enough to be allies; we shouldn't be enemies. Instead of keeping me mostly in the dark, you could let me help—instead of just forcing my brother to."

"I don't need anything from you, except for you to mind your own business, and stay away from me." He turned and strode back toward the east corridor.

"Wait …" Bel hurried to catch up to him. "Are you going to alert United Watch?"

He kept walking. "I'm not going to do anything."

"I know it was wrong to do what I did—all of it." Bel panted, struggling to keep up with the pace of his long stride. "But *you're* not exactly—"

He halted and turned toward her so abruptly she almost slammed into him.

"Just … *stop*." His nostrils flared. "I don't want to hear it. I don't want to see you. I don't want to think about you."

"You're the one who insisted I stay here."

"A necessary evil."

She glared up at him.

His expression was hard as stone. "Keep out of my sight until this is over."

Bel stood in the hallway alone, watching the cyborg disappear around the corner. Her heart pounded furiously, a great throbbing force that filled her whole body with heat. Her eyes pricked, trying to wet themselves against her will, but she fought them, curling her fists.

No, she thought. *This is over* now.

She wouldn't wait until Mateo figured out whatever it was the cyborg wanted to know. She was going to leave the Submundo—immediately.

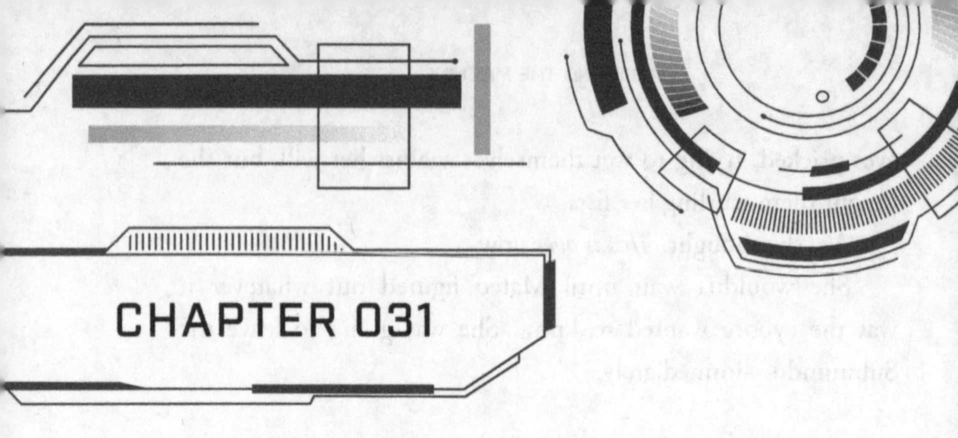

CHAPTER 031

BEL FOUND HER EMPTY BACKPACK lying on the floor of her room, right where she'd left it the day she'd arrived. She called Lucius, whose settings panel was still open. Only the video frames had been closed, but the terminal was still up, along with her Atmo accounts and the looped camera feed. Her stomach churned, imaging the cyborg looking at all this, what it must have made him feel to see her intrusion.

But it was ridiculous for him to be hurt, she thought. Maybe they weren't completely enemies, but they weren't friends, either. She wouldn't have cared who he was or what he was involved in if it didn't affect her own safety and Mateo's. She would have gladly left him alone and gone back out into the wilderness.

Although, she had to admit, it had been nice to have a clean place to stay, and food. To know United Watch couldn't find her here—at least as long as she cooperated. Her skin was still dry and tender from all that time out in the sun, and the thought of sleeping under the meager cover of trees with mosquitoes eating her alive definitely didn't sound better than where she was now.

Still, she'd gone too far, and she couldn't stay with the cyborg anymore. She kept remembering the look on his face, his horror at finding her in the folders where he kept all his secrets. Had he really been planning to let her talk to Mateo? If that was true, then maybe he really had done all of this out of fear, not because he was a bad person. It didn't matter, though. Mateo could still finish the mission; he could hold up his end of the deal, but there was no reason for Bel to be at the Submundo anymore.

With the camera feed still on loop, it would be safe for her to gather supplies. She went through the closet and found herself some sturdier clothes—a pair of jeans, some hiking boots, a hooded sweatshirt. She packed a pair of shorts and a tank top, too, so she'd be prepared for any kind of weather. Then she went down to the pantry and stocked up on a bit of food and filled a water bottle.

From the Medical Resource Room, she filled her backpack's outer pockets with some rudimentary first aid items and from the Armory she took one of the small blaster pistols, the silvery blue Pulsar 13.

According to cameras, the cyborg was in the lounge, so Bel hacked into his office and gathered a few supplies from the closet. Batteries, a solar charger, a holopad, and most importantly, an InVisor. Back in her room, she programmed the InVisor with a new identity for herself and had Lucius scan her against the UW database to make sure she came up with the new alias.

Finally, she went to the garage. She looked over the vehicles, the selection of large skimmers.

She shook her head. *Too much.*

Her gaze fell to one of the Lightfoot F1s hanging on the wall. They were compact. *Like a bicycle without wheels.* She could take one out the West Entrance without having to open that huge hatch on the east side, and even fold it up and carry it onto the Mag once she got to the closest city with a depot. She'd be able to cut the whole trip down to an hour and a half if she went by maglev for most of it.

When she was finished preparing everything, she stood in the Common Room, taking one last look around the magnificent space. Despite the opulence of the furniture and the windows and the gardens beyond, she felt the weight of the few stolen items she was carrying in her backpack, and the Lightfoot in her hand. Even though these things were probably nothing to someone as wealthy as the cyborg, she couldn't help feeling like she was as much a criminal as the news had made her out to be. She was taking things that didn't belong to her—after hacking into a ruined man's haven. Now that she'd heard his side of the story—even though she still didn't know his enemies' side—it was a lot harder to look at him the way she had before.

She chewed her bottom lip as she reached into her backpack's side pocket, where she'd stashed her drives and digibank. With a flick of her hand, she detached the bank and gripped it tight. The outer shell was cold against her palm. It was everything she had. Everything she'd earned as ReBELi0u5, all her money for school, for her future. She set it on the center table.

"Lucius, can I leave a message with this?"

"Yes, Mirabel. What is your message?"

It was just before dawn, and a wet chill prickled the skin of Bel's hands. She was glad she'd brought the hooded sweatshirt. Despite the morning cold, she inhaled deeply, grateful for the pure, outdoor air. She held it in her lungs for a long moment, savoring it.

There was dew on the grass. Bel walked a ways, carrying the Lightfoot, before she kicked it open and mounted it. Using the holopad, she logged in to her Atmo account, where she'd saved the information on Mateo's location, which she then programmed into the Lightfoot's routing system. As she prepared to speed away, she felt like there were rocks in her stomach. She glanced back at the Submundo's West Entrance, which was just a pinprick of light on the rock wall from here. The cyborg was all alone in there, having been violated in so many ways, including by her watching some of his grueling personal history. A part of her wished she'd at least said goodbye. But what would have been the point?

She inhaled again, slowly, then gave herself a decided nod, and pressed the Lightfoot's accelerator.

By the time she'd ridden two miles or so, the sun was rising, diffused red light spreading out behind dark clouds, murky. It was going to rain. The smell in the air made her certain.

She rode through the trees and soon reached a clearing. Being out so far in the open made her a little nervous, away from the protective cover of the ponderosa pines; being *out*, in general, prompted a fear she hadn't been expecting. It was a complicated mess of emotions, but she realized she'd felt safe in the Submundo, safer than she'd felt in a very long time, even if it hadn't completely been her choice to stay there. There'd been no looming pandrones or panopts, and it was the first time in years that she hadn't worn InVisor. The cyborg had called her by her own name. She'd even told him real things about herself and her old life—piano music and her mom, her dad's books—things she hadn't even told Aly.

Thunder clapped in the distance. It shook the earth, tickled Bel's bones. Gray clouds slowly turned to black. No lightning, but the air was moist and heavy.

Rain drizzled at first but condensed quickly. Bel pulled her hood up over her head as she rode, the sounds of thunder easily overpowering the Lightfoot's quiet vibrations.

And then, hidden among the claps of thunder but evident between them was another sound Bel recognized—a persistent whirring sound.

I have an InVisor, Bel reminded herself. But that didn't keep her pulse from thrumming or her stomach from clenching as the drones came into view.

What were they doing there? And so many of them? Surely that ranger hadn't gotten a good shot of Mateo's face the other day. Besides, he'd damaged its sensors with the handgun, hadn't he?

Unless shooting it had been enough for authorities to dispatch *more*.

They'd known Mateo was out here somewhere. Having lost him, they might think a damaged ranger warranted further investigation. Especially if the ranger had been able to transmit footage of getting shot down. They would have seen it was intentional damage—and who else would do that? Not some recreational backpacker.

So they must still be looking for him. And, technically, her as well.

She kept her distance, trying to predict the pandrones' path so she could avoid it. Not that she needed to. Mateo must have encountered them too, on his way back, and his InVisor had protected him. At least, she assumed it had, or the cyborg would have said something—wouldn't he? If her brother hadn't contacted him upon arrival in Dorado?

Distantly, the pandrones combed a cluster of trees. They moved methodically, spread out, flashing their lights. Nothing to see here.

Bel continued onward, hoping to slip past unnoticed, but as

soon as she approached, the drones changed course. The noise of the Lightfoot—however subtle—must have caught their attention, she thought. But it didn't matter; they'd scan her and find nothing suspicious. Another meaningless name like all the ones she'd had linked to her face before.

She steeled herself as they roved over her. Scanning. Scrutinizing.

Beep.

"Citizen: Halt! You are in violation of West California law. Please remain where you are until higher authorities arrive. Estimated time to arrival: Approximately nine minutes."

Bel veered off to where the next hill sloped down, deep and out of the way, picking up speed.

With swift, drastic movements, they followed.

She sped into the next wooded area. They followed her still, hovering over the canopy.

The rain stung her eyes, but she made it to a good spot under a dense collection of branches. The pandrones buzzed above her, waiting, circling.

"Citizen: Halt! You are in violation of West California law. Please remain where you are until higher authorities arrive. Estimated time to arrival: Approximately eight minutes. If you do not comply, this device is authorized to administer a projectile tranquilizer."

It was dark, the overcast skies blocking out the morning sun, made even darker by the green boughs above. The drones flicked on their lights. Small beads of water shone in the beams.

The InVisor was still in place; Bel felt it with her finger, a soft bump on her forehead. She must have programmed it wrong. She reached into her pack for the blaster and clutched it to her body, waiting, trying to determine what to do.

One of the drones dipped down, testing the space between the trees where she hid. The space was too narrow; the drone tested another area, and another, until finally it found a place to enter.

Bel swerved just as the drone came at her, while the other drones followed, six in total.

"Citizen: Halt! Please remain where you are until higher authorities arrive. Estimated time to arrival: Approximately seven minutes."

Bel zoomed through the trees, zig-zagging, swerving again to avoid hitting trees. The drone lightbeams aided her sight, although she would have preferred to stumble alone in the dark than rely on the illumination of robotic predators.

The drones have a hard time under the trees, Bel thought. And for good reason. The canopy was denser here, and she'd trapped them under it with her—but that didn't mean all was lost. She scanned the way ahead for narrow spaces.

She spotted a thick tree and zoomed toward it. The drones were on her tail. "Citizen: Halt!" At the last second, she jerked the Lightfoot to the left. Two of the drones, unable to reorient in time, crashed against the tree and clattered to the ground, broken propellers thwacking uselessly against the damp dirt, damaged and distorted commands fading out.

She zoomed toward another tree, trying for another juke, but it didn't work this time.

"If you do not comply, this device is authorized to administer a projectile tranquilizer," the drone voice said. "This is your final warning."

When she had a clear path, she leaned to the side so she could angle back and shoot—but she paused, never having shot a weapon before. Mateo had shown her how with the mechanical handgun, but only up to the point of pulling the trigger. As the drones loomed closer, however, Bel didn't have any more time to second-guess herself. She grimaced and fired the blaster.

Zing.

The kickback shook her, and she missed, but went for it again.

Zing. Another miss.

Zing. A hit, just barely. The laser skimmed the surface of the closest drone, which dropped, but regained position quickly.

The other drones continued their pursuit. Bel shot twice more. Another miss, then a hit that appeared to have damaged a sensor. The drone was still functioning, but hovered aimlessly, disoriented, and fell behind.

She tried another juke and lost one more drone. Two to go.

"Administration of tranquilizer."

Bel was calculating her next shot when the drones, catching up, seemed to have finally locked onto her and began to fire back with the tranks.

The tranks zinged past, narrowly missing Bel again and again. Some of them struck the trees, spewing wood chips.

She wove through the woods, trying to put distance between herself and the drones again, to give herself a chance to aim better.

Another trank cut past her, snagging her sleeve. Startled, she lost her hold on the blaster and it thumped to the ground, lost behind her in a blur as she raced on.

Only two more drones, she told herself. Despite no longer having a weapon, she still might be able to lose them. Never mind that she had no plan for how to make it to the city without a working InVisor; but she had to make it out of these woods alive first.

As if they had heard what she was thinking, another pair of drones appeared—the others must have dispatched them. The new ones stayed above the trees, but they added more light and they fired more tranks.

Bel glanced over her shoulder to see one of the drones flying alarmingly close. In a moment, it would hit her with a trank and knock her flat.

She tensed, not daring to look back.

She waited. Seconds passed like minutes. She hovered and ducked and cringed.

A high-pitched, mechanical squeal. A strobe of light.

What?

But she was still riding. Still untouched. Dodging trees.

Bel looked over her shoulder now. The drones that had pursued her below the canopy were gone. Behind them, a young man on a full-sized skimmer carried the Relámpago Z-101 laser rifle.

"Keep moving!" The cyborg aimed at the two remaining pandrones that followed above the branches.

Bel nodded and continued.

The cyborg shot several times. Smoke curled from nearby branches as rogue laserbeams singed them. The air smelled like campfire.

One of the drones fell, tumbling through rough branches and catching on them, coming to a rest, suspended lifelessly above.

The final drone was tenacious. The cyborg couldn't seem to hit it. Bel found an opening and circled around it, drawing the drone toward her to give the cyborg a clear shot. In giving him a clear shot, however, she had inadvertently given the drone a better shot at *her*.

The dart struck the base of the Lightfoot.

Sparks flew as the metal turned hot under the soles of Bel's shoes.

A small burst shook the vehicle, throwing her balance, and she hurtled down.

The ground came up to meet her—and then everything went black.

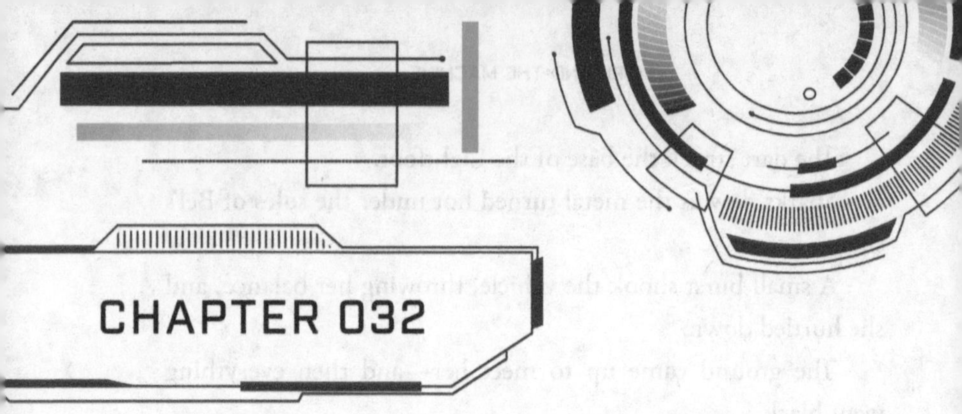

CHAPTER 032

BEL FADED IN AND OUT OF CONSCIOUSNESS, dissolving, reemerging, then dissolving again. It was similar to being only half-awake, where dreams and reality mingled and became senseless.

She imagined herself as a little girl again, running down Santa Monica Pier trying to catch up to Mateo. He'd said he could get to the Ferris wheel before she could. Both parents shouted for them to slow down. Bel tripped and scraped her knee. Her father came to her side, covered the wound with his hand and whispered the same rhyme he always did when she was hurt. "*Sana, sana, colita de rana, si no sanas hoy, sanarás mañana.*"

A burning sensation in Bel's leg grew stronger, radiating from a central point on her thigh.

She lay on the ground, cold and wet. The cyborg's face appeared over her. No drones, no noises but the rain-patter on the earth beside her throbbing head. The cyborg must have shot the last drone.

He was tying something around her leg, tightening it. Her jeans on that side were torn clear up to her hip.

Now his hand was on her face, inspecting her. He held her eyelids open and moved a finger on his other hand back and forth. Somewhere in the blur beyond his finger, Bel sensed that his chest was bare, although for a moment she couldn't figure out why. Then she realized that while the material tied around her leg was rough, it was not rough or thick enough to be the excess denim from her torn jeans; he must have made a tourniquet from his shirt.

Bel tried to sit up.

"No, no, no," he told her, encouraging her back down and propping up her legs on the backpack.

He said something about bloodflow to her heart and brain, but Bel lost full clarity on the words. *Don't go to sleep. Concussion.* She sat up anyway, involuntarily, as her stomach heaved and she vomited into the grass. After that, back to darkness.

She realized she must have blacked out again, because when she opened her eyes there was something tented over her. Small, kind of a faded gray with cargo pockets. A men's jacket—the one the cyborg had been wearing as he'd ridden up—propped up on sticks. Bel felt warmer, if only slightly, but still damp. She wondered if the cyborg was cold, whether he could sense temperature the way she could. The rain had slowed to a drizzle.

The cyborg appeared again, still bare chested. The parts of him that weren't metal—most of the skin on his right side clear down to the navel—were smooth and dark with rain beaded up on them. The parts that *were* metal were also smooth, and also dark, but silvery and lit up from behind. Bel thought he should be careful so that he didn't short circuit in the rainwater—but also, most electronics these days had been designed to *resist* fluid damage. If holopads could do it, an advanced-tech cyborg should certainly be able to.

Even being ultra-human, though, he wasn't obnoxiously muscular. He was trim, with only subtle definition on his arms and abs.

He checked her leg, which stung and burned like nothing she'd ever felt before.

"Bleeding's stopped," he said.

"What …." Bel croaked. "… happened …?"

"Lightfoot blew on impact. The crash threw you on the way down, so you didn't get the full force, but you took a piece of busted motor components to the leg, almost like shrapnel. Gave you a pretty deep cut, and burned you in the process."

He started packing up things around her. She lay still, sucking in air as the pain sank in and she became more aware of it.

Then, with as much of her help as she could give him, he hoisted her onto his skimmer and climbed on behind her. He braced her between his bared arms as he held the skimmer's handlebars, steadying her.

"Just lean back," he said.

She rested the back of her head on his shoulder and, with a jolt, they headed back to the Submundo.

The cyborg walked Bel all the way to the elevator and up to the lounge, half-supporting her, and began to set her up there. It was smaller than the Common Room, cozier, and closer to the East Entrance from which they'd just come. The fireplace lit purple as they entered. The flames reflected off the metal inside his chest, highlighting a device nested inside where his heart would have been, if he'd been fully human.

"Take these." He handed her some pills and a glass of water. "For the pain." He left and returned with a pile of clothes—some shorts and a dry t-shirt for her, and another hooded sweatshirt for himself, which he pulled over his head as he spoke. "I'm going for medical supplies. Change into these while I'm gone."

Bel regarded the shorts with confusion.

"I'll need access to your leg so I can stitch it," he clarified.

"Stitch it?" she repeated. "You … know how to stitch?"

He didn't answer, just left her alone for a few minutes. She didn't want to think about adding a needle to her burning flesh, but she changed, slowly and with difficulty.

When the cyborg came back, he was carrying a container full of supplies. Gauze, tape, antiseptics, a thermoscanner. After checking Bel's temperature and asking her to complete a few basic tests—following his moving finger with her eyes again, repeating a list of words—he pushed his sweatshirt sleeves up to his elbows, sanitized his hands, and put on a pair of disposable gloves.

"Oh. Wow," said Bel. "You're getting really serious here. I don't know if—"

"Try not to freak out when you see it."

He knelt beside the sofa where Bel sat, and removed the homemade tourniquet, revealing the wound. There was a chunk missing from the flesh, maroon like dried jam, thick around the edges. The burning persisted, a hot, swollen sensation throughout the entire limb.

Bel gritted her teeth when he touched it. He sanitized the area surrounding the wound and, even without him touching the wound itself, Bel winced.

Then he prepared a syringe. "Local anesthetic. Ready?"

Bel couldn't say that she was, but she held herself firm as he performed the injection. Her entire upper leg was tender, the pain extending far beyond the wound site, but the anesthetic worked quickly. The cyborg sanitized inside the wound.

Despite the fact that Bel was mostly numb now, the cyborg was gentle. Bel watched him and his delicate movements. He swiped away congealed blood. Next, he prepared a curved needle with suture. As he stabbed into her skin, she flinched, although she hardly felt anything. It was more the idea that he was piercing her so casually.

He focused on the sutures, working the curved needle with his mechanical hand. "I'm not technically trained to do stitches, by the way," he said quietly. "Hope you're okay with that."

"You sure *look* like you're trained."

"I practiced on a lot of grapes." He went in for another stab.

Bel tried to imagine him doing this on a grape. Those robotic hands trying to handle something so small. Of course he hadn't looked like this before, according to his videos. Still, he handled the needle and suture surprisingly well for someone with his physical limitations.

"There's a VR app for training on sutures," he added, "and with the haptics it does come close to the feeling of puncturing skin … but it's not the same. I like the sensation of doing it on something organic."

"Why did you come after me?" she asked.

He made a few more punctures, then used a pair of small scissors to cut the excess suture material.

"I was in the area."

He applied some ointment.

Bel replied flatly, "Of course. What was I thinking."

"Yeah—what *were* you thinking?" A protective tenor came over his voice. "Going up against an entire fleet of pandrones by yourself …"

"That was *not* part of the plan."

He shook his head, then looked as though he was trying

to decide if the wound warranted more ointment. "Well, you certainly did *plan*," he admitted. "Every detail."

He looked at her for a second, set the ointment bottle on the table, then prepared some bandaging supplies.

"How did you know to come for me?" she asked.

With a bundle of gauze, he covered the wound and began wrapping it, delicately lifting her leg each time he went under for another layer. Her skin tingled at his closeness.

"There are always a few padrones in the area," he said, "patrolling the forest. And I knew there might be even more now, still searching for your brother. When I saw that you took an InVisor, I figured you'd be fine, but ..."

"I tested the InVisor before I left," Bel clarified. "I have no idea why it wasn't working."

"You also took a Pulsar 13."

Suddenly Bel recalled what Lucius had said during the tour of the Armory. *Pulsar 13s are powered by coin cell vidrinium batteries ...*"

"Remember when I told you the vidrinium inside me interferes with InVisor masking signals?" said the cyborg.

Bel covered her face and groaned.

"Anyway," he said, "I went out and looked for pandrones. Luckily, they make a lot of noise. And your blaster shots were helpful too."

Bel felt her face go pale. "You risked getting blown up to come after me."

He was reserved as he finished up the dressing. "I guess I did ..."

She stared at him, shaking her head. Who was he? "You could've just let me face my consequences."

"I could have," he agreed. "But I didn't think you deserved

to *die* out there."

"And what, exactly, made you think I was worth saving all of the sudden?"

"I'm not as cruel as you probably think I am. But also …" He reached into his jeans pocket and removed her digibank, setting it gently on the side table, staring at it. "This must be everything you have."

Bel had already forgotten about that, along with the message she'd told Lucius to leave with it.

Mr. Steele,

I'm sorry for hacking your thoughts. I guess it's fitting that I only have pennies to give you for them. Still, I want you to have this, and I hope it's enough to cover the Lightfoot and a few other things I needed.

For what it's worth, thank you … for everything. I'll make sure Mateo finishes the assignment to the best of his ability.

Mirabel

"Yeah …" she replied quietly.

"You knew the things you took wouldn't be worth anything to me. And I'm sure you were pretty angry with me, after everything. But you left this anyway, as part of some weird little code of honor or something." He scoffed. "I would've gone after you anyway, but, I don't know … This just made me feel like … maybe I *could* trust you."

"Really bad people can still have codes of honor. Like how Hannibal doesn't eat people he respects, or how the Kingpin refuses to work with Nazis ..."

"Do you want me to trust you or not?" He almost smiled as he cradled her bandaged thigh, looking over his work, evaluating the wrap. "Anyway ... I think this looks acceptable for now."

Bel paused at his phrasing. There was also something familiar about the way he held her, inspected her. The same way he'd been inspecting something during the call he'd made the other day, the one she'd assumed had to do with drug trafficking or some other corrupt exchange. *Esto parece aceptable por ahora. This looks acceptable for now.*

Bel glanced down. The work on her leg was professional, wrapped with just enough pressure, tucked neatly at the edges. He'd handled her with care.

Suddenly she saw the whole thing through a new lens.

Let's take a look. Not inspecting a product, necessarily, but perhaps a wounded limb.

You'll need to be more careful. Your line of work is dangerous. Not necessarily because the listener's line of work was illegal, but maybe because it was physically strenuous.

Obviously what I can do from here is limited. A fact when operating digitally out of a remote location.

"You're an eMT ..." Bel put her hand on her forehead. "Little *e*. I saw a video about that last year. Those med techs that operate electronically—virtually—in other countries."

He raised a brow. "Holomédico. Yeah. I thought you knew that."

"How would I know that?"

"You were there during one of my calls."

"I just got the audio. It didn't even occur to me that you could be treating patients a world away. After I saw the Knight Crew motto in your notes ..."

"Knight Crew? As in, the crime syndicate?"

She nodded. "'Metallum foris, metallum intus.' When I hacked your personal holopad, I found a text document with notes … and the words 'metallum intus.'"

"It was something I overheard once, before I came here," he explained. "Because of its translation, I thought it might be relevant." He flexed his metal fingers.

"'Metal within,'" Bel said. "Or … 'metal on the inside.'"

"Right."

"I think the Knight Crew likes it for the metaphor," Bel said. "Metal without, metal within. Durable. Impenetrable. Like a knight's armor. And hardened on the inside, too; no sympathy, no mercy. A theme. A play on the name. I thought maybe you were affiliated with them. Maybe a member of one of the wealthy crime families—someone who got targeted by a rival group or something. I thought that's why you were hiding here, why you would even own a place like this."

"You've seen too many films."

"I *wish* it were the stuff of fiction. My life has been ruined by groups like that. That's why *I've* been hiding."

He stopped to look at her. Stared, like he was analyzing her deeply. "I never even thought to ask."

"Ask what?"

"Why you're here. How you ended up this far out in the forest. The long version."

Bel hesitated. "I guess that's true."

"Tell me."

She tucked a stray bit of hair behind her ear. "My dad, and Mateo, they were working with VOLT. Trying to intercept one of the Knight Crew's operations, gather evidence, that sort of thing. The team succeeded in exposing a huge part of the network, but they wrecked their cover in the process. Mateo got away safe, but my dad … he didn't make it."

"I'm sorry …"

Bel shook her head. "I should say, Mateo got away safe *physically*. But … the Knight Crew ruined him. Manipulated records and documents. Made him a criminal. VOLT couldn't fix it, so they hid us instead, relocated us multiple times, gave us fake identities, InVisors. We tried to look as normal as possible—other than the fact that my older brother was my legal guardian, and that I've been to three schools in less than three years. But I screwed up. I exposed us. So, who knows if I'll ever be able to even *pretend* to be normal again." She scoffed. "I thought I'd at least manage to graduate high school …"

"You've missed quite a bit now," he said.

"Yeah." She sighed. "Anyway … I'm glad to know you're not Knight Crew. But, I can't believe what happened to you. Seeing it on video …"

He averted his gaze. "I've learned to live with it."

Bel hesitated, thinking about what she'd done. It seemed so much worse now that she was talking to the victim of her crime, experiencing his humanity up close. "I know what I did was … a violation. In one of the worst ways. I looked into your mind without permission." She played with the edge of her bandage. "And you weren't wrong about me. I'm used to knowing everything—or at least knowing enough about people to figure out their motives or guess what they're feeling. With you, it was different. For the first time in a long time, I had to deal with someone who didn't have their whole life accessible to me … and that scared me. A lot."

"Well, you don't have to be scared of me." He picked up a few of the medical supplies and started to gather them. Without looking at her, he added, "I was scared too. But it was wrong to blackmail you into staying here."

"It was, but—"

"As soon as you're ready, I'll help set you up to go—safely this time. I'll let your brother know the mission's off and you can figure out the best place to reunite."

"Oh. Um ..."

For two weeks, all Bel had wanted was to leave and find Mateo, and now the cyborg was not only going to *let* her go, without consequence, he would actually help her do it. But things were different now. Before tonight, she hadn't known exactly what the cyborg had been through, why he'd ended up here or how he'd suffered along the way. She hadn't even considered how he might have been hurting, what the rest of his side of the story might have looked like. If she left, she'd never find out.

"Now that you've been awake a while," said the cyborg, "and shown you can carry a conversation, it's safe for you to go to sleep—if you want. Your pupils look okay, and except for the gaping leg wound, I think you can walk normally. Both good signs. So, I'll let you get some rest."

As he reached down to pick up the rest of the first aid supplies, with his sleeves still pushed up, Bel noticed that the wires in his forearm were torn and detached in a few places.

"What happened?" she asked.

He glanced at the arm. "Oh. That's no big deal. The last drone tried to come for me after I shot its trank discharge. It got me with the propellers before I was able to completely kill the motor."

"That doesn't affect the function of your arm?"

"Just the sensory function, which is mediocre on a good day. No different than usual."

"Let me fix it."

"It's fine. Seriously."

He turned to leave but she grabbed him by the elbow. "Please?"

He brought her soldering equipment, which he'd kept in his office, and set it up on one of the end tables. "Guess I shouldn't be surprised that this is yours too, and not your brother's."

She examined his wounded arm, an intricate mechanism, although raw and unmasked. She turned it, taking in the details: ossteel bones, hydraulic actuators, graphene-rubber composite tendons, wires running through like capillaries, some type of veining system, synthetic muscles, a flexible hinge at the elbow, shiny plating …

She touched the tip of the butane iron to two tips of exposed wire to heat them, then brought in the solder to bind them together. She cleaned the iron and repeated the process for another broken wire.

"I would've just left it," he said.

The iron sizzled with each repair.

"I'm sure you would have," said Bel. "But you don't have to deal with everything alone, you know." She let up for a second to melt more solder.

"After what happened to me, can you blame me for not wanting to trust anyone? I mean, look at me." He held up his robotic hand in demonstration.

Tentatively, Bel touched her fingers to his. "Can you … feel that?"

He shook his head. "Not really. Barely."

Awkwardly, Bel withdrew her hand. After a few more wires, she finished and turned off the iron and tucked the wire bundle back down into the arm.

"You don't look so bad." She took a cloth and wiped off excess solder from the surrounding metal.

He scoffed. "Thanks."

He evaluated the repaired forearm, fiddling with the wires inside, tucking them further in as if they had anywhere else to go. Once he seemed satisfied that they wouldn't fall out, he left them, then rubbed his non-metal wrist.

"Why do you do that?" Bel asked, nodding at his movement. She must have seen him do it a dozen times by now.

The cyborg glanced down. "Shooting pains. Electrical impulses or something, I don't know. It's been happening since the beginning. Since they … rewired my insides, or whatever."

Bel reached for him and took his wrist in one palm, then pressed her free fingers gently to his skin. She made small circles as she'd seen him do. "I thought it was hard not to have control over being myself—even just in name—but it must be a lot harder not to be yourself physically."

He looked down at her fingers. "I might not have known I was any different inside, if it hadn't been for the explosion and the fire. Except for the exposed parts, the rest of me feels pretty normal."

"Yeah?"

He nodded. "Just little things are off; things that wouldn't make much difference to anyone else."

She continued making circles on his wrist. "Like what?"

"Like … my eyesight is a little better than I remember. The texture of my hair's a little less coarse. I don't have as many marks on my skin—freckles, moles. Whatever they did to me—if they broke me down and reconstructed me or who knows—it was thorough. I do still have *most* of my original marks. My skin can still be wounded and heal—unless it's severely damaged, like my face, and then it has a strange, temporary sealing effect. I can even eat and digest, but I don't have to."

"You don't have to eat," she said. It was kind of a question, but not a question either. She'd never seen him eat, and Delessio had confirmed that no one had tried in months.

"The battery gives me all the energy I need. And food, well … it doesn't really taste like anything to me. Kind of makes me sick, to be honest."

"That must be … strange. Awful." She shook her head, still holding his wrist. She let up the pressure but didn't let go yet. "Does that feel any better?"

"Actually, I probably should have mentioned that the pains come and go. It hasn't hurt since you started." One corner of his mouth quirked up.

She released him. "Oh …"

"Sorry. I guess I … didn't want you to stop." He shoved both hands into his sweatshirt pocket. "But I didn't just say that."

A flush of heat crept over her skin. "Right … of course not."

"It's easier if I just resent you for being here—even though I'm the one who made you stay. And, anyway, I'm sure you'll want to leave again soon. Your brother must be dying to see you."

She cleared her throat and readjusted her position on the couch. "Look … whatever the circumstances, we made a deal. I want to help you get the answers you need. I want to stay. That is, if you'll let me. I—" She wrinkled her brow and touched her bandaged thigh, then looked at the cyborg.

"What's wrong?" he asked.

Slack-jawed, she untucked the bandage and peered at the wound. "You … How did you …"

Bel wasn't looking at a bloody gash. She was looking at a partially healed, pink scar. She snatched the ointment from the table and read the label.

Sanaflamm
Ointment USP, 8%
For dermatologic use only

"This stuff never made it to the general public," she said. "I remember reading about it. Vivorex was working on it, but …"

She stared deeply into his face. The same dark skin, the same Afro-Latin features.

The cyborg was clearly a wealthy young man, someone with enough money to be important. Apparently not a criminal. But she hadn't heard anything about anyone like that on the news. People should be looking for him.

Except people wouldn't look for someone they believed to be dead.

She remembered the panopt with the In Memoriam. Elodie Acero. Head of Vivorex. Developer of Sanaflamm. Two years since her death. Her son's suicide a year later.

"What do I call you?" Mateo had asked him.

"You can call me Mister Steele."

The coat of arms flashed in her mind. An armored knight. Except the family's name was not indicated by the knight himself, but rather what he wore … The *metal* of his suit.

The cyborg had told her his name that first day—the Spanish word for "steel" was *acero.*

"You're Elodie's son," she said. "You're Andro Acero."

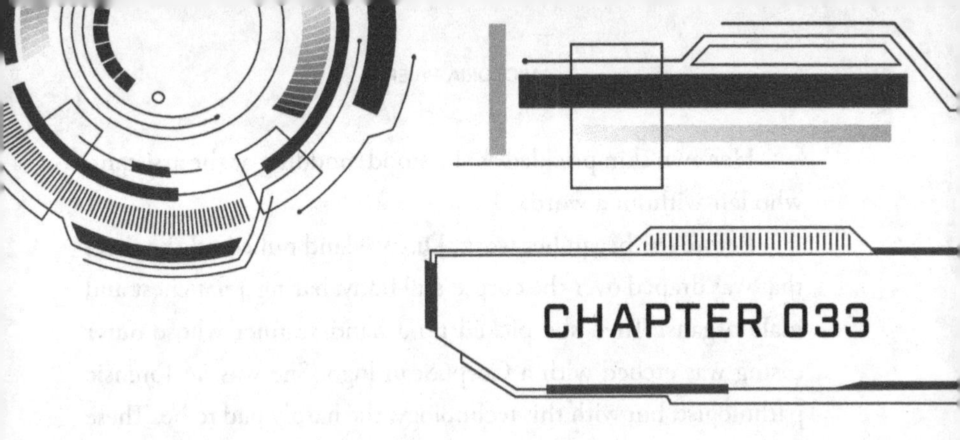

DR. ELISABETH WAYLAND STRUGGLED to keep her eyes open. The clock at the top corner of her holoscreen changed from 4:59 a.m. to 5:00 a.m., perfectly timed with a deep yawn. Even after six months, she still hadn't gotten used to the new schedule.

She tucked an auburn strand of hair behind her ear and looked up from her holoscreen as one of the assistants wheeled in another body—every hair shaved off the skin, as usual. It was supposed to be for sanitary purposes—that's what the lab policy stated anyway. But it certainly didn't hurt that it made the bodies more difficult to identify, should there ever be an unlikely breach of the database that held all their photographic and video documentation.

Not that bringing them in here was *wrong*, of course. It was a gray area, sure, but the Immortality Projects maintained that it was a much greater sin to waste a human life. For those who spent their living, waking hours doing harm or participating in activities detrimental to their health, it was better that they should serve the greater good. It was better that the marvel of the human body be studied in every capacity, not only for medicine but to learn of its true potential—and to replicate and enhance that potential as quickly as possible.

Her own skin prickled as she stood, nodding at the assistant, who left without a word.

Before she began her work, Dr. Wayland pulled off the sheet that was draped over the corpse-still body, baring a flat chest and male organs. Then she picked up a hand scanner whose outer casing was etched with a CorpuScan logo. She was no forensic pathologist, but with this technology, she hardly had to be. These scanners could parse just about any detail related to the human body and spit out the numbers in less than a minute.

The scanner beeped as Dr. Wayland moved it over the body, beginning with the feet, then moving to the legs, pelvic area, abdominal cavity, chest cavity, and head.

A pause while it analyzed the data.

GENERAL
Biological sex: male
Racial Origins: 86% Europe West, 12% Iberian Peninsula, 2% Other Regions
Age: 24 years, 2 months, 3.4 days
Weight: 187.6 lbs
Height: 5 ft 11 in
BMI: 26.2

Dr. Wayland scrolled through several more categories and lines of grossly detailed information that included bone density, blood volume, skin type, hydration level, muscle mass, body fat percentage, and even which hand was dominant. Internal systems contents analysis (ISCA) came up negative for amphetamines and opiates, positive for cannabinoids and trace amounts of cocaine. All results culminated in a final analysis.

PHYSICAL STATUS
Consciousness: 0%
12 hours deceased
DETERMINED CAUSE OF DEATH
Pulmonary embolism

Dr. Wayland repeated the same process again—part of her new orders, along with the new, earlier schedule—and received the same results, and transmitted the data to her holoscreen and exchanged the first scanner for a second. This scanner did not have any markings on its exterior, as it was never used outside of this laboratory. She scanned using the same method, however, and most of the results were the same, except for two.

CHEMICAL
Other: positive
PHYSICAL STATUS
Consciousness: 18%

"You're one lucky bastard," she said to the body, transmitting the new data. It was pointless to talk to the source units, of course, but it made these sleepy shifts a bit less lonely. Some of the bodies came in registering "forty-eight hours deceased" on CorpuScan, but "consciousness two percent" on the lab's private scanner. She couldn't imagine how hungry they must be. After all, no one fed the dead—or at least those who *appeared* to be dead. "Don't worry … we'll pump some fluids into you pretty quickly here." She went back to her holoscreen, where a frame popped up comparing results from both scanners. She typed a quick report and marked the transaction as "acceptable."

As she pulled open a second frame to begin preparing the

body for assignment, the elevator dinged on the other side of the doors, muffled and a bit distant.

Her shoulders tensed. These constant visits were becoming a nuisance, and she never knew when they would occur. But it was her own fault. If it hadn't been for her oversight, they wouldn't be necessary.

A few seconds later, the doors swung open and a man entered.

Dr. Wayland stood to greet him. "Mr. Acero."

Soto Acero glanced at the body.

"I'm just barely finishing up the scans," Dr. Wayland explained, taking her seat again in front of the holoscreen.

"Everything coming up favorable?" Soto asked.

"Looks like it," Dr. Wayland replied. She gestured at the frames. "CorpuScan reads cause of death like a pulmonary embolism, but our scanner picks up the falsifier 'other' chemical and registers the body as living. Consciousness reads above five percent but below twenty-five."

"Excellent."

Dr. Wayland nodded and continued working while Soto looked over the body. He didn't like her to waste time even if he was there distracting her.

She synced all the information and waited for the system to bring up assignment needs.

PROJECT CRATIS
Source Units Needed: 2
PROJECT EXEMPLUM
Source Units Needed: 3
PROJECT MACHINA
Source Units Needed: N/A

PROJECT MENDACIUM
Source Units Needed: 7
PROJECT METO
Source Units Needed: 2
PROJECT ITERUM
Source Units Needed: 0

The scanner beeped behind her. Soto didn't always check her work for her, but when he did, she found herself clenching her jaw until he left.

She looked over the numbers. Project Mendacium needed source units the most, but this body had already undergone a falsifier—an "assigned" unit rather than a volunteer—otherwise it wouldn't have registered the way it did on the scanners, which could alter the data when testing the efficacy of new and in-development falsifiers. With that in mind, and having already noted that this body had a very nice bone structure that would be excellent for the ossteel modeling software to analyze, she selected Project Exemplum.

ASSIGNED OR VOLUNTEERED?

Dr. Wayland tapped "assigned," which resulted in the body's identification number: A819

"How many times did you scan with the CorpuScan device?" Soto asked.

Dr. Wayland turned in her chair warily. "Twice …"

"I'm getting a different reading this time. CorpuScan consciousness reads one point four percent."

Furrowing her brow, Dr. Wayland came to take a look. The data on the scanner did indeed read 1.4 percent.

Soto looked over at the holoscreen. "You were going to assign him to Project Exemplum."

"I was. The techs over there told me they were looking for strong specimens, and since it would be redundant to place him in Mendacium, I thought—"

"Do you want a repeat of the last incident?" Soto barked. "A body still registering any percent 'conscious' to a CorpuScan device—even at one point four percent—is at a much greater risk for waking during procedures. You should know better by now."

"I'm sorry, Mr. Acero. I promise I'll be more thorough next time."

Soto narrowed his eyes. "If you screw up again there won't be a next time. Remember that. I've been gracious with you. Millions of dollars in lost units and a compromised location. I've prioritized your brilliance over my own assets, and I better not regret it."

"Yes, Mr. Acero."

She felt a sense of dread seep through her limbs. There had been a good chance that this particular slip would have gone without consequence, especially with the new monitoring procedures in place in the Project Iterum division. But of course Soto had to be here now to catch this. With Dr. Wayland's luck, she'd have twice as many random visits from him now, and she'd have to scan every body twenty times before he'd be satisfied.

"Assign the unit to Project Meto," said Soto. "As you can see from the numbers, we could use the organs and tissues over there. Tissues, especially."

"Oh?"

Soto gave a curt nod. "I'm having the Meto techs focus more closely on external sensation. Tactiperone has been losing effectiveness if the subcutaneous tissue is exposed or damaged. We can't have field units unable to sense things every time they get a cut."

"Right. Of course."

"The self-sealing effect has held up, though," he added. "Better than ever in this last batch. Edges are closing up within seconds. Our units are superhuman."

Dr. Wayland forced a smile and selected Project Meto from the list to reassign the current source unit, giving the body a new number. Soto looked over her shoulder as she did it, as though her past mistakes suddenly made her incapable of tapping a holoscreen correctly.

The odds that something like last time would happen again were incredibly low. It could only have had to do with her own experiment, a risk she'd taken in hopes that she might be able to develop an antidote to the falsifiers.

Falsifiers would essentially render someone cataleptic, and simultaneously mask the signals that might alert CorpuScan to any active brainwaves or otherwise undetectable breathing, meanwhile mimicking the presence of specific toxins (depending on the type of falsifier and its mendacium blend).

If there was a market—albeit a black one—for drugs that could make a murder look like a suicide, then surely there was a market for a drug that could reverse its effects, and she'd hoped to impress Soto with her initiative. But after testing the antidote on a small batch of bodies—mostly those that had been intended for organ modeling, during a time when that department already had too many specimens—she'd only been able to rouse *one* of them to a reasonable level of consciousness, and the CorpuScan data was still coming out all wrong. So, she'd given the young man a serum to quell his consciousness back to an unreadable state and then sent the body off to Project Iterum, which had been in dire need of new units at the time. She'd never imagined it would lead to the destruction of half the Iterum division. But it seemed that any level of source unit consciousness could be a sufficient stimulant.

To this day, even though she knew it was risky, she still kept several units in a separate location, looked after by a small team she'd put together to help with the work and do further research on other potential anomalies, thinking that she might redeem herself if she ever managed to develop something noteworthy. Unfortunately, she barely had the time to keep up with her current assignments, let alone pursue additional feats with what she had once optimistically called Project Inversa.

"Also," said Soto, "I'll need you to stay a little longer this morning. A special specimen is going to arrive around 11:30. Make sure it goes through Project Exemplum first for thorough modeling, then send it to Iterum—no exceptions.

Dr. Wayland nodded and tried to steady her hands, which had begun to tremble.

A special specimen. That meant Soto had targeted that person for a specific reason. Usually, the bodies were just those of criminals or derelicts, people the world was better off without, whose organic components could serve a greater good. That's what Dr. Wayland told herself anyway. It was for the cause of groundbreaking, world-changing science. But once in a while, Soto would bring in a body that meant something. It was personal, part of some more sinister plan. She could see it in his eyes. She just couldn't figure out how he could be so menacing when he wasn't even willing to kill someone directly. That was part of a personal rule he had or something. All life, no matter how ill-lived, was sacred, and couldn't be taken without going through the proper protocol of analyzing and taking advantage of its full usefulness.

"And if there are any processing issues," Soto added, "the next person who rolls in here on an assessment table will be you."

CHAPTER 034

"AND CHECK THIS OUT ..." said Bel's holomorphic head, speaking to Mateo from his holopad. Her head faded out, and then her whole body appeared three-dimensionally, a tiny, projected version of herself standing on the holopad screen.

Mateo had heard that this tech was in development—something to do with advanced fish-eye lenses that could see in a hemispherical way, paired with software that could interpret and re-render the image of a person or an object as intended—and as usual, the cyborg managed to possess it ahead of everyone else.

"There's a little tab on the side when you're on a call. It's called 'fill mode,'" she told him. "Your device has it too."

That made sense, considering where he'd gotten the thing.

Andro Acero? Mateo still couldn't believe it. Although everything was starting to make more sense now. The money, the connection to Vivorex, the biotechnical implications of a human body with ossteel bones inside.

"You're a little too spry for someone who's got a concussion," Mateo told his sister. "Which I'm still mad at you for, by the way."

"I know. I'm sorry ..." Bel bent down to pick up her holopad off the floor—the requirement for fill mode to be able to capture a full body—and tapped to convert her likeness back to a regular holomorphic headshot.

Mateo sat down on the apartment couch and held the holopad on his lap. "So, he's just going to *let* you talk to me now?"

"It's kind of a long story," said Bel. "But I'm safe. Everything's okay—for both of us."

"What's that supposed to mean?"

"I can leave whenever I want, and he won't tell anyone about us. You can drop everything you're doing. We can go anywhere."

"Oh …" Mateo chewed the inside of his cheek. A week ago, he would have been relieved. Now, though, he'd begun to feel responsible for all of this somehow. He'd gotten so deep into the assignment. He was so close to getting answers.

Bel climbed into her bed and smiled. "But you don't want to quit …"

Mateo lowered his voice conspiratorially, regardless of the fact that he was alone. "The thing is … I think there might be a chance that the syndicates, and whatever's going on in the background at Vivorex, are connected. I think whoever's running that project might be working with the Knight Crew. Or maybe the Knight Crew is financing it, or benefiting from it somehow."

Bel paused and stared at him. "'*Metallum intus.*'"

Metallum foris, metallum intus. Yes. Mateo was familiar with it. Every time the news showed those bastards' faces, they plastered that logo and that motto right beside them. "What about it?"

"That was one of the clues Andro had listed. He's got detailed notes, research, even video memories."

"Video memories?"

"Something in his body keeps memories as footage. Based on that, there was a lab with dozens of other bodies like his, all hooked up to monitors. There was big imaging equipment, lots of advanced tech. Probably twenty-four-seven staffing, based on the time of night he woke and how many techs he saw. He's got street names and a general location, but whatever was there before is gone now. They must have relocated after the explosion because of the attention it would have drawn."

"Damn …"

"Anyway, what makes you think there's a connection to the syndicate?"

"I've been going through Veronika Mandersloot's old emails and looking at all the file attachments, several of which were purchase orders with vaguely named companies: Bay Supply Co., SF Distributors, Kirkpatrick Inc. A lot of the items on them were just run-of-the-mill lab supplies—syringes, antiseptics, disposable gloves. Pretty decent coverups, from what I could see. But then I found another set of purchase orders—a year's worth—all to a company called Cinco Industries."

"Cinco Industries," Bel repeated. "Why does that sound familiar?"

"From when I was working with Dad, with VOLT, and we were looking into Knight Crew shipments. The crew was targeting warehouses all over the Bay Area trying to steal vidrinium from other traffickers and hide it under a fake company. Cinco Industries. And now, there are only a handful of buildings registered to it that I still have to investigate before I will very likely know *exactly* where to start digging for the next round of information on Project Iterum."

"So what I'm hearing is that this has become personal."

Mateo sighed and scrubbed his hands over his face. "Apparently it has."

"I'm glad you still want to do it. That's what I wanted to hear."

"'Wanted to hear'? Don't tell me you're making friends with that guy. Yeah, he's got money, but he still—"

"He still saved my life," said Bel.

Sure, Mateo thought, but that didn't completely absolve him of all the coercion and intimidation. Although a picture was beginning to form in Mateo's mind, now that he had a name to go with the cyborg's face. Suddenly the guy keeping his sister wasn't just some strange monster; now he was a boy with a traumatic past, a victim of something bigger that might be affecting others.

"And I'm well aware," Bel added, "of your aversion to the idea of making friends."

"You're really okay over there? We're both safe?"

She nodded. "Trust me."

"Last time I did that, we walked into *this* whole mess."

"A 'whole mess' that you don't really seem to want to tear yourself away from."

He rubbed the back of his neck. "I guess I don't."

"Then don't."

"Fine. But now that you're allowed to help, I'll need all hands on deck."

"Great. Count me in. I'll be in touch as soon as I've got anything."

"Sounds good. Love you."

"Love you too."

Her head disappeared and the holoscreen faded to black. He slipped the device into his back pocket and stared out the window. The world bustled below him, hundreds of people back and forth between buildings, working, sightseeing.

Even though he and Bel weren't completely out of the woods yet—Bel not at all, technically speaking, what with the

Submundo's national forest location—he couldn't deny that he longed to be out in the midst of civilization, and not only watching, alone, from a distance. For the past two years and nine and a half months, he'd survived on the lie that he didn't need anyone, other than Bel, and that he was content to survive on the basic human necessities as long as it kept them safely hidden. But he was only human. He wanted to walk without looking over his shoulder. He wanted to smell the asphalt and the fog and the food trucks. He wanted to stand on the pier and feel dominated by the sheer volume of water in front of him. He wanted to go get a coffee.

Mateo mentally conjured the view of his route to The Circuit, during which he'd passed Wholly Ground, right on the corner before crossing the street. He couldn't do *everything* he wished he could—not yet, anyway—but he could do the last one. It was only three blocks. It was a step toward taking back a bit of himself.

Wholly Ground was an automated marvel, similar to the Submundo's kitchen, although more simplified. Two rows of five holokiosks took orders, while customers waited in line to use them. A conveyor countertop delivered orders from the kitchen, which was a self-sustained factory that brewed and blended with unprecedented precision. Behind large sheets of glass, customers could view some of the process, as cups dropped into moving holders and were shot off to different filling stations, receiving twelve ounces of this, a shot of that, a decoration of cream or foam. Mateo inhaled the warm scent of roasting beans and took his place in line.

Despite the metal and glass that made up the majority of the modern space, there were touches of chestnut throughout, complementing the earthy vibes of the coffee itself, along with a few sections of living greenery wall.

When Mateo's turn came, he selected an Americano, venti, and tapped through to pay. Prior to payment, the screen prompted him to enter a name for the order. Thinking of his conversation with that girl the other day at The Circuit, he typed GAEL, then scanned the digibank.

Thanks, Mr. Steele.

He went to the "kitchen" viewing window. When his cup dropped into place, a small robot arm popped up and rapidly printed his name onto the side. He followed the rest of the process all the way to the end, where a soft, artificial voice said, "Gael, your order is ready."

Mateo picked up the coffee and took a sip, relishing the warmth in his mouth. How long had it been since he'd had anything but instant coffee from a dying, old pot? He couldn't even remember. Years.

As he turned to exit, however, he tensed at the woman who stood directly before him.

She nodded at his cup. "Nice name you've got there."

This time, her eyeshadow was some kind of dark pinkish color (magenta?), and her shaped eyeliner made her look like a very lovely cat—which was appropriate (because, Kat). Her hair was French-braided up one side of her scalp, running in a curve over her three-times-pierced ear.

The universe really had a twisted sense of humor.

"Let me guess," she said. "Gael ... *Mendivel?*"

He did his best to play along. "'Database Administrator at Blair Investments.'"

"I thought we decided on 'Blaise' Investments."

"Uh … sure. Whatever you say." He cleared his throat. "Are you, um … following me?"

Kat smiled sardonically. "As much as I'd love to spend my days traipsing after awkward strangers who don't seem to want to talk to me … No, I'm afraid not. I work just down the street. This is my nearest Wholly Ground and, to be honest, I practically live here. The odds of you running into me on any given day at this place are high." She patted his shoulder. "Sorry to put a pin in your balloon."

The AI barista voice said, "Kat, your order is ready" and delivered another cup, along with a blueberry scone, on the belt.

Kat took her items. "Well, *Gael*"—she rolled her eyes with dramatic flair—"it was nice to see you again. Good luck on all your financial endeavors." She started to weave through the mass of people.

Bel's voice murmured through Mateo's head. *I'm well aware of your aversion to the idea of making friends.*

His sister had been in good spirits, safe and unharmed. Her usual mouthy self. Could it really be true that they didn't have the threat of discovery hanging over their heads anymore? At least as far as the cyborg was concerned? It wasn't enough to let Mateo lower his guard completely, but it gave him the guts to speak up.

"Come on, don't be like that." Mateo followed Kat, raising his cup so as not to accidentally crush it against another customer and spill it everywhere.

"Like what?" Kat barely turned her head to acknowledge him.

"Like … offended that I like my privacy."

"You must not like it *that* much"—she moved out to the

sidewalk with Mateo right behind—"or you wouldn't still be talking to me."

He held the door for the next three customers while she waited with crossed arms, coffee held against her elbow.

"We all have our secrets." He released the door. "Sometimes we don't even *want* to keep them, we just … have to."

"And you think your secrets are better than everyone else's?"

He raised his eyebrows thoughtfully, then took a sip from his cup. "Yeah. Kind of."

"You're unbelievable." She shook her head and turned to walk away.

Mateo groaned and caught up to her, then moved to block her path. "Look," he said, as she stopped and held her cup in both hands, tapping the paper with acrylic rainbow nails. "Honestly, in another life … if I wasn't dealing with the things I'm dealing with … I would have asked for your Atmo already. I just want you to know that."

"So, you're just going to let your circumstances control you."

"Sometimes that's the only choice."

"Okay." She smiled and pushed past him.

Once again, he fell into step with her. "What does that mean?"

"It means 'okay.' I accept your choice to live in fear."

"Caution isn't the same thing as fear."

"It can be."

"I'm not afraid. I'm just … I'm …" He groaned. "It's not that simple."

"Okay."

"Stop that."

"Stop agreeing with you?"

"You're not agreeing. You're patronizing me."

She stopped suddenly and looked at him with an intense stare. "Do something about it, then."

"What do you want me to do?"

She looked him up and down and cocked her head. "Come with me."

"Where?"

"To my cosmetics studio."

"Why?"

"The appointment-scheduling software hasn't been working right for weeks now and all the cosmetologists are having to input everything into the calendar manually—like pioneers." She shrugged. "After what you did for me at The Circuit, I figure you could probably help. That way you can keep following me, but you can feel less guilty about it … because it's just business, right? My boss will even pay you for it."

Mateo chewed the inside of his cheek. Was Bel right? Was he paranoid beyond reason? Being forced into the Los Padres had certainly made him feel vindicated in his paranoia, as had the whole debacle after breaking into the Submundo. But all of that had also uncovered—or at least *begun* to uncover—secrets that needed to see the light of day. So maybe not all risks were in vain. Maybe not all risks were that risky.

He looked at Kat, with her bold style and her bright, expectant gaze, and finally said, "Alright."

He followed her for two blocks. Neither of them said anything the entire time. Mateo gazed up warily at the surrounding panopts, which mostly played music videos or ads for clothing stores and beauty products, with the occasional break for news.

Kat went straight to a storefront with **KOSMETIKOS** in neon over the entrance and stepped inside. A girl with pink hair greeted her.

"Katherine. Nice of you to join us."

"I'm only a few minutes late." Kat slipped off her pleather jacket. Underneath, she wore a sleeveless, silky blouse in a dark plum color, accented by a long gold necklace with an elephant charm on it.

The other girl threw a glance in Mateo's direction. "And you picked up a stray?"

"Well," said Kat, "I did *name* him, so he's not really a stray now. This is 'Gael from Blaise Investments' and he's going to fix our scheduling system."

Mateo nodded his greeting, which the girl met with an indifferent expression before Kat led him to her workstation, where a digital nameplate glowed at the corner of her mirror.

KAT SEOK, SENIOR COSMETOLOGIST

"Wow," said Mateo. "*Senior* cosmetologist."

Kat scoffed as she straightened a few tools on her workstation table and pressed a touch panel that warmed up all her docked hair irons simultaneously. "Who's patronizing who now?"

He glanced around. The interior design was a blend of chic industrial with touches of advanced tech. Exposed brick walls and corrugated metal siding on counters and stations. Smart mirrors and wireless hair appliances and holographic menus showing all the latest look books. The same Kosmetikos logo from the outside of the studio had been duplicated in neon on the back wall.

Below the neon sign hung a series of holographic photos

featuring celebrity faces. Popular actors and athletes, musicians and politicians. The kind of photos that a lot of restaurants and dry cleaners and other businesses displayed so they could show off which famous people had been there and partaken of the local products and services. It was kind of a small studio—and not that well located—to be able to claim it had seen so many famous people up close, but Mateo figured it must have been some well-kept secret.

"So, you work here full time?" said Mateo.

"Nine to five, Tuesday through Saturday. Extended hours during holiday seasons when everyone wants to be all done up for parties and galas and whatnot. Super glamorous life, right?"

Mateo picked up a container of reddish eyeshadow from the station table and sniffed it.

"It's made from blood oranges," she said. "From a special line that only uses plant pigments."

"Fascinating …" He put the lid back on and set it down.

She put on an apron, tying the string behind her waist. "Might be a little too granola for some people, but I like it. Anyway, now that I'm set up, let me show you our malfunctioning system."

Back at the main desk, the girl with pink hair had left, now leading a client to her chair. A large holoscreen floated above the desktop with an open calendar application. Kat flicked over to a scheduling system and put a hand on her hip. "There you go. As you can see, the appointments are being received through our website and app, but they won't register in our appointment book. Think you can get it to work right?"

Mateo tapped a couple of icons. "Yeah, I think so. I might need to delete the whole thing and reinstall, if that's okay. I'll back up the data first, though."

"Whatever it takes," said Kat. "I'll be right over there if you have more questions."

Before Mateo went to his task with the system, he also opened up his own holopad, so he could look over his research while he backed up the studio's data before reinstalling.

In between all this, Kat saw several clients. Mateo couldn't help spending a few seconds here and there to watch her process, the delicate way she stroked someone's eyelids with a brush, or the way she pressed her lips together when she concentrated on a manicure design, or even how she deftly tidied up the station, tossing brushes and blenders into a container of cleaning solution and setting out new ones.

Meanwhile, a panopt droned in the background, its audio muffled through the studio's sheet glass window but still managing to filter into Mateo's ears, and he found himself half-listening to it out of habit.

Celebrity boxer Aidan Liota reveals he and longtime girlfriend Bretta Omo secretly got married last year in the Riviera Maya

Largest wildfire in all Six Californias explodes as hot weather threatens new blazes

Try DiMaggio's Flavor Explosion and taste the difference for yourself

As Mateo set up the program to reinstall, another client came in asking for very specific facial contouring. She pulled up holoscreen photos of model-turned-actress Renata Vu for reference, a few different angles with different lighting.

Kat analyzed the photos. "You got it."

It took about half an hour, and Mateo found himself

watching for longer stretches this time, fascinated by the way shadows and highlights could change the entire look of a person's bone structure. By the time Kat was done, the client's face compared side by side with one of the photos was uncannily similar.

"All you need now is a pair of green contacts and you're all set." Kat flicked her brush like a magic wand.

The girl thanked her and offered a generous tip before calling up one of her friends on the way out.

"You get those kinds of requests a lot?" Mateo asked. But before Kat could answer, his eyes fell to the celebrity photos on the back wall. It suddenly occurred to him that they didn't look like traditional celebrity headshots, which might come from various sources; they all had the same background—the same dark cloth—and studio lighting. "Wait a second ... Are those not ..."

Kat shook her head. "Nope. Those are *not* really celebrities." She grinned. "It's actually sort of a joke we have going on around here. Most people who come in on a regular basis know about it. A parody—but also sort of a gallery of our art. We have a holographic photo booth set up in the back, although we only do pictures if it's a celebrity face we haven't already recreated."

A quick scan of the images confirmed this. Renata Vu was already on the wall.

Kat's pink-haired co-worker walked past and scoffed. "That's not even the half of what Kat can do. Paparazzi have photographed multiple 'celebrities' that were actually clients of ours." She pulled her personal holopad out of her apron pocket and opened the holoscreen, navigating to an older issue of *People* magazine and landing on an entire spread of paparazzi photos. One of them showed soccer legend Ronan Oachs coming out of a McDonald's. "That's actually some guy named Eldon. Kat's handiwork."

When Mateo looked to Kat for confirmation, Kat gave a little bow with a hand flourish.

Her co-worker turned off the screen and grabbed a broom to sweep up the hair around her own workstation.

Mateo shook his head and went back to the installation. "You're really talented, but … I guess I just don't understand why anyone would want to be someone else if they didn't have to. People don't realize what a privilege it is to walk around being yourself."

Atmo platform disables accounts of NYU team looking into political ad targeting said the panopt outside.

"Maybe if you're a tall, dark, handsome guy in his twenties with the ability to fix holopad errors in a couple of taps. But for some people, being themselves all the time, completely unfiltered, would be hard. Some people don't feel worthy of being looked at in their natural state."

"And you help cover them up? Wait—did you just say you think I'm 'handsome'?"

"I *embellish* them," she corrected. "And I believe I also used the words 'maybe' and 'if.' Plus, you're not that tall, so really the accuracy of the whole sentence is questionable."

Mateo frowned.

The installation still had a couple of minutes left, so Mateo took the opportunity to keep working on Andro's case.

He stared at a map he'd pulled up, which noted every building in the city registered to Cinco Industries. He'd already marked off the ones he'd investigated in person, a few of which were empty while the others held actual practical equipment and supplies, probably left over from whoever had used those buildings before. It wouldn't be farfetched to imagine the Knight Crew buying up buildings they'd never even touched, holding onto them until they needed them. He looked at the overwhelming number of locations and considered how he might narrow them down, but the information was mentally exhausting.

To give his mind a break from that particular set of information, he did a quick search on Andro Acero, just to re-familiarize himself with the details of his history.

Andrónico Vicente Acero
Born: October 18, 2067
Died: June 9, 2086
Location: Cupertino, Dorado, U.S.
Education: Himmerholt Preparatory Academy
Parent(s): Elodie Acero
Associations: Vivorex Labs

Mateo verified that Andro Acero had, allegedly, overdosed at a club called Paragon almost one year ago. He scanned the news pieces, trying to extract some sense of logic from the details. The coroner's CorpuScan report had checked out. Then it had been cremation, followed by a small family-only funerary service. No photos of the body or the service, "out of respect for the Acero family's privacy during this grievous period." Soto Acero, Andro's uncle, had supposedly given the eulogy. By all accounts, Andro was dead. And yet …

"I don't want to sound cliché," Kat added, "but you look like you just saw a ghost. Like, blood drained from your face, glossed-over look in your eyes, the whole shebang. You need some water or something?"

Mateo took a deep breath and combed his fingers through his hair. "You're not far off with that ghost thing."

She handed him an aluminum bottle of water, which he accepted, chugging it like it could wash down the bad taste his mouth seemed to have acquired.

What kind of sinister plot was Andro Acero a part of? And if someone had wanted to get rid of him, why not just have him killed? Why fill him with wires and metal? Mateo's stomach churned at the thought. Sure, the guy had blackmailed him into helping with this, but he wasn't much older than Bel. So young, and already his life had been completely destroyed. And for what?

A lab with dozens of other bodies like his, all hooked up to monitors.

Big imaging equipment, lots of advanced tech.

Twenty-four-seven staffing,

Mateo shook his head. This was big. Run by incredibly powerful people, with ridiculous amounts of money, who had the means to relocate what was likely billions of dollars' worth of equipment and probably mostly non-consenting test subjects at a moment's notice without batting an eye. And the electrical energy alone that would have been required to operate something like that ...

Mateo gasped. *That's it!*

Kat eyed him suspiciously but kept twisting sections of her next client's hair into swirls and pinning them up.

A ding told Mateo the installation was complete. With a sincere effort to pull himself away from testing his bright idea, he tapped a couple of settings to link the studio's backed-up data, and suddenly all the missing appointments flooded into the slots in the interface.

"Did you fix it?" Kat asked.

"Looks like it," said Mateo.

She excused herself from the client for a moment to come take a look. "Awesome. Thank you. What do we owe you?"

"Don't worry about it." Already with his mind back on the electrical energy component of his search for Project Iterum, Mateo tapped on his holopad and typed in a few commands to pull up the city's live power grid. From here, he could compare the amount of electrical power that every building was using at any given moment. He could even tap into its historical data to compare all the Cinco Industries buildings' energy usage.

"You sure?" said Kat.

Eyes still glued to his holoscreen, he robotically replied, "Yeah. It was nothing."

As he'd suspected, the buildings he'd already visited were using minimal to no energy—what with empty shelves or supplies just sitting there. And as he'd suspected, there were only a handful of them using large amounts of energy. Three, to be exact—with one far outranking the other two.

"Gotcha," he whispered.

Kat raised an eyebrow. "'Gotcha'?"

"I'm really sorry." Mateo minimized the holoscreen and tucked the holopad into his jeans. "But I have to go. I can't tell you anything else. I wish I could, but—"

"No, it's fine," Kat replied. She returned to her client and inserted another hair pin and popped her fist onto her hip. "I should have expected that by now."

"Thanks for"—he glanced around, locked eyes with the client for a second, then set his gaze back on Kat and offered her a faint smile—"this."

Kat's mouth flattened into line. "No problem. Thank *you*, I guess. For fixing the scheduling."

Mateo wanted to say more, to come up with some good excuse, to make some kind of promise to see her again. But the client in her chair made the whole thing even more awkward than it already was. And Mateo, although emboldened by Bel's newfound safety, still wasn't in a position to make promises to girls he met at electronics stores—or anyone else for that matter.

"I really—"

Kat waved him off like it was no big deal, although a sense of disappointment flickered behind her eyes. "Go. Do what you need to do. It was nice ... *not* knowing you?"

He hesitated, but finally just nodded and rushed out.

Once he was out in the open crowd, he maneuvered through as quickly as possible. He'd already sent the location of the building to his watch and wanted to start navigation. Overhead, the panopts overlapped, different voices fighting for the attention of the audience below, reminding him that he needed to get somewhere more shaded so that he could ease the anxiety of wearing his own thinly veiled face in public.

Still, he couldn't keep his ears from automatically picking apart the sounds, listening for warnings, for potential dangers to his or Bel's safety, for anything useful.

Live at the Holoworld Arena on July 23: Waivelength, featuring The Cobalts and New Division Girl

Metropolitan Outfitters presents the Everywhere Bag. Compact. Convertible. Durable.

BroadwaySF presents Star Wars: A New Musical. Purchase tickets on Atmo for 10% off.

Official reports state that Dorado senator Kella Quintero has now been missing for more than 72 hours, with no clues as to her whereabouts …

Mateo stopped in his tracks, pivoting, searching for the panopt reporting the news. He found it and turned to face it.

… while the senator's publicity team has been working to keep the mystery quiet until more information is known.

The senator's headshot took up a third of the screen—that of a middle-aged, olive-skinned woman with a single streak of gray running through her brown hair—while reporters continued to speak beside it, detailing the events leading up to her disappearance, followed by the process that had determined she hadn't left by choice. The screen then transitioned to a clip of the senator speaking at a recent event.

"We need to pass this bill," she said. "These criminals are operating freely, right here in our cities. Bringing dangerous bioweapons onto our streets. Profiting from our societal vulnerabilities. We cannot allow this to continue another day."

Many speculate that Senator Quintero may have been targeted by former members of one of these crime organizations, which Quintero has been working to eradicate for almost a decade.

Mateo fought off a bout of nausea. He couldn't be sure this was connected, but the story sounded familiar. Someone important gone missing, criminal organizations' suspected involvement. The only question was, why hadn't they staged a death? Why had they let the public believe Quintero was still alive somewhere?

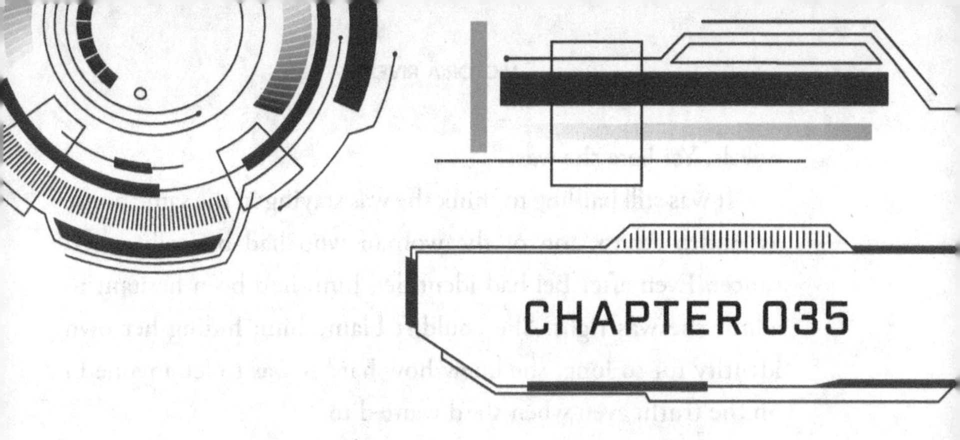

CHAPTER 035

THE BEDROOM HOLOSCREEN PLAYED an old, flickering film. One in a list of "100 Greatest Films of All Time" that Lucius had recommended—most of which were slower paced and less visually overstimulating for Bel's current condition. Despite feeling fatigued and having a mild but ongoing headache, the only other symptom she'd noticed after her head injury was that focusing seemed to be a lot more work than before. Like some odd, mental hangover. So, she'd asked for the films list on shuffle and watched whatever ended up on the enormous frame.

This one had started with a monochrome scene on a farm. A girl in a gingham dress with her hair in two braids, carrying a basket while a little black dog followed her up the path between wooden fences. She was running away from someone and trying to frantically explain the situation to her relatives, who were too busy to listen.

"Dorothy, please," said an old woman, sorting through a crate of baby chicks, "we're trying to count."

Bel lay in bed, propped up on pillows. She'd been mostly cooped up in her room for the past couple of days, recovering from her traumatic brain injury. That's how she had chosen to think about it anyway, because "mild concussion" didn't seem to warrant the kind of bedrest she'd only read about in Jane Austen novels. Yet here she was.

It was still baffling to think she was staying in the same house as Andro Acero, son of the woman who had basically cured cancer. Even after Bel had identified him, he'd been hesitant to admit she was right. She couldn't blame him; hiding her own identity for so long, she knew how hard it was to let anyone in on the truth, even when she'd wanted to.

Shortly afterward, having revealed a bit more of the truth, he'd gotten weird. Distant. Not the way he'd been before when he was a tangle of dark secrets avoiding daylight, but instead like he'd been trying to protect her from something. From having to look at him with new eyes that might compare what she knew of his former self to the man-machine hybrid in front of her, and from having to come to terms with her disappointment or something.

Onscreen, a tornado funneled in the background, kicking up dust and hay. Dorothy walked against the wind and forced her way inside the house as the door broke off and flew away. After receiving her own bump on the head—*traumatic brain injury*, Bel thought—Dorothy landed on the bed and started hallucinating. Bel couldn't help but laugh at the scene, which was clearly a screen of another film of flying objects shown through the set window, made to look like the house swirling around inside of the tornado's winds.

On her bedside table, Bel now had a holopad at her disposal, brand new and hers to use for whatever she wanted in the privacy of her room. She'd been funneling information to Mateo as fast as she could think of it—anything Andro had told her that might be of use to his mission. Andro had given his consent for this, something Bel was determined to respect from now on.

As far as she knew, Andro had been taking extra eMT shifts

and keeping himself busy. He came to check on her once in a while and insisted on bringing her very specific, nourishing meals.

"Brain food," he'd said, over a salad of kale, avocado, and mixed berries with pomegranate seeds and an açai vinaigrette. There had also been Moroccan salmon in aioli sauce with a side of asparagus, butternut squash soup garnished in herbs, and a dark chocolate tart flaked with salt. "Good fats, plenty of antioxidants and vitamins. And dessert, because I know you love dessert."

"How do you know that?"

"Delessio keeps a log of every order that goes through the kitchen."

With a sardonic tone, she'd replied, "Of course he does."

He'd poured a lot of energy into helping her recover, but he didn't seem to want to stick around. As though her knowing who he was suddenly made him want to start hiding his face again, as though she hadn't seen everything before—all his wires, and the burnt edges of his skin peeled away from his ossteel bones.

She couldn't stop thinking about the other day, though. How he'd taken her back to the Submundo and so methodically treated her wounds. The gentleness in his care. The boyish look on his face when he'd admitted his wrist was actually perfectly fine.

I guess I didn't want you to stop.

Bel replayed it in her mind as the movie played in her room, all the words and scenes from real life and fiction blending until she finally dozed off.

When she woke, the film was in color.

Bright greens and a rich, golden road.

Dorothy and a living scarecrow, who appeared to be her

traveling companion, came across a man made of tin, rusted firmly inside his own body and unable to move.

"You're perfect now," said Dorothy, once she'd oiled the tin man's joints so that he could move again.

"Perfect?" he replied. "Bang on my chest if you think I'm perfect."

His chest responded with a hollow reverberation.

"It's empty," he explained.

"No heart?"

"No heart."

Bel pictured the visible portion of Andro's metal ribcage, the brief glimpse she'd had of it when he'd been shirtless the day he rescued her. Nothing but wires and lights and metal machinery inside.

The tin man proceeded to sing a forlorn song about all the things he wished he could do if he "only had a heart."

Bel watched the scene drearily, but it wasn't lost on her. A few minutes later, she gathered her strength and went downstairs to the VR dome.

This time, Andro didn't have the windows blackened. But, this time, Bel wasn't so fast to try and figure out what he was doing.

He didn't seem busy right this second, standing there almost like he was waiting for something. She decided to try the intercom, and pressed the microphone to start it. "Hey."

Andro turned around and tapped his headset off so he could see through the VR. He didn't quite smile. "Hey."

"Um … I just wanted to …" Bel realized she hadn't thought

this far ahead. In fact, her whole thought process had been hazy. Tin men and ossteel men and virtual realities on screens. All she could think was that she wanted to be back in that lounge with him again, with the purple fire crackling.

"Everything okay?" he asked. His voice was echoey, eyes brimming with concern.

Bel didn't answer. She stared back at his image and nodded silently, forgetting he couldn't see her.

The doors parted and he glanced back at the empty dome before asking, "Do you … want to come in? I'm expecting another call any minute. But you could sit in and watch."

"Sure," said Bel, relieved to not have to explain herself when she didn't have any explanations to give. Not that she was capable of articulating at the moment, anyway.

Andro let her in and handed her a second headset. As she pulled it over her face, a whole other room took over her view. It was small—bigger than the back of an ambulance would be, she guessed, but still compact. There were four metal walls, a bed, an examination chair, a couple framed pieces of art (a waterfall, a closeup of birch tree trunks) for ambience. Andro's avatar stood before her wearing a medical mask over his nose and mouth, although underneath he seemed to look mostly himself—some "corrected" version, without any metal showing. He wore a set of navy-blue scrubs and athletic shoes, waiting as she took him in.

"Do you really need a mask?" Bel said. "I mean, since you're not actually having any physical contact with the patients?" She doubled-tapped for the menu to alter her own avatar's clothing options, selecting a set of purple scrubs.

"The illusion makes the patients more comfortable. Especially in some of these countries that suffered a lot from past pandemics."

A digital ring interrupted them, lighting the entire booth with a white flash. The name of the location appeared in the air.

Andro touched ACCEPT.

An older man, probably in his mid-sixties, entered through the virtual doors.

Andro greeted him in Spanish and introduced himself by first name only. He introduced Bel as his assistant. The man, called Castel, shook both their hands and took a seat on the medical chair.

Still speaking Spanish even to Bel—for the benefit of the patient, who didn't speak any English—Andro explained to Bel that identical booths had been installed in various cities throughout the world, by a company called Holomédico, which had also developed the VR software to match, so that patients could sit in a physical chair in a physical booth that would line up perfectly with the virtual chair in any VR location. The booths were also outfitted with scanners and projectors to scan the entire physical form of each patient *and* project the med techs into the booths with them, to give the look, feel, and comfort of a real-life interaction. Techs were volunteers who signed in and were randomly assigned a patient (paired by preferred spoken language) and then virtually connected to that location for evaluation.

Castel nodded and told them it was a great resource, although the wait times for the booths were long and he had almost thought better of trying to get in. But the wound on his hand, which had occurred during his work in construction, wasn't healing properly, and his inability to work at full capacity made it difficult to afford a doctor's visit.

With the same care Bel had seen before, Andro looked over the man's hand, asked him a few questions, and determined that there was a circulation problem, which was affecting his ability to heal. He recommended elevating the hand when not at work, drinking plenty of water, and applying an antibiotic ointment that could be found at most drugstores.

After Andro had treated a few patients in a row, Bel gathered from the whole process that this kind of treatment was inherently limited. There was no administering of medicines, no bandaging or stitching. The "e" in eMT was for "electronic," not "emergency," and most patients were looking for help with basic illnesses or injuries. The most Andro could do from this distance was observe, ask questions, and offer advice. His knowledge of the various medical facilities in different cities was impressive, though, as was his ability to offer suggestions as to where patients might be likely to find any financial aid programs available, or in-person physicians that were flexible with payment terms.

Near the end of the shift, a middle-aged woman entered, with warm brown skin and gray hair in soft waves. She was dressed in a pink shirt and khaki slacks, patching in from La Romana, Dominican Republic, 18.4326968,-69.042561.

Her name was Aury, she said. Fifty-seven years old, non-smoker, 154 centimeters tall, 63 kg.

"*He estado sufriendo de dolores en el pecho.*" She placed her hand over her heart.

Chest pains.

Andro had her recline in the chair and began with his questions.

Does the pain come on suddenly? Or gradually?

Have you fainted?

Do you have a family history of heart problems?

Do you feel dizzy or lightheaded?

Are you short of breath?

Are you under extreme amounts of stress?

To the stress question, she said, "*Pues, sí. Es mi hijo. Ha estado desaparecido durante dos semanas.*"

Her son had been missing for two weeks now. He'd gone to work one morning and never returned. He wasn't answering her calls. It wasn't like him to not respond. Naturally, this had been affecting her sleep. She spent every waking minute worrying about him, and every minute outside of her employment obligations looking for him, asking people if they'd seen him. It was tearing her apart.

Andro put a hand on her virtual shoulder. "*Creo que está sufriendo de ansiedad. Y por una buena razón.*"

Anxiety—and for good reason.

Aury took a slow, trembling breath. The rims around her eyes reddened and she pursed her lips, nodding.

He told her he knew it was impossible under the circumstances, but she had to try to rest. He instructed her on how to perform breathing exercises and also gave her a list of foods to eat to keep up her strength.

Heart food, Bel thought. But of course it wouldn't help her get her son back. It wouldn't ease the pain of losing someone she loved so much.

They discussed how she might sleep better, and while she was detailing her work schedule—which sometimes involved late nights—Andro stole a glance at Bel. Helplessness filled his eyes. In his case, *he*'d been the missing son, and his mother hadn't even been alive to search for him—probably a pain he was glad she hadn't had to bear. But this woman did have to bear it, and she bore it alone.

Bel's mind began to fill with her own kinds of evaluative questions. Where did her son work? Was it in the city, or out of the way? Did any of the nearby buildings have security? What about government panopts? Most major metropolitan areas around the world had national surveillance systems similar to United Watch, although sometimes not as extensive or as secure—but that might also make them easier to hack. If there were any organizations Aury's son was affiliated with, or places he frequented, there was a chance he'd left a digital trail. It was just a matter of getting into the right records, accounts, feeds. Connecting the dots.

Tentatively, Bel stepped forward to interrupt. "Señora, disculpe … Creo que puedo ayudarla."

I think I can help you.

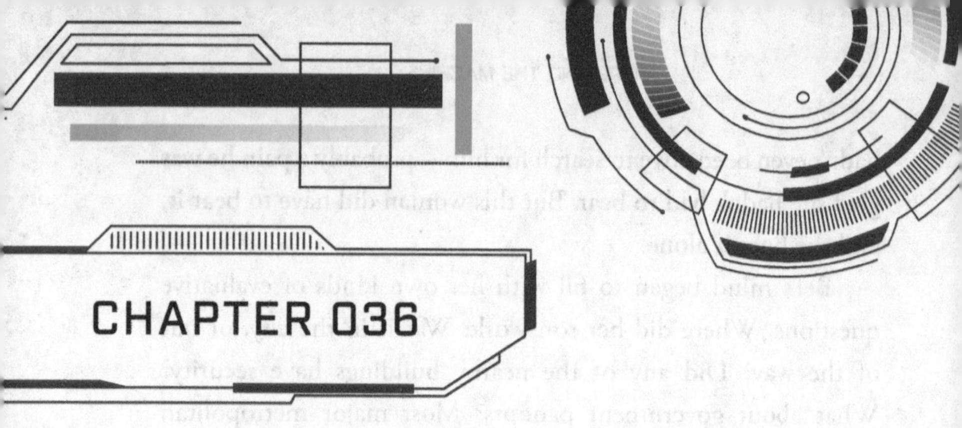

CHAPTER 036

BEL IMMEDIATELY SET TO WORK on a search. She exchanged contact information with Aury and then brought a holopad to the Common Room, where she opened an ongoing message to ask Aury questions as she thought of them. Andro sat beside her on the sofa.

First, Aury explained that her son, Bernardo, worked as a mechanic at a factory outside of Higüey. Bel then used the contact information on the company's website to send an email containing a Trojan program which, when opened, would help grant her access to the entire factory's database. It took over thirty minutes for one of the employees to open it, but from this, Bel learned that the building used an outdated key fob system, which she was easily able to infiltrate to verify that Bernardo had scanned in to work the day he disappeared. She also sifted through the building's low-quality security footage, which existed only outside at the supply loading bays, to find that Bernardo had been abducted into a different company's vehicle—that of a water delivery service called Cristalagua.

"You think it's him for sure?" Andro asked.

"I can't be *completely* sure," said Bel, "but I would hope abductions from this particular factory aren't so common that it could have happened to multiple employees on the same day."

"Good point."

After more than an hour of additional research, Bel discovered that Cristalagua was the latest front for an electronics smuggling network—in a constantly shifting series of coverups. Bel relayed this information to Aury, who confirmed that it was possible her son was involved in something like that to make extra money, and that he may have gotten in over his head trying to protect a friend who had leaked information to the local authorities.

Bel then used the abducting vehicle's license plate number to gather enough intel to get its individual GPS location and track it to an old butcher shop about ten miles from the factory. From there, she tapped into a government panopt near the butcher shop to observe some of the comings and goings of the network operatives, until she confirmed that someone fitting Bernardo's general description was inside. While she worked to break through their wireless internet encryption and reverse their own computer cameras in order to see closer, Andro brought her a tall glass of water and reminded her not to overdo it; after all, she was still recovering from a head injury. She tried to rest her brain while they waited for things to happen, but it was difficult to keep her thoughts from seeking out new ideas to get more information.

Once Bel's inside view was active, it seemed that Bernardo was being held for questioning. Shortly after, his captors brought him out for a quick beating.

"That's definitely him," said Andro, looking from the video feed to the image Aury had sent in the message log.

Grimacing as the captors struck the man again, Bel nodded. She sent Aury all the information she would need in order to alert her local law enforcement—address, background info on the business front, and a heads up about the kinds of weapons they had on them—and then, she and Andro waited.

They watched as Bernardo was questioned aggressively and then returned to the back room, bloody and bruised, but safe for the moment.

Shakily, Bel drew her hands back from the keys and rested them on her knees. Her head throbbed.

"It's going to be okay," Andro told her. "You've done everything you could possibly do."

Bel noticed he wasn't wearing his sweatshirt anymore. He sat beside her in a black t-shirt, his mechanical arm and its innards in clear view. As she thought about it, she realized he'd taken off the sweatshirt sometime during the long scavenger hunt for information, but she'd been too busy to think anything of it in the moment. Looking at him now, he seemed almost … comfortable.

"You hungry?" he asked.

It had been most of the day since she'd eaten, and she'd drained her water an hour ago. "Starving."

"What would you like?" Andro invoked Lucius to put in an order to Delessio.

Bel groaned at the prompting to make a decision. She'd used all her brainpower on the hunt for Bernardo and couldn't fathom trying to come up with something to eat. "What do you recommend?"

"You want *me* to pick something? The guy who doesn't eat?" he asked.

"Well you *used* to eat, didn't you?"

He sighed and told Lucius, "Bring us number five on my favorites list, would you?"

After Lucius dissipated, Bel returned her attention to the video feed, chewing her lip as she kept her eyes pinned to the scene inside the butcher shop. Her past forages for information had been easier to detach herself from; it had been easy to ignore the *people* she was researching, to look at them as screens of data or walls of code. But this was real.

Andro slid his non-metal hand on top of hers, enclosing her trembling fingers. Somehow that didn't help her apprehension, but she sensed that was for a different reason. Her pulse quickened as she looked up at him. A calm expression passed over all his features, both ossteel and flesh. Just as the moment turned awkward, the sound of distant sirens broke their mutual silence.

The colors on the video feed took on a flashing, red overlay as the sirens grew louder. A voice on the police intercom demanded that the shop's occupants show themselves. Inside, however, the men scuttled around, preparing weapons, shouting orders at one another. They dragged Bernardo and three other captives up to the front, where they displayed them as hostages at gunpoint.

Bel squeezed Andro's hand.

Gunshots sounded. Officers flooded the shop. Several of the men inside fell to the ground, while officers manhandled the others. Within a few minutes, all the men operating Cristalagua were either dead or in handcuffs. One of the captives had been shot, but Bernardo and the other two were released, and everyone left the premises.

Still shaky, Bel let out a breath of relief. Andro drew her up against him and whispered, "He's safe. You did it."

When the food came, sliding in on an automechanical cart, Andro stood up. "I've got a few things to take care of, so … I'll let you eat."

The smell of warm spices and steaming root vegetables was almost enough to make Bel forget everything else, but as Andro went to leave, she snapped alert. "You're not going to stay?"

He slipped his hands into his jeans pockets. "Not like I can join you."

Bel deflated. "Right. I know, I just thought … I mean, you have to tell me what I'm eating here. Your fifth favorite food, apparently?"

"One of five dishes tied for first," he clarified. He hesitated a second, but then sat back down.

Dipping a spoon into a bowl of what appeared to be some kind of stew, Bel said, "So, what is it?"

"Sancocho Dominicano, de *siete carnes*."

"Seven meats?"

"Some of them come from the same animal, to be fair—like the pork and the bacon—but yes. It's kind of a special occasion type meal, but some people say it's good for a hangover, too."

A few discs of corn on the cob floated on the surface of the broth like sunbursts, while avocado slices were fanned out at the edge of the bowl. The stew was thick and hearty, with rice bulking up the liquid.

"And you really can't eat any of it?" Bel asked.

He shook his head. "The signal transmission to my brain, I guess, doesn't come through with the same complexity that it does for a normal person. I don't get the hunger sensation so much; it's more the *desire* to eat, which I can't really fix when it doesn't taste the same."

Bel felt guilty with her mouth full of sancocho, the chunks of salty beef and a vegetable she was pretty sure was yucca—something her *abuela* used to cook with when she'd still been alive.

"I'm sorry," she said.

He nodded at the dish. "I thought you might be able to enjoy it, though, even if I can't."

She felt her face flush. "Couldn't your body at least metabolize food? For more energy or something, even if it doesn't taste like anything?"

"Not very efficiently. I tried that in the beginning, to see what effect it had on my battery life, but it barely nudged the numbers. Choking down three meals a day for a week boosted me one percent. Didn't really seem worth it. Especially since I don't know my battery's degradation rate, so a single percentage might be worth even less down the line."

"That makes sense, I guess."

Andro was quiet for a while as Bel ate. She made a mental game of trying to figure out everything that was in the stew; there was chicken and yams, russet potatoes, possibly two kinds of plantains, peppers, onions, garlic, cilantro. It was warm in her stomach, a comfort from the inside out.

With an amused expression, Andro picked up a wedge of lime that was tucked between the bowl and the plate beneath it, squeezing the juice into the bowl. "Almost forgot."

Bel stirred the contents of the stew to blend the new addition.

"What you did was really great, by the way," Andro added. "What you did for Aury. I hope you know that."

Pausing with her spoon in the air, Bel said, "Oh. No, that was pretty basic stuff. For me, I mean. I know it seems like a lot, but … it was really the least I could do. She needed help, I had the skills. It's good for me to do something useful for once, you know?"

"Mirabel. You just rescued a whole human being. More than one. From thousands of miles away and across the ocean."

Bel liked the way her name sounded in his voice. She liked the sound of her own name, her real one, which she'd missed. The first time Andro had said it, it had been contemptuous, and she'd still been wary of its use. But now … Now she felt like she could revel in it.

"I guess I hadn't really thought of it like that," she said. "I was just digging for information. It's a habit."

"Yeah, well, to the rest of us, it looks more like a superpower."

She smiled. "Maybe. I'm sure you've saved a lot more lives than me, though. You're the one taking care of sick people all the time."

"I tell people to stay hydrated and get more sleep. I'm a glorified mom."

Bel laughed, then inclined her head. "How are you a medical professional at your age, anyway?"

"Well, the Holomédico program has such a huge demand for medical volunteers, they actually start training kids at fifteen. By sixteen, you can work with patients under supervision, and by seventeen you can take patients on your own, as long as you keep passing all the tests. But obviously you can't mess up a whole lot, considering you can't physically treat wounds or draw blood or anything too crazy."

"So, you started when you were fifteen?"

He nodded. "I was planning to do pre-med at Stanford and I wanted all the experience I could get. By now, I'd hoped to be an actual EMT—capital E—but … well, you know the rest."

She nodded.

If he only had a heart.

If he only hadn't lost so much of himself.

She glanced at his chest, covered with black stretch cotton, hiding his non-heart pump. Yet he had more heart than a lot of people. She only hoped she and Mateo would be able to help him somehow. "I think it's time we get back to working on *your* case."

CHAPTER 037

BEL AND ANDRO STOOD ON OPPOSITE SIDES of an enormous chessboard, with alternating neon pink and teal squares. The VR sky was dark except for the light pollution of the surrounding cyberpunk city, with its enormous curving skyways and vehicles hovering like lit-up insects between buildings in the distance.

"Your move," said Andro's avatar.

His whole torso and upper limbs were made of silver metal, with a chest plate molded to the shape of chiseled abdominals. On his lower half, he wore black military-style pants and combat boots. He had a mechanical eye that lit up teal, rimmed with layered gears that twisted and whirred whenever he turned his head and focused on something.

Bel smoothed her virtual pink hair, shaved off on one side with the top swooping drastically over. She pointed to one of her knights—a burly character with broad shoulders, high-tech goggles, and guns for arms—then pointed to the square she wanted him to go to. He moved in his L-shaped path, shooting the character that was occupying his new spot. A man in a dark trench coat and brimmed hat, clasping a straight sickle that buzzed with electricity, fell to the ground, flickered, and disappeared.

Andro scoffed. "I knew you were going to go for the bishop." He looked over the chess board, glancing at an avatar that looked just like Bel's except for her teal hair. She stood in the corner, protecting him diagonally.

Bel smiled. "Anyway, so you were saying about Paragon …"

His eye gears rotated while he figured out his next move. "Right. The club." He directed his rook to attack. "So, I used an InVisor to get in, of course. There was this girl at the bar who started talking to me. I got us a couple of drinks, and next thing I know, everything starts to blur. I feel sick. The lights are too bright. I can't tell up from down …"

A giant, helmeted creature in a teal-toned metal suit with a laser weapon came stomping out of its place, shoving past several three-foot robot pawns.

"After that, it's pretty hazy. I have these vague memories, but I'm not sure if they really happened or if it's that kind of thing your mind comes up with when you're half-conscious, ideas that don't make any sense when you try to explain them out loud, even though they feel true."

The rook settled on one of the pawns and lifted a wide, armored foot, bringing it down on the pawn's head with a metallic crunch. The pawn released a few beeps and blips, its neon lights crackling until they went out. Now the rook had a clear path to Bel's king.

She sighed.

Andro cleared his throat. "I swear I heard people talking over my body like I was a corpse. About tox screenings and 'cause of death,' all the results that were coming up on a CorpuScan. I couldn't see anything, but I felt … cold. And hungry like I hadn't eaten for days. And they said my name, so I knew it was me. The last thing I heard was a discussion about what would happen to my ashes. But then … I woke up. Like … this."

"You think maybe your uncle paid some people off to fake your death?"

"That's what I thought at first. But with everything I experienced between blacking out and waking up in the lab, I've started to think he was more thorough than that. Almost like … like he had some way of making me *look* dead. Convincingly dead. Enough to fool professional medics."

Bel paused as she considered whether to move forward another robot pawn for a block or pull back her bishop to attack. "You think that's possible?"

"Of course that's possible. My mother found a way to use nanotechnology to heal burnt human flesh in a matter of minutes. You don't think there's some way to fake someone's drug overdose?"

Her pulse sped. "No, I do. I just … wanted to believe it was crazy. Because that would make things easier to deal with."

"What things?"

Bel decided on the attack, directing her bishop. "My mom's death."

They both watched emotionlessly as the bishop withdrew the charged straight sickle from his trench coat and slashed at the giant helmeted rook, slicing its throat until a neon teal fluid leaked out.

"She was a surgeon, at Menlo Park. She had this friend, who was also a patient," Bel explained. "The guy worked in commercial real estate—industrial, mostly. Warehouses, cold storage, that sort of thing. He used to talk about some of the unusual things he'd seen, or suspected, at least. And then, one day, he just … died of a heart attack.

"But it didn't add up. My mom knew him, knew his medical

history. Testing these days makes it a lot harder to miss diseased arteries and all that. She just had this … gut feeling. So, she started asking questions, doing research, begging my dad to look into some of the properties the guy had been selling and to whom. Against her colleagues' advice, she tried to file for a manual autopsy—which sounded completely insane."

"Right," said Andro. "I'm guessing you'd have a hard time even finding someone who *could* do one anymore. Not when CorpuScan tech has basically eliminated human error."

Bel nodded. "But before she could get the MA approved …"

All the characters on the board besides Bel and Andro fidgeted during the pauses. Brandishing weapons, pounding fists into palms, tilting heads and cracking knuckles. Bel watched some of their movements, letting her unfinished thought hang in the air.

"She met a similar fate," Andro concluded.

"Hers was an aneurysm," said Bel. "All the screenings confirmed it. But none of us—me, Mateo, my dad—could help thinking that the timing was too convenient for whoever had something to lose from her suspicions."

Andro just looked at her, no longer seeming to care about the chess board. He didn't make his characters retaliate. As with all the games, despite the spatial distance, his voice came in her ear like he was standing right next to her. "I'm so sorry."

"My dad was already working with the VOLT initiative," Bel continued solemnly. "So, after what he'd learned before, they were convinced it was the Knight Crew syndicate. He was determined to take them down, to get some sense of justice, but … that obviously didn't end well." Bel let her gaze wander for a moment before turning it back on Andro. "Anyway. The point is, you didn't actually overdose, and I'm pretty sure my mom didn't actually have an aneurysm. So that means someone is manufacturing some biotechnical way to manipulate medical screenings." She scoffed. "I mean, I guess I shouldn't be surprised. I know how easy it is to hack machines, to scramble signals."

"To make it look like a body doesn't have any active brainwaves flowing," Andro added. "Or to mimic the presence of toxins. Like the way vidrinium interferes with InVisors."

Bel nodded quietly. "It must be laughably easy. Your move."

Andro deliberated, but ultimately pointed to his queen.

Bel's teal-haired doppelgänger sauntered ahead enough squares that she was still protecting Andro's avatar horizontally, but now also threatening Bel diagonally, with Andro's remaining rook backing her up.

"What was your family dynamic like?" Bel didn't react to the new threat. "Did you always feel like your uncle had it out for you?"

Her own king, doppelgänger to Andro's avatar, with his mechanical eye lit pink, blinked slowly. She took a step back until she was standing directly in front of him; if Andro's queen killed her, she'd be pushed to the sidelines to watch and control the rest of her players, but then she could make her king avenge her and Andro would be left queenless.

"Actually, we were close," he replied. "He was my mother's twin. In a lot of ways, he was the father I didn't have."

"I guess I never thought about you having a father. Elodie always seemed so ... self-sustaining."

"She was never interested in marriage. But she did want to be a mother. And, true to her love of biotechnology, she lived her life in such a way that those two desires were not mutually exclusive."

"What happened with Soto, then?"

"After my mother died, we drifted apart some. I think neither of us really knew how to cope, or how to lean on each other. But we managed. Things went back to normal—as much as they could. It wasn't until the Veronika Mandersloot scandal that something really shifted between us."

"Mateo mentioned going through her emails. I remember when she got fired; it was all over the news, and social media—although I don't remember all the details …"

Andro didn't pull back his queen, but he didn't attack either. He directed one of his robot pawns forward two squares, a move away from killing one of Bel's and breaking down the fence that protected her pieces.

"It had to do with the human test subjects for several of the projects she was overseeing. Not following the proper protocol for legal consent."

"Sounds familiar …" said Bel.

"Yes. Anyway, after Soto fired her, it was like a switch flipped. Suddenly it was like he was a different person. I figured maybe he and Veronika had had a secret relationship. Something intimate. There had always been hints of that. A sexual tension between them. They'd started going out of their way not to be seen together, not even casually. It was like they thought if they were never in the same room at the same time, nobody would pick up on it. And then when things went south—when he had to force her out of the company—he got bitter. Angry."

Bel looked over the board again, biting her lip. "Wait. So, Soto was running Vivorex … just until you turned eighteen?

"I was originally set up to inherit the company, but I didn't want anything to do with it. I mean, the medicinal aspects of it, sure, and developing cures. But I've never had any interest in business. Soto's great with that. He knew I would never try to get rid of him."

"So, you don't think he was trying to, like … make you disappear because he thought you were going to take Vivorex from him …"

He shook his head. "Absolutely not. I only suggested *once* that my mother might not like the way he was running things. He'd been acting suspicious, starting new projects he wasn't telling me about—he always told me everything before, even when I was too young to fully understand. I may have subtly reminded him I had some sway if he didn't come clean. But that was it."

Bel killed Andro's pawn with hers. The two robots shot electrical pulses at each other, a clash of blue and pink, before Bel's finally won out and Andro's exploded into a billion tiny chunks that turned to dust in the air.

"Do you think Veronika was still in contact with him?" she asked.

He rubbed his wrist. "It would make sense. She seemed to have some special hold on him, I could never figure out why. Kind of like chess. You'd assume the king is the most powerful, but he's not; it's the queen who can really work the board."

Bel locked eyes with her doppelgänger, who glared back. "So maybe he only fired her for appearances' sake, but kept working with her on the side."

"Maybe even let her keep access to company data for reference," Andro agreed. "Or funneled company money into whatever she was working on."

"And somehow *you* ended up in one of those projects."

Andro pulled out his second bishop but only enough to add an extra layer of protection on the queen. "I guess so."

"Why didn't they just kill you?"

"That's the question I keep asking myself."

Above them, the sky flickered. The image of the light-polluted sky split open for a second, revealing a part of the real-life dome.

Bel jumped. "What just happened?"

"Looks like one of the sensors," said Andro. "Might be wearing out. Broken ones can't accurately sense the dome, so then they can't manipulate the virtual space and it just shows up as a 'hole' in the simulation. I'll check on it when we're done. It probably needs replacing."

Sending forward her own bishop, Bel said, "Anyway, I'm guessing you already tried to see if you can still access company files?"

"My login was disabled. Not that there would have been anything useful anywhere that I'd be able to look. That's why I need your brother; he can get to the files that even the highest-level executives don't know exist."

"What about the Knight Crew connection?" she asked, watching another one of Andro's pawns attack another one of hers. "What could they have to do with all this?"

"One day, I overheard Soto on a call, and he said, 'It's fitting, isn't it? *Metallum intus.*' That's why it was in my notes. At the time, I didn't know what that meant, as far as its relation to the crime syndicate, but after what you and Mateo have told me, I think it's possible they've helped fund some of the projects, or benefitted from them somehow. If my uncle or Veronika worked on developing something that could fake any cause of death, the syndicates would probably eat that up; they always need to get rid of *someone*, right? I'm sure they'd love not to have to start a war every time by causing an obvious scene with it."

The malfunctioning sensor caused another flicker but Bel

and Andro ignored it. Suddenly, Bel spotted an opening on Andro's side—a spot he'd tried to protect with his rook but which he'd made vulnerable again by moving a robot pawn. She smiled and stepped forward, crossing several squares until she stood right beside Andro.

"Checkmate."

The board and all the characters and Andro's and Bel's virtual uniforms all separated into individual pixels and swirled away, along with the city itself, landing them back in the reality of the gray dome. Bel squinted, her eyes having adjusted too well to the game's nighttime scene.

"Why do you have it set up to just end the whole game after a loss?" said Bel. "No 'play again' button? No 'demand a rematch' or anything?"

He shrugged. "I don't like to dwell on what I've lost. Game over is game over."

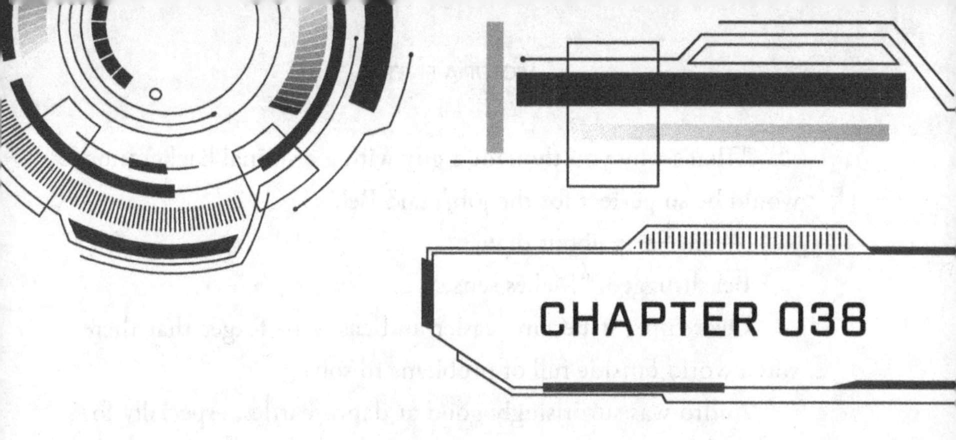

CHAPTER 038

BEL AND ANDRO SPENT THE NEXT WEEK interacting mostly within the vast library of VR games and, in between action, going over the details of Andro's experience *ad nauseam* but struggling to come up with any new conclusions.

"You really don't think the authorities would be able to help you?" she said. But of course he didn't. Otherwise he would have contacted someone right away after he escaped.

"They're not as powerful as they seem. Soto will have ways of covering his tracks. I've never known him to be cruel, but he definitely has the power to make evidence disappear if he wants to. Plus, I'm supposed to be dead. All the records check out. Who's to say I'm not just some clone or something, making wild claims?"

"They could probably protect you, though, at least. Help with the investigation."

"Maybe. But they'd have to do everything by the book. Requesting records, which could easily be tampered with. Interviewing employees who are too scared to say what they know, if they know anything at all. Getting warrants before searching any affiliated locations. Nothing that would allow hacking the databases, spying on them, doing whatever it takes to get in."

"That's why you thought a guy with a criminal background would be so perfect for the job," said Bel.

"Yeah. Sorry about that."

Bel shrugged. "Makes sense."

Over time, it became easier and easier to forget that there was a world outside full of problems to solve.

Andro was surprisingly good at dance battles, especially for someone full of metal. Bel took the lead, however, when it came to slashing airborne music boxes with laser swords at high speed.

Wild West sharpshooting was quite literally hit or miss for either of them, and they ended up laughing at the sheriff NPC's cheesy puns more than actually shooting. In response to a miss, the sheriff might say something like, "Nice try, cowboy. Turn the *udder* cheek and *moo*-ve on!" while a hit would result in a comment like, "Hoo-ee! Any quicker on the *draw* and you could win an art contest!"

Eventually, they found their way to less competitive activities.

Sometimes they worked together to explore other planets by spaceship and fight evil aliens, or played different members of a superhero league to apprehend common villain enemies.

They used the suspension cables—which dropped down from hidden ceiling panels—and the haptic suits to engage in fighter pilot air battles, a setup that provided not only the sensation of sitting in a cockpit but also taking sharp nosedives and even flying upside down.

Occasionally, they took a break from such dynamic adventures in favor of quieter experiences.

Andro suggested a carnival simulation called All's Fair, which likewise used the suspension system, but for the effect of making users feel like they were riding carousel horses or cascading down rickety rollercoasters at a sharp decline. There were the requisite ring tosses, Skee-Ball, funhouses, and virtual musical performances, too.

They strolled through the Louvre and the Smithsonian, rode bikes through Central Park, and visited the tops of most of the world's monumental skyscrapers.

Bel also assisted Andro as he took more Holomédico calls. After one particularly long round of treating patients virtually, Andro said, "What do you feel like doing today?"

Bel scanned through the system icons until she found the one for the map, which she pulled up. The world came up three dimensionally before her and she closed her eyes and spun it, putting out her finger and blindly landing it.

"That's the middle of the ocean," said Andro.

Bel opened her eyes. "Okay, but I got *close* to land." She zoomed in to find that she was only a short way off from the western coast of Africa, near the island nation of São Tomé and Príncipe. She tapped on the island, and then the system dropped her and Andro right onto the sand of the beach.

Smiling, Bel sat down cross-legged.

The sun was high over the water, bright and white against a cloudless sky. An endless canopy of palm trees swayed behind her and Andro, who sat beside her.

He picked at the imaginary sand. "Pretty cool we can do all of this from one place, isn't it?"

Bel nodded. "I'd have lost my mind by now if I couldn't at least *pretend* to go other places."

Andro said, "Same."

"So, the Submundo has just been here all this time, waiting for someone to … need it?"

"Basically."

"It just seems so elaborate. There are very wealthy people

who don't have homes this nice as a *regular* home, and yet this is your backup. How is that?"

"My mother designed the Submundo to protect us—herself and me—in the event of … well, anything, really. Natural disasters, global pandemics, threats to our family. She was so preoccupied with the future, and she went above and beyond to prepare for any and all potential outcomes. She planned not only for our needs, but for the needs of anyone who might ever live here. Partners, kids. There was no way to know when we would need the Submundo, whether it would be today, or twenty years from now."

"She was certainly thorough," said Bel.

"I never thought I'd be so glad it existed, until I got here in this … condition." He looked down at his chest. "Honestly, though, I kind of thought I'd just be here until this body couldn't go on anymore."

Wind whipped Bel's virtual hair over her face, a sensation that felt as real as it looked. "That must have been really hard."

"It was. There were moments when it felt so bad, I just … wanted it to end. Wanted to *make* it end, even."

Bel felt a chill run up her spine. She hesitated. "You mean you … tried to kill yourself?"

"Well, I guess 'try' is putting it too generously. I never got very far. Even looking like I do, having to hide underground, apparently some part of me still wanted to survive."

"What do you think it was," she asked, "that kept you from … taking your life?"

He paused for a moment, as though he was trying to recall something. "'Life, although it may be an accumulation of anguish, is dear to me.'"

It sounded like a quote, but Bel wasn't sure.

"Mary Shelley. Frankenstein," he said.

Bel narrowed her eyes. "And you call this place the Submundo. The 'Underworld.' You really do think you're some sort of monster …"

He turned his face, flexing his jaw. "I'm ugly. Frightening. A twisted version of whatever I used to be—altered in a lab. And that's only what you can see on the surface."

"Is this the part where you tell me you're dangerous, and that I should stay away from you?"

His expression darkened. "This is the part where I tell you that you're already in too deep."

"I'm not frightened by you," she told him.

"Well, you should be."

"I don't scare that easy."

"And that just may be your downfall, Mirabel Solís."

Despite his eerie tone, Bel thought she saw a hint of amusement on his lips, stoking her own amusement. Even all stripped out and burned up and filled with metal, there was something … perfect … about him. She imagined how he might respond if she were to tell him that.

Bang on my chest if you think I'm perfect.

She glanced at his chest. "Do you … have a physical heart?"

He shook his head. "I don't know.

"But there's something in you pumping fluid to the rest of your body …"

"There must be." He tapped the metal casing where a flesh heart would have been. "But I'm a pretty sleek piece of tech, so it's not exactly 'beating.' Whatever it is, it's electric—and quiet."

"What about the vidrinium battery? That must supply you with a lot of energy, especially since you can't really sleep."

"Yes. Everyone else wishes they could have those extra hours, to not get tired. Turns out you have to replace your insides with machinery to achieve it."

"It's all machinery anyway, though," said Bel. "Organs are just pumps and filters. Veins and arteries are pipes with valves. The brain is a computer. It doesn't really make that much difference what it's made of or where it's located."

"You know what," he said, slipping his shirt over his head, "if I feel for it just right, I can actually"—he pushed under the edge of the skin, temporarily breaking through its seal until his fingers were inside, making Bel cringe visibly—"touch it."

Bel tried to make sense of what she was seeing. It wasn't real, she told her mind, because they were in the VR. But the VR had copied Andro's every visible cell, and everything corresponded to his actual body. So, he really was sitting in front of her, touching these internal mechanisms.

He glanced up at her. "It would just take a screwdriver to remove the brace and then the battery would slip right out."

"Apparently you've thought about this," Bel observed.

"When I thought about ... ending all of this ... I figured all I'd have to do was take out the battery and I'd get my wish."

Bel pressed her lips together. "I'm glad you didn't."

"I'm glad you showed up here," he said quietly. "But ... I didn't just say that."

Looking at his precisely placed fingers and filled with a sudden, courageous curiosity, Bel said, "Can *I* touch it?"

He nodded, removing his own hand and taking hers. She let him guide her to the battery. First a soft *squelch* and then she felt the warm metal, the outline of the bracket—a rectangular frame open at the front—the battery's smooth surface, which vibrated gently.

His gaze lingered on her for a second too long and she

found herself short of breath. He still held her by the wrist as she touched him in this incredibly intimate and simultaneously disturbing way, and some part of her thought the space between them had begun to narrow, but if it had, it was happening so slowly she couldn't be sure.

The waves crashed and the wind rustled palm fronds and the sun warmed their bodies, a warmth that transcended the virtual so much that Bel felt it in her actual bones.

Fluid in pipes, Bel thought, as her blood rushed. A flood of chemicals. Her elbows and knees were hinges, bent and angled where she was sitting. Her muscles were cords in a pulley system, tightening at the thought of how close she was to Andro, wanting to pull him closer.

A flicker tore the sky's perfect blue, putting them both at attention.

Andro released her with a hurried "sorry," prompting Bel to remove her hand.

"That's okay," she said, a flush of warmth leaving a distinct afterburn inside of her.

The edge of Andro's skin made a quiet hissing sound as it re-sealed itself.

"I should … check your brother's status," he said, standing. He tapped the air and pulled up the menu again, exiting the VR. The ocean, the trees, the sand, all dissipated back to gray walls. "I need to see if he's made any progress on that building location."

"Right. Of course." Bel remained seated on the floor, trying to catch her breath.

Stupid, she thought. He'd only been indulging her curiosity; he hadn't meant anything by it.

She watched as Andro headed for the doors, wishing he'd come back.

Then, he stopped and turned. "You know, I never really thanked you for what you did. For Aury. I'd like to do something for you."

"That's really not necessary," she told him. "I've got a long way to go to make up for some of the *other* things I've done. I don't deserve a reward for it."

"Well … I'd still like to. Meet me back here tonight. Eight o'clock. Please?"

He waited until she nodded, then nodded back, and left the dome.

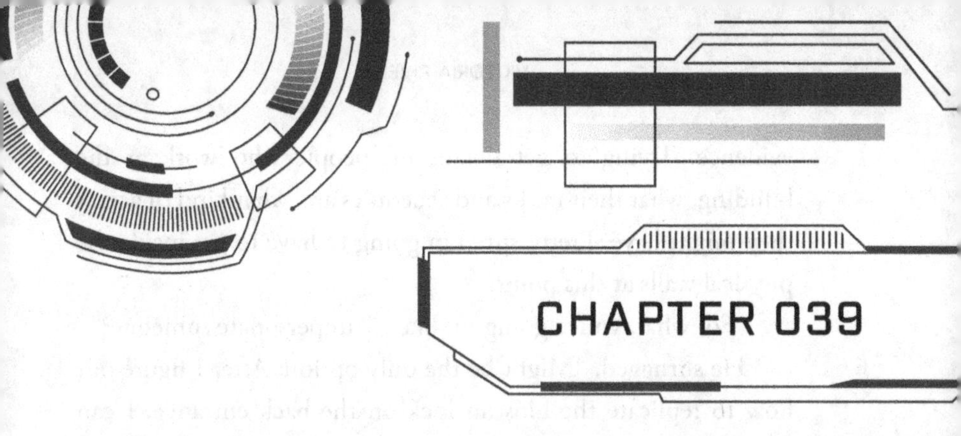

CHAPTER 039

BEL SAT ON HER BED with the holopad on her lap. "How's it going over there?" she said to Mateo's holomorphic head. "Andro said you found the right building."

"I did. And even better, I've been combing Veronika Mandersloot's old messages—which, up to this point, had only been giving me vague clues as to which companies may or may not be fronts for her questionable business operations—and I found an interesting attachment."

"Like what?"

"A training program application. No details as to what the training program *is*, but all applicants are required to complete an invasive background check, sign an NDA, and take a detailed personality test. I mean, sure, with some of the work Vivorex does, they might want to protect patent-pending technology or other sensitive information, but the extent of these requirements seems ... I don't know. Excessive."

"But you don't have any information on actual applicants yet?"

"I just barely got into a server this morning that has some additional HR files. So now I have to see if I can find a link between any of them and the trainee application package. Shouldn't be too hard. But I'm still gathering intel and verifying evidence. Trying to get details on people who work at the building, what their ranks and schedules are, what kind of access they might have. Pretty sure I'm going to have to get inside the physical walls at this point."

"So, what, you're going to, like … impersonate someone?"

He shrugged. "Might be the only option. After I figure out how to replicate the bioscan lock on the back entrance, I can walk right in there—but if I get caught, they'll know I'm not an employee."

"I wish I could be there as backup." She dragged her fingers through her hair.

"You're safe where you are. Don't get any ideas."

"I've already *had* ideas, remember? Since when have I ever stayed out of something you wanted me to?"

"You're staying put. That's that."

"Fine, but—"

A ping came with a popup notification and hung above Mateo's head.

It was a message from Andro.

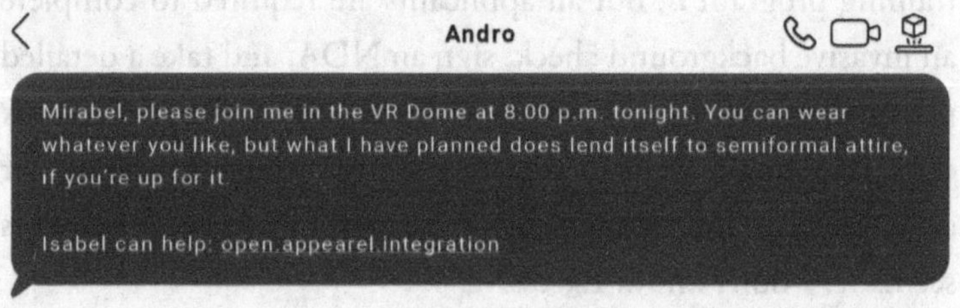

"Mateo," said Bel as she read over the text, "I have to go. But keep me updated."

"Sure thing. Love you."

"Love you."

As soon as Mateo's image faded, Bel tapped the link in

the message. It opened an app called Appearel, which opened into a graphic representation of the Wardrobe and appeared to be integrated into the system that had already taken her measurements in the closet, presenting an avatar of Bel at the center and allowing her to sort clothing by style and category, and virtually try items on.

Most of the dresses were simple, solid colors. A black velvet sheath, a maroon satin wrap, a white halter A-line, a navy poplin with a banded waist, a lace fit-and-flare, a few variations of maxis. It wasn't until she landed on a knee-length, champagne-gold dress—a silk A-line with a sparkling gossamer overlay—that her heart gave a little stutter. The silk ended at the neckline, while the gossamer continued up over the shoulders, forming short, sheer sleeves. It was like fairy magic. She selected a pair of black, open-toed heels with ankle cross-straps to go with it.

Bel showered quickly, then dried and styled her hair in loose waves. Then it occurred to her that she hadn't seen any makeup in this house, so she asked Lucius, who revealed an entire drawer in the bathroom vanity with all the basics in multiple skin tones. She chose a light dusting of shimmer powder, then lined her eyes thinly and added a few strokes of mascara before swiping a bit of almond oil on her lips.

She checked the clock—five minutes to eight—and hurried off to the dome.

A chair outside the VR dome had a headset resting on the seat, so Bel picked it up, placed it over her face, and turned it on.

The doors slid open as she stepped toward them.

"Close your eyes," Andro said. Bel felt his non-mechanical

hand in hers, leading her to what she guessed was the middle of the dome.

He released her and tapped the side of her headset to change its view. "Alright. Open."

It was nighttime. They were standing on a rocky bit of island, dusted with snow, jutting out over calm waters. There was a chill throughout the space, not enough to cause discomfort but enough to give the feeling that they were outdoors. The air seemed to hold a certain energy, the faintest buzz of an electric charge, and when Bel looked up, she understood why.

Hazy ribbons of green and purple light wafted across the star-specked sky, slithering, dancing. Fading thinner and lighter, then coming brighter again. Bel gazed at the aurora, lips parted, chest swollen with a breath she couldn't fully take in or fully release. It was like some otherworldly, invisible being was holding a brush and making enormous, three-dimensional watercolor strokes, each hue bleeding into the blackness on the edges and pooling up at the center line.

The colors shimmered in reflection on the water, which stretched outward for miles like inky, frosted glass. And the stars, millions of white pinpricks, domed over them, some of them still and others streaking by.

Mountains rose from behind, rocky and powdered.

The delicate, sulphuric scent of the sea came through in a gentle breeze.

Breathless, Bel turned to Andro. "I don't even know what to say ..."

Still entranced, it took her a second to realize that Andro wasn't himself. Or, more correctly, that he *was* himself, just not the one she'd gotten used to.

He stood before her in a slim-fit, navy-blue suit with no tie, a white dress shirt unbuttoned at the collar, brandy leather lace-up Oxford shoes with a matching belt, and his own unblemished, pre-cyborg face. His chin was clean-shaven, and his hair was grown out a bit, coarse and black with gentle ripples.

But he didn't bother looking at the view. He looked directly at her. "You like it?"

"*Obviously*," she said. "Who doesn't want to see disturbances in the trajectories of magnetospheric plasma?"

He smiled. "You look nice."

"So do you. But … just so you know, you don't have to do *this*"—she gestured at his whole form—"for me. I never wanted you think I had a hard time with—"

He took both her hands to keep her from continuing to move them around dramatically. "Just … let me feel normal for once, okay?"

She sighed. "Okay."

He was handsome, Bel had to admit it, even though she worried it would take away from what she'd come to feel for him in his previous form. He had warm brown skin, a bit of a dimple on one side when he smiled. Strong brows and full lips. And eyes the color of raw umber. Still, she was used to the faint discoloration of his left eye, the raw edge that usually ran down the middle of his right cheek, all the dark metal with the lines of blue light peering between panels, the glint of the wires. They were a part of him, the only version of him she'd known. She felt a twinge in her chest at the thought that he must hate his face, must ache to see this "better" one instead, must think she could hardly stand to look at him without the filter.

"I can't believe you did all this," she told him. "Even with the VR, you still had to have it scan everything and add skins. And maybe I'm crazy but this whole place just looks … I don't know … *extra*, somehow."

He bowed his head a little. "I did fine-tune the graphics and the sensifiers. I wanted the colors to be especially vibrant—true to life—and for everything else to *feel* as real as possible."

Bel's heart rate kicked up a little when she realized he was still holding her hands, swallowing as she processed the sensation. "It feels pretty real."

"Come on." He pointed his head toward a spot on the ground and led her over with him. When he stopped, the ground faded to a terrace that stretched several yards in every direction. A few trees—not enough to block the view of the sky—manifested around the perimeter, with twinkly lights strung between them.

After a moment, music began to play from some unseen place, prompting Bel to look around—but of course it was coming from everywhere, from the surrounding speakers built into the dome's walls.

The opening chords were familiar, the synthesizer and the deep bass. Then the lead singer of Waivelength sang the lyrics.

It doesn't matter
What state of matter you are
We fill the universe
We're all made of stars

"You remembered," Bel said.

"I also remembered reading some of the intersphere reports about the night you ran away from Orwell," Andro told her. "Seems like you left your senior prom a little early."

A few dozen NPCs faded in around them, all paired off, formally dressed, slowly swaying to the music.

It was a much more elegant scene than the one she'd run

from two and half weeks ago, and for once—unlike Andro—she was glad *not* to feel normal. All of this was so much *better* than normal.

"Would you like to … dance?" he asked.

Bel nodded.

She wasn't sure how to go about the whole thing, hesitating before she reached up and put her arms around his neck. Her body warmed when she felt his hands on her waist.

It's kinetic
The way your energy sweeps
Over the atmosphere
And pulls me in so deep

Bel gazed past him at the water, all dark and slick, with the reflection of the Northern Lights slicing through it. The surface texture, the way it moved. She could almost forget she hadn't really been transported to another place.

"You really like it?" Andro asked.

She nodded again.

"I wanted to take you away from the Submundo. Out of the dark underground and somewhere real. As real as possible, anyway. Not just another scene in a game."

"What's wrong with games?" said Bel. "I've liked our games."

His hand flinched against her lower back. "We've been playing games since we met—and not just in the dome. Maybe it's time to stop playing."

"But you're still wearing a mask …"

He shook his head. "In the real world, my whole body's a mask now, synthetic and fabricated. You've only known me as some deformed machine. This, what you're seeing right now, is who I actually am. Who I'm supposed to be."

"But you can't define yourself by your face. Literally anything can happen to a face. And it does. Not just injuries or tragic disfigurements, but disease, or skin breakouts, or age. No matter who you are or how well you take care of yourself, that face is going to get marks on it one way or another. Those marks are part of who you are too, like … tangible memories. They're not always good, but they're things you've survived, things that have shaped and affected you. You don't have to like them—and sometimes you shouldn't— or even be grateful for them, but you have to accept them."

"No. Why do I have to accept it? I didn't ask for this. Aging is *normal*. Skin conditions are *normal*. Getting a gash on my forehead from some idiot move at the skate part as a ten-year-old is *normal*. This"—he gestured to himself—"isn't." He released her and turned his back, scrubbing his hands over his face, perfectly filtered and hiding the exposed metal.

She took a step toward him and brushed her fingers against his elbow. "I want to look at you."

He turned toward her again, sullen.

"No, I mean I want to *really* look at you." She doubled-tapped for the menu settings, looking to Andro for any objections. He just stared at her. With another tap, she disabled the filter, along with the NPCs that danced around them. The NPCs faded, and within a few seconds, the system had re-scanned Bel and Andro and removed any enhancements. They stood face to face under the stars, under the color casts of the aurora, Andro with his marred face unfiltered.

She watched him for a moment, not saying anything, heart pounding. His eyes were sad and pleading, but her attention fell to his lips. Those were exactly the same as they'd been before, parting slightly before he pressed them together again.

"Isn't this harder to look at?" he said darkly.

She pointed at her own face, a blemish on her chin that she knew was clearly visible. "Is *this* hard to look at?"

"Stop. You know that's not the same thing." He moved her hand away but held onto it. "I understand what you're trying to say, but I don't buy into the whole 'it's what's on the inside that counts' idea."

"What about *my* insides? Do those count for anything? Or did you only set up this thing for me tonight because my skin's intact?"

"Sure, it's because your skin's intact. And because your hair looks like the ocean at night. And because you don't let anyone tell you what to do. Because you know about magnetospheric plasma, and you have the skills—and the heart—to help someone a world away, and you're not intimidated in the face of danger—to a fault, in fact—and you don't let anything stop you when you're determined to figure something out. And because, for whatever reason, you can look right at this shredded excuse I have for a face and not recoil in horror. It's everything. And it's so … *frustrating*." He shook his head. "No one else was ever supposed to come to the Submundo, and with everything that's happened, I know I need to keep my distance from you. But all I want right now is to …"

Bel didn't bother to try and hide her trembling. She didn't move or look away.

He let go of her hand and reached for her cheek, but paused, mid-air, and curled his fingers. "I promised your brother I'd never touch you …"

She took his wrist and guided him to her, letting his palm rest against her warm skin. The wavering aurora glimmered green in the metal just below his left eye.

"I want you to."

Her heart pounded as his fingers slid up under her hair and he stepped in. His chest rose and fell in a rhythm syncopated to her own, and she wondered what chemicals flowed through him, what impulses shot between the different parts of his body. Her own impulses, the electric currents in her brain, were firing wildly.

As he watched her, she tried to decipher his expression. It was … calculating. Like the way someone might try to gauge the distance between two points in a jump to know how much force to use, the angle from which to approach it, how much of a running head start to get. Except he looked like he was standing on the ledge of a skyscraper, aiming for the next building over. Too high up. Too far to fall. Ready to back away.

"I … don't understand why you'd want anything to do with me," he whispered.

He kept his other hand, all metal and actuated joints, in a fist at his side. It flinched, like he was trying to remind himself not to move it. Bel remembered the first time they'd played Neon Sniper, how he'd held her off with that hand—maybe without thinking—pulling back once he'd realized, hiding it.

Bel took that hand too, and brought it to the other side of her face. "I want *everything* to do with you."

His gaze trailed over her for an instant, and then finally, he kissed her.

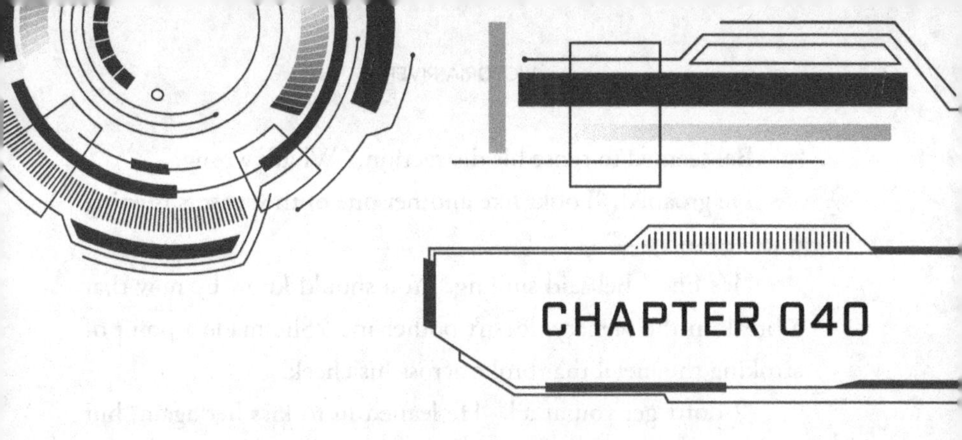

CHAPTER 040

EVEN THOUGH HE WAS DOUBTFUL as to what percentage of him was still human, Andro felt more human than ever. Both hands tangled in Bel's hair, kissing her, his whole body pulsing with an overwhelming energy. She was flushed and warm. Her arms drew him close, fingers pressing gently into his shoulder blades. For a moment, he could forget about the metal, like it wasn't any different than flesh or bone, just some inconsequential part of him. He was whatever he was, and Bel was whatever she was, and none of it mattered except for the points of contact between them.

They paused for a second, both breathless and coy. Andro opened his mouth to say something, but he suddenly couldn't form a complete thought. Bel brushed her thumb over his lips and kissed him again, making his battery hum. All the while, the stars watched over them—sharp, bright points, some twinkling or flickering, others steady—while the aurora snaked slowly past. It was only in his periphery, in the water's dark reflection, that Andro saw the break in the sky.

The VR scenery flickered as it had done once before, reminding him he'd forgotten to replace the failing sensor. The gray panels of the dome tore through, like a rip in the fabric of spacetime bringing through a glimpse of another dimension.

Bel seemed to sense his distraction. "What's wrong?"

He groaned. "Looks like another one of the sensors is going out. I'm sorry—"

"It's fine," Bel said smiling. "You should know by now that a break in the scenery doesn't bother me." She made a point of stroking the metal that broke across his cheek.

"I don't get you at all." He leaned in to kiss her again, but the break in the sky turned from a soft flicker to a steady, bright streak. He stopped and looked over.

"That's going to bother you ..."

"I know it's stupid, I just ... I wanted this all to be perfect for you. And I'm sure you're going to insist you don't care, but—"

"I could help you switch it out."

"No, you should stay here. Enjoy the scene—just face the other way, maybe? It'll only take a few minutes. I'll grab the replacement and be right back."

"You sure?"

He nodded. Before he could walk away, though, she grabbed the front of his shirt and pulled him against her, kissing him one more time. The force of it almost made him stumble, but he caught himself and let himself sink into it.

With his forehead resting against hers, he said, "On second thought ..."

Bel laughed and shoved him away. "Go."

Andro moved through the corridor with a sense of elated urgency. Long before he reached the storage zone, he'd already been mentally mapping out his way through the space so that he wouldn't have to think about which turns to take down which rows when he got there.

Left at the cleaning supplies, another left at the housewares, right at the first of the electronics.

His artificial lungs seemed to swell with more air than he could handle. What had he been thinking? He was never supposed to get close to this girl. But of course he'd never expected her to want to be close to *him*. Because of that, he'd let his guard down. He'd opened himself up.

Despite the risks, though, Andro couldn't deny that for the first time since arriving at the Submundo, he could envision a life for himself outside these walls. It would never be the same as it had been—he was fundamentally different now, and nothing could change that—but if Mateo Solís could get him the right information, he could leave this place and crawl back out into the light. He wouldn't have to hide anymore.

He didn't know what it would entail, to maintain himself, to restore his lost energy and continue living, but now there was a very real possibility that he *could* continue living. That had been the main problem, not knowing how long his battery was going to last. Knowing it was only a relatively short matter of time before he lost power—both a machine's death and a human one.

For this reason, he'd dismissed hundreds of ROSE notifications, not daring to see the drop in the numbers.

He must be down to 70 percent by now, even 60 or 50 thanks to efficiency loss. It would be disheartening to see.

Except that the difference now was that there was hope. Hope to bring down whoever did this to him. Hope to be repaired. He'd never be fully normal again, but he might come close. A new normal. He still had time—another few months at least, he guessed—to figure it out.

Inside the storage room, passing the housewares, he could

already see the red glow of the ROSE meter screen casting up between the aisles.

He *should* look at it, though, for reassurance. What irony, he thought, that in this moment, knowing could be more reassuring than discouraging. But it wouldn't be knowing how much of his life force had slipped away, it would be knowing he had a bit more time to get things in order.

With a deep breath, he forced himself to turn down the appropriate aisle.

When he saw the number, he stumbled backward. He slammed into the shelf behind him and sent a cascade of boxed device cases crashing down. Panting, he gripped the edge of the shelf and pulled himself up, staring hollowly at the device.

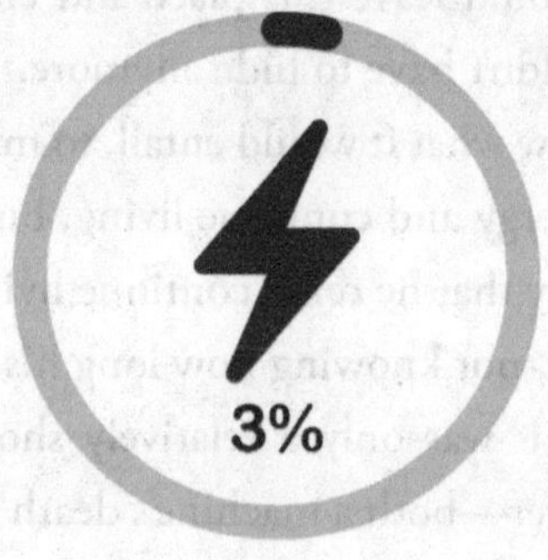

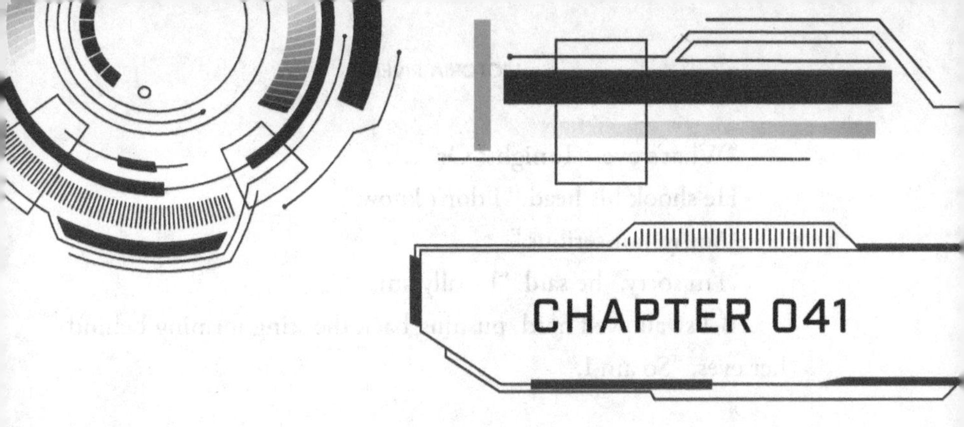

CHAPTER 041

BEL WAITED ON THE ROCKY RIDGE of the land close to the water, hugging her knees. Andro had been gone longer than she'd expected, and she found herself desperate for his return. It was pathetic, she thought, that she couldn't stand the few minutes she'd spent without him, how she couldn't stop thinking about the feel of his fingers—metal or flesh—on her skin. She watched the Northern Lights lazily, her gaze somehow falling past the entire scene and barely processing it, her mind delightedly elsewhere.

The dome's sliding doors startled her, parting the virtually distant mountainside and letting the corridor's light leak in. Andro stood there in silhouette. Bel went to him immediately, stopping short when his expression told her something was wrong. He hadn't brought a replacement sensor with him.

She wanted to ask him what had happened, but somewhere in the sudden shift, she couldn't find it in her to speak. And so, they stared at each other a moment before Andro finally said, "It's getting late."

"Late?" said Bel. "It can't even be 9:00." She pursed her lips. "And since when does time even exist in this place? You barely sleep, and—"

"Fine. It's not late. But this is over … okay?"

"What's over? Tonight? Or …"

He shook his head. "I don't know."

"You're not serious."

"I'm sorry," he said. "I really am."

Bel swallowed hard, pushing back the sting forming behind her eyes. "So am I."

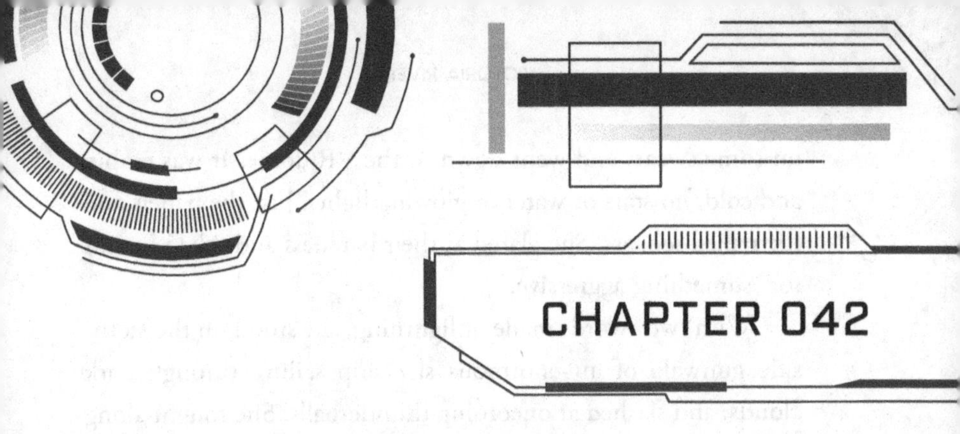

CHAPTER 042

BEL HAD SET THE VR SCREENS in her room to mimic outside conditions the way the Terrarium did, and so the dawn light faded in with true morning. She'd tossed and turned in that big, luxurious bed, playing the night over and over, looking for clues. All Andro had done was go to the storage room for a few minutes. What possibly could have happened along the way? And then, more than the questioning, Bel had fought with herself … because she'd known it would only take a couple of clicks to get an answer. She'd only have had to pull up a holoscreen and hack into the security feed and she'd be able to see where else he might have gone, what he'd seen, the exact second when everything had gone wrong.

But she wasn't going to be that girl anymore—a girl so desperate to satisfy her own curiosity that no one else's feelings or privacy mattered. The worst of it was that, for the first time, she felt like she genuinely *needed* to know—not out of idle curiosity, or as part of some high school revenge scheme, or even for her own protection—but so she could comfort Andro in some way, let him know he wasn't alone. This information was so much more valuable than the data she'd stolen before, and now she felt there was nothing to do but leave it alone.

When Bel couldn't stand to lie in bed any longer, she threw

on some sweats and went down to the VR dome. It was empty and cold, no stars or water or glowing lights. Just the panels and the naked sensors. She glared at their bareness and asked Lucius for "something aggressive."

With two swords made of lightning, she stood on the stern-side gunwale of an enormous sky ship sailing through dark clouds, and slashed at oncoming thunderballs. She fought along with an NPC crew behind her made up of aliens and humans dressed like space pirates, while swelling techno music played in the background. Five minutes in and she was already sweating as she stabbed the lightning sword directly in the center of a thunderball and watched it explode like a firework, with a boom that rattled the entire dome. She hit several more in a row and roared each time she made contact. A strike. Another strike. Another roar. Soon, they weren't coming fast enough. She climbed up onto the gunwale, precariously balanced, while the suspension cables in the dome supported her and lifted her higher as the simulated ship reached a new altitude.

Slash. Slash. Slash. Boom. Slash. Slash. Slash. Boom.

"Come *on*," she growled.

Finally, she couldn't take it anymore. She leapt up, meeting a huge thunderball mid-air and slashing it to explosion. The burst filled her ears and shook her body. And then, she hurtled down out of the sky toward the tiny city below. Forgetting where she was in real life, she relished the fall, welcomed it. She could already feel herself plummeting through miles of air, hair whipping her face, followed by an instantaneous destruction, the crush and snap of her every bone, the relief as her life seeped out of her. Only it wasn't really far below; it was a dozen or so feet, and the cables pulled taut and stopped her short of the floor. The forceful way they stopped her made her grunt, and she hung limply—pathetically—amid wisps of drifting cloud.

GAME OVER

The whole game disappeared, and she released herself from the cables. She dropped the remaining four inches and hit the cold, mesh-metal grating. Panting and defeated, she lay there, pressing her cheek against the hard surface. She was not okay.

For the next two days, she continued to busy herself in a similar way at the dome (careful to avoid Andro's shifts with Holomédico), or holed herself up in the library, or stayed in her room. If Andro had once again been using surveillance to make sure they didn't encounter one another, it was a wasted effort, because Bel wouldn't have known what to say to him anyway. The Terrarium sun rose and fell, rose and fell, and finally, on the second evening, as she lay on the grass, listening to artificial crickets and watching the all-too-realistic clouds float past the full moon, she knew it was time.

Bel found Andro in his office, staring at a set of building schematics on the holoscreen. Something he must have gotten from Mateo, who was still working on the details of his plan to infiltrate the Project Iterum site in person.

Andro looked up as she stood in the doorway.

"Do you want me to leave the Submundo?" she said.

He ran a hand over the short spikes of hair that he'd allowed to grow in lately, and chewed his inner cheek. "I don't think it would hurt for you to see what your brother's been working on."

"You said you didn't want to play games anymore," Bel added. "So why can't you just tell me what's going on?"

"I thought you might have already figured it out by now. You have ways of doing that."

"I don't *want* to figure it out. I want to hear it from you. That's not the kind of information I want to steal—not anymore."

"I appreciate that. But it's better this way, trust me."

"What way? Pretending like the other night didn't happen? I know you care about me. I'm brave enough to say that, even if you aren't."

"That night was a literal fantasy. We were pretending to be standing in a place neither of us has ever been in real life. And we were pretending we could be something we … can't be."

"Says who? Nothing and no one can tell us what we can or can't be to each other."

"It's not that simple." He shook his head. "Even if things were different … If I weren't trapped here without answers … Whatever I could be to you, it would only be partial—a *virtual* reality. And I think you've had enough of that. You deserve something real."

"It's not up to you to tell me what I deserve."

"You're right. But it is up to me to tell you what I think is right. And I think it's better that you don't get any closer to me."

"No," she said. "You're not going to do that. You're not going to tell me to stay away from you. You said I was already in too deep, and you were right."

"You've pulled yourself out of worse, I'm sure."

"If you were so set on holding yourself back from anyone—

from me—then why all the nice gestures? Why open up to me, take care of me, do things to make me happy?"

"Because people are inconsistent. Sometimes we want two things at the same time. Our natural instincts go against our better judgment. We gravitate toward the things and the people that make us feel good, even when it's not safe to. We rationalize one small thing after another until it's too late."

"That's not a good enough reason."

"You're a whole, incredible, human girl, and I'm just a … mutilated machine. We don't make any sense together," he said. "How's that for a reason?"

Bel clenched her jaw, trying to keep her emotions in check. She could see she wasn't going to change his mind. She just wished she knew how everything had shifted so quickly.

"I guess you weren't kidding," she said. "Game over really is game over for you."

Andro didn't seem to be showing much emotion. The only thing Bel could detect was a subtle movement at his throat, a tension as he swallowed. "I really am sorry."

"Well," she said, wiping her cheek as a tear broke loose and tracked down, "I guess it would only make sense if … if I left."

That's what Andro wanted, Bel knew it, but that didn't stop him from looking at her like she'd wounded him by saying it out loud.

Finally, he replied in a strained whisper. "Yes. It would only make sense."

Bel's backpack was full again, with everything she could possibly need to make it out of the forest and down to the nearest Mag, pressuring the pack's seams and threatening to bust out the zippers. She unfolded the Lightfoot—she'd insisted on taking the cheapest vehicle Andro owned, despite his protests—and pressed the ignition, watching the entire vehicle raise itself several inches off the ground in a slow, building motion.

She looked at Andro.

"I know you can handle yourself, but, in case you need me for some reason," he said, handing her a mini holopad, "this has my main device number programmed into it. I'll … try to be available for you."

"Thanks." She slipped the holopad into the back pocket of her jeans. "Mateo will still hold up his end of the deal. I'll do my best to help him get you the answers you need."

They stared at each other for a moment, neither of them really seeming to know how to approach this farewell. Andro absentmindedly pressed his thumb to his wrist. Bel took his wrist in her own hand, making those same small circles with her first two fingers—the smallest act of comfort she could offer. No matter how angry she was, she didn't like the idea of him being in pain, even if it was dull and he was used to it by now.

"You know, the human fingers," he said offhandedly, "can differentiate between textures as small as thirteen nanometers."

Bel thought about this as she pressed her fingers to his skin, paying attention to the texture, the feel of the realistic veins, the permanent creases from bending and movement. She inhaled and gazed out at the woods and wilderness before her, sinister as ever and painfully familiar after her time trying to survive in it with Mateo.

Andro drew back his hand just enough to clasp Bel's, stopping her motion. He stroked her knuckles gently with his thumb, a pensive look on his face.

"You know, it was inevitable that I would fall for you," he said. "I'm literally made of metal. And you're ... magnetic."

Her face warmed and her heart pounded and her eyes stung. "But you didn't just say that."

He nodded solemnly. "Right."

Bel mounted the Lightfoot, which dipped beneath her weight.

Andro waited beside her, and Bel was somehow stitched to the spot, not wanting to move, wishing she could be here and out there and everywhere at once. She ached to see her brother, to be in the city again ... but she didn't want to leave either. How could she leave the protective fortress that had kept her for weeks that had felt like months? Leave the closest thing she'd felt to home in years? Just ride away from a prison-turned-shelter, and from the boy who ruled over it in anguish, whom she seemed to have already begun to harbor inexplicably deep and complicated feelings for? As if he could read her mind, Andro stepped in front of her, his face a canvas that bore the brushstrokes of uncertainty and sorrow, and he kissed her one last time, deeply and without shame. Then encircled her in his arms, holding her for several seconds, like he was trying to absorb her, taking a deep breath that he trapped inside himself for a long moment before letting it go.

"You saved my life," she told him.

"And you saved mine," he said. "At least ... what was left of it."

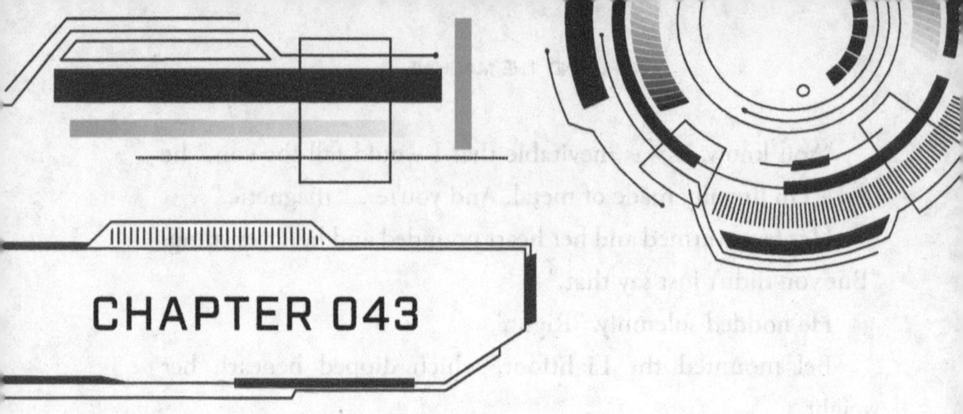

CHAPTER 043

ONCE BEL REACHED THE EDGE of the Los Padres, it would only take about thirty minutes to get to Santa Maria, at which point she would be able to get on the Mag and travel the remaining 225 miles in about seventeen minutes.

Her eyes were red and swollen, and she felt hollow. As she moved through the last of the rural outskirts, small farms and emerald vineyards striped the earth, bordered by a series of brown hills, prickly with sagebrush and dry grass and a few trees that were hardy enough to survive in such conditions. Little by little, bits of civilization appeared. A rundown vehicle charging station. An old diner. Small towns with a few amenities, medium towns, and larger towns that all ran together until they turned urban. The air had a different smell. Bel inhaled deeply.

This was going to be bittersweet.

Entering the main streets, panopts blared from every surface, newscasters' faces looking down on the citizens, products spinning to show off new features, block letters and logos bursting off the screens. Bel's finger instinctively scoured her hairline, feeling for her latest InVisor to make sure it was still there. These were the first panopts she'd seen in more than a month, and the sight twisted her stomach. Having been safe in the Submundo and free to walk around without an InVisor, she was no longer hardened to the presence of their watching eyes.

The Lightfoot adjusted to current traffic conditions and rerouted to a quicker way to the Mag station. Once there, Bel folded up the Lightfoot and used her digibank to purchase a ticket, carrying her vehicle and sitting on one of the side-facing benches along the Mag car's interior. A few minutes later, the San Francisco skyline greeted her.

Bel could hardly see the lead-up for how fast the Mag slid into the local depot, everything passing like a smudge on the windows, but she caught glimpses of familiar skyscrapers and bodies of water amid the haze of smog. She stepped out to another crowded station, a terminal with Arrival and Departure holoscreens and more panopts at every turn. From here, she unfolded the Lightfoot and input the coordinates to Mateo's apartment. She zoomed through busy streets alongside delivery vehicles, medical transport, private town cars, novelty cable cars, and other hovercrafts like her own. The traffic was heavy, so much thicker than the forest she'd just traversed.

The buildings were glass and metal behemoths looming over her, with panopts attached almost end to end among them, adding stark, intensive colors to the silvery panorama of the Bay Area. Models stepped out of the screens, posing, pantomiming; alien heads promoting *Saturnians III* gnashed their teeth; electronics, beauty products, and fast food menu items bulged out like parade balloons; the noise of these ads, mingled with news reports, shingled itself and created a grating dissonance.

Before she realized how far she'd gone, she spotted the Vivorex building.

The enormous double helix glimmered among its straight-edged neighbors, a wonder that visually honored the work of its inhabitants. Bel had to pull over and gape at the view—the metal and glass that somehow managed to represent this flowing, organic entity—gazing up to where its sky deck disappeared into the smog.

After that, it was only one more block until she'd reached the apartment building, a tall and luxurious thing, but no match for what she'd just seen. Still, she thought she should have paid a visit to the Wardrobe before she'd left the Submundo, because she was clearly very underdressed for the setting.

Andro had remotely added her to the apartment's digital account so that the scanners would recognize her and let her up. When the elevator door opened into the apartment, Mateo was standing there waiting for her.

Bel smiled flatly. "Hi."

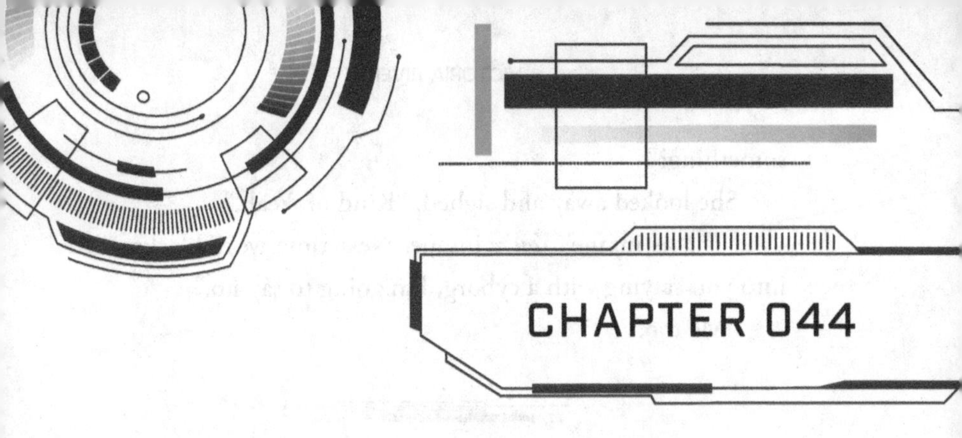

CHAPTER 044

MATEO DREW BEL INTO A HUG so tightly against his chest she looked like she could barely breathe. Then he pulled back abruptly to examine her, checking her for signs of damage.

Bel moved past him and into the apartment. She gazed up at the high ceilings, squinting at the fluorescent light, taking in all the straight edges, clean lines, all the steel and tile and marble.

"I see you haven't been suffering too much," she said.

He shrugged. "Not on a superficial level, no." He frowned. "I had no idea you were coming."

She dropped her backpack and took a seat on one of the couches, running her hand over the buttery leather that covered it. "Me neither."

"Everything okay?"

Bel didn't last a minute before breaking down. She told him everything—all she'd learned about Andro's memories and speculations, ideas they'd discussed about Project Iterum, and even a skimmed-over version of the events that had led her to want to stay at the Submundo and subsequently pushed her away from it.

Mateo listened without interruption, doing his best to stifle his knee-jerk response to hearing all of this.

"Wait a sec," he said. "Are you, like … in *love* with him or something?"

She looked away and sighed. "Kind of. Yeah."

"This is insane. *You're* insane. Next time we're blackmailed into you staying with a cyborg, I'm going to say no."

"Me too."

Mateo woke with his face sticking to the leather of the couch, his pillow somehow having fallen to the floor during the night. He'd insisted Bel take the bed, but he'd figured she would want to sleep in. Instead, she'd gone off somewhere early, then started making noise in the kitchen the second she'd returned. Soon the whole place smelled like melted butter and warm corn tortillas and scrambled eggs.

He rubbed his eyes.

"Do you want some *huevos con tortilla*?" Bel asked. She turned the contents of a frying pan over with a spatula. "I thought we could use a little comfort food."

Mateo meandered up to the bar and pulled out a stool. The scent took him back several years, to when their mom would cook eggs like this for breakfast. Melt butter in the pan, cut tortillas into small pieces and fry them, then add the eggs.

Bel handed him a plate and scooped a huge pile onto it.

"Are you feeling better?" He looked around for a fork just before Bel stuck one into his waiting hand.

She sighed. "Not really. But I'm dealing with it … as you can see."

"Glad to hear that." He chewed a large mouthful. "Now that you're here, you might as well make yourself useful. We've got a lot of work to do."

"So, get me up to speed." She turned off the burner and sat next to him with her own plate of eggs.

"I've got the schematics of the building where Project Iterum is operating. But, as Andro suspected, the building is on a WLAN, and even has an additional wireless security shield, so I can't intercept any signals from the outside."

"And then there's the bioscan entry panel."

"Right. So, I've been working on a way to bypass the bioscan and I just had a major breakthrough yesterday afternoon. It's pretty complicated, but I've been working on writing a program to hack it."

"Okay. Badass."

"Thank you. Once that's done, we're in, only there's just one small problem."

"Is it … walking into a building full of employees who will immediately know you're not one of them the second they see you?"

"That's the one."

"Bummer."

"I've already worked out a way to get an authentic lab coat—I spied on some of the employees coming and going to make sure I've got any logos or details correct—and scrubs like the ones they wear, because they all match and they're made by a supplier downtown. Same kinds of shoes and ID tags, all that stuff. But if I get stopped by anyone who wants to check my fake ID, I'm screwed."

"Why not just program a whole person and headshot and fake profile into *their* database so it comes up if they scan you?"

"Sure, but I can't access that database in advance. I'd have to be inside to do it, and it's not safe to go inside without it. It's paradoxical."

"So, you don't know anything about anyone who works there, other than what you've seen stalking them from the alleyway before and after a shift."

"Correct."

"What about employees who aren't technicians? Custodians, maintenance workers, IT? People whose information isn't important enough to be protected from hackers ..."

Mateo shook his head. "The only 'less important' people related to this project I know anything about are ..." he paused with his fork mid-air.

Bel raised an eyebrow. "Who?"

"Trainees." He slapped the table and grinned. "That's it—the students!"

"What students?"

"Remember how I mentioned the trainee program application I found in Veronika Mandersloot's messages? And how I was able to get into some of the HR data? I have all the trainee applicants' information. It wasn't protected yet because they hadn't officially been selected at the time."

"Okay, but you'd still have to impersonate one of them."

Mateo deflated. "Oh, right." He set down his fork and dragged his holopad over to himself, opening up a new holoscreen frame. He tapped through several files until he came upon copies of the applicants' information—the ones he was certain belonged to Veronika's figurative "yes" pile—then turned the screen so Bel could see.

She scanned the information, tapped between different documents, stopped to analyze photos. There were fifty in total. "Pretty diverse group. More women than men, a couple non-binary, but basically every race. Except I don't think you could pass for any of these guys. Very pale or very dark, and the one

guy who's about your color is a totally different body type."
She tapped back and forth to look at some of the others again,
passing over the females.

"Wait," said Mateo. "Go back."

Bel tapped to the previous applicant profile. "Yesenia Perez?
You really think you could pass for—"

"Not *me*, dummy."

Frowning, Bel gave the photo a closer look. The girl's hair
was different than Bel's—darker, and tightly curled—and her
skin tone was a bit lighter, too, but her facial features were
similar. She scanned the girl's physical details. Same height, and
her weight was only about ten pounds off.

"You want me to stop protecting you?" said Mateo. "Here's
your chance to walk into the fire."

Bel turned pensive for a moment. Mateo could see the
wheels turning in her mind. It was one thing to hack an identity
when all actions took place behind a keyboard; this would be
a live performance. It was much more danger than Mateo was
comfortable with, but he knew she wanted it, welcomed it,
would probably find a way to get into trouble regardless.

"What about the skin and hair?" said Bel. "And I don't *totally*
look like her. Her nose is narrower than mine, and her lips are
fuller. Cheekbones are a little higher too. I mean, the glasses are
easy to fake; I could just pick up a pair at the drugstore. But she
looks older—easily a grad student—and I'm clearly still in high
school."

Mateo took a deep breath and puffed out his cheeks. There
was an obvious solution to this; he just had to be willing to get
past his reservations.

"That won't be a problem," he told her. "Let's just say 'I
know a guy.' Or, more specifically … a girl."

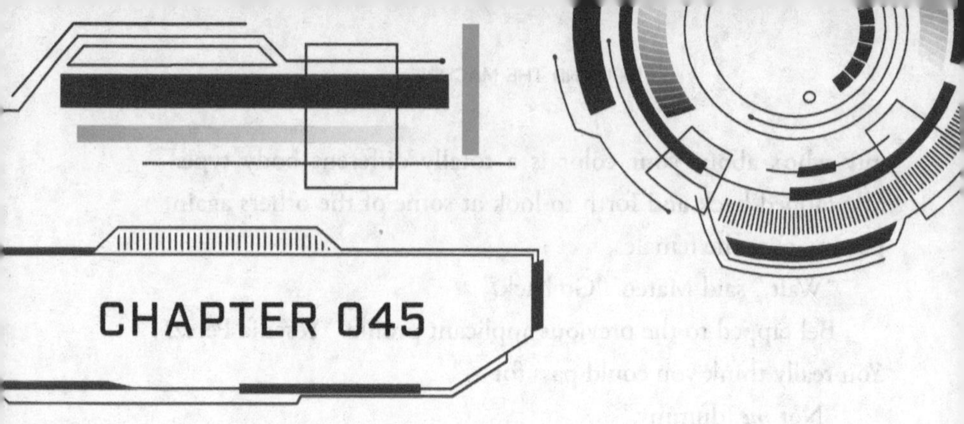

CHAPTER 045

"I DON'T KNOW ABOUT THIS." Bel trailed behind her brother through the usual morning horde along the sidewalk. People spoke to small holomorphic heads on holopads or sipped coffee as they walked.

Mateo said over his shoulder, "This is the hardest part. The rest will be easy."

"It feels a little creepy, how much we're going to have to stalk this trainee—intercepting her emails and all that."

Mateo had explained his plan the night before. The details of Yesenia's work with Project Iterum were a mystery, but her personal life was up for grabs. They could hack her email, set up a false emergency to cause her to leave town, then intercept her inevitable message to the lab to excuse herself for however many days, before her superiors would see it; that way, the people at the lab would never know to not expect her. From there, it was a matter of forging a trainee ID tag and having Bel take the girl's place. Between the class of fifty trainees and the masks they'd have to wear during their rotations (as laid out in the training materials), the whole thing should be ridiculously simple. She'd sneak away the first chance she got and start hacking the network, recording everything she saw and digitally feeding it to Mateo as she received it through a pair of Vues. The high-tech lenses would double as intel-gathering equipment *and* part of her disguise as the trainee.

Bel added, "And you really think this girl you met at The Circuit can make me look enough like Yesenia Perez that people who've been studying with her for *months* won't notice I'm a completely different person …"

"You haven't seen Kat's work. She's been able to get the paparazzi to sell photos of 'celebrities' to *People*—and *People* doesn't give away the green for celebrity lookalikes. If she can fool the media, she can definitely fool a bunch of lab trainees. Besides, the students have to sign an agreement not to socialize with their peers beyond what's reasonable for communicating basic information related to projects—so they might not talk to her that much anyway—it's in their application. Which is a huge red flag in and of itself that something's off with this whole thing."

A few minutes later, they reached Kosmetikos. The girl in question was working on a woman's hair, with a cloud of hairspray slowly dissolving around her.

The cosmetologist looked up, her long lashes bordering mauve-shadowed eyelids. She wore a black apron and stopped mid-tease when they came in. Smiling wryly, she flicked her gaze to Bel. "So you *do* make friends once in a while."

The client in the chair regarded Kat's guests but ultimately turned her attention to whatever was playing on her holopad, a music video with a lot of strobing lights.

"This is my sister," said Mateo. "And I'm really sorry for how we left things last time, but … I was hoping maybe you could help us with something."

Kat inclined her head, then continued teasing the client's hair, fluffing up a load of platinum blonde and spraying it heavily.

"Trying to get you to talk is like peeling off acrylic nails—and now you just show up here out of nowhere and you want me to drop everything to … *help* you?" She set down the can of hairspray and crossed her arms.

"Not drop everything," Mateo muttered. "Whenever you're available next. And we'll pay you for your time."

She picked up a different comb and returned her attention to the client's hair. "No thanks. Not interested."

Mateo looked at Bel like he wanted her to do something, but she only shrugged. What could she do? She didn't know this woman—although she loved her mustard Peter-Pan-collared blouse and the messy-chic topknot in her hair. Plus, she could only imagine what the girl's interactions with Mateo had been like. Frankly, Bel was surprised Mateo had managed to interact with Kat enough in the first place to even know where she worked.

"I really am sorry." Mateo stepped closer. The client threw him a glare but said nothing. "I know I made a terrible impression, and I don't deserve anything from you. I left you hanging more than once. But this is important."

She ignored him, not even sparing him a glance as she sculpted the hair, smoothing out the top surface to create a dome that did nothing to hint at the tangle underneath.

Bel gazed up at the celebrity photos along the wall. "No way. Is this your work?"

"Yep."

"Wow," said Bel. "It's incredible. I can't believe you can just—"

"My name's Mateo," her brother blurted, grimacing as soon as the words left his mouth. He'd left the name like an offering—a piece of meat for a wild animal he wasn't sure would respond kindly. A gesture of good faith.

The cosmetologist paused, her brows pinched together. Her lips parted, but she waited like she expected him to elaborate. When he didn't, she repeated his name. "Mateo." She let another moment pass as though she were letting it sink in.

"Mateo," he repeated.

She folded her arms again and narrowed her eyes like she was analyzing him to see whether the name fit.

Yet another long moment passed.

"Look, I really need to be able to trust someone right now," said Mateo, "and … I really want it to be you."

At that, she seemed to soften. Her lips broke into a gentle grin. Finally, she replied, "Okay."

"Okay?"

She nodded.

"Meaning … you'll help us?"

She twirled her comb and slipped it in her apron pocket like a gunman in a western holstering his weapon, then put her hands on her hips. "What can I do for you?"

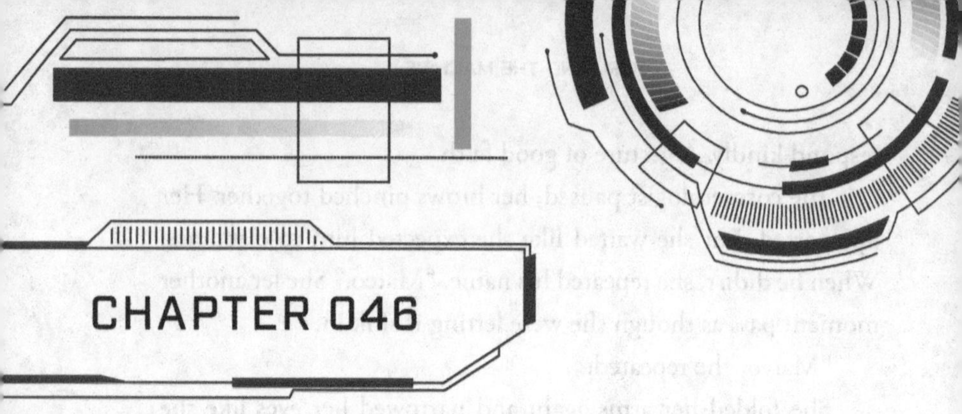

CHAPTER 046

THE FACE IN THE MIRROR was not her own. Bel wondered if this was what it had been like for Andro—in some sense—the first time he'd seen his reflection after escaping the lab. It was surreal. The strange girl blinked when Bel blinked and tilted her head when Bel tilted her head, and it was her, but it wasn't her either. She was a few years older, with a lighter glow to her complexion and a golden tone to her eyes—a look she'd had to wear contacts to achieve.

Kat appeared in the mirror behind her. "What do you think?" She slid her open holopad over, with Yesenia's photo three dimensionally projected. "Pretty damn close."

Bel let her fingers graze her newly curled and dyed hair, black spirals that framed her new face. "She's gorgeous. But I kind of feel like I'm in a horror movie. Like I just woke up to find out someone did some crazy body-switching experiment on me." At least it wasn't her own face mutilated, though, she thought. That would have been much more horrific.

The studio was eerie, and empty except for Bel and Kat. After hearing the gist of what this whole operation was about, Kat had decided it would be best to work on Bel early in the morning before normal business hours.

"You're like, a literal artist," said Bel, leaning toward

the mirror and poking her own cheek. "Like you just did a photorealistic oil painting—but with makeup—using my face as the canvas."

Kat crossed her arms and smiled. "That's basically the idea. Optical illusion. A mask that fits as closely to your face as a mask can possibly get."

Bel blinked away the discomfort of the contacts sitting on her eyes and twisted one of her new curls. "It's amazing."

A soft, digital chime sounded from the doorway, startling them both.

Mateo entered, then froze mid-step, his jaw slacking. "Whoa," he breathed. "For a second, I almost thought …"

Kat spun Bel's chair so she was facing her brother instead of the mirror and pulled off the black salon cape. "Let's hope that effect lasts for more than a second on these lab techs you're trying to fool."

Smiling flatly, Mateo nodded and took a slow breath. Bel knew this was hard for him, letting someone else in on their secrets. Despite Kat's surprisingly positive reaction to the explanation that they were "going undercover to get information and take down a corrupt operation allegedly abusing human test subjects," Mateo continued to be wary, like Kat might turn on them any minute. But as far as Bel could tell, Kat was thrilled just to know anything about Mateo, let alone be a part of this attempt at vigilante justice.

"Hey," said Kat, approaching Mateo and placing a hand on his arm. "You're safe. Okay?"

He scoffed. "I've heard that one before."

"Well, I can't guarantee you'll get out of that whole undercover situation unscathed, but I promise you I'm no threat." She glanced back at Bel. "I can tell you really care about your sister, and this friend you're trying to help. And all the people affected by whatever's going on in that project."

"Thanks."

"And you were right," she added. "Your secrets *are* better than everyone else's."

Bel approached the back entrance of the building, where a small panel on a rusted door flashed a scanner light. She touched her ear and the hidden comm device came alive with Mateo's voice.

"Okay," he said, the crown of his head barely visible above the ledge on the next building's rooftop where he was situated. "My program's already running interference with the bioscan, feeding it data that ties your bio signature to Yesenia's trainee profile. Give it a sec and you should hear it click."

As part of their plan, Bel had arrived early to avoid any direct contact with other trainees. She couldn't arrive *too* early—that might look suspicious—so she'd have to do this quickly.

"Don't freak out," Mateo had said, "and don't get distracted. Your job is to find any company device, make sure it has access to the closed network, then clone it and get the hell out of there. We'll do all the rest from the outside."

"Right, right. I'm just a Trojan."

"Exactly. Plus, anything meaningful you get on video. But that's just a bonus; don't waste time looking around."

Bel adjusted the glasses on her face—high-end Vues, which were fitted with an invisible camera and also operated as a tiny screen that could display almost anything a holopad could. Everything had been set up to stream footage back to Mateo's device so that he could see what she was seeing, as well as save a cloud copy of the footage. They weren't a perfect match for Yesenia's eyewear, but "I got new glasses" was a simple enough excuse if anyone happened to notice. Especially considering that this disguise was just a precaution anyway—in case Bel was stopped or questioned for any reason—and hopefully to blend in well and not draw attention in the first place.

Her pulse thrummed as she waited, not knowing what to expect once she was on the inside. Their limited information—having managed to obtain digital trainee orientation packets from a few months ago—had told them only that trainees were to report to Lab A, which Bel and Mateo had determined from the schematics most likely corresponded to a room on the second floor on the north end of the building.

Click.

Bel pulled open the door and entered.

Her gaze immediately rose to the height of several aisles of blue and silver struts, towering over her with boxes. Bright, fluorescent bulbs striped the corrugated ceiling, their light reflecting off the polished, concrete floor. It was all so enormous and overwhelming that Bel almost forgot to put on her mask. Quickly she secured the bands and adjusted it over her nose and mouth. She tucked her student holopad under her arm and squared her shoulders.

Just pretend you belong.

"Remember," said Mateo, "Get what you need and get out."

In the distance, the hushed voices of other employees spoke in foreign, technical terms. Bel tensed at the sound, paying attention to every inflection. Slowly, she moved through, following the schematics that displayed on the inner side of her lenses. As she passed aisle after aisle, she caught glimpses of technicians milling about wearing lab coats, some carrying open holopads and dragging three dimensional items through the air. A few manual laborers hauled covered equipment back and forth. A couple of security guards with stunners patrolled lazily along the outer wall. Thankfully, everyone seemed to be too busy to notice Bel—and no doubt assuming anyone who had managed to make it inside could only have done so with proper access.

She passed rows and rows of pallet racks lined with white and brown boxes holding unidentified contents, some of them shrink-wrapped, others out in the open.

"Must be part of the front," said Mateo's voice in her ear. "Cinco Industries."

Once Bel turned a corner, there should be a short hallway and an elevator. She held her breath until she reached it, not letting it out until she was safely inside, and pressed her back against the wall. The doors were an inch from closing when someone's hand slipped between them, coaxing them back open before a couple of techs walked in.

Bel's pulse quickened but she stood still. She could practically hear Mateo holding his breath on the other end of the comm.

The techs held coffee and discussed "Test Batch 6" and neither of them looked at her.

"You can see here," said the female, swiping at projected frames to open a page of graphs, "that the sensory reception is improving, but it's still falling short of our goal."

The male nodded along and analyzed the graphs with her. "See if your team can raise the level of Tactiperone in the somatosensory networks by another six units without any negative side effects. If that doesn't work, we may have to reconfigure the neuronal process altogether. Hopefully that won't be necessary."

"Hopefully," the other agreed. "Soto wouldn't be happy to hear that. We're already behind schedule on this batch."

The elevator reached the second floor and the doors slid open and the techs moved out. Bel waited a beat, then followed. She heard Mateo release a breath.

The second floor smelled of ammonia and iodine, bleach and camphor, and then a few other things Bel couldn't really define—vaguely human odors. Techs swarmed the floor.

"Don't just stand there," said Mateo.

Bel wanted to tell him she wasn't about to go charging in some random direction without calculating her next steps first; the last thing she needed was to bump into someone or walk into some area where Yesenia wasn't technically allowed. But she'd have to be careful about how she communicated with Mateo; she also couldn't be caught looking like she was talking to herself.

Familiarizing herself with the layout—the details that the schematics didn't show—she scanned for computers and other devices, for offices and server rooms, anything that might grant access to the information she needed. The main area was taken up by a curtained-off zone, although the majority of the techs were clustered together along the outer edges or moving between rooms.

The curtains bared glimpses of what might be between them, items draped in white sheets and flashes of holoscreens. As far as offices, most of the doors were closed, and those that weren't revealed technicians working at desks or talking to other technicians, which obviously wouldn't allow Bel to walk in unnoticed. The curtained area was her best bet; there seemed to be several devices back there.

Casually, Bel approached the curtains. Peering through the break in the blue fabric and the metal rod that suspended it, her throat tightened.

Several bodies were laid out in rows. They lay on thick beds with flashing lights. Male and female varieties with no hair. Each bed had a holoscreen next to it showing moving graphs that must have been monitoring vitals. Two techs moved from bed to bed, each holding their own holopads, tapping on charts like they were making notes or maybe checking off assessment items.

Bel whispered to Mateo, "What about one of the monitors?"

"Risky," he replied. "Features might be limited. Plus taking one could set off an alarm or something—it could cut off the stream of data from whichever body it belongs to and alert everyone in the building."

Not sure what to do, Bel waited, watching the techs. Eventually, the two techs came together.

"Units A602 and V311 are meeting all requirements for rem-con," one said to the other.

"I'll send over the units' info and let the staff know to prep the sources."

They parted and the first went out through a break in the curtains on the opposite end of the space. The second set her holopad into a docking station before heading off somewhere else.

"Are you all clear?" Mateo asked.

"Just about."

As soon as the tech was gone, Bel sprung to action. She pushed through the curtain, wove through the laid-out bodies, and kept her head low until she reached the holopad dock, quickly slipping the holopad inside her lab coat, then following the schematics to the nearest supply closet.

The light flicked on as Bel secured the door behind her, revealing mobile mop contraptions, giant brooms, vacuums, and floor buffers, and shelves with towelettes on rolls, cleaning chemicals, and sanitary gloves. Behind all the supplies, there was a small nook at the end of the shelves in the corner, where Bel slipped in and sat cross-legged on the floor, pulling off her mask and opening up both holopads.

"Shut down the lights," Mateo told her.

"I know." She used the local holopad to shut down the automatic lights. That way, if anyone were to come in, she'd have a reasonable amount of time to hide everything before anyone found her—or time to get out, if possible—while they tried to figure out the lighting problem.

Once that was taken care of, she opened another one of Mateo's software programs and connected her holopad to the other, preparing to clone.

"It should take about fifteen minutes," Mateo reminded her. "Assuming we're dealing with the kind of system I'd expect them to have."

While she waited, Bel started her foray into the local network's security feed, preparing to delete any footage of herself stealing the holopad—ironically, using the same holopad to do it.

"Got it," she said as she typed. "So, I just have to hope no one figures out there's a holopad missing, connects it with the trainee who's missing, and happens to check this closet."

"Right."

Bel located the second floor's main security camera, highlighted a clip of herself staring through the curtains and subsequently entering among the bodies, and tapped DELETE. She did the same for another camera's feed on the opposite side, where she could be seen coming out.

When she'd finished, the progress bar for the cloning process was still only at 27 percent.

"I'm going to have a look around while this finishes up," she told Mateo. "Might as well get a heads up on what kind of data we'll be sifting through, if I have to sit here until it's done anyway."

"Fine. But don't get too caught up in whatever you find. Pay attention to the holopads. You don't need to be in there a second longer than it takes to finish it."

A few documents were available without any special clearance. Mostly basic medical protocols, HAZMAT safety guides, information on how to replace a lost ID, and other boring and useless information.

There were also waivers for each test subject, and other legal documentation, to indicate prior knowledge and acceptance of the high risks involved in these tests, which was also spelled out *ad nauseam* (coma, permanent loss of sensation, brain damage, blindness, tumors, several other debilitating conditions, and of course death). Enough to allow employees the privilege of a clear conscience about their work. Bel wondered how many of the signed waivers had been forged.

Regardless, Vivorex had protections in place. Of course they did. A company like this wouldn't take these things lightly, which is why they were on a private network; it was the reason that basic information on the project was difficult to find even from within Vivorex itself, and the reason Bel hid in an office building that looked completely unaffiliated with Vivorex from the outside.

Another directory, titled Reference, contained documents with some of the following titles:

- *Cybernetics and the neuronal process*
- *Application of Shape Deposition Manufacturing (SDM), Smart Composite Microstructure (SCM), and three-dimensional multi-material printing in the construction of soft-robotic humanoids*
- *Sensory reception through synthetic somatosensory networks*
- *Spectral computed tomography and osteoreplication*
- *Metals in three-dimensional skeletal printing: steel, ossteel, titanium, and graphene composites*
- *Limitations of vidrinium in long-term batteries*

Mateo's voice buzzed in her ear again. "'Cybernetics,' 'skeletal printing,' 'sensory reception' ..."

"Are you going to read everything I'm looking at?" Bel said.

"Yeah. I'm going to read everything you read, watch everything you watch, keep my eye on your every move and my ear on your every noise. My ass is clenched so tight I'm probably going to implode—and I'm not going to let up for a second until I see you come safely out of that building."

"Okay. Yikes. Chill."

When she tried to access a folder of images, a frame popped up requiring a passkey. She pulled up a terminal to enter a string of code, which allowed her to break through easily.

Suddenly she was staring at thousands of detailed body scans, full color and three dimensional, all from different test subjects with an assigned number. Test Subject A304, Test Subject V517, Test Subject A102. Scans of real people that served as some type of blueprint, the exact size and shape of every bone, muscle, and organ.

"Must be how they recreate such realistic body parts," said Mateo.

There were endless images that featured 3D printed bones using different metals, prototypes and proofs of concept. More with actuators, synthetic ligaments and joints, muscles, and finally, the "functional integumentary tissue"—*skin*, Bel thought—layers building upon layers that told a long and fascinating story about the creation of humanity in a completely new way. From the broad and relatively simple skeletal structure to the fine intricacies of nerve networks. And the power behind its motion: vidrinium.

She skimmed dozens of pages on the production of vidrinium batteries and wires and how they could be utilized in test subjects.

Vidrinium (Vr) provides a new method for energy storage with an incredibly slow efficiency loss.

With a reasonable voltage, we can expect to power a single unit for up to a year, depending on energy output required.

There were diagrams for creating synthetic neural pathways, and a process for combining electronic signals with a chemical called Tactiperone to aid in tactile sensation.

"Tactiperone," Bel said. "The techs in the elevator were talking about that."

"What's the progress at?" Mateo asked urgently.

Bel glanced at the other holopad. "Fifty-eight percent."

"Seriously, Bel. The second it hits a hundred, you're out of there. There'll be plenty of time to look over all of that later."

She tapped around through a couple other directories, but there were too many. She wasn't sure where to start to get the best information. But mid-tap, she stopped herself. She knew what it was she wanted to see, and there was a way to narrow down to it immediately. She'd almost forgotten that Andro had a unit number. Fingers flying, Bel performed the search: A309.

The first thing that came up was an incident report.

INCIDENT REPORT
Supervising Technician: Elisabeth Wayland, Ph.D.
Date: September 10, 2086
Time: 11:30 p.m.
Location of Event: Site Q, Floor 3
Name(s) of Other Persons Involved: Technicians Sandra Persimmons, Aidan Longmire, Kyra Oh, Hector Chase, and Neil Hidalgo

Incident Type:
|x| Injury - First Aid
|x| Injury - Medical/Emergency Treatment
|x| Property Damage
|x| Equipment Failure
|_| Theft

Emergency Service or Police Called? Y/N
No

Reason Why or Why Not?
Discretion Protocol

Incident Description:
Unbeknownst to staff members, unit A309 woke. He soon fled from medical technicians who attempted to subdue him, causing a disturbance that led to the explosion of an oxygen tank, resulting in a fire that moved throughout the laboratory and spread to the surrounding area before staff members on duty could contain it. Several staff members were injured and

hospitalized. Several units were lost to the fire.

Estimated Damage or Loss Amount
Approximately $19.8 million

Types of Damage or Loss
Includes but is not limited to seventeen monitoring stations, nine test subject units, twelve holopad computers, and numerous miscellaneous devices and products of lesser value. All lost units accounted for via Sequitor® tracking data. Lost units: A302, A303, V304, A305, A307, A309, V310, V311, A312

So that confirms it, Bel thought. She'd never doubted Andro's video memory of events, but seeing it written out rooted her in the truth. It pulled at her, like a lace tightening across her chest.

She couldn't believe it was real, the idea that his body had been forced to become a "test subject," flayed open and mutilated just prior to this explosion.

With Andro's Sequitor® destroyed before he'd even left the premises (therefore emitting no signal and showing his last location as Site Q) and his body counted among these "lost assets," the lab would have no reason to believe he was still alive.

"Was that him?" Mateo asked.

Bel nodded, forgetting he couldn't see her face. But her Vues must have shown a shaky camera view because he then said, "I'm sorry."

She didn't say anything. It was too awful to dwell on right now when she still had work to do. She could let it sink in later, when she wasn't in the middle of a place she wasn't allowed to be, among the kind of people who butchered other people to test the authenticity of synthetic corporal systems.

Additional Notes:

All data and network assets salvaged, all source units removed prior to long-term damage of the facility.

"'Source unit?'" she wondered aloud.

Bel moved on to the next item that came up in the search, hoping for more context. This one was a video. The second she tapped it open, she gasped.

"Is that …" Mateo trailed in her ear.

It was a clip of Andro lying on a table, naked except for a cloth draped over his hips. It was like looking in on a morgue, only the body had more color than a corpse. Still, to see him like that, lifeless, motionless, made Bel's stomach churn. The table had an indicator; Bel could only guess that it doubled as a charging station, to replenish the battery that ran so many of his mechanical parts.

A woman in a lab coat stood over the table where Andro's body lay flat, and examined one of his limbs. Another person came to assist her. The body didn't appear to be breathing. The assistant touched a panel on the table's edge and the body began to make small movements—flexing fingers and toes, turning the head just slightly back and forth, the belly rising and falling almost imperceptibly. The woman spoke directly to the camera now.

"Test Subject A309, ready for rem-con."

Rem-con.

"The techs from earlier," said Mateo. "They were saying that about the test subjects behind the curtains …"

The assistant brought in a second body on a regular table—no charging indicators, just an IV and a few electrode attachments—and placed it beside the first, but blocked the camera's view while she situated it. Meanwhile the technician rattled off the details of Batch 3 units, how they differed from Batch 2, what new methods had been implemented, and what they hoped to improve upon. Batch 2 had had flaws in sensory reception, energy conservation, and connection strength, she said.

When the assistant moved out of frame, Bel felt like the life had drained right out of her. She covered her mouth.

Another Andro, identical, lay on the second table.

"What … the … *hell* …" Mateo whispered.

Bel stared at the two bodies on screen. Perfectly matched. Not a single discrepancy in the dark tone of his skin, in the shape of his face, in muscular definition or body composition. Even the mole on his shoulder—one Bel hadn't seen because the skin there had been burned away before she'd known him—and a scar above his knee.

Together, the technician and her assistant attached the appropriate connectors, opened frames on the holoscreen, and positioned themselves to observe what happened upon final procedure.

"The time is 8:04 p.m.," said the tech. "We will begin remote connection now."

With that, the tech tapped something on the holoscreen.

Andro's body—what Bel presumed to be the original, on the table without the charging station—convulsed for several minutes, his vitals spiking on every graph available, beeping rapidly. It scraped her nerves raw to watch. She cringed until, finally, after several long moments, his body relaxed, vitals calming and graphs leveling off. Now the graphs that corresponded to the android began to show change, a rise that settled into a steady rhythm.

Then, a soft robotic voice from the holoscreen said, "Remote connection complete."

"Bel ..." said Mateo. "This is bigger than we thought. This is ..."

Then Andro's doppelgänger—the android version of him—came alive. He remained comatose, but his chest rose and fell, his head turned slightly back and forth, his fingers flexed.

Bel felt lightheaded as she watched the techs monitor the connection and make sure there were no problems. They then began to prick and prod different parts of the android, measuring the response electronically. The tech reported each result and provided numerical specifics to support her assessment.

Then the tech told the assistant, "Please return the source unit to maintenance." She turned to the camera again. "This concludes the connection procedure for Test Subject A309, source and android units."

Bel stared at the screen, unable to form words. Andro hadn't been mutilated after all; instead, his mind had been captured and held hostage in some hyper-humanoid robot version of himself. Not a cybernetically enhanced body, but an entirely different body made up of synthetic parts. No wonder his "brain" had been able to store video footage of everything he'd seen. No wonder he couldn't sleep.

Finally, she choked out, "Maintenance ..." Her pulse beat in her ears. If the real Andro was still somehow "connected" remotely to this other body—the one that was made up of machinery, presumably the person she'd met at the Submundo—then that had to mean his original body was still alive somewhere. "Mateo ... What if Andro's body wasn't cut apart and fitted with a bunch of machinery? What if there's another version of him somewhere—whole? *Maintained.*"

Mateo pulled Bel from her churning thoughts. "Hey. *No.* Listen, I know you've just seen some pretty messed-up stuff, but I still need you to focus, okay?" He waited a beat. "You with me, Bel?"

Bel glanced at the holopad's progress bar, which was now full, reading 100 percent, but she couldn't seem to move. A numbness spread through her whole body. Horror clashed with hope.

It was possible for Andro to get his life back—the only thing he'd wanted all this time. Despite the nightmare he'd experienced, he could still come out of this physically unscathed. Bel just had to find out where his real body was.

"Bel. What are you doing? I just saw the progress through your Vues. You're done. Get out."

"It doesn't make any sense." Bel scrubbed back through the video of Andro. "They think the second body—the artificial one—was destroyed. Would they bother to keep the real one alive if it supposedly wasn't 'connected' to anything anymore? But if they *didn't* keep it alive, he couldn't just be walking around at the Submundo without a real consciousness, right? I mean—"

"We can talk about this later. Get up *now.*"

Bel was about to start collecting the devices when she saw that there was a third item in the search for Andro's unit number. It had come up as a tag, along with several other unit numbers, as a "related item." Her fingers seemed to move independently of her, tapping on the video.

"I'm going to go in there and kill you myself," said Mateo.

At first, the video appeared to be more of the same—an android body undergoing demonstrations and tests—but as Bel continued to watch, it became clear that this was something else entirely.

The tech in the video spoke over two bodies again, side by side, except that they weren't identical this time. In fact, they were complete opposites—one Caucasian male, one Black female. The female was hooked up to wireless electrode monitors and an IV line—a full human—while the male rested on a charging station, implying that he was an artificial unit. An android.

"We will now begin rem-con from the secondary source unit," said the tech, tapping a few buttons on the holoscreen.

Like in Andro's video, the human female began to convulse. Bel waited, forcing herself not to react. And as before, the woman settled back down into a usual rhythm and the computer voice said, "Remote connection complete."

And then, the male android began to breathe and move—again remaining comatose—shifting like someone reacting mildly to a dream in the night.

"This can't be real …" Bel whispered.

"Come on," said Mateo. "I've got that whole thing cloned, okay? No matter what happens with the network, we have more than enough information. Let's go."

Bel collected everything, securing the holopads under her lab coat and putting her mask back on. She crept out of the closet, keeping alert of who was coming and going nearby. As soon as the way was clear, she speed-walked toward the elevator, looking back and forth between the schematics on her Vues and the turns in front of her. There were several people along the final stretch before she would reach the elevator doors, but she maneuvered through them, keeping her head down.

She only had to make it a few more feet before she'd be able to get in, ride down to the main level, and book it out of this place before anyone had a clue she'd ever been there—and that's when she collided head-on with a woman in a white coat.

CHAPTER 047

BEL APOLOGIZED QUICKLY and tried to keep walking, but the woman blocked her path. She was about six inches taller than Bel, with stern features and auburn hair in a tight, low bun. She frowned as she looked at Bel's ID tag, which read "trainee" in bold lettering.

"Why aren't you in training right now?" the woman asked. Her own ID tag read "Dr. Elisabeth Wayland."

Wayland, Bel thought. *Where have I seen that before?*

Supervising Technician: Elisabeth Wayland, Ph.D.

"Sick," Mateo said in her ear. "Tell her you got sick and had to leave for a minute. Schematics say there's a restroom around the corner, so it'll check out."

"I was feeling sick," Bel told Dr. Wayland. "I had to excuse myself to the restroom. Didn't want to vomit all over the lab."

Dr. Wayland crossed her arms and frowned. "You know the rules. You should have called to excuse yourself instead of coming in."

"It came on really suddenly. If I'd felt that way earlier, I would have called, I swear."

"How about now? Still feeling sick?"

Bel shook her head. "Much better."

She heard Mateo smack his forehead. "No! You tell her you're *still* sick so she sends you home."

"Fine," said Dr. Wayland. "Head back to the lab, then." She nodded in the general direction.

The rectangular plate outside one of the doorframes was labeled LAB B. Bel hesitated, wondering if it was too late to follow Mateo's advice. "Actually, maybe I should—"

"Before you miss anything else," Dr. Wayland said.

"Right. Thanks."

Mateo growled through the comm. "Whatever. Just go in, keep your cool, and you can try to sneak out afterward."

Entering the lab, Bel scanned the five rows of student desks, and dozens of trainees typing notes on holopads while a man spoke at the front. She located a single, empty seat and walked briskly until she reached it.

"And what's great," said the presenter, who nodded at her once to acknowledge her arrival, "is that the functional integumentary tissue, or FIT, doesn't need to replace human skin to its full extent, especially when it comes to regulatory functions, since the bodies we're working with are mechanical and artificial and—in many ways—actually quite superior to the true human form. This afternoon we'll be looking at the process of membrane placement on an android unit and then we'll compare the results to its corresponding live test subject."

A young man raised his hand. "But there is virtually no way to tell the difference, correct? Between real human tissues and the FIT?"

"Not to the average person, no," said the presenter. "To those of us who know what we're looking for, yes. But the FIT is basically alive; it looks, feels, and acts like regular skin, works with follicles, it wounds and heals just as you'd expect. With the exception of large-scale flesh wounds that destroy its basal layer completely, of course. In that case, we'd have to use a FIT graft, or even fully replace the membrane, in order to repair the android externally. Any other questions?"

Another hand went up. "So, the outer appearance of each android is a near-perfect replica. But what about the behavior? I've been reading some of the reports on rem-con and I'm curious whether there's any discrepancy there. Any delays in natural response, trouble synchronizing, that sort of thing?"

The presenter nodded. "Good question. Remote connection and control has been a very long and complicated process, but thankfully the preliminary testing and proofs of concept were able to work out most of the errors prior to our experimentation with human test subjects. Any synchronization issues were resolved in Batch 2, along with the majority of sensation issues—although not all—after fine-tuning the sensory signals that are replicated and relayed to the source unit's brain, which allows the android to react to stimuli in a timely and appropriate manner. Batch 3 proved to be our most successful round of tests and propelled Project Iterum to its current stage, from which we've already begun testing field agents—without any issues to date."

A couple of the trainees started to applaud, a gesture that caught on until the whole class was clapping.

"Thank you," the presenter said. "We're very proud of how far we've come. And now you all get to be a part of what comes next. But just know that no matter the incredible technology you've witnessed, it would be nothing without the human consciousness. It's the consciousness that brings the most lifelike essence to each machine, the quality that completes the indistinguishability of these androids. Earlier technology lacked that defining element. But we have the pieces in place to ensure that field agents are able to essentially project consciousness from source unit to android unit on demand, in order to remotely control the android unit. The possibilities coming out of Project Iterum are endless."

Another hand went up.

"Yes?"

"Is there any way to track the source unit through its remote connection to the android? Say someone were to capture an android field agent. Would they be able to trace it back to the source unit's location and find the source unit?"

The presenter shook his head. "That would compromise security. Obviously we use the Sequitor® tracking system for our own purposes, while we're in the experimentation phase, to make sure all our android assets are accounted for—and thank goodness, since we had a close call with one of them last fall—but as far as the signals between source and android, those are heavily encrypted. Without Sequitor® trackers, we wouldn't even be able to track our *own* units." He smiled. "Any other questions? Yes …"

"What happens if rem-con is disrupted unintentionally?" a young woman asked. "Say an android unit is killed, or damaged irreparably. The source unit simply wakes?"

"In our most recent test batches, yes. Initially, though, we discovered that the sensory kickback from an abrupt—or unintentional—disconnection was enough to fatally damage the source unit. A shock to the brain. We resolved this issue in Batch 5. Without that resolution, the project would have failed to serve one of its major purposes: to create bodies that can be used to preserve or prolong human life. That's why this work is so important. Imagine entire military troops whose bodies could be compromised, but whose sources—already well educated and trained—could live on to fight in another body in another battle. Having 'but one life to lose' for your country would be a lament of the past. And there are countless other applications. Costs, of course, are high at the moment, but we hope that with time, we'll be able to turn android manufacturing into a common, sustainable practice."

A digital trill sounded from somewhere above them and everyone closed their holopads and rose from their chairs.

"See you all in thirty minutes," the presenter said over the noise of movement. "Be ready to discuss the properties of ossteel."

Bel followed her fellow trainees as they filtered back into the main area, but veered away as most of them headed for what she could only assume was a type of break room. Mateo urged her onward in her ear.

As she reached the elevator, though, her footsteps felt heavy.

"Why are you slowing down?" said Mateo. "You wanna get stopped by another technician? What's wrong with you?"

Bel touched the hard surface of the lab's holopad under her coat and slowed to a complete stop. If she left, and Mateo's attempts to hack into the network from the cloned device didn't work, she might not get another chance at the information. At some point, the lab might figure out there'd been a breach— when Yesenia came back and her attendance record didn't line up with her absence. Impersonating a trainee likely wouldn't work a second time. She was already in the thick of it; she had to take advantage of this singular opportunity.

"I'm sorry, Mateo," she whispered. "But I have to find him."

"Bel, please don't do this."

She looked over the schematics and pulled back, redirecting

to a nearby stairwell.

It should be pretty safe, she figured, with everyone using the elevators. Stairs were a formality, for electrical malfunctions and fires. Safely ensconced, she opened the lab holopad again.

Frantically, she searched through another mess of documents. Everything she could find on maintenance, what that meant and where the source units might be kept. She found something called "Protocol for Source Unit Maintenance."

Whenever possible, source units undergoing maintenance are to be stored in subterranean conditions, for the purpose of added safety and security, and must always be protected by Tier 5 clearance.

"Subterranean," Bel read aloud. She glanced at the schematics. "The basement."

She typed at full speed, entering one command after another to break through the limitations on Yesenia's ID number and give her Tier 5 clearance.

"Is there nothing I can say at this point to change your mind?" Mateo asked.

Bel shook her head. "Nothing. Sorry."

Following the stairwell—her safest bet, rather than going back into the fray of lab techs or braving the elevators again— she hurried to the lowest level. The door opened into an empty lobby, with another set of doors separating it from everything else. She waved the ID over the scanner panel and the door clicked, allowing her to push it open. A dark room stretched out before her, with special lighting on several rows of machines.

Bel's stomach dropped. The sight was like something out of an old science fiction film, with strange contraptions keeping human bodies alive inside them.

Source units were positioned within complex apparatuses, which appeared to provide electronic and chemical stimulation to the body, particularly muscles—probably to avoid atrophy and deterioration—but it looked like something alien, a disturbing violation of the human form. There were also IVs connected to drips of bright purple liquid—some advanced nutritional content, maybe—and tubes that seemed to be draining the waste from it. All vitals were being closely monitored, and each apparatus had a collection of UV-type lights at the top.

The men all had facial hair at various lengths. It looked like someone had been keeping them only minimally groomed. All wore the same clothing: a gray top and bottom, similar to scrubs but with snap buttons in a few areas for the convenient placement of wires, tubes, intravenous lines. Each had a wristband on the left wrist with a unit number and barcode. Several more bodies lay beyond.

Bel cringed as she approached a blond, bearded man with his limbs strapped to mechanical levers, electrodes stuck to his skin. Once in a while, the levers shifted, aiding circulation through forced movement of arms and legs like strings on a puppet.

The method made sense, though. The presenter had said the project expected units to be able to transfer consciousness on demand. It was likely they'd want to be able to connect a source to an android for weeks or even months at a time, and then disconnect and have a source that could get up and walk around without issue—unlike certain coma patients who might require physical therapy to recover.

Bel eased down the aisles between machines, peering warily into each one. Each time, she looked for Andro. Did this body have his skin tone? Did that one have his hair? Was that his jawline? Were those his shoulders? But one after another was too pale or too short or too old or too female.

Another set of machines were sectioned off from the others. She wasn't sure at first what made them worthy of their own special zone, but upon closer inspection it became clear. Aside from the fact that this particular set of people were shaved clean of any hair—nothing on the head or face, not even eyebrows—they had another important distinction: They weren't connected to anything. While all the others had monitors with a green indicator that read "connected," these did not. Their monitors only showed vital signs.

"Maybe they're *waiting* to be connected," Mateo offered.

"Maybe." Bel stood over a middle-aged woman with olive skin and a mole on the right side of her chin. The woman seemed vaguely familiar, but Bel couldn't place her, not in her current state. And anyway, the odds that she would have met one of these people wasn't likely.

At the end of the row, another holopad sat in its dock, with a login screen waiting for input. Bel inched toward it, brow cocked.

"You thinking what I'm thinking?" Mateo asked.

Looking around to be sure she was still alone—aside from dozens of unconscious bodies—Bel withdrew the holopad with Mateo's software on it and brought it beside the docked device, wirelessly analyzing the access point.

"Only if you're thinking the devices down here aren't on the same network as the rest of the building."

The software brought up an alert.

ACCESS DENIED
Tier 6 Clearance Required

"No way would we have been able to get into this with the cloned holopad." Bel whispered through the comm as Mateo's software began to crack an entirely different set of restrictions.

After a few minutes, Mateo had to interfere with the cracking attempt, instructing Bel on a few commands that were advanced even for her, before finally breaking through.

The login screen faded to reveal another database. And of course the first thing Bel did was search A309.

The results came fast—a single line that sank her.

Test Subject A309: Source Unit - Terminated from Project

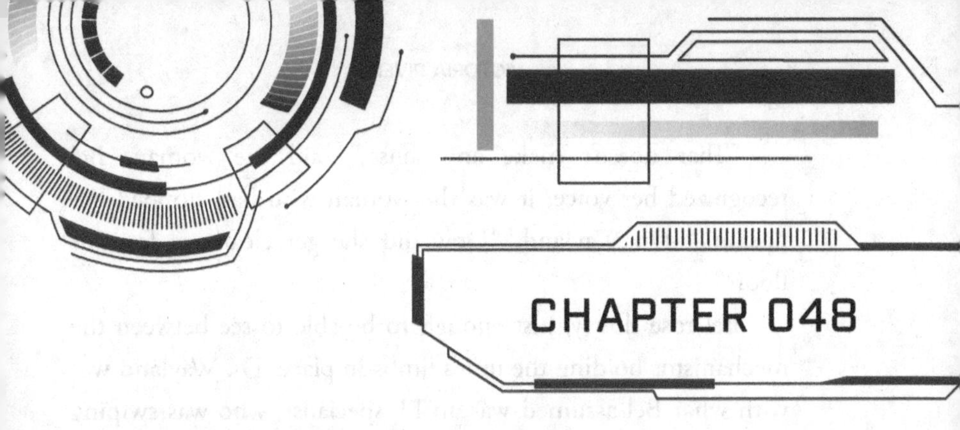

CHAPTER 048

BEL STARED AT THE WORDS on the holoscreen for longer than she should have.

Terminated from Project?

What could that possibly mean?

Andro was alive in his android body, so there had to be a source unit—the real Andro—controlling it from somewhere. She was certain it wasn't possible for his entire consciousness to have transferred to the android and simply stayed there if his organic form had been killed. That wasn't how remote control worked.

The source unit had to still exist—but where? The one thing that would have given Andro hope, and now Bel was back at square one in terms of finding it. She didn't even know where to *start* looking. Not if his unit number was no longer in the database.

Then a voice echoed from the lobby. No—two voices. A man and a woman. She hadn't heard them come in.

Pulse quickening, Bel searched for another closet, for anywhere to hide, but there was nothing she could get to that didn't pass the lobby's view.

She ducked behind one of the machines.

"What's going on?" said Mateo. "Is someone there?"

"That doesn't make any sense," said the woman. Bel recognized her voice; it was the woman who had stopped her upstairs—Dr. Wayland. "How did she get clearance for this floor?"

Bel rose slowly, just enough to be able to see between the mechanisms holding the unit's limbs in place. Dr. Wayland was with what Bel assumed was an IT specialist, who was swiping through data on a holopad supported on the crook of his arm.

Mateo muttered a string of curses.

"I have no idea." The IT specialist typed something one-handed. "But her profile says she's been granted access. Recently."

"How recently?" Dr. Wayland asked, peering around the room, squinting into the darkness. "Lights on," she demanded.

The room lit up and Bel ducked back down.

"Less than twenty minutes ago," the specialist told Dr. Wayland. "It also looks like she's been accessing test subject video logs that she normally wouldn't have clearance for."

Dr. Wayland released a huff of frustration. She spoke again, this time to someone else, like she was using a comm. "Yes, can you please send Yesenia Perez to my office?" she said. "And I'd like a security guard as well, in case there's any resistance. Thank you."

Mateo said, "Just hang on. Stay still."

Bel held her breath. Her pulse was thick and heavy, like it might burst her veins.

"Soto's going to have my head for this," Dr. Wayland muttered to the specialist. "*Another* disaster on my watch?" she shook her head and huffed. "Come on. We're done here."

"Wait," he replied. "This entry log … It says she never swiped out."

"So, she's still on the floor?"

Silence now. They were both on alert. Watching, waiting.

In her crouched position, Bel started to tremble, struggling to remain compact without breathing audibly.

"Cancel that," said Dr. Wayland to her comm. "Send security down to Level One. Immediately."

"Bel," said Mateo, "You need to try to reach the holopad …"

How Bel longed for a simpler time, when her worst crime was remotely locking down the biology lab at her school so she didn't have to dissect a fetal pig, or tampering with the exam software to get out of a history test that—in her opinion—was a test of inaccurate and incomplete curriculum. Aly had joked once about having her set off a fire alarm during finals, but of course that would have been a Class B misdemeanor so she never would have actually—

Wait, she thought. *Alarm!*

She repositioned herself so that she could operate the holopad again, typing until she tapped into the building's electrical system. She pulled up a control panel, looking at a live diagram of the floor. Everything was marked and visible, all the doors, the activated locks, the security requirements for individual machines, the lights.

"Good girl," said Mateo.

One tap and the room fell dark, as before.

"Lights on," Dr. Wayland said.

Bel tapped them off again.

Dr. Wayland growled. "Lights *on*."

Off.

"What the hell is going on?" Dr. Wayland said.

"Someone else must be controlling it. Would this girl know how to do that?"

While they discussed the possibility of an entry-level lab

trainee controlling the lights, Bel located the back door alarm. As she moved to set it off, the security guards entered, their heavy boots much louder on the concrete than Dr. Wayland and the IT specialist had been with their more sensible shoes.

The high-pitched alarm sounded from the opposite side of the floor.

"She's going out the back," Dr. Wayland informed the guards.

The pattern of stampeding footsteps faded to that direction. Bel stood, blood returning to her legs where they'd been tightly bent. Everyone was gone. She made a mad dash for the lobby. The doors wouldn't open. She grunted as she pulled out her ID pass—but when she swiped it, the screen beeped a negative tone.

"What?" She tried again.

Another beep.

A flashing red light.

The specialist must have revoked Yesenia's clearance while he was looking at the activity log.

With holopad still in hand, Bel opened the terminal to try to regain access, wishing she'd left that frame open from before. Yesenia's employee profile came up again, giving Bel the chance to enter the code to change the clearance level.

Before she could update it, though, the doors opened independently of her. Without thinking, she rushed forward and slammed directly into a pair of security guards.

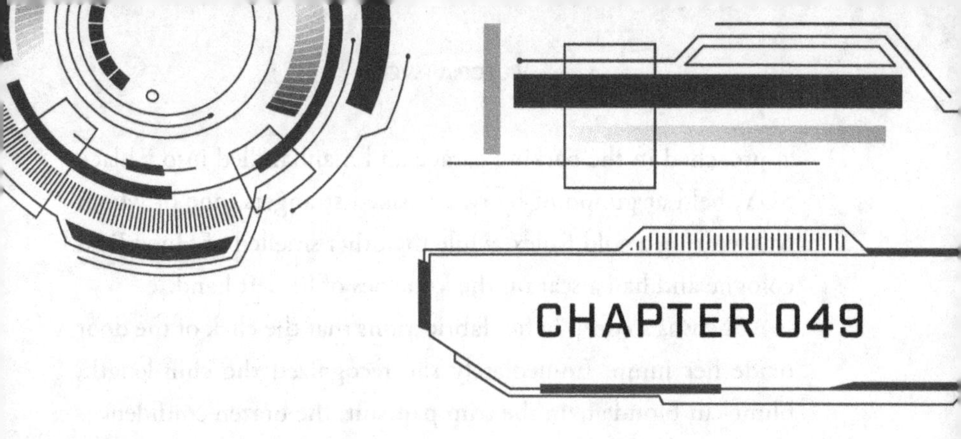

CHAPTER 049

THE GUARDS LEFT BEL IN A SECURED ROOM, dark and windowless with a metal table and two chairs. A few incandescent lights cast a dim glow on her as she waited, handcuffed.

They'd searched her, taken both holopads, the Vues, and her communication device. It was disappointing, but thankfully the footage she'd filmed wasn't stored on the Vues themselves and was safely in the cloud under Mateo's care. She also trusted that Mateo had severed his connection to her devices and made sure his own were untraceable. She didn't, however, trust that he'd made himself scarce; he was probably lurking around the outside of the building, trying to find a way to rescue her.

Bel groaned and tried to rest her head on her cuffed hands. She could still try to make some excuse when they questioned her. Her current story, which she'd rehearsed mentally several times now, was that she was being blackmailed into using her position within the lab to gain information for a mysterious enemy. She would claim that she'd never seen the man who'd put her up to it and that she had no interest in hurting the company—she only cared about the safety of her sick mother, who lived in a nursing home in Sacramento. She'd tell them she was happy to give them any information she could to help them find the real culprit. This would require some other lies, like how she'd been approached in the parking garage and manhandled into a black SUV, held at gunpoint by two masked strangers, one of whom was wearing a gold Rolex, while the other smelled of Hugo Boss cologne and had a scar on the knuckles of his left hand.

She was so deep in her fabrications that the click of the door made her jump. Immediately she recognized the chin-length, blunt-cut blonde hair, the trim pantsuit, the brazen confidence.

Veronika Mandersloot.

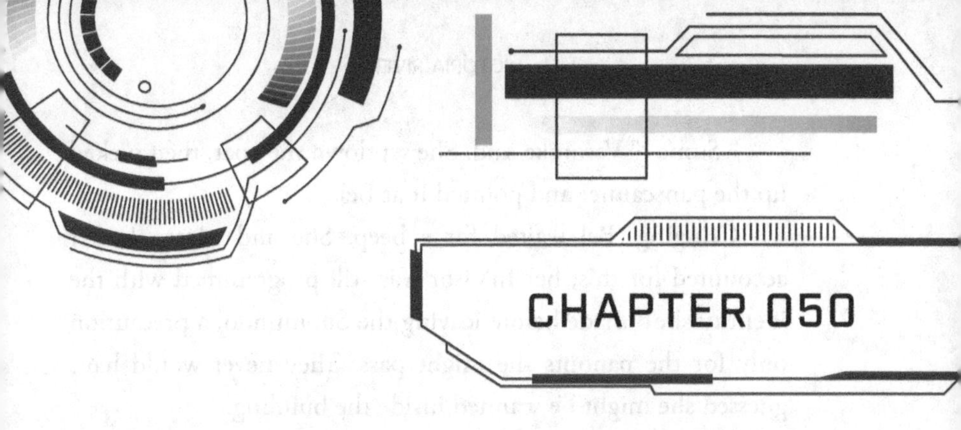

CHAPTER 050

"YOU RECOGNIZE ME," Veronika noted.

Bel parted her lips, but no sound came out.

Veronika smiled, although it didn't quite reach her eyes, and extended her hand. "Veronika Mandersloot, as you know."

"Yesenia," said Bel. It was hard to shake someone's hand in cuffs. "I know this all looks really bad, but I promise you I was acting under duress. I meant no harm to—"

The door clicked again and the security guard stepped in, carrying the lab coat Bel had been wearing, along with the ear comm, the Vues, and some kind of scanning device. "Ms. Mandersloot, we weren't able to recover any footage, but here are the trainee's items, and a panscanner, as requested."

Panscanner, Bel thought. Like pan*opt*, pan*drone*?

A *portable* panoptical scanner?

"Thank you," said Veronika. She placed the three devices on the table and examined the lab coat. When she came to a few colored streaks on the collar, she paused. "You wear a lot of makeup?"

Bel shrugged and said, "Some." Yesenia's face in her photos had been relatively bare; Kat had made sure to give Bel the no-makeup look, despite the fact that, ironically, Bel was wearing more makeup than a *Saturnians* cosplayer.

"'Some'?" Veronika said. She set down the coat, then picked up the panscanner and pointed it at Bel.

Cringing, Bel waited for a beep. She and Mateo hadn't accounted for this; her InVisor was still programmed with the identity she'd made before leaving the Submundo, a precaution only for the panopts she might pass. They never would have guessed she might be scanned inside the building.

When the results popped up, Veronika narrowed her eyes. She looked at Bel, then back at the scanner. "Guard!"

A second later: "Yes?"

"Bring me a damp rag."

The guard raised an eyebrow but returned after a moment with something that looked like it had come from the custodial closet.

Veronika handed it over, pinched between her index finger and thumb. "Wipe your face."

Reluctantly, but without much choice, Bel did as she was told. The cloth came off bearing blotches of the same color Veronika had seen on the lab coat, with several other tones from Kat's contouring.

Scowling, Bel dropped the rag with a wet slap.

Somehow Veronika managed to maintain her poise as she took her own seat across from Bel, a fierce and stylish executive in this second-rate interrogation room. "Tell me what you're doing here, posing as one of my trainees."

"*Your* trainees?" Bel said. "Weren't you fired from Vivorex? How can you still be running one of their labs?"

Veronika ignored the question. "I don't believe for a second you're doing this under duress. If someone wanted to target this project through an employee—or future employee—they'd have coerced someone who actually works here, not gone undercover.

Who are you working with?"

"I'm working alone," Bel lied. She hoped Mateo wouldn't burst into the building any minute, proving her wrong and endangering them both.

Veronika gave her a sideways look. "And what, exactly, is your objective here?"

"To make sure what you're doing is ethical."

"Really," Veronika said with a laugh. "And what did you conclude from your ... *research*?"

"I think you already know."

"Humor me."

Bel ran her tongue over her teeth and took a breath through her nose. "I think this is a butcher shop."

Pursing her lips, Veronika crossed her arms and leaned forward. "That ... is ... exactly what I wanted to hear."

Bel wrinkled her eyebrows. "What?"

Veronika put both hands on the table and lowered her voice. "You're right—I was fired. But not for the reasons the media would have you believe. I've opposed this project— and all projects like it—from the beginning. But I trusted the wrong executives, made some poor choices, spoke out when I shouldn't have. They wanted to keep me quiet. So, when word got out about some of the practices going on, I'm the one they blamed. After that, all they had to do was fire me publicly and they were free and clear of guilt—at least as far as the public was concerned."

"Then what are you still doing here?"

She whispered. "Isn't it obvious? I'm 'cooperating.'"

"What do you mean?"

"I apologized. Begged for another chance. Told them I'd work anywhere I might be needed, do anything they wanted, that I'd overlook my personal biases and focus on the importance of the work, even if that meant sacrificing a few ethics in the process. I convinced them I could do better, be better, that I had a brilliant mind and they couldn't let it go to waste. It took a bit of persuasion, but eventually Soto let me run this lab—as a test of my loyalty. So, *officially*, I am no longer affiliated with Vivorex. Unofficially, well … I'm here, aren't I."

"I still don't get it …"

"Look," said Veronika, "I admire what you're trying to do. Really. It's an incredibly brave thing, walking in here like you did, risking so much to expose the truth because you believe it's what's right. But I already have this covered."

"So, then … you're trying to expose Soto too?"

Veronika nodded. "I can't say much else, but yes, basically. I'm only telling you this because I believe it would be ridiculous not to trust someone who's gone to this much effort to infiltrate my lab. You're clearly very passionate about the cause against what we've been doing here. Which I appreciate." She glanced toward the door. "But I *am* going to have to ask you to let me handle this. Whatever footage you've streamed out of here, whatever evidence you may have seen … Releasing it could compromise everything I've worked so hard for. I've been earning Soto's trust, building a full directory of hard evidence—enough to end all these experiments, bankrupt Vivorex, and put Soto away for the rest of his life. I'm already well on my way to taking down this whole operation. And what you've seen, I need you to keep it to yourself. If you really care about stopping it, if someone you care about was hurt by it, whatever your reasons are … Please let me finish what I've started."

If someone you care about was hurt by it.

Bel took a deep breath, trying to work through all this

information. Andro's history with this experiment was horrific enough, but all the lying and scheming and entanglements were hard to wrap her head around. She supposed it made sense, the way people in power would have tried to silence Veronika, the way Veronika was forced to publicly take the blame. And here she was, continuing to fight them from right under their noses. Bel couldn't help but gawk at her.

But also, it occurred to her that knowing that Veronika was secretly working against the whole thing could be helpful. This woman had information that might otherwise take weeks to find.

"Can you at least tell me," Bel asked, "what might have happened to some missing source units?"

Veronika narrowed her eyes. "*Missing* source units?"

Bel nodded. "I was looking for one in particular. When I searched the unit number, it came up empty. 'Terminated from project.'"

Sighing, Veronika softened. "Look, I don't know what this person meant to you, but, unfortunately, 'terminated from project' is a nice way of saying"—she grimaced—"that that unit is … no longer with us."

Sinking in her chair, Bel once again, racked her brain for the logic of this. It had to be a coverup. It didn't make any sense.

"What if I know for certain—or almost certain, at least—that that can't be true?" Bel said.

"We keep track of every source unit and every android unit. All units accounted for, at all times. If the record says 'terminated,' the unit is either dead or destroyed. I'm sorry."

"And you're sure there's no way anyone is keeping additional source units hidden somewhere else? You don't think Soto or one of the upper-level technicians could be doing other experiments without your knowledge?"

Veronika crossed her arms and looked at Bel sharply. "I suppose anything is possible. But that's not something I can afford to look into right now. Any suspicious behavior on my part could ruin everything I've been working for. Even your presence here is a threat to my position. You understand that, don't you? If I'm going to expose this whole operation with any real impact, I need your full cooperation."

"How long will it take to expose Project Iterum and make sure Soto is held accountable?"

The woman shrugged. "I can't say with any certainty. I can only tell you that I'm *very* close to getting the justice that I—and all the victims here—deserve. Weeks away, if we're lucky."

Weeks, Bel thought. Weeks would feel like years, knowing what she knew now. Imagining Andro's source unit hooked up to those mechanisms, feeding him purple fluid through tubes, artificially stimulating his muscles and joints. And not just him, but all the others who, like him, had been taken against their will.

"Once you've exposed everything, will you be able to find out what happened to my missing source unit?"

Veronika scoffed. "*Your* missing source unit?" She looked her over, analyzing her. "You're tenacious, I'll give you that. It's possible, yes, that I might be able to find more information once I've fully opened the Pandora's Box that this company has created."

"If you can do that, then ... I guess I can leave it alone, for now."

"No—you have to leave it alone *completely*. You don't know the kind of people you're dealing with. If they find out who you are, what you know, they can destroy you. From what you've seen today, you should have a pretty good idea of the least they could do. Believe me, it can get so much worse."

"People have tried to destroy me before. My family, at least. I've managed to survive this long …"

"That doesn't surprise me. But like I said, you need to let me handle this. I'm closer to the enemy than you are. Okay?"

Bel sighed. "Okay."

Veronika smiled sympathetically. "You know, you really had me fooled with all that makeup. You're so young."

"I guess I am."

Standing, Veronika smoothed any potential wrinkles from her pantsuit. Bel stood too and waited.

"I'll sneak you out the back. Your visual state right now," she said, gesturing around Bel's partially made-up, half-wiped face, "will cause a scene if we let any of the employees or trainees see you like that."

Bel touched her own cheek. "Right."

"I'll make sure everyone finds out that I 'dealt with' you. They'll assume the worst, and that'll be that."

After entering a digital code on Bel's handcuffs to unlock them, Veronika led her through a labyrinth of abandoned shelves and supplies until they reached the backside of the building, then released her into the alley behind the building.

"Thanks," said Bel, still a bit rattled.

"If you really want to help," Veronika told her, "you can contact me with any new information you've found. Any other leaks, or leads on something you think I might not know about. Just call the Vivorex main line and ask for Dr. Wayland; she can put you through to my private extension. Honestly, the best thing you can do is supplement the pieces I've already put in place. I mean, why work separately when we're on the same side?"

"That makes sense."

"Great. Good luck." Veronika shook Bel's hand again and winked, then went back into the building, the door clicking shut behind her.

CHAPTER 051

VERONIKA'S HIGH HEELS CLACKED on the cement floor as she walked with angry determination.

"Ms. Mandersloot," said Dr. Wayland, smoothing the sides of her pulled-back hair. "I'm so sorry I didn't catch that trainee sooner." She fell into step with Veronika. "I never would have imagined anyone would be capable of infiltrating the lab like that."

Not bothering to stop, Veronika simply said, "Forget it."

"You won't tell Mr. Acero, will you? I'm on thin ice with him."

Scowling, Veronika rolled her eyes and kept walking. "Neither of us has the mental bandwidth to deal with your oversight right now. I handled the situation."

Dr. Wayland frowned. "I didn't see any guards. You just escorted her from the building yourself?"

"That's right—and don't let that get around the lab. Not everyone will understand."

"I don't really understand either. Who knows how much information she must have streamed out? Not detaining her leaves us vulnerable to exposure."

"Yes, but if I were to keep her here—torture her, even—to try to find out who she's really working with, I'd only encourage the other conspirators to begin releasing data. I could spend hours interrogating her, while our videos could be leaked in seconds. Now she thinks I'm her ally, that I'm already furthering her cause and that she has no need to be so hasty. I've persuaded her to delay her exposé, which buys me some time to investigate. I have her identity in the panscanner's memory and I'm getting my best associate on it right away."

"So, there's nothing to worry about …"

"Nothing at all. We'll find out everything there is to know about her and we'll make sure anything she's got on us disappears from every device she owns. As it turns out, there are *many* advantages to working with the Knight Crew."

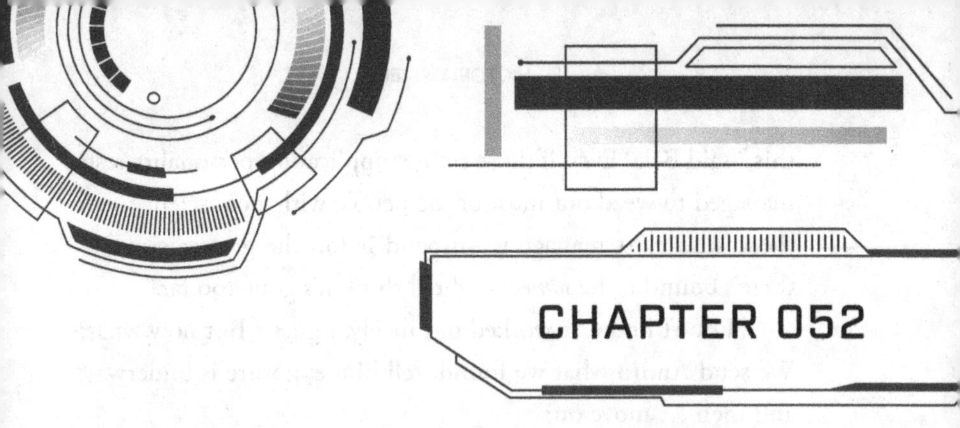

CHAPTER 052

"YOU HAVE GOT TO BE KIDDING ME," said Mateo.

Bel had found him on the building's roof, tampering with the door lock, but luckily he hadn't gotten very far because he was still trying to dismantle the alarm digitally. He'd been so relieved to see her, and they hadn't stuck around longer in case the whole thing had been too good to be true and someone was on their way to apprehend them, so it wasn't until they'd returned to the safety of the apartment that he began to question her more closely.

"I thought it was crazy too," Bel replied "But she's working on it from the inside. A *true* insider, not like me. She already has clearance for almost everything, and everyone completely trusts her. Mostly, that is. I think Soto might still have his doubts."

"And we're just … not supposed to release any information until *she* does?"

"She wants to put Soto away for good. And I think that's for the best. After what he did to Andro …" Bel felt sick now that she had a moment to process everything. The videos she'd seen, the details of the lab work. How could someone do that to another human being? And worse, to a family member?

Mateo pulled at his hair. "This is exhausting."

"Of course we're not going to be the only ones looking into

this," said Bel. "Even if those trainee application personality tests managed to weed out most of the people with a conscience—or those who can't manage to suspend it for 'the greater good'—there's bound to be *someone* who'll think it's gone too far."

"I don't know. It worked out nicely, I guess. But now what? We send Andro what we found, tell him exposure is underway, and then ... move on?"

Bel shook her head. "I don't want to tell him anything yet."

"What? Bel. That's literally the whole reason we risked everything to get this information—so we could tell him all of it *as soon as possible*."

"Sure, but what's he going to think when he finds out what's really going on? When he sees that there are *two* of him? He's immediately going to wonder if there's a chance he still has a source unit somewhere, and where it is. Since I don't have an answer to *that* yet, I don't want to open that door for him. Not until I have a better idea. Veronika said she might be able to help, although ... that could take a few weeks."

"Weeks," Mateo repeated bitterly.

"I thought we could do some digging on our own in the meantime. Maybe we can figure it out before she does."

"Fine, but we need to get in touch with VOLT and set up new identities right away. If Veronika Mandersloot panscanned you, that means other people at that lab could get access to your current alias background, which could lead them to any of the places you've been since you came into the city. Anywhere there's been a panopt. Even though it's not really you, they could still find 'you'—and as a result, me. Veronika may have turned out to be an ally, but we can't say the same for other employees working on Project Iterum."

Bel scratched at her InVisor. "You're right. Good thing I

never bothered to get used to this name."

After a while, they ventured out to the street, stopping for coffee on the way to Kosmetikos. Kat had been messaging nonstop, wanting to make sure they were okay, asking for more details—and Bel was eager to get her face and hair back to normal.

They paused at the intersection, waiting for the light to change.

An anchor from UW news spoke from the panopt directly across the street attached to a bank skyscraper's grid of glass windows. "But after Senator Quintero's mysterious reappearance yesterday morning, the public has begun to question her motives."

Mateo wasn't paying attention. He was typing a reply to Kat, with a quirky grin on his face.

The light changed and Bel nudged him onto the crosswalk with the other pedestrians.

"I assure you," said the senator on the panopt screen, speaking from a press conference pulpit, "This was all just a horrible misunderstanding. I experienced a personal emergency that I was forced to attend to very suddenly, with no time to communicate my absence to family and friends. I truly, sincerely apologize for any distress this may have caused."

Halfway across the street, the camera view zoomed in on Quintero's face and Bel stopped dead.

"Bel!" Mateo looked up from his message as another pedestrian stumbled against her from behind.

Bel grunted and caught herself before she plunged toward the pavement.

"Watch where you're going!" the man shouted.

Mateo hooked Bel's elbow and steered her to the connecting

sidewalk. "What's the matter with you?"

Bel gazed up at the panopt, her chest tightening at the sight of the senator up close. Female. Middle-aged. Olive skin. And a mole on the right side of her chin. And then, when the frame switched to a wide angle, it got worse.

Senator Quintero nodded as she listened to a question from the audience, pressing her thumb to the inside of her opposite wrist. She rubbed in a circular motion three times before Bel felt her own face go pale.

"Wait …" Mateo squinted at the woman's face.

Bel tucked a large curl behind her ear and swallowed hard. "I don't think we can wait for Veronika Mandersloot to take care of this."

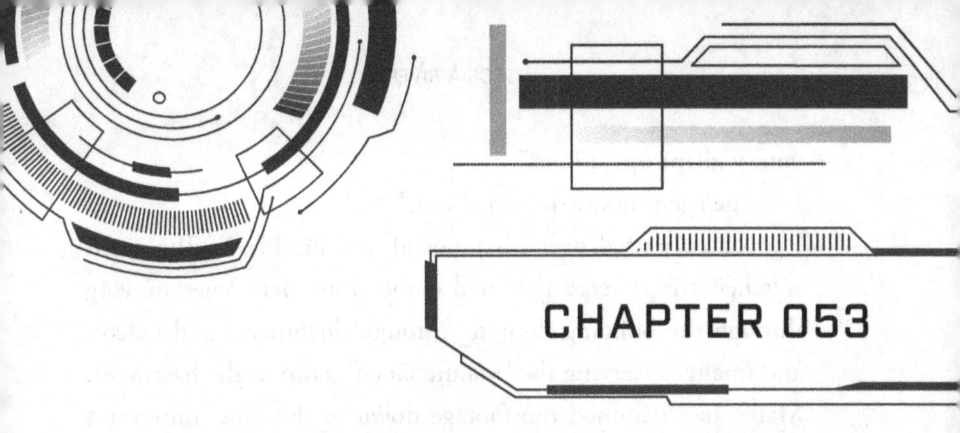

CHAPTER 053

NIGHT HAD FALLEN OVER THE CITY AGAIN and Bel rode behind Mateo on the back of his skimmer. They rode until the buildings got small again, where the panopts were fewer and the traffic dwindled. Soon, they reached a small grocery store on the corner and parallel parked on the curb.

"This is where we're meeting?" Bel asked.

"What'd you expect? A five-star restaurant?" said Mateo.

Bel shrugged. Before she could answer, a limousine pulled up and an older Black man in a blue suit stepped out to greet them.

"You here for the meeting?" the man asked.

"Yeah," said Mateo.

The man nodded. "Very good. This way, please."

He ushered them into the vehicle and closed the door.

"I'm Agent Grayson," he told them. "I understand we lost touch with you several weeks ago after a failed connection in the Los Padres. We apologize for the breach. It seems our agent was intercepted on her way to meet you; her navigation data was compromised and used as a starting point to locate the two of you. After that, we were unable to locate you."

"We've been a little busy," Mateo admitted. "Got sort of … detained. But we have some information for you, in terms of your vigilant operations."

The agent nodded. "Go ahead."

Mateo passed over his holopad and hit PLAY. The agent watched the footage that had come from Bel's Vues moving through the building, looking through documents and videos, and finally, observing the "maintenance" setup in the basement. Mateo had trimmed the footage down to the most important parts.

When it finished, the agent turned to Mateo and Bel. "I'm impressed you were able to obtain this footage and still come out alive."

"I got lucky," said Bel. "I met an unexpected ally at the last minute. She said she was handling it, but I don't know if she's aware of what's going on *beyond* that place right now."

The agent adjusted his suit lapels. "Well, this is a whole new kind of identity theft."

"And they're using it on government officials." Bel reached over and scrubbed the video back to the basement footage of the source units. "Senator Quintero, who just went missing not too long ago and reappeared yesterday … I saw her body in that basement." She tapped the screen to pause it on Quintero's face. "Right there."

His brows pinched together as he analyzed the screen.

"And there's a thing with the wires in the wrists," Bel added. "A malfunction that causes pain there. Quintero seemed to be having the same pain at the last press conference she gave, which means she has to be …"

"A duplicate," said the agent. "While someone else is controlling that body."

Mateo took back the holopad. "These android duplicates run on vidrinium. There's tons of it in multiple warehouses owned by front companies, and if you investigate them based on some of the data I have, they might be able to lead you to Damian Knight *and* the Knight Crew—who seem to be helping finance the project. Is this something VOLT would like to handle? Or should we go to the local authorities?"

The agent shook his head. "The authorities aren't going to believe it."

"That's what we figured," said Bel. "They might be able to uncover some vidrinium, but as far as the whole of Project Iterum is concerned, these bodies are created so perfectly, it would be impossible to tell them apart from the real thing with common methods. From the papers I read, it looks like they've used real DNA from the sources. The 'integumentary tissue' that makes up the skin has cells that would show up like the senator's on a lab test. Same with hair and saliva."

"Not to mention it sounds completely insane," said the agent.

"What about the video evidence?" Mateo asked. "I mean, I know we obtained it illegally, but ..."

Pointing to the holopad, the agent said, "Video files are inherently untrustworthy to the public anyway. Unless people can see things for themselves, with their own eyes, no lenses between them and the evidence, whatever we try to show them would be worthless. You'd need something more compelling. A way for the authorities, maybe even the public, to see it for themselves. But I'd venture to guess these criminal doctors and scientists know how to get around a search warrant. Or how to disappear before anybody can put one to use."

Bel thought it over a moment, imagining Quintero at the pulpit. Perfect hair, perfect pantsuit. Captive audience none the wiser to the fact that she wasn't true flesh and blood, that instead of a beating heart she had a volatile, metal rectangle keeping her alive.

Volatile …

"Actually," said Bel. "There might be a way to prove it to *everyone*—all at once."

Both the agent and Mateo looked to Bel with confusion.

The agent raised an eyebrow. "What do you have in mind?"

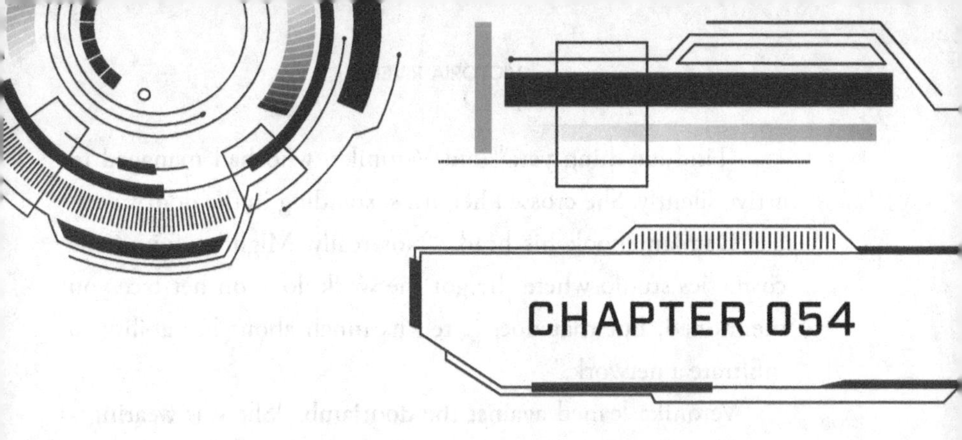

CHAPTER 054

DAMIAN KNIGHT PUFFED ON A CUBAN CIGAR, filling the small office with a haze that carried a rich, woody aroma. He sat at a rusted, metal desk with his sleeves pushed up to his elbows, a holoscreen open to the UW Database of Persons. He'd only barely scratched the surface on the girl, a quick search based on the profile he'd been given.

Andrea Losada | Cupertino, Dorado
Age: 18
Address: 351 Masterson Street, Apt 204

She'd been spotted by several panopts in the Perla Luna District, and close to the luxury apartments at 89 Wentworth, along with several other public places, but nothing that gave much insight into her undercover activities.

Panopt WC7-391
2087-06-04 06:22:52 UTC.
Nearby Businesses: Kosmetikos Cosmetology Studio, Urban Outfitters, Pho Getta Bout It, Taqueria Bermúdez, Page Me Books & Gifts, CVS

"Find anything yet?" said Veronika, who had managed to arrive silently. She crossed her arms, standing in the doorway.

Damian shook his head. "Not really. Might've found the cosmetics studio where she got the work done on her face you mentioned, but that doesn't tell us much about her ability to infiltrate a network."

Veronika leaned against the doorjamb. "She was wearing a comm and a pair of Vues. My suspicion is that she was working with someone else who actually knew what they were doing. It's possible she had skills of her own, but I doubt she managed to access Tier 6 classification without help."

"And what about the Vues?" said Damian. "No data stored on those?"

"None that we could find. You can look them over yourself to be sure, but apparently they were set to stream without storing any data. My on-site IT specialist told me he traced the path of its data stream to some other device and gave us a last-known GPS location for it, but it dead-ended in a dumpster about a block away. Completely destroyed. Otherwise we'd have been able to get an account code for whatever cloud service is holding the information they copied."

"Pretty clean," Damian said before taking a long drag on his cigar.

Veronika fanned the drifting smoke away from her face. "So, what do you think? Can we find her?"

"Of course we can." He typed something that brought up a map of the city, with several dots scattered over various areas, each with dates and timestamps. "Finding out just how much information she has, who else has it, and where it's being kept … that's a different thing."

Veronika came forward and analyzed the information on

Damian's screen. "Her last sighting was last night outside a grocery store on Meridian Avenue. Shouldn't there be something after that? On the way back to this apartment complex where she's been spotted multiple times?"

Damian held the cigar between his first two fingers and blew a stream of smoke at the screen as he read over it. "Should be. Unless she stayed out there all night and most of today. Or …" He narrowed his eyes.

"Or what?"

"Or she's even more proficient than we thought." He scoffed. "She's using an EchoMask, or an InVisor. She switched herself up on us."

CHAPTER 055

FROM ONE OF VOLT'S OFFICES, Bel watched the video again, for the third time.

In it, Senator Kella Quintero—or the likeness of her, at least—rubbed her wrist just before shaking another hand, crowded by guests at the meet-and-greet that had taken place that morning in the lobby of a Radisson. If Bel squinted, she could see the VOLT operative moving through the horde, a man tasked with planting a specially formulated, odorless and invisible incendiary substance on Quintero's clothes—a product made from the same base chemicals as Sparkfyre.

As planned, the scuffle broke out, an event choreographed by a couple of other VOLT operatives scattered throughout the lobby. The first operative, now close to the front of the line, taking advantage of the commotion, pretended to stumble directly into the senator.

Security rushed to pull him off, to contain the growing madness as audience members panicked and scattered.

"I'm so sorry," said the operative. "I'm so embarrassed—"

The video cut out.

"Got it?" said Mateo, taking the holopad from Bel.

She nodded. Mentally, she memorized the spot on Quintero's blouse. Unbuttoned to the skin, enough to give Quintero room to breathe but to still allow her a "professional" appearance. Humming right below that skin was where the vidrinium battery should be. And that skin was primed to react instantly to a laser.

Crowds murmured outside the UC Davis Pavilion. A digital sign read "Live Tonight: Senator Kella Quintero."

Once inside, Bel adjusted the sleeves of her three-quarter-sleeve blazer over her red button-up top and touched the new InVisor—which VOLT had programmed with yet another alias—at her hairline. Kat, who was staying behind the scenes with Mateo and the other VOLT hackers, had done Bel's makeup again, although this time much more subtly.

Again, Bel wore a pair of Vues, streaming everything she saw to the VOLT crew. Her comm hummed softly in her ear with their background noise as they prepped devices and muttered amongst themselves.

Bel took her seat, high up and out of the way, the closest VOLT had been able to get her to the stage and with a good angle on Quintero. She took several deep breaths.

"Welcome," said the announcer, a suited man with graying hair at the temples. "We are so pleased to hear from Senator Quintero tonight, who will address us on the issue of transportation resources."

Someone on Bel's comm said, "Preparing to take over the screens. Red Flame, on your mark."

The announcer went on for a few minutes about Quintero's accomplishments and her tireless work to clean up the crime syndicates and networks. He reminded everyone of the upcoming elections in the fall. Finally, Quintero came out onto the stage, to the sound of raucous applause. Bel clapped halfheartedly as the speech began.

Quintero read from the teleprompter. How convenient

for someone masquerading as another person, Bel thought, to have all their words prepared for them in advance. Whoever was controlling the body—Soto or one of his allies—would have an easy job puppeteering any elected official.

But Bel could hardly focus, thinking about her task. She kept her eyes fixed on Quintero's collar, where the accelerant had been placed. Even with the precise beam of a laserlighter, Bel feared she might manage to miss. Her hands trembled. She knit her fingers together for a moment to steady herself.

Quintero went on to discuss how high-speed magnetic levitation trains had connected the major cities of the nation in unprecedented ways, but how every advancement of society came at a cost, often presenting new problems.

"The niobium industry is unstable," said Quintero, "and with Brazil controlling most of it, this makes it difficult to obtain sufficient materials for the vast supply of superconducting magnets necessary to install new maglev routes throughout the country ..."

"Numbers are in," said one of the VOLT hackers through the comm, startling Bel to attention. "Maximum remote viewership. The most eyes we're going to get on the broadcast via livestream, plus a full house in the Pavilion. Now's the time, Red Flame."

Bel nodded. Inching forward in her seat, she withdrew the laserlighter from her pocket. Without pressing the laser just yet, she aimed at Quintero's chest.

Silently, Bel counted.

One.

Two.

Three.

She pressed the button. A wavering, red dot appeared above Quintero's collar for an instant. A tendril of smoke curled up from her skin.

Then, the woman's chest erupted in flames, burning back the flesh that separated the laser beam from her vidrinium battery's outer casing.

The crowd gasped.

A small explosion echoed throughout the auditorium.

Quintero stumbled, now missing one side of her torso and half of her face while flames licked her clothing and charred additional integumentary tissue. She screamed, bracing herself with her single, remaining arm against the podium, while security and assistants rushed to her aid. Exposed wires shone in the light of the flames while fluids seeped out and bubbled in the heat.

Buzzing with adrenaline, Bel stood and moved through the people, watching the holoscreens flanking the stage to see whether the VOLT hackers had taken over them yet. Quintero's melting face remained zoomed in for all to see.

The magnification screens went black for a moment, and then the lab footage filled them. The view through Bel's Vues looking over the bodies in the lab, pausing on Quintero's face. Voiceover explained what was happening, calling out Vivorex. Then the test subject video logs came on, footage of a source unit waking in a different (android) body.

Amid the chaos, Bel pushed through the crowd, hurrying to the stairs, and found her way out of the building. The panopts outside showed the whole thing as breaking news, interspersed with clips to provide context.

"Kella Quintero appears to be some sort of artificial intelligence," said the newscaster, "while additional footage suggests that the real senator may be held hostage in an unknown location. Police are working to find out who was behind the exposure and what the attacker hoped to gain with this horrific public display, while also investigating potential suspects in the senator's abduction."

Bel rushed to the street where a limousine awaited her. The door opened as she approached.

Agent Grayson smiled as he watched everything unfolding on a holoscreen from within the vehicle. "Well done, Red Flame."

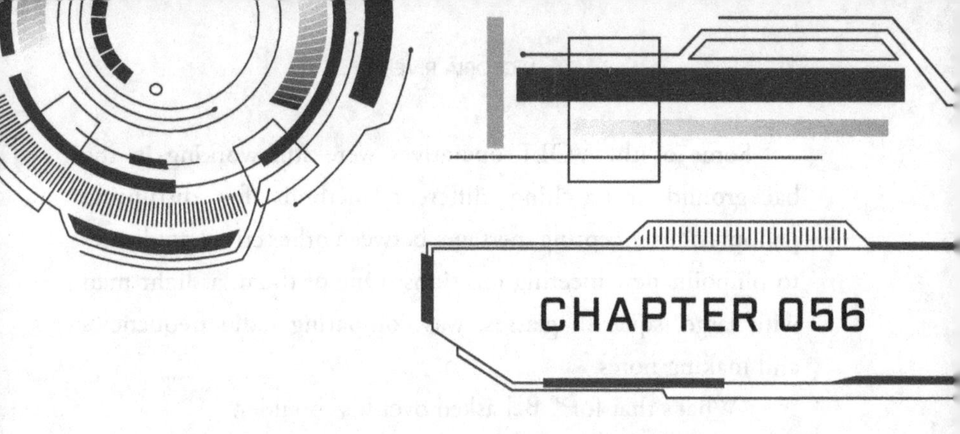

CHAPTER 056

AS SOON AS BEL RETURNED to the VOLT office, Mateo was there to meet her. He squeezed her so tightly she couldn't breathe, and said "You're done with this kind of stuff now, okay? My anxiety can't take it."

Kat put a hand on his shoulder and smiled.

Bel pried herself away and glanced at the other hackers, who sat around a table with their holoscreens open. "How's the rest of the plan going?"

Mateo ran his fingers through his hair and pushed out a tired breath. "Good. We've leaked every bit of information we had—the info on the shell companies dealing vidrinium, the emails and the applications that tie the lab trainees to Vivorex, all digital activity that leads authorities directly to Soto Acero, along with the footage of test subjects, blueprints for android bodies, everything. Right about now, authorities should be tracking down whoever was controlling Quintero's doppelgänger."

"I'm going to check UWN," said Kat, pulling out her own device. "They'll be broadcasting every step of what happens next."

Over the next few hours, Bel sat with Kat, Mateo, and the VOLT operatives, drinking coffee, eating Indian takeout, and watching the updates.

Some of the VOLT operatives were still working in the background, researching different methods for disrupting panopts or intercepting messages between other crime syndicates to pinpoint new meeting locations. One of them, a slight man with large, squarish glasses, was comparing radio frequencies and making notes.

"What's that for?" Bel asked over his shoulder.

"My department's in the process of building an app," the man said, "that will confuse panoptical sensors with specific sound wave patterns."

"Sound waves?"

He nodded. "Sort of a backup plan in case an InVisor fails on one of our charges or operatives. We call it RIPL—Radio Induced Privacy Layer. It's similar to a dog whistle, in the sense that it would be inaudible to those around you, but the panopts would pick it up. You can see here …" The man pulled up the data, showing the frequency comparison and pointing to the holoscreen. "Any sound within this range, when emitted in these particular patterns, will disrupt signals to a panopt, a pandrone, even a handheld panscanner."

"Nice," Bel said. "That would have been a good app to have a few weeks ago."

"We're actually doing beta testing right now. If you have a device, I can install it for you if you want."

She nodded and handed over her mini holopad. Between her experience with Thane, and then what had happened with the drones outside the Submundo, she was eager to take every extra precaution available.

Once the man was finished, Bel went back to watching the news coverage with Mateo and Kat and the others, just in time for an update. Authorities followed VOLT's information back to the lab, where they apprehended dozens of lab employees and eventually uncovered the now-severed connection to Quintero's android body—not able to verify whose consciousness, specifically, was inside when she blew. Many lab employees had already fled, while several remained, trying to protect assets or remove data from the vicinity.

"After questioning lab employees, police have been informed that the experiments resulting in Quintero's duplicate belonged to Vivorex Labs, under the authority of current CEO Soto Acero—who, in recent years, publicly dismissed Vice President Veronika Mandersloot for malfeasance. Investigators speculate that Mandersloot was a scapegoat for Acero's illicit and unethical procedures, and that her dismissal was part of a large-scale coverup."

The newsroom view cut to law enforcement—including FBI and Homeland Security—ushering a very confused Soto into a police vehicle outside Skyline Towers luxury condominiums while members of the press crowded the scene and shouted overlapping questions.

The man looked hollow, his dark skin wan and his eyes sunken. He squinted at the bright lights.

Voiceover stated, "Soto Acero has now been taken into custody to await trial, as a potentially decades-long scandal involving a trail of vidrinium and a gross abuse of power, has come to its fateful conclusion."

Everyone in the VOLT office applauded.

Bel, however, could only think of Andro, what this meant for him—and how hurt he would be to know that his suspicions were true, that his own uncle really did all this, to him and to everyone else involved.

CHAPTER 057

ANDRO SAT IN THE LOUNGE, with a holopad resting on the arm of his leather chair. His vision blurred slightly as he stared at an open holoframe, looking over the list of detected nearby devices to locate his own memory—whatever data was stored in his enhanced brain. He confirmed connection security, and then began to sort through the footage that his own eyes and ears had captured over the past several days. Because he never really slept, it should have been difficult to locate what he was looking for among months of audiovisual recordings, but thankfully everything was timestamped so that all he had to do was look for the date and the hour.

His vision blurred again as he selected a range of footage to download and waited for the computer to receive it. A wave of drowsiness crept over him and he paused, allowing himself to feel it, to analyze it.

How long had it been since he'd experienced this?

The holoscreen pinged with a notification.

Download complete.

Andro tapped it open.

The video memory of Bel's face came onto the screen, looking up at him, the colorful glow of the aurora shifting across her cheeks.

Instinctively, he reached out to touch the image, his metal fingers passing through the holomorph as though she were a ghost.

Again, his vision blurred. A fog seeped into his consciousness.

He struggled to stay seated upright, slumping from the chair and onto the rug, inadvertently dragging the holopad with him.

For the first time in almost nine months, his body—not just his mind—seemed to ache for sleep. Finally, he could power down. Finally, he could close his eyes and let his mind slip into darkness and rest.

Except, now, with the ROSE and its single digit number looming in the shadows of the Storage Zone, he feared that if he truly slept, he might never wake up.

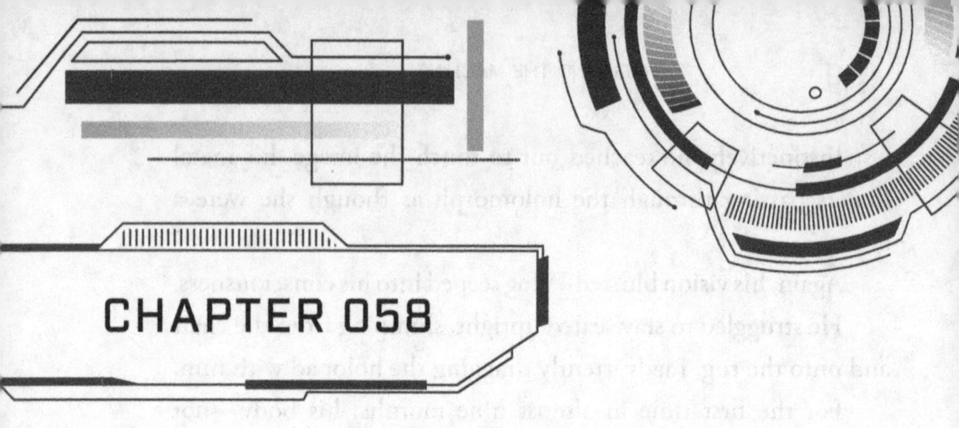

BEL WAS EXHAUSTED BUT COULDN'T SLEEP. She sat up on the side of her hotel bed in a room provided by VOLT— temporary until they could make more permanent arrangements for her and Mateo now that they'd been reassigned. Since the night they'd met Agent Grayson, they'd been programmed as Lily and Luís Veray, and Bel hated the identities already. The operatives were considering a remote town in Wyoming for them, a place called Greenhill, but as Bel tapped through photos on the intersphere, she grimaced, thinking there was absolutely nothing green about it. It was rocky and dusty and brown, with nothing but highway and old train tracks for miles. She didn't even allow herself to entertain the thought that she would be far away from Andro, and had convinced herself, at least for the moment, that she might be able to sway VOLT into letting her and Mateo stay in West California, or at least one of the other Californias.

Bel closed the images and groaned. She had to tell Andro the truth, before he found out some other way. He didn't watch or read the news much, so he probably wouldn't have a clue about what had happened with Quintero. She didn't want to tell him in a message, though. Even a call didn't seem the right way. She wished she could see Andro in person, talk to him face to face.

And then she thought about his face, that first moment when it had been so close to hers, the chills that had racked her spine. Maybe she could go back, just to tell him what she'd learned— and what she still hadn't learned yet.

What had he been doing these past several days without her?

Restless, she opened her holopad and re-read some of the documents she'd copied—screengrabs from the streamed footage converted to text and pictures.

She skimmed over the notes on the process for creating human body blueprints, the details on rem-con and maintenance, and finally a scientific article that provided the results of some testing done on the strength and life of vidrinium batteries implanted in android units.

Study found, however, that the batteries in these units are unable to save sufficient energy during Suspension Mode. Further programming is required to ensure that Suspension Mode—colloquially referred to as "android sleep"—results in a true suspension of the android unit's electrical activity. Current units will inevitably see a more rapid battery drain due to an unintentionally consistent usage of power, drastically shortening the projected "life" expectancy.

Bel had to go back to read it a second time.

Suspension Mode.

Further programming required.

Unintentionally consistent usage of power.

Andro had told her something similar. *"My body doesn't 'power down' all the way. Literally or figuratively."*

Rapid battery drain.

Shortened life expectancy.

He didn't have any idea how much time he had left.

Or *did* he?

Before everything had suddenly changed, the last thing he'd done was look for a replacement sensor in the Storage Zone.

Bel's eyes went wide as she remembered the mysterious device that had shown up on the Submundo's back-end diagram: ROSE

A quick search brought up the acronym's meaning: Remote Observation Status Emulator, an application that could read energy levels in connected devices.

"No …" she whispered.

She bit her lip, a crease forming between her brows. Her breath quickened.

She'd promised herself she would let Andro keep his secrets. But this was different—wasn't it? If his life was hanging in the balance?

"What happens if rem-con is disrupted unintentionally? Say an android unit is killed …"

"We discovered that the sensory kickback from an abrupt—or unintentional—disconnection was enough to fatally damage the source unit. A shock to the brain. We resolved this issue in Batch 5."

Andro's unit was created in Batch 3. She'd figured out that much from the videos she'd hacked.

But he already knew he was running out of time. He had to. That's why he'd pushed her away. He'd seen it with the ROSE app. And because he didn't know he had another body—his *real* body, intact—he would have thought it was the end for him. Except that it still *might* be if his battery ran out and the sensory kickback malfunction killed the source unit. If she could find it, she could wake him before it was too late, but she had no idea where it was.

Bel argued with herself for a few minutes, pulse racing in a panic.

How much time did Andro have left?

She needed to know. This was about more than Andro's privacy. Even if he didn't want to be with her, he could still live, maybe return to some sense of normalcy one day. But only if she gave him a chance.

Once she downloaded the ROSE app, she set to work on hacking into its user database. Andro wouldn't have used his real name to purchase or operate it, but thankfully she found a user registered under the one alias she happened to know he had: Adam Steele. She set up a password cracker and was soon able to log into his account. The app was remotely connected to one device, and she suspected it was Andro's battery meter, although it didn't have a name, just a serial number. She tapped on it, bringing up a dashboard interface with a circular meter at the center.

What she saw made her blood run cold.

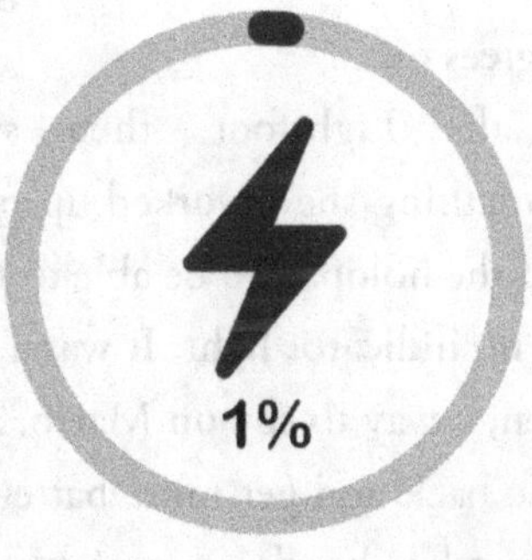

CHAPTER 059

BEL FIDGETED AS SHE DOUBLE-CHECKED the location on her holopad. She was standing outside a warehouse, albeit a smaller one, and Veronika was five minutes late.

"I know you might not want to talk to me after all this stuff with Quintero," Bel had told her on the phone, "but I was hoping that by some miracle, I could get your help."

Veronika had been shockingly compliant and agreed to meet with her.

The streetlamps gave the night sky an eerie, orange glow, and despite the summer months ahead promising warmer nights, it was a chilly 50 degrees out.

She parked the Lightfoot, then switched holopad applications to something she'd worked up prior to her arrival. She'd programmed the holopad to be able to record video in the background, with no indicator light. It was a hack she'd learned when she was seven, a way to spy on Mateo. She didn't know if she'd need to come back and get more batteries later; whatever she was about to get her hands on tonight would be likely to drain as quickly as Andro's original battery, so it wouldn't hurt to have a record of where to go—and how to get in—to have access to a full supply without having to involve Veronika again. Especially not knowing how long it would take to find Andro's source unit. More batteries would buy her more time.

Slipping the holopad into the front pocket of her jeans with the camera lens peeking out, she felt the bottom of the device click against something else. She fished around until she found what it was—the laserlighter, still tucked away in her jeans from earlier. Pushing away the memory of the horrific scene she'd caused with it, she shoved it into her other pocket and leaned against the wall, hoping Veronika would get there soon.

A few minutes later, an electric town car pulled up. The door opened and Veronika stepped out, coming toward Bel with a tight-lipped smile.

"Thanks for meeting me." Bel tried not to shiver. She didn't imagine it would be much warmer inside—after all, the place was holding vidrinium and would need to be kept relatively cool to avoid a hazard—but the protection of the walls could only improve the temperature.

"That was quite a story about your friend," said Veronika. "Incredible, in fact. And it explains so much—why you were so adamant about shutting down the project. Now that it's all out in the open, hopefully we'll be able to find his missing source unit soon."

"I'm sorry I didn't listen to you," Bel told her. "As soon as I saw Quintero on the news, my gut just told me to act fast."

Veronika shrugged. "Well, it all worked out. My reputation's on the mend, and Soto's going to be locked away. I suppose I should thank you. The FBI would have been more discreet, careful about the information they shared with the public. But I can't say I don't like your style—and now my hands are clean of it." She held out her hands as if in demonstration of their cleanliness.

Bel swallowed, eager to get to the batteries, and forced a

hollow laugh. "Glad I could help."

She followed Veronika to a heavy, metal door with a panel for entrance. Veronika waited for the bioscan to accept her. The door clicked.

Inside, only security lights were on. Bel looked over the racks, filled with boxes, and wondered whether they were all vidrinium or only some of them, whether they were batteries or other vidrinium products.

"So," said Veronika. "Let's get your friend his battery, then. Do you know what batch his body came from? Batches 2 and 3 use the same battery model, but Batch 1 batteries are smaller and Batch 4 are a bit larger."

"Three. A309 would be Batch 3, unit 9, right?"

"Yes, that's correct. This way."

Bel nodded and trailed behind, trying not to let the dimness agitate her. Veronika had insisted they keep a low profile, in case there were any vengeful employees lurking around. Considering what time of night it was, and the fact that Mateo didn't know she'd gone anywhere—lest he try to stop her while Andro breathed his last android breath alone—Bel was more than happy to lie low, especially while was skulking through a warehouse full of banned vidrinium products.

"Ah," said Veronika, tapping the exterior of a box. "There should be some in here." She slid it from its place and opened it up, slicing the tape with a sharp fingernail. Several pieces of packing material separated the batteries.

"So, your friend ..." Veronika said while she unwrapped the first layer of batteries. "Who was he? Why do you think he was forced into the experiment?"

"Why was *anyone* forced into it? To be made to disappear. To provide healthy bodies and bypass regulations, right?"

"That has been the trend, yes." She worked on removing a layer of shrinkwrap next, which held several batteries together at once.

Bel's fingers grazed the edge of the holopad, which still stuck out of the front pocket of her jeans, its camera cataloging the exact row and shelf where the batteries were kept.

Veronika broke open the plastic enough to remove a single battery. She extended it to Bel.

It was cold and hard against Bel's hand. Not the warm, smoothness she remembered when Andro had let her feel the battery already installed in his chest. But Veronika didn't let go. Bel pulled, but Veronika held tighter.

Then someone came from behind and wrapped an arm around Bel's throat.

"Took you long enough," said Veronika.

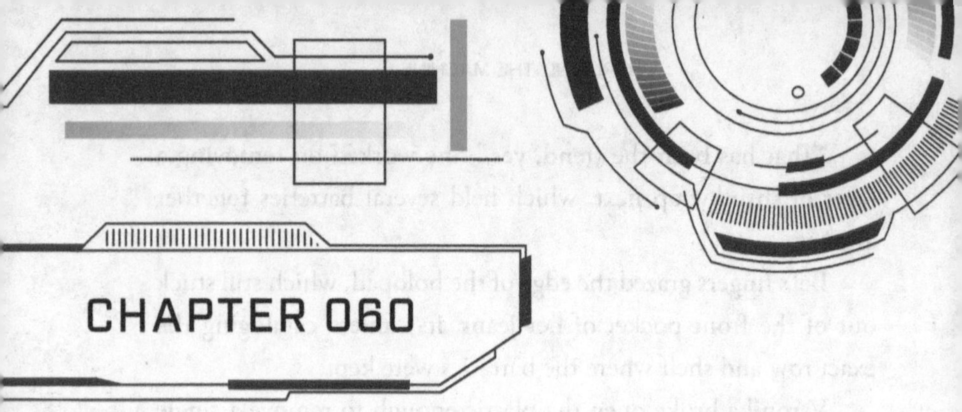

BEFORE BEL COULD REACT, her arms were tight against her body behind her, with a plastic band cutting into her wrists. Veronika tossed the battery back into the box and came forward. Twisting her head back, Bel caught a glimpse of the man who held her captive—a tall, menacing creature with white-blond hair, who smelled of cigars. Her chest seized.

She recognized him only from his mug shot, but his name had haunted her nightmares for years. He wasn't fully real to her, just a shadow on dark nights, an evil force that had ruined her life invisibly: Damian Knight.

For a second, she couldn't breathe—couldn't think. And the battery she'd touched with her own fingers couldn't have felt farther away, even though it lay in a box just a few feet from where Damian held her.

The man's thick hands gripped her shoulders, shoving her face against the racks. He slipped the holopad out of her pocket.

In her periphery, Veronika tapped on the screen. "Now, let's find out who got loose."

"What?" said Bel.

"Your android friend."

"How exactly could one of them 'get loose'?" Damian asked. "I thought they were controlled by source units."

Veronika tapped through to the contacts list. "That's what I'd like to know. As far as I'm aware, there's no source unit that happens to be missing its android—unless one of my employees has been lying to me."

"You said we were on the same side," said Bel.

"I said what I needed to say to get you to keep quiet until you could lead me to whoever you were working with. But you gave us a run for our money; it was pretty hard to track you through the panscanner data on a false identity. Thankfully, though, I have someone on my team who specializes in gathering hard-to-find intel"—she glanced at Damian—"and then you made it even easier for me by meeting me here in person. I truly, truly appreciate that."

"Glad I didn't wait for your permission to expose the project, then." Bel flared her nostrils.

Veronika ignored her, still tapping through the holopad's information. She located the contact history.

Call music rang from the device.

Bel grunted and struggled, but Damian shoved her again.

The holopad seemed to ring for an eternity before a voice finally silenced the music. It came out groggy. "Mirabel?"

Damian manhandled Bel so that she was facing Veronika now, who held the holopad, with Andro's image hovering.

Andro's face fell when he saw her, with her hair mussed and what was sure to be a bruise forming across her jaw, in the clutches of Damian Knight.

Veronika's mouth gaped. "Now *this* I did not expect …"

"Who is he?" said Damian.

"I can't believe I'm saying this," said Veronika, cradling the holopad in both hands and bringing Andro's holomorphic likeness closer, like she was observing some strange specimen under a lens, "but it's … Andro Acero."

"Acero," Damian repeated. "As in—"

"Except that's impossible," said Veronika. "Project Iterum lost assets in an incident last September, but … Soto's nephew was recruited to Project Cratis—where they study nerve networks in order to recreate them synthetically. He would have been poked and shocked until he was all used up, and then they would have incinerated what was left. How the *hell*—"

"Drop the call, Andro," Bel said, jerking against Damian's grip, which only made him hold her tighter. His fingers dug into her arms. "Destroy your device. She's working with Soto, and this guy knows how to track—"

Damian clamped a hand over her mouth and pressed the barrel of a blaster to her throat. "Shut. Up."

"Let her go," Andro said through a thick swallow. Wherever he was, he seemed to be hunched over, trying to brace himself. "You don't need to involve her in this. If you want me dead, your wish is about to come true."

A grin spread slowly across Veronika's face. "That's right. I almost forgot … You've got a low battery. Dangerously low." She put the holopad on "fill mode," then set it on the floor and tapped "expand," making Andro appear full size as though he were in the room.

Bel gasped when she saw where he was—on the rug in the lounge, trying to push himself up off the floor.

"I blackmailed her … into doing this." Andro took full breaths between every few words. His eyes were glazed over, head lolling. "She's just … taking orders." Another full breath through his nose. "She's innocent in all of this. You have to let her go …" He was shaking, the lights behind his wires flickering. "I'll tell you exactly … where you can find me. I have … coordinates …"

Bel screamed into Damian's hand and shook her head furiously. He let up pressure on the blaster, waiting for Veronika's response.

"The Submundo …" Veronika said. She must have seen the look of shock in Bel's eyes, adding, "Soto mentioned it once. We were close."

Through an agonizing grunt, Andro said, "Get that blaster away from her … *Now*. You know … where I am."

Damian released his grip and tucked the blaster away, but did nothing about the zip ties on Bel's wrists.

"Andro, I'm sorry," said Bel. "I know about the ROSE app. I was trying to get back to you with another battery—tonight, but …"

Weakly, Andro steadied himself. "You have to … let me go … Okay? There's no time. And … no reason for you to … get hurt … because of"—he coughed—"because of me."

Bel turned to Veronika. "What do you have against him? He doesn't have to die!"

"He *does* have to die. I've gotten all I could out of him, and I can't have him walking around telling everyone what he knows about me. My work isn't finished yet."

"Then I guess it's safe to say you're working with Soto," said Bel angrily. "You let me think you wanted to take him down."

"Who says I don't? Although you've already done that *for* me, haven't you, 'Red Flame'?"

"If you don't, then what were you doing 'cooperating' with Project Iterum? And what are you doing *now* with vidrinium dealers?" She shot Damian a glare. "If you and Soto aren't in this together, then …"

Bel shook her head. It didn't make any sense. This was all getting too complex.

She glanced at Andro, who was taking deep breaths through his nose and slowly releasing them between narrowed lips. Whatever energy his battery still had left was barely enough to keep him conscious.

They'd started going out of their way not to be seen together. That's what Andro had told her in the VR dome.

Never in the same room at the same time.

The context had been different, though. The aftermath of a messy affair. Avoidance—the pressure of their peers and the public.

But what if it had been because they *couldn't* have been in the same room at the same time? Literally—physically—couldn't? Externally, they looked different, but *internally* ....

"Wait ..." Bel said. With everything she'd seen and learned in the past few weeks, there was no reason not to believe it, and yet she struggled to wrap her mind around it. It sounded crazy—but what was 'crazy' anymore? What was really implausible now, when people could wear other people like a mask? "You *are* Soto."

Andro sucked in air with difficulty, unable to respond to the accusation.

"I'm such an idiot," Bel said to Veronika. "You have the ability to *duplicate bodies*. You can walk around in any skin you want—blame anyone you want for your crimes, and everyone will believe it because you look exactly like them. You can be *you* when you need to, and then when it's more convenient, you can remotely control a body that looks like the woman you wanted to silence. And meanwhile, you put her away, hid her in some basement all hooked up to machines. That's why some of the source units in the basement weren't connected to anything."

Laughing again, Veronika pushed a few strands of hair away

from her face. "Oh, you really are an idiot."

"She's not … Soto …" said Andro, in a strained voice, barely above a whisper. He clutched his chest as his internal lights continued to flicker.

Bel longed to reach out to him, to hold him up, to beg him to stay strong, but the blue tone of his holomorphic figure reminded her she was more than two hundred miles away and he may have only minutes left.

Looking at him, another memory came to her. Standing on that checkered floor, everything lit up in neon. *You'd assume the king is the most powerful, but he's not; it's the queen who can really work the board.*

Bel remembered the way Soto had appeared on the news, haggard and confused. Sunken eyes, body thinner than she'd seen him at his last public appearance. If he was currently impersonating Veronika Mandersloot—with his real body hooked up via rem-con—he'd have wanted to make sure the man taken into police custody only *looked* like him, but was not, in fact, him. But that man on the news, handcuffed and scared … That couldn't have been an android. It had been more like a man who'd just woken from the dead. More importantly, a man who'd *woken*.

These androids couldn't sleep.

"No," Bel agreed through a ragged breath. "It's the other way around. You're not Soto in a Veronika suit; you've been Veronika all along, only masquerading as Soto while you committed the worst of your crimes."

"Soto was never a part of any of this, was he?" said Bel. "And now he's going to take the fall."

Veronika smirked.

The flickering throughout Andro's body grew more severe,

wires shorting out. Instinctively, Bel wrestled against the zip ties, like being free of them would suddenly give her the ability to teleport to where Andro was.

"Any minute now, right?" Veronika nodded at Andro. "And he's from an early batch. The second he disconnects, the kickback will kill his source. Wherever it is."

"Andro," Bel pleaded. She took a few steps toward his holomorph, her eyes filling with tears. She didn't care that she hadn't figured out how she would save him yet, how she would get out of this warehouse without her captors trailing her. All she needed was for him to stay alive just a little bit longer.

When nobody stopped her, she kept going until she was standing right in front of him, and then she knelt so they were face to face. Tears tracked down her cheeks.

Wearily, and flickering more violently than ever, Andro reached toward her. Had he been there in person, his fingers would have brushed her face. Bel imagined she could feel them.

"Andro—"

One final short, and then his body collapsed.

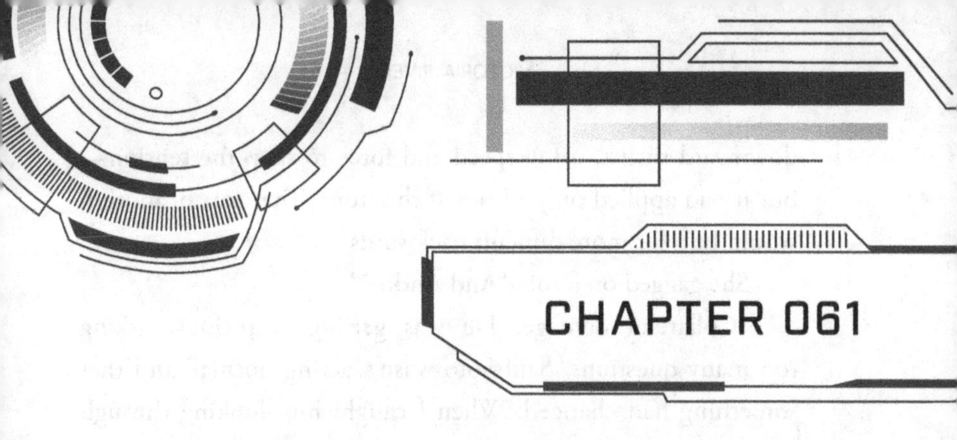

CHAPTER 061

"YOU BROUGHT THE PANSCANNER, RIGHT?" Veronika said to Damian. The call was still connected, the holomorphic image of Andro's dead body lying on the concrete.

Bel shivered, panting. Hyperventilating. Sobbing, now. This wasn't real. Andro wasn't dead. He couldn't be. Not when she'd been so close to saving him.

Damian nodded and handed over a panscanner he'd apparently been keeping on his belt, obscured by his jacket.

"Why didn't you just kill Soto yourself?" Bel demanded hoarsely. "Why all these calculations? All this scheming?"

Veronika scoffed as she turned on the scanner. "I didn't just want him *gone*—I wanted him to *suffer*. He disrupted world-changing work—work that I've spent my career perfecting—and then he painted me as a monster to the media, to the public, to the colleagues that used to respect me. It wasn't a coverup like the media's been saying; it was an exercise of Soto's false sense of ethics. He deserves to be destroyed publicly, the way he destroyed me ... the way he *tried* to destroy everything I've built."

Silently, Bel twisted her wrists behind her, testing the tightness and strength of the zip ties. In all her safety and self-defense training, she'd seen a demonstration before on how to break them once—raising the wrists high, followed by a quick, downward thrust, using speed and force to snap the tension—but it had applied only to ties at the front. That sort of motion would be a lot more difficult backwards.

She gagged on a sob. "And Andro?"

"Collateral damage. He was getting suspicious, asking too many questions. Said Soto wasn't 'acting normal' and that something had changed. When I caught him looking through Soto's files, I knew it was time to put a stop to it."

"So you drugged him and threw him into an experiment that you knew would kill him."

"*Utilize* him. His flesh, his neural pathways, his bone structure models. The Immortality Projects are designed to *prolong* life. It wouldn't make sense for me to destroy a life without getting all the benefits I could out of it—for future generations. They'll be grateful for the sacrifice, even if you—and so many others—are not."

"So *that's* your villain code?" Bel concluded. "*That's* where you draw the line? Life is sacred, but only for what the flesh can teach you? The body is priceless but the soul is disposable?"

Damian waited for a nod from Veronika before dragging Bel to better lighting and gripping her head tight. For the second time, Bel's InVisor was pried from her skin. It burned, the spot where the tiny device had been, raw from the strong, waterproof adhesive that wasn't meant to be removed in such an abrupt and careless manner.

While Damian analyzed the tiny dot that now stuck to his finger, and Veronika prepped the scanner, Bel took the opportunity to thrust her hands down against her tailbone, trying to recreate the same method she'd seen on Vidverse. It wasn't enough, though, and the ties dug deeper into her skin. She had to bite her tongue to keep from screaming at the pain, inhaling slowly to calm herself.

Then came the beep of the panscanner on her bare face.

While a scan of her InVisored face would have brought up limited information, Bel's unscrambled face would have brought up her entire life. Every family member, every address she'd lived prior to VOLT's reassignments, even a list of news stories or articles that had involved her.

She tried the thrust again while Damian looked at Veronika expectantly, waiting for her appraisal of the data. Another fail. She clenched her jaw, burying the pain deep inside herself as it shot up her forearms.

Veronika shrugged and handed the device to her accomplice. Whatever it said wouldn't have meant anything to her. But Damian …

He froze.

"Solís …" he whispered.

Bel angled her wrists for maximum tension. One more thrust. She braced herself for pain, but this time, it was brief— and relief came fast. A soft snap. The strip of plastic hung loose.

Veronika turned on her, suspicious. Bel caught the broken zip tie before it fell, enclosing it in her fist, keeping her wrists tucked behind her as though nothing had happened, and stared at Damian with new determination.

"That's right," said Bel. Her heart raced as she tried to keep her cool, wrists throbbing. "You might remember how several innocent people got shot when your crew opened fire on your rivals. My dad's dead because of that."

"Several of my key officers were imprisoned, or driven across the border, thanks to his interference. Billions of dollars lost, an entire faction of my network destroyed—a network that employs hundreds of thousands of workers."

"Traffickers and criminals," Bel spat.

"They do what they have to do to eat," he barked. "And I provide them that opportunity."

Bel looked away from him. The very sight of him was enough to make her blood boil. She averted her gaze, focusing on an exit strategy. How many rows had they passed on the way to the Batch 3 batteries? How many turns to the door to the outside? As she considered all this, a small flicker of light caught her eye—coming from Andro's collapsed body. It was deep in his chest, and barely visible, but it was there. Her own hope flickered just as faintly.

Veronika looked from Bel to Damian. "Wait, you actually know this girl?"

"Her family," Damian clarified. "Brother and father were helping VOLT set up a sting operation a few years ago. It would have worked if we hadn't already been on edge when a couple of other syndicates attacked our shipment and we had to rain fire on everyone—including undercover operatives hiding out nearby. Took out the girl's old man, but the organization managed to save the boy. He must've been barely eighteen at the time."

"Where's your brother now?" Veronika asked.

Bel didn't answer.

"That's fine," Damian said to Veronika. "I'll find him. It's a simple matter of checking the location tags on the girl's previous identity and looking for similar tags on anyone she's been associating with. If I run into any problems ... I have ways of getting answers out of people."

"Haven't you done enough to him?" Bel said, discreetly massaging her sore wrists behind her. She eyed the open box of batteries a few yards away. How many seconds would it take her to get to it? Then she'd need to get around the corner—

fast. Damian's blaster was tucked away; he'd have to realize, then react, then grab it. That might be enough time.

Andro's faint light still shone. Bel steadied her breath.

Damian sneered. "Not nearly. He's going to give me everything he knows about VOLT—leads on locations, operatives, weaknesses. And if he makes it difficult ... he'll have to watch you die."

Bel opened her mouth to protest, but a beeping device cut her off.

"Sorry," said Veronika, checking her holopad messages. "Looks like it's about the next shipment. It's coming early."

Damian gave Bel a warning glare before he joined Veronika to see about the shipment details. With their backs half turned, they muttered about who to send to the loading dock at the last minute, whether they'd be able to get someone easily on such short notice, if they should bring it here or take it to their Starck Street location ...

Bel inhaled slowly. Her brain hummed with nervous energy. Never had her feet felt so leaden before—but there wasn't a fraction of a second more to waste. She sprinted for the battery box, snatching the battery that Veronika had tossed back inside. Damian turned to look just as Bel pivoted and ran the opposite direction. She caught sight of his blaster as he pushed his jacket aside to reach for it.

A blast zoomed past her head. She braced herself on one of the racks, then turned the corner and raced down the next aisle. Damian was on her heels before she could get too far, firing at her back. She ducked and dodged as the blasts streaked through the air. Between the boxes on the racks, Bel caught glimpses of Veronika moving along the next row, following her path.

They were trying to corner her.

At the end of the aisle, Bel made a sharp turn and ran perpendicular to the rows, passing several before she hid down another one at random. From there, she crept quietly, peering between cracks and small spaces in the racks looking for movement. Damian had his blaster in position, slowly scanning the area, but Veronika had disappeared. Bel crouched behind a high stack of boxes that were precariously balanced on a wooden pallet still attached to a forklift. Holding her breath, she waited. She was sure there were only a few more rows to reach the exit, but she wanted a sighting of both Veronika and Damian before she risked another sprint.

Then, unexpectedly, the stack of boxes began to tip. Bel dove out of the way right before the tower slammed to the ground, bursting the cardboard and spilling medical supplies and spools of wire. The weight of it would have killed her for sure—and it hadn't been an accident.

"Over here," shouted Veronika, hurrying after Bel, who picked up one of the punctured boxes and flung it into Veronika's path. Veronika stumbled, giving Bel time to get halfway down another row before Damian reappeared and started firing again. One of the blasts grazed Bel's shoulder. She cried out and veered to the side but kept running.

At the end of the row was a straight shot to the exit now, but the area was too open. There'd be nowhere to duck, no way for Bel to protect herself.

Instead, she made a sharp right, back toward where Veronika had initially led her. It was a roundabout method, but they probably wouldn't expect it. It would confuse them, and then she could get them off her tail. There might also be another exit on the other side of the building.

Bel sucked in a breath through her teeth, grimacing as she

took cover when she reached the batteries, and clutched her wounded arm. The blast had burned clear through her jacket and shirt, another deep gash to her flesh not unlike what she'd experienced the day with the pandrones.

From a distance, Damian seemed to be shooting blindly in Bel's general direction now, like he was hoping to get lucky. Bel flinched when one of the shots came close, trembling as she crouched lower, all but crawling. He didn't know exactly where she was, but he was probably less than a minute from figuring it out.

Okay, so this was a bad idea.

It was hopeless. She was outnumbered, and she didn't have a weapon. She glanced around, looking for anything she might be able to use in self-defense. A discarded wrench, a loose pipe, some piece of metal from the rack system she could detach.

Her eyes fell to the box in the middle of the aisle—the one that the battery in her pocket had come from. Her hands tingled at the realization.

She *did* have a weapon.

The weapon was all around her, shrink-wrapped and boxed up, but highly volatile. And she had a trigger—the laserlighter. Now all she needed was to get her captors back into the line of fire.

Andro's hologram still projected from the holopad on the floor, showing his faintly glowing metal. Bel didn't want to take her eyes off of it, for fear he would fade out while she wasn't looking, but she minimized the image and tucked the device next to the battery in her pocket. Then she crept over to the battery box and peeled away the rest of the torn shrink wrap, opening the package enough that the batteries could fall loose. There must have been at least three dozen stacked together.

After locating a hiding place on the bottom rack between a couple of other boxes, Bel flipped the battery box upside down, scattering batteries noisily across the floor. Footsteps followed as Bel tucked herself away and drew out her laserlighter.

Veronika and Damian both rushed to the scene, tiptoeing amongst the batteries that littered the aisle like a minefield. Bel pressed the laserligher's button and aimed the lens at a small pile of batteries directly between where Veronika and Damian stood apart.

Damian spotted the red dot and immediately ducked, but it was too late.

The batteries burst from within, spewing metal and fumes. Bel covered her nose and mouth with her shirt. The first explosion set off others, as fiery bits ignited the volatility of more nearby batteries. Veronika flew backward, thrust into the racks, while Damian was thrown across the floor. Clothes lit up in flames. Veronika shrieked, collapsing and flailing. Another explosion blew the woman's hand clean off. Damian, who was now missing chunks of both legs, dragged his body through the fire, which had caught on the cardboard of several boxes along the row.

Bile rose in Bel's throat. She'd never seen anything so gruesome.

She was also seated between more vidrinium; she had to get out *immediately*. Shoving her way through, she couldn't avoid crossing Damian's path, and even in his mutilated state he managed to grab hold of her foot.

Bel tripped, catching herself on her hands. She kicked at him but he held on and then reached for his fallen blaster. He fumbled with the trigger, which gave Bel a chance to wriggle harder against him. She'd just broken free when he got a handle on the weapon. All she could do was roll out of the way, but that would put her directly into the fire that was rapidly spreading across the floor as burning acid oozed. The only thing left was to get up and try to dodge the shot.

Shakily, she pushed herself up to her feet. Her leg muscles flared, propelling her forward at full speed. She listened for the *zing* of the blaster, but instead it was a violent *boom*. The other boxes had burned all the way through and the batteries had ignited.

Bel kept running. The heat swept over her back, urging her on. She didn't stop until she reached the exit, pressing furiously at the panel to open the door. It was only as she came to the Lightfoot parked outside that she collapsed to her knees, panting.

Another *boom* from the inside of the building shocked her from her respite, and she powered up the Lightfoot, climbed onto it, kicked the accelerator, and sped away into the night.

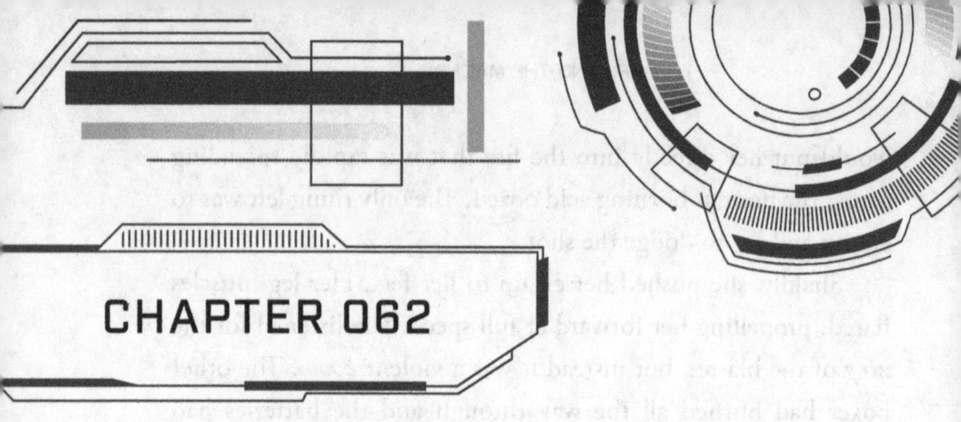

CHAPTER 062

DESPITE TRAVELING AT 760 MILES PER HOUR, the Mag could not go fast enough. Bel had raced to the Mag depot and nearly forgotten she wasn't wearing an InVisor, but thankfully remembered the RIPL app and kept it open on the holopad as she reached panopt-heavy streets, allowing the sound wave patterns to disrupt the scanners.

Now she sat in the back corner of one of the Mag cars with her Lightfoot leaned against the armrest of her seat, wishing she could still watch Andro's holomorph. Unfortunately the call had dropped when she'd pocketed the device. She'd tried to reconnect several times without success, knowing full well that Andro certainly couldn't be conscious enough to accept another call—but she'd had to try.

When the Mag pulled into the Santa Maria depot, Bel was already waiting at the doors. She practically leapt onto the platform and started the Lightfoot back up.

The woods passed in a blur as Bel hovered across the landscape. She was grateful she'd been able to simply reverse the travel route from the day she'd left the Submundo, otherwise trying to find the hidden mansion in the dark would be a lot more difficult.

Once she got close, the LED light in the rock and moss

let her know she'd arrived before the GPS did. With Andro unconscious, she'd have to hack the security again, but this time she had a holopad. She was able to manipulate the rolling code much more quickly than she had with the Ecker. However, her fingers were anything but nimble at this point, trembling after the events at the warehouse and lack of sleep and hours of fearing for Andro's life and her own. More than once, she hit the wrong keys, resulting in code errors that set her back.

Finally, the earthen door moved open and allowed her passage to the tunnel.

Lights flicked on. Lucius appeared. She was in.

Bel found Andro in the lounge, collapsed on the rug next to his holopad, which lay flat beside him.

"Andro." She touched his face, jostling him for signs of life.

She grunted at the force of his weight as she rolled him onto his back to get a better look at his chest. The last remaining light she'd seen on the call was gone.

"No. *Please.*"

With difficulty she pulled his shirt up over his head and tossed it away. Fearless this time, she pressed her fingers under the border of flesh to locate the battery panel, feeling around for the screws. However, it was clear she wouldn't be able to fit a screwdriver comfortably into that space. She'd have to cut him.

She returned with a surgical knife from the Medical Resource Room, along with a small screwdriver.

Now she had to brace herself; even though his body was synthetic, she couldn't help feeling like she was cutting into something organic—and without a shred of surgical experience.

She desperately wished for her mother's expertise and steady hands right now.

When she made the cut, it looked and felt the way she imagined a real surgical cut would, although the blood that trickled out was a darker shade of red than human blood. Using her thumb, she peeled back the skin first, followed by a layer of synthetic muscle, until she'd gained full access to the battery panel. After removing the screws, she used the edge of the surgical knife to pry the battery out.

Almost there.

Bel fumbled for the new battery, hands shaking as she locked it in and replaced the panel.

She waited.

The lights inside Andro's exposed parts flicked on. Bel's pulse pounded in her ears. Next, movement in his toes and fingers, flexing gently. With eyes still closed, he turned his head. Bel nearly choked on her excitement, clasping Andro's hand and mentally urging him to look at her.

But that was it. His movements slowed, then stopped altogether. His lights remained on, some energy moving through them, but he didn't open his lidded eye.

Bel realized she'd seen these motions before. From the bodies on the video logs, the test subjects booting up before connection, the movements they'd made before any consciousness had remotely connected to control them.

"Andro …" she pleaded.

His chest rose and fell in a perfectly rhythmic and subtle way. He could easily be asleep, if Bel didn't know better—but she did. He *couldn't* sleep.

He was like a device on standby, insides fully charged and whirring, but without any program running. Connected to nothing. A machine without a ghost.

He was gone. Really gone.

Game over.

CHAPTER 063

THE NEXT TIME BEL OPENED HER EYES, she found herself blanketed in a virtual sunrise.

Everything from the previous night blended together in her memory—explosions and lasers, the Mag and the woods, panic in the city after the exposé.

Andro's death.

After patching up the cut she'd made on his chest, she'd walked his mindless vessel to the VR dome before powering it down and transporting them both to a peaceful scene. Getting him someplace else—pretending she could take him far away from the Submundo, even though it wasn't really *him*, only the body he'd inhabited for all the time she'd known him—gave her a sense of comfort. She couldn't bear the thought that he'd not only died inside this prison of a mansion but also died inside this prison of a body. Any release, or fantasy of freedom for what was left of him, seemed appropriate.

His body lying beside her was her full reality check. It had all happened, and it was all irreversible. The body's source of consciousness was dead somewhere, and Bel felt herself falling apart all over again, but this time she was too numb to cry anymore. She rested her head on his lifeless chest as a single tear slipped down her cheek.

She'd almost fallen asleep again when a voice made her stir.

"Mirabel ..."

Slowly, Bel lifted her head, turning her ear toward the sound.

Was she even awake?

No. This was definitely a dream.

Andro's voice, speaking her name. "Mirabel?"

Beside her, the Andro she'd tried to rescue was silent and still. And the voice was more distant. It had an echo.

"Mirabel?"

Bel pushed herself up to a crouch, then rose slowly.

There.

Beyond the virtual trees, walking over the virtual grass.

It was him. *Another* him.

She didn't dare believe it. It was just a trick of the system like everything else in the dome. Lenses and lights, CGI, pixels and projection.

He'd left her a recorded message in the VR memory, scanned his likeness as a hologram. That had to be it. She couldn't figure what might have triggered it to open; maybe it had been on a timed release. He wore the same filter as the night before she'd left, the one that had shown his original, organic face. None of what he'd considered his cybernetic "imperfections."

Except there were other "imperfections." His hair was grown out, and his face wasn't shaved. It didn't look like a style someone would wear on purpose—it was more like the result of neglect, wild and unkempt. And he wore gray scrubs with snap buttons, and a barcoded wristband.

Bel's heart skipped a beat.

He approached her and he was whole. Everything he'd been when she'd known him and so much more. No burns, no blemishes, no wires or metal, and—if she wasn't hallucinating—

not a simulation.

How?

She moved to meet him, slowly at first and then building up speed, closing the distance between them at a run. She nearly knocked him over as she threw her arms around him, holding him with a fierceness that could only come from not believing someone was real. His arms were tight around her too, his lips on her hair, and his warmth was different from before, not the warmth of a machine but a warmth that was radiantly and unmistakably human. They stood this way for a long time, neither of them ready to let go. With Bel's ear to his chest, she could hear it—a heartbeat, a pulsating rhythm within him, giving life to his body, fueling his organic machine. Her own heart thumped so loudly she thought it must be audible a mile away.

Finally, Bel took off her VR headset and drew back enough to look up at him, touching his face, tracing what would have been the edges where, before, flesh bordered metal. He was sweaty and his eyes were tired, and although he was genetically sound, he was sprinkled with flaws—eyebrows ungroomed, skin dry from months under lamps, a scratch on his cheek—glorious human flaws.

"Is it really you?" she asked

He nodded. "I think so."

"But ... how did you know ..."

"You said you were coming for me. That was the last thing I remembered. As soon as I woke up, I got a skimmer and came straight here."

"Your consciousness was trapped here at the Submundo for *months*. You could've gone ... anywhere else."

"I wanted to see you. And make sure you were okay."

Bel thought of Andro's other body, how she'd seen him collapse onscreen. Then she thought of those maintenance machines, what he must have looked like hooked up to one of them, what it must have felt like to wake there. "*You* wanted to make sure *I* was okay?"

Andro raised a brow. "I guess you have a point. But … *are* you okay?"

She nodded. "I am now."

He pulled her against him and kissed her—the kind of kiss that made the room spin, putting his whole body into it. The force she felt from him was like a superconducting magnet, an energy she couldn't and didn't want to pull away from. And now, she didn't have to.

1 **Excerpt Transcript of Proceedings**

2 **Testimony of Elisabeth Wayland**

3 **August 8, 2087**

4 **Before the Honorable Judge Leland P. Shaw**

5

6 **(Oath was administered)**

7

8 **Direct Examination**

9 **By Ms. Telles**

10 Q: Good afternoon. Would you please state your

11 name for the court?

12 A: Elisabeth Wayland.

13 Q: Thank you. And what was your position at

14 Vivorex?

15 A: Head Technician overseeing the Immortality

16 Projects.

17 Q: Can you please list the projects?

18 A: Project Cratis, Project Exemplum, Project

19 Machina, Project Mendacium, Project Meto, and

20 Project Iterum.

21 Q: You assisted both Mr. Soto Acero and Ms.

22 Veronika Mandersloot during the same period, is

23 that correct?

24 A: Yes, that's correct.

25 Q: And what was your understanding at the time,

26 of the relationship between the two of them?

27 A: I understood that they were both my

28 superiors, that Soto was the creator of the

1   Immortality Projects and that Veronika—Ms.

2   Mandersloot—was his second in command.

3   Q: What about Ms. Mandersloot's public

4   dismissal? It didn't strike you as strange that

5   they were continuing to work together?

6   A: (Shaking head in the negative.) The other

7   technicians and myself were told that Ms.

8   Mandersloot's firing was a PR stunt. Soto Acero—

9   or, I guess it was actually the android body of

10 Soto Acero controlled by Veronika Mandersloot—said

11 it was the only way we could continue with the

12 projects, and that Veronika would still be running

13 the lab behind the scenes.

14   Q: Did she come to the lab often?

15   A: Yes.

16   Q: When she appeared as Mr. Acero, you had no

17 idea that Ms. Mandersloot was controlling an

18 impersonation of him?

19   A: No idea whatsoever.

20   Q: During your employment, did you ever come

21 across anyone you recognized when bodies entered

22 the lab for evaluation?

23   A: No. The bodies were shaved clean and it

24 would have been difficult to recognize anyone. And

25 I wasn't supposed to be looking for that. The

26 important thing was the work.

27   Q: So, you weren't aware that Mr. Acero's nephew

28 had been admitted to the projects?

1   A: No. I'd never met him. He also didn't make
2   a lot of public appearances—and in my line of
3   work, with how busy I am, I don't watch a lot of
4   television—so I wouldn't have known, regardless.
5   And, again, the bodies were always shaved clean
6   before I ever came into contact with them.
7   Q: And you were running some of your own
8   experiments on the side, is that correct?
9   A: Yes, that's correct.
10 Q: What kinds of experiments?
11 A: Falsifier antidotes.
12 Q: What did those experiments entail?
13 A: A lot of the bodies that came in had been
14 rendered unconscious by a falsifier—basically a
15 sedative that can make someone appear dead, and
16 mimic signs of a particular cause of death for
17 a CorpuScan device. The falsifiers were always
18 administered by one of our agents in order to
19 recruit new subjects to the project.
20 Q: When you say "recruit" you mean … ?
21 A: Abduct. Anyway, our specialized scanners
22 could detect falsifiers, so that we could test
23 their efficacy. But I would occasionally set aside
24 a few of those bodies and inject my antidote
25 prototypes.
26 Q: Did you see any positive results?
27 A: Not as far as I knew.
28 Q: One of the bodies you used for these

experiments was the body of Andro Acero?

A: Yes, but like I said, I had no idea. I was just doing my job.

Q: And your experiments … ?

A: I considered the experiments a part of my job. Although Mr. Soto Acero—or, Ms. Mandersloot— had not assigned them to me, I knew it was important to cover all of our bases, to see the technology from every angle. If falsifiers were to fall into the wrong hands, we would need to protect ourselves. I pride myself on going above and beyond.

Q: There's an incident report dated September 10th of this year that states Andro Acero's "android unit"—A309—woke unexpectedly and, in a panic, set off an explosion that destroyed his android body and that of several other units. Was that the result of your experiments, in your professional opinion?

A: I believe that my antidote serum must have caused a malfunction to the source unit's consciousness, which thereby overstimulated the connected android unit's neural response and woke it from stasis.

Q: But you believed his android body had been destroyed during this incident?

A: Yes. His and eight others. The Sequitor® tracking signals to all of them were lost, which

1 | implied the androids were no longer functioning.
2 | Q: The documents state that Andro Acero's
3 | source unit—his human body—did not appear to be
4 | disconnected, though. How did your lab explain
5 | that?
6 | A: We thought it was a phenomenon. Or at least
7 | my colleagues did.
8 | Q: You weren't able to trace the connection?
9 | A: (Shaking head in the negative.) That's what
10 | the Sequitor® was for—so that we could keep track
11 | of our units. The remote control ability, when a
12 | consciousness is connected to an android, that's
13 | a traceable signal in theory, yes, but the units
14 | are highly protected. Think of it like a VPN, only
15 | much more secure. These androids were designed
16 | to have the potential for field work—soldiers,
17 | espionage. If one of them were to be captured,
18 | the ability to trace their brain signals would
19 | completely compromise the source.
20 | Q: So, then, you kept Andro Acero's source unit
21 | for observation?
22 | A: Yes. I thought he might provide some valuable
23 | insight later on.
24 | Q: Why?
25 | A: Because the other connected source units had
26 | a clear reaction to the disconnection, but his
27 | didn't.
28 | Q: What is the expected "reaction" of a source

unit—also known as the "human" body—when an
android unit is destroyed, or otherwise abruptly
disconnected?

A: Typically we expect the source unit to simply
wake up, but …

Q: Typically?

A: That was the idea. The android bodies were
meant to serve as a protection. Their fatal
experiences should have no bearing on the person
driving them. But some of the earlier batches
had a malfunction. A sort of kickback effect. We
learned it was due to sensory overload, something
that essentially would shock the brain and kill
the source unit. We lost several source units that
way. But Unit A309—Mr. Acero's nephew—didn't die
or wake. His monitor said he was still connected,
even though we believed there was no longer any
android to be connected to, and the kickback
malfunction didn't seem to have affected him
either. The other technicians found it strange,
but I was sure it had something to do with the
experimental antidotes I'd injected.

Q: So, what happened to the body? What did you
and your colleagues do with it?

A: I terminated him from Project Iterum and
transferred his body to another lab for what we
called "maintenance." That's when we would place
bodies in a special machine to keep them in

1 working condition—stimulating muscles to avoid

2 atrophy, aiding circulation, et cetera. I wasn't

3 sure whether his consciousness was suspended

4 somewhere, stuck between the two bodies, so

5 to speak, or if that was even possible. But I

6 thought it best to keep him and observe him.

7 It wasn't officially documented because I was

8 already on probation for the first incident; but

9 I also couldn't waste an opportunity for further

10 research.

11 Q: And what happened on September 10, 2087?

12 A: I wasn't in the lab that night because of the

13 events that occurred during Senator Quintero's

14 speech. Most of the employees were evading

15 investigations and I wanted to stay out of the

16 way until everything had been cleared up. But

17 according to the security cameras, Andro Acero's

18 source unit woke, and basically … walked right out

19 of there.

20 Q: Because of your antidote experimentation?

21 A: No. I'd like to take credit for it, but

22 I believe it was actually the result of the

23 September 10th incident. His android injuries. The

24 fire damaged a lot of his sensory receptors on one

25 side. Somehow that severely dampened the kickback

26 … and saved his life.

27

28

NEWS AMERICANA

Vivorex employees to serve time for complicity

A number of Vivorex employees stood trial this past month for crimes related to what is now known as the Iterum Scandal. Charges include misappropriation of company funds, abduction, unlawful confinement, and unethical experimentation.

THE GAUGE

Vivorex CEO's nephew found alive after unwilling participation in covert android production project

Andro Acero (son of late Vivorex founder Elodie Acero), believed to have committed suicide in early June of 2086, was found alive after spending months as an unwitting participant in Project Iterum, a secret project with the purpose of developing outwardly indistinguishable android clones of human test subjects.

The project began under the direction of ex-Vivorex Vice President Veronika Mandersloot, who was killed in a vidrinium explosion at a warehouse just outside Silicon Valley.

For approximately eight months, Acero remained remotely connected to his android unit, unaware that the body he controlled was, in fact, a duplicate of his own. Within the android unit, Acero took refuge in an elaborate safe house built underground at a family inholding in the Los Padres National Forest.

With the help of siblings Mirabel and Mateo Solís, who stumbled onto the safe house while lost in the wilderness, Acero was able to gather additional information from the outside world and eventually uncover the truth about his condition.

Acero states that once his android unit lost power, he awoke in an old factory in

READ MORE

Cupertino, a building that once belonged to the textile company Bian Industries, which more recently served as one of several covert locations for the Immortality Projects' assets. "Being transported like that," said Acero, "my mind closing off in one place and then reopening itself again several hundred miles away, I felt like I'd just teleported."

According to Dr. Elisabeth Wayland, who recently testified in court, Acero should have been killed immediately due to an electrical kickback malfunction that technicians had discovered in the early development of the androids, and since resolved in more recent iterations. "Any abrupt disconnection of the android caused a shock to the brain. A sensory overload," Wayland explained.

Fortunately, Acero's android unit had been maimed in a laboratory explosion and fire, which technicians believed had dampened his sensory functions and, ultimately, protected him.

Vivorex to continue Immortality Projects under ethical terms; Acero family seeks balance

While the scandal surrounding the Immortality Projects has revealed a large number of legal and human rights violations, its potential applications in reducing mortality rates are undeniable.

Military, search and rescue, and law enforcement are a few sectors that could greatly benefit from the protections of remote-controlled vessels that function seamlessly as human bodies. In a joint statement, the Vivorex CEO and his nephew declared that they would strive to continue the project, while adhering to laws and ethics. However, it will be "a precarious balance," said the elder Acero, "to ensure that the technology is not misused."

"Pandora's box has already been opened," stated Andro Acero, 19, who fell victim to Mandersloot's version of the project last year. "There's nothing we can do to change that. But we can try to control the chaos, to direct the tech in such a way that it can be a positive resource rather than a vehicle for crime."

THE DORADO REVIEW

Knight Crew crime syndicate leader killed, victims exonerated

San Francisco (AP) – Damian Knight, the third of seven Knight siblings whose extended families belong to—or live under the protection of—the crime syndicate known as the Knight Crew, was killed in a vidrinium explosion, along with ex-Vivorex Vice President Veronika Mandersloot, in a warehouse on the night of June 9.

According to holopad footage produced by Mirabel Solís, 18, along with her written statement, the explosion occurred during an act of self-defense after the teen had been threatened, held against her will, and pursued with firearms.

Mirabel Solís is the sister of Mateo Solís, 21, whose criminal record made him a subject of news coverage multiple times in late May and early June of this year. During the investigations that surrounded Project Iterum's exposure, Solís claimed his personal history had been altered by Knight to reflect false criminal charges in order to punish him for the involvement of his late father, Gabriel Solís, in the interception and obstruction of Knight Crew transactions that occurred in 2084.

Solís's attorney, provided by Vivorex, called for a deep dive into the syndicate's activities.

Following Knight's death, authorities were granted a warrant to investigate Knight Crew properties and records, which brought to light several instances of identity tampering, including that of Mateo Solís. Evidence was sufficient to convict Nicander Knight, the second-eldest Knight sibling, while other members of the crime family face further investigation.

Meanwhile, Solís and other victims have been exonerated and absolved of all criminal history.

Advanced drug manufacturing mimics natural death, murder victims revealed

In close connection with the notorious Iterum Scandal, authorities were informed of the true source of nearly one hundred confirmed deaths once believed to be due to natural causes.

For several years, drugs known as "falsifiers,"or "phakes," have been covertly circulating among crime syndicates thanks to the development of mendacium, a substance used by Project Iterum pioneers to gain victims for experiments without drawing attention.

"It was easy to use the bodies," Dr. Elisabeth Wayland explained during questioning. "No one ever went looking for them because, as far as anyone knew, they were dead. CorpuScan confirmed."

However, not all victims were slated for use in the Immortality Projects. "Many were killed to keep things quiet," an anonymous source told *The Dorado Review*. "People that needed to be 'removed,' so to speak, so they didn't compromise syndicate operations. It was better that way—it didn't start as many conflicts. When a crime family kills someone, it sends a message; it breeds retaliation. But making it look like an accident, or better yet, an act of God? No backlash, no authorities looking into it, nothing. Problem solved."

Among victims whose causes of deaths were wrongfully determined was Liona Solís, the mother of Mateo and Mirabel Solís (both of whom played an integral part in helping bring the Iterum Scandal to light).

A candlelight vigil will be held at Golden Gate Park on July 26 to honor the deceased.

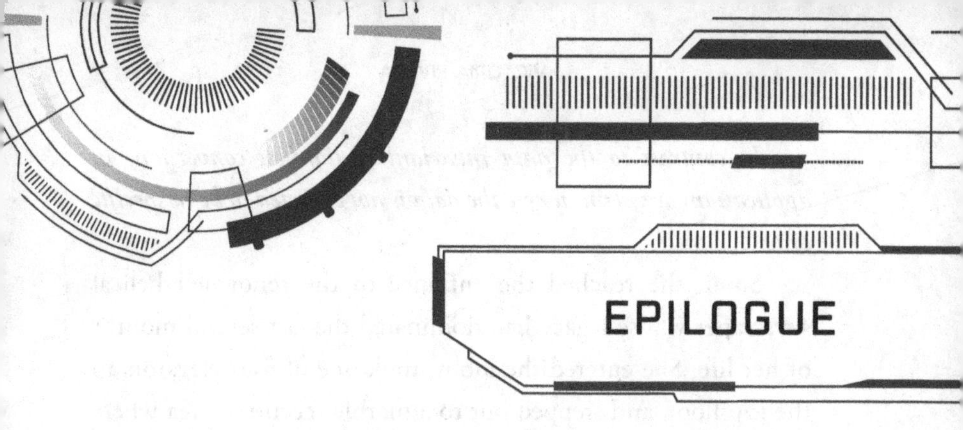

BEL NUDGED HER WAY OUT OF WHOLLY GROUND, barely making it through alive with everyone around her clamoring for their caffeine. She held a drink carrier with three cups in it, labeled "Mateo," "Dr. Acero," and "Mirabel." She glanced up at the panopt across the street. As usual, she felt the urge to touch her hairline, but she caught herself and smiled, reveling in the fact that nothing was stuck to her skin. The front strands of her hair were braided out of the way, in a style that Kat had shown her, baring Bel's full face to the world.

In her other hand, she held her small holopad, careful not to spill any coffee on the Caltech sweatshirt she wore.

Aly's holomorph smiled from the device. "So, I'll see you this afternoon, then?"

"Yep. My last class ends at 3:30."

"Perfect. A new DiMaggio's just opened a few blocks from my dorm and anyone who gets there before 5:00 gets a free slice."

"Can't wait. I'll head down to Ventura the second I'm free," said Bel.

"Sounds great. Talk to you later!"

"Bye."

Bel pocketed the holopad and slipped an earbud into one ear, streaming an audio textbook as she approached the crosswalk.

In contrast to the data invariant endianness conversion, in applications or systems where the data is not expected to be in specific order …

Soon, she reached the entrance to the renowned helical skyscraper whose legacy had dominated the last several months of her life. She entered the lobby, took one of four elevators to the top floor, and stepped out to a marble reception area where four employees worked behind a long, joined desk. On the wall behind them, the silver, mounted letters spelled out *Vivorex.*

One of the employees looked up from her holoscreen. "Nice to see you again, Ms. Solís."

"Hi Ava," Bel said cheerfully. She went past the desk toward the offices that lay beyond, passing three doors before she stopped at one whose nameplate read "Andro Acero."

The door was open. Andro stood by the window, facing out with his hands in his slacks pockets. Bel knocked lightly on the door jamb.

He turned to see her, and grinned. "Hey."

She stepped in and handed him his coffee, which he accepted as he kissed her.

"'Dr. Acero'?" he raised the cup.

Bel shrugged. "It's inevitable, right?"

He laughed and took a sip. "I told Mateo you'd be here any minute. He's coming to install his new software. Not that I'm going to be using it much. This whole me-having-an-office-here thing is just a formality."

"Well, it's good to be at least *kind of* involved in your family business, even if you're going to insist on a different career path. Your uncle knows things would be a lot different at Vivorex if you hadn't survived."

"My survival wouldn't have meant anything without you

and your brother …"

Mateo's face appeared in the doorway, an ID tag dangling from a lanyard on his neck.

Mateo Solís
Chief Technology Officer

"Did somebody say 'brother'?" Mateo hugged Bel and took his coffee without asking. He nodded at Andro. "Shouldn't you be getting a head start on those textbooks? I saw the Stanford email with your class schedule; you've got your work cut out for you."

"You're reading my emails now?" said Andro.

"You left it open when I did your last update. I *glanced*."

"Well, I guess it's a good thing I don't have any secrets anymore," said Andro. "With the two of you around, they'd be impossible to keep."

"I just briefed Soto on the software," Mateo added. "Everything should be up and running by tomorrow afternoon."

Andro nodded. "Great."

Mateo's watch buzzed.

Bel leaned over to read Kat's name on the screen.

"Sorry you two," said Mateo. "I gotta take this. Mind if I come back in fifteen?"

Bel and Andro shook their heads as Mateo slipped out. After he'd been gone a few seconds Andro said, "Would you like to see the rooftop garden?"

The rooftop may as well have been the top of the world. Bel took a deep breath, and even though the air was smoggy, it smelled like home.

Andro took her hand and slid his fingers between hers. "How long does it take you to get to campus on the Mag again?"

"Twenty-seven minutes."

"God, I love modern transport. Would've taken half a day before the Mag."

"Yeah, and I wouldn't be able to see you before class. Or after."

Bel's device pinged several times before she silenced it.

"How's the app going?" Andro asked.

"Good. We've added another hundred volunteers to the network—although we're barely keeping up with requests. But we found thirty-seven missing persons, just yesterday."

He smiled. "I'm really proud of you."

She peered down at their hands, admiring the shape and bend of Andro's fingers. *Levers*, she thought. Bars on fulcra. Through them, she could feel his pulse, which she had felt so many times now, reminding her of the complex, organic pump in his chest that powered him.

So much of the human body was machine. The hydraulics of the heart and veins. Muscles like pulleys. Teeth like wedges. And the brain was a magnificent and nuanced computer, while consciousness was a wireless data stream that even the best minds still hadn't fully been able to harness.

She was glad, though, that consciousness remained such a mystery. It was good that there were still some things that couldn't be replicated—or stolen. Some things that were ceaselessly bound to the human condition and unhackable.

Of course that made it pretty much impossible to delete the less desirable parts—imperfections, weaknesses, fears, annoying tendencies—the natural code of the individual. Even in the most favorable circumstances, the question "who are you?" would always be a loaded one.

But there was beauty in that composition, both in products of chance and in consequences of choice, in the best parts and the broken parts, in aptitude and malfunction, in roses and their corresponding thorns.

Plain and simple, though, to *love* something made it beautiful, Bel thought. End of story. She looked at Andro and she knew she loved that beautiful, imperfect machine—and more importantly, the man who lived inside of it.

♥

ACKNOWLEDGEMENTS

First and foremost, to my husband: Thank you for being willing to take this leap with me as I chose to start my own business (twice) and finally just publish my own books. There were many risks involved, but you have believed in me from start to finish. Despite all my fears and reservations, you have continued to encourage and support me, let me brainstorm with you, analyze movie plots and characters with me, listen to my rants, comfort me when I cry (which I know can be a lot!) and provide constructive feedback somewhere in the midst of all your cheesy jokes. You are the love of my life, and you push me to be my best self.

Rocco and Bellamy, I know you won't read this until you're older, but thank you so much for your patience as I've navigated the ups and downs of my career(s). I have not always balanced everything perfectly, and for that I hope you can forgive me. You two are my everything, and you both inspire me so much!

Dad, you have always championed my every creation with so much enthusiasm, even though I'm sure you didn't know what I was talking about half the time. Your positive affirmations, pep talks, and good energy have carried me through many tough days.

Mom, it was your love of reading and writing that first introduced me to books and the power of words. I'm grateful for those early days that shaped my mind. Also, thank you for always letting me try new things ad nauseam to build my skills and find out what I'm capable of.

Mamita Lina, aunque ya no estás en esta tierra, siempre has sido una de mis mayores inspiraciones. Estoy muy orgullosa de compartir tu nombre y tu amor por la escritura. Me enseñaste que nunca es demasiado tarde para nada. Gracias por tu legado ♥

Graciela y Felipe, muchísimas gracias por apoyarme como si fuera su propia hija. Su generosidad me ha permitido la flexibilidad de explorar las posibilidades de mi carrera, primero en diseño gráfico y ahora como autora. Estaré eternamente agradecida de tenerlos a ustedes como mis suegros.

Daicy, gracias por tu amor y apoyo, por quitarme un peso de encima cuando necesitaba ayuda. Cuando me sentía sola y agotada, llegaste con optimismo y energía. Siempre estaré agradecida de que hayas pasado a ser parte de mi familia (y lo serás siempre).

To my writing group, the Keystrokes, thanks for reading my work month after month for years. Thanks for seeing me through some of my messier writing and my weirder ideas, and for tolerating my long Discord messages. I can't believe we're still together (especially with the added irony of physically being far apart). Special thanks to Walker and Zach who critiqued this whole book!

Kristin J. Dawson, my first author friend, the extrovert who adopted me so many years ago, thank you for being such a great example. Thank you for reading some of my earliest work (*cringe*) and not telling me to quit! You have always been a positive force in my writing brain, even though we've often had long lulls in communication. Also, congratulations on your recent book news! Each and every one of your successes is well deserved.

Morgan J. Muir—look what you made me do! Thank you for encouraging me to go to 20Books, for not mocking my trad pub dreams or trying to talk me into indie publishing. You let me figure it out for myself. You invited me to join you in such an incredible author environment where, for the first time, I felt validated and powerful as a writer. Without that, I would not be publishing this book right now. Your encouragement and your willingness to share your wealth of knowledge changed my life. I can never repay you.

Speaking of 20Books, thank you to all those who organized and presented. There are too many to name, but I can't imagine where I'd be mentally as a writer without this conference. Probably still moping in the query trenches and wallowing in self-deprecation.

Everyone at AutoNetTV, especially Brandon and the production team, thank you for taking a chance on me as a baby graphic designer in 2015. Working with you was my first major step into freelance work, and then remote work, which allowed me to have a career while also being able to be with my young children. The flexibility you gave me helped keep me sane while I juggled all my responsibilities and tried to make time for side hustles. My Photoshop and graphic design skills grew exponentially thanks to you guys. Plus you were all just amazing to work with!

Brooke, my twin soul, thanks for always popping up out of nowhere when I'm having a bad day. It's like you know telepathically! Or would it be *empathically*? I'm so grateful for your friendship and our shared love of writing.

Brianna, thank you for listening to all my lengthy Marco Polo messages! Thanks for trying to read my stuff and for talking bookish things with me. You, too, have popped up out of nowhere right when I've needed a boost.

Violeta, even though we only talked once, like six years ago, your words helped set me on the path that led me here. I always knew I wanted to write, but I got distracted by so many other shiny objects. You told me to get clear on my goals.

Alexia and Matthania, thanks for beta-reading this!

Tiffany, Lara, StephAnn, and Ivy: Thanks for being my first ARC team! It's always awkward letting other people read my stuff (which is ironic, since that's literally the goal). Thank you for your enthusiasm and encouragement as I fight this ongoing battle with my insecurities :)

ABOUT THE AUTHOR

VICTORIA RIVERA is a graphic designer and mom of two kiddos. She has a bachelor's degree in English and has worked as a copy editor, proofreader, and designer at newspapers and magazines.

She developed a love for science fiction at a young age while watching movies with her dad. She was born and raised in Oregon but currently lives in northern Utah and misses the rain.

When she's not writing, she enjoys doing DIY projects, playing Beat Saber, rage-cleaning to good music, and reading (obviously).

For updates on upcoming books, subscribe to her email list at www.toririv.com. Follow her on TikTok (@tori.riv) for a glimpse into her day-to-day activities and other bookish things.

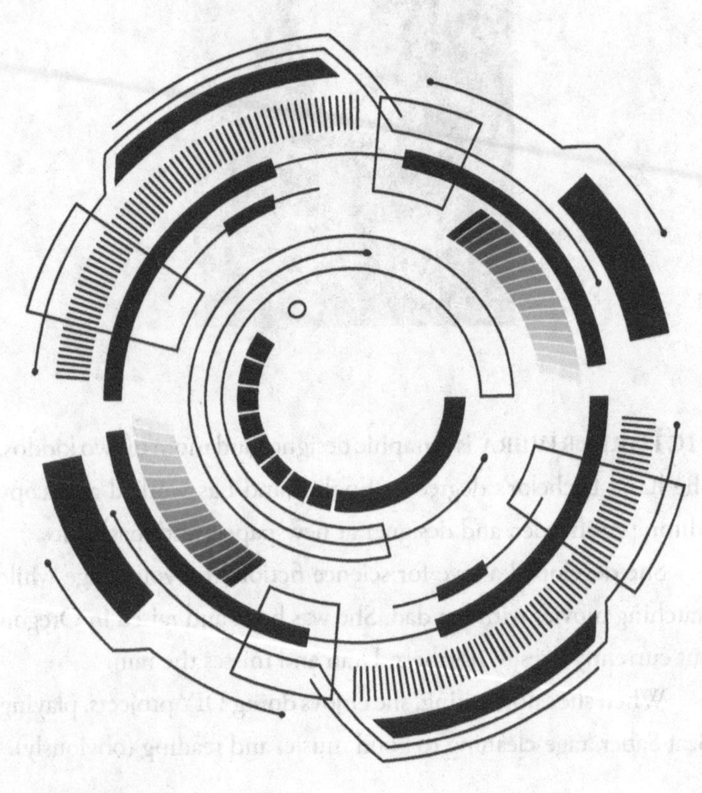